Praise for Trisha Ashley:

'Trisha Ashley writes with remarkable wit and originality – one of the best writers around!'
Katie Fforde

'Trisha Ashley's romp makes for enjoyable reading'
The Times

'Full of down-to-earth humour'
Sophie Kinsella

'A warm-hearted and comforting read'
Carole Matthews

'Fast-paced and seriously witty'
The Lady

'Packed with romance, chocolate and fun, this indulgent read is simply too delicious to put down'
Closer

'A lovely, cosy read'
My Weekly

'Fresh and funny'
Woman's Own

www.penguin.co.uk

Trisha Ashley's *Sunday Times* bestselling novels have sold over one million copies in the UK and have twice been shortlisted for the Melissa Nathan award for Romantic Comedy. *Every Woman for Herself* was nominated by magazine readers as one of the top three romantic novels in the last fifty years.

Trisha lives in North Wales. For more information about her please visit her Facebook page www.Facebook.com/TrishaAshleyBooks or follow her on Twitter @trishaashley.

Also by Trisha Ashley

Sowing Secrets
A Winter's Tale
Wedding Tiers
Chocolate Wishes
Twelve Days of Christmas
The Magic of Christmas
Chocolate Shoes and Wedding Blues
Good Husband Material
Wish Upon a Star
Finding Mr Rochester
Every Woman for Herself
Creature Comforts
A Christmas Cracker
A Leap of Faith (*previously published as* The Urge to Jump)
The Little Teashop of Lost and Found
A Good Heart is Hard to Find (*previously published as* Singled Out)
The House of Hopes and Dreams
Written from the Heart (*previously published as* Happy Endings)

THE GARDEN OF FORGOTTEN WISHES

Trisha Ashley

BLACK SWAN

TRANSWORLD PUBLISHERS
Penguin Random House, One Embassy Gardens,
8 Viaduct Gardens, London SW11 7BW
www.penguin.co.uk

Transworld is part of the Penguin Random House group of companies
whose addresses can be found at global.penguinrandomhouse.com

First published in Great Britain in 2020 by Bantam Press
an imprint of Transworld Publishers
Black Swan edition published 2021

A CIP catalogue record for this book
is available from the British Library.

ISBN
9781784160944

Typeset in 11.52/14.4 pt Adobe Garamond by Jouve (UK), Milton Keynes.
Printed and bound in Great Britain by Clays Ltd, Elcograf S.p.A.

The authorized representative in the EEA is Penguin Random House Ireland,
Morrison Chambers, 32 Nassau Street, Dublin D02 YH68.

Penguin Random House is committed to a sustainable future
for our business, our readers and our planet. This book is made
from Forest Stewardship Council® certified paper.

For Mum, who so loved my books
Mary Turner Long
5/7/1925 to 7/1/2020

1 Tall Beds
2 Mid-Level Beds
3 Lawn Walkways
4 Beds with Lavender Edging
5 Herb Beds
6 Poison Garden
7 Yew Tree / Caged Rosary Pea
8 Water
9 Wetland
10 Veg Style Long Plots
11 Paths
12 Gates / Pagoda / Poison Fence
13 Wooden Walkways

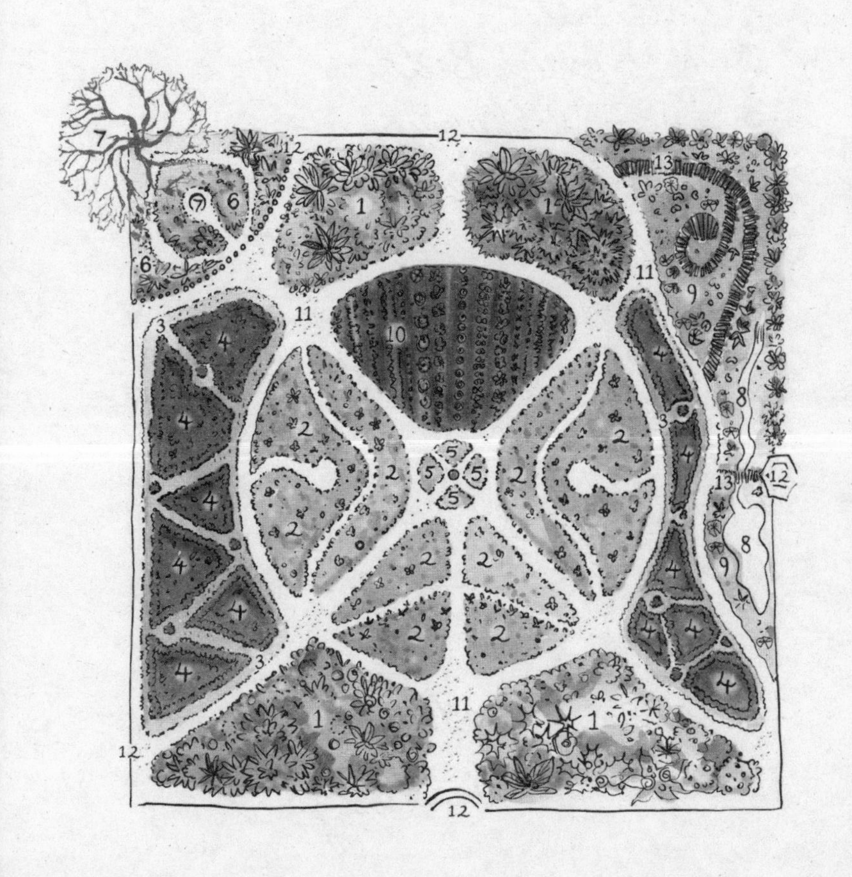

12
7
12
6
1
1
13
6
11
9
3
11
4
10
4
4
2
8
2
2
3
5
5
5
5
2
2
4
13
12
4
2
2
8
4
9
4
2
2
4
4
3
4
2
2
4
1
11
1
12
12

Prologue

Passing Places

1993

'Tell me about when you were a little girl at Jericho's End,' I said. It wasn't that I needed to hear her stories again, for they were engraved on my memory for ever, it was just that her thin, silvery thread of a voice was all that seemed to keep her connected to life – and to me.

After the last round of chemotherapy, her curling, red-gold hair had returned in the form of an ashy down, and her hand in mine, once so strong and capable, seemed to have turned into a bird's claw, dry as a bundle of fine twigs and cool to the touch. Painkillers had smoothed out the lines in her hollowed face and clouded her blue-grey eyes with vagueness.

'It's me, Marnie. Can you hear me, Mum? Auntie Em's dropped me off after school, but she's going to come in and see you later, when she picks me up.'

'Marianne, not Marnie,' Mum corrected, with an echo of the old touch of reproof.

The hospice was so quiet that you could hear the bees buzzing among the lavender bushes in the garden, and only the purposeful footsteps of the nurses going briskly and competently about their work broke the drowsy spell.

'Mum?' I tried again. 'Remember when you were a little girl and lived at Jericho's End, and what you and your friends saw when you were playing among the stones by the Fairy Falls? Tell me that story,' I pleaded.

'Jericho's End . . . ?' A light seemed to glimmer in her eyes for a moment and the fleeting ghost of a smile touched her lips.

'Ice-cream . . . and angels,' she sighed ecstatically on an exhaled breath, as if she'd had a glimpse through the doors of Heaven, and spotted the Angel Gabriel driving the celestial version of a Mr Whippy van – and then, in an instant, she was gone.

Even at twelve, you know when the butterfly has flown and the chrysalis is an empty husk, but I sat there holding her hand and wondering if the journey from birth to death wasn't a straight line at all, but a circle, until Aunt Em came to fetch me.

1

French Leave

Early 2017

When my mobile rang, I was digging up early potatoes in the walled garden of a vast and castellated French château, though not the one belonging to my adoptive family, the Ellwoods, which was an altogether more modest affair about forty miles away, in the Dordogne. I fished the phone out of my pocket with an earthy hand.

'Marnie? Good news!' announced Treena Ellwood, who filled the dual role of my almost-twin sister and best friend, sounding as if she was standing next to me, rather than back in the UK. 'I just heard on the grapevine that Mike got married again early last year. I thought there must have been a good reason why he suddenly agreed to the divorce.'

'He's . . . remarried?' I repeated, slowly. I spared a fleeting thought for his newest victim, but my overwhelming feeling was that one final shackle holding me to the past had finally fallen away. I found I was staring at the ice-blue sky, wondering if I still remembered how to fly.

And as I stood there, phone in hand, the memory of my

brief marriage escaped the dark corner of my mind in which I'd hidden it and slithered out to taunt me for the reckless, loving fool I'd been.

It had been a whirlwind romance and I'd blithely followed a trail of rosy delusions right up to the altar within two months of meeting Mike Draycot. I'd assured everyone that despite the short time we'd known each other and the age difference – he was ten years older – we were true soulmates . . . though, later, I found it hard to think of anything we shared.

But then, I wasn't the malleable, emotionally damaged person he thought I was; he just caught me at a low ebb. I was strong, prone to be acerbic and fiercely independent, and yet Mum's death when I was twelve had left me with a deep feeling of insecurity. My adoptive family's recent decision to sell up their home and garden centre business in the UK, and to relocate to an old château in France, had stirred up that feeling all over again. Somehow it felt like a second betrayal.

Mike had seemed so understanding and sympathetic. I'd told him more about how I felt than I'd ever revealed to anyone, even Treena, and since his first wife had died tragically young, we seemed to have a bond of loss in common.

He was charming, very clever and emotionally manipulative in ways I'd never even thought of. I had no idea what I was letting myself in for.

Mike was a wiry man with the deceptively skinny physique of the runner, and had attractively spiky silver and black hair, bright dark eyes and an engaging smile.

He owned the veterinary practice in Merchester where Treena was providing a year's maternity cover for one of the staff, which is how I came to meet him. Treena, however, was the only member of the family who *didn't* think Mike was the perfect man for me, right from the start.

'He's a good vet, but the animals don't like him,' she'd warned me, before the wedding. 'And he's the only vet I know who doesn't have pets of his own.'

She herself had two dogs and three cats, and for the last year I'd shared a small rented cottage with her and her menagerie on the edge of Merchester, where the Ellwoods ran their garden centre. Just before I met Mike, my adoptive family had fallen in love with the rundown Château du Monde in France, which came with extensive grounds and outbuildings, a lake and campsite. With hard work, it would provide a home and a living. Unlike her married older brother and her sister, Treena herself had decided to stay put in the UK and I'd been in two minds whether to go or stay. There were gardens to restore at the château and the Ellwoods hoped eventually to set up a garden centre there, too. But moving to France had never been *my* dream. In any case, I was successfully working my way up the gardening hierarchy of the Heritage Homes Trust, and had just been offered a promotion at a property in the North-East.

Falling for Mike scuppered both those options, though he seemed to understand my ambition to become a head gardener one day, as well as sharing most of my aims in life . . . and really, I can't *imagine* how I got that impression, because it wasn't long before I realized that he was intent on making me over in an entirely different pattern of his own design.

But of course, the benefit of hindsight is a wonderful thing. And at first he was very subtle in his technique: one small thing after the other, each designed to isolate me from family and friends, undermine my self-confidence and independence and lead me further and further under his control.

It didn't help that in public he showed a different face, so that for a long time he fooled everyone (though never Treena) into thinking he was the perfect husband and I the ungrateful and difficult wife.

The very first pinprick to start deflating the rosy bubble of romantic delusion had come right after my small wedding, which was a close 'family and friends' affair. Aunt Em (I continued to call them Aunt Em and Uncle Richard, even after they adopted me, as they were friends as close as any family) had made my beautiful white silk dress herself, a floaty boho affair, and instead of a veil I just wore my long, black wavy hair loose, with a circlet of flowers on my head.

I'd noticed Mike hadn't smiled at me when I came down the aisle, or said anything other than to make the responses during the ceremony, so when we went to sign the register I asked him if he liked my dress . . . to which he'd replied coldly that he would have preferred something more sophisticated that made me look less like a child bride.

In that instant, with that casually cruel remark, I saw a stranger in his eyes and my world rocked. Then just as suddenly, he was giving me the old charming smile and turning away to speak to someone else, leaving me wondering if he could have meant it as a joke. If so, then it wasn't kind. I mean, given his wiry, skinny physique, his sharp-shouldered suit made him look a bit as if he was dangling from a wire coat hanger, but I wouldn't have dreamed of hurting his feelings by saying so.

At the reception in a small hotel, he was so very much the happy bridegroom, saying how delighted he was with his beautiful bride and introducing me to his elderly, but strangely cowed parents, who had travelled up from Hastings for the occasion. He left me alone with them only for a moment, during which time they wished me happiness, though not as if they were optimistic about that outcome, and said they were sorry they would have to leave early to catch their train home.

I had a sudden unexpected urge to ask them about Mike's first wife and especially what she'd died of, but before the question could leave my lips, Mike hurried back and bundled them off into a taxi.

Treena cornered me a little later and asked me what was the matter. 'And you can't fool me, I know something's up.'

'Oh . . . it's nothing really. I just took something Mike said in church the wrong way, but I'm sure he meant it as a joke.'

She insisted I told her what he said and then frowned over it. 'That was a stupid and cruel thing to say. Why on earth should you dress as if you were the same age as him?'

'Well, I did think the child bride bit was silly, considering I'm a lot nearer to thirty than twenty. That's why I thought he must have been joking.'

'Huh!' she said disbelievingly. 'I just heard him telling Mum that he hoped you'd be starting a family very soon and giving up your job. Mum was surprised.'

'So am I!' I stared at her. 'He *knows* I want to wait a couple more years before I take maternity leave. I've already given up the chance of promotion with that job near Hexham, but there should be an opening where I am in the next year or two, if I hang on in there.'

'I suspect he might not have quite grasped that,' Treena said drily.

I looked at her uncertainly and then said after a minute, 'I wish the family wasn't moving abroad. Thank goodness *you're* still going to be around!'

'Yes, I'm definitely accepting that partnership in the Great Mumming veterinary practice, so even after I move, I'll only be about twenty miles away,' she agreed.

'Will you have to move? It would be nice having you in Merchester.'

'I know, but I'd find the commute a bit of a pain down all those small country roads and, anyway, I'd like to settle there, near Happy Pets. I'll move Zeph to a livery stables nearby, too.'

Zephyr was a dappled silver and lilac-grey mare that reminded me of an old-fashioned rocking horse and Treena adored her.

'If you're going to move, then I ought to clear my stuff out,' I said. Not only were a lot of my belongings still at the cottage, but some of the things that had been Mum's were stored there. There wasn't room in Mike's small and minimalist flat in a former mill building, though we planned to buy a house together.

'I suppose I'll have to put a lot of things into storage until we move to somewhere bigger.'

'There's no rush. I can just take it with me when I move, so you can sort it out later, if you like,' she said. 'By the way, you do realize Great Mumming isn't far from that village where your mum came from – Jericho's End?'

I looked at her in surprise. I was so used to thinking of Jericho's End as some fabled, forbidden Shangri-La that I'd almost forgotten it was a real place.

'I suppose it is,' I agreed.

'When I've moved, we could go and have a look at it,' she suggested. 'Aren't you curious?'

'I don't know,' I said honestly. 'I loved hearing Mum's stories about it when I was little – it seemed such a magical, wonderful place – but then, she made me promise never to go there. She said . . . it would be dangerous.'

Treena's blue eyes widened. 'You never told me that! What kind of dangerous?'

'I don't know. Perhaps it was something to do with her family. Remember I told you her parents belonged to some small, strict, religious sect I'd never heard of, who sounded as if they came straight out of the Dark Ages by way of *Cold Comfort Farm*? They disowned her after she got pregnant with me, so perhaps she just meant they'd make me unwelcome, or put a curse on me, or something.'

'Yeah, right,' said Treena.

I recalled the urgency with which Mum had made me promise not to visit Jericho's End, which seemed a bit over the top . . . but then, so had her upbringing. 'I'd hate to bump into any of my Vane relatives,' I said.

'It wouldn't matter if you did, because you're an Ellwood now, and anyway, you don't look anything like your mother so they won't guess if they're not told,' Treena pointed out.

This was true, since I was medium-sized and had the black wavy hair and pale olive complexion of my Italian father, while Mum had been a tall, Titian-haired beauty. We did share a heart-shaped face with a broad brow from which sprang two wings of curling hair, and eyes of an unusual light grey-blue ringed with black, but that was it.

'Well, I expect I'll have to go there with work at some point. I'll tell you what it's like, and then if there aren't any Vanes running around with axes, we could go and visit it,' she suggested.

The promise Mum had extracted from me did seem a bit silly now and these future plans comforted me. I told myself that I had lots to look forward to. I had good friends, loved my job and, if the family were moving abroad, at least that gave us somewhere nice to go for holidays. And Mike had his own work, as well as a passion for early morning running that took him for miles and seemed to be almost an addiction.

There were bound to be minor misunderstandings at the start of our married life, when Mike and I had known one another for so short a time, but since we loved each other, I was quite convinced any little difficulties would soon be ironed out.

Only I didn't realize that it was me who was supposed to be ironed out, and then refolded into a state of submission, fear and obedience . . . I wasn't going down without a fight, however.

Sarcasm had always been my weapon of choice. The first time Mike gave me a list of things he wanted me to do while he was at work one Saturday, I looked at him in astonishment and said, in a robotic voice, 'This android is not programmed to take your orders.'

He didn't find that funny, and was grouchy for the rest of the weekend. Then he apologized but I knew he was still punishing me when I began to be excluded from social arrangements or he totally overrode household decisions we'd already agreed upon. I began to see a pattern, and again, he wasn't amused when eventually I said that if he'd wanted a Stepford Wife he should have married one. I really wanted our life together to be everything it had once promised to be but I knew I had to choose between saving the so-called marriage or saving myself in the end. Before he destroyed my love for him, I wasted too much time trying to make things right between us, but when I finally took my courage in my hands and told him I thought we'd been mistaken in each other and should separate, he flew into one of his terrifying cold rages, which by then had much the same effect on me that the Dementors had on the characters in the *Harry Potter* novels, and threatened that if I ran off to Treena for help, he'd blacken her professional reputation.

That stopped me in my tracks. She'd moved to Merchester by then and taken out a loan to buy into her friend's family veterinary practice, not to mention a mortgage on a small terraced cottage. I couldn't risk any action that might harm her.

Mike had already made very sure he'd alienated me from any other friends I might have turned to, and the family were too far away to see what was happening. I had casual friendships with my gardening colleagues but, due to Mike, I no longer even went to the pub with them after work . . . and his habit of suddenly turning up at the garden where I was working didn't endear me to my employers, either.

He'd known Treena was the one person I could turn to and so, once that was impossible, I felt trapped and hopeless.

Now, of course, I find it hard to understand how I came to be so much under his thrall, but one thing followed another in a spiral of descent, until I began to feel I was losing both the fight and my mind, and there was no way out but one – until Fate and Treena intervened to set me free and I became the Runaway Bride.

Now, five years later, here was Treena telling me that Mike had remarried and moved on.

I realized I was still holding the phone in one hand and Treena's voice could be heard faintly asking me if I was still there. I felt as if an hour had passed, but the same small white cloud above my head had hardly shifted and I knew it must have been barely minutes. I took a deep breath and let it out in a long sigh, then put the phone to my ear again.

'Yes, I'm still here, but I think I just had a near-death type experience, where the dodgier parts of your life rush past your eyes.'

'No, that one must have been a new-life experience, because

there's no reason to put off coming back to the UK now, is there?'

'I expect he lost interest in me long ago anyway and there was no reason why I shouldn't have come back after the divorce was finalized,' I said. 'But now he's remarried it somehow feels . . . safer.'

A sudden wave of homesickness swept over me for the rolling farmlands, upland moors and little market towns of west Lancashire, where I had been brought up. I wanted to walk on the flat, pale golden sands at Merchester, with the wind blowing stinging sand against my bare legs and the taste of salt on my lips.

'He's got someone new to work on now he's remarried,' Treena said. 'Sylvie, my receptionist friend, said his wife is a vet too, and she's joined his practice so he's going to be able to keep tabs on her all the time. She's only a couple of years older than you were when you got married – he seems to like them much younger than he is.'

I shivered, though that might have been the icy breeze winding around me.

'So, when are you coming home, Marnie?'

'As soon as I can find a job, though not with the Heritage Homes Trust, because after Mike managed to convince them I'd had a breakdown, alarm bells and whistles would go off if I sent in an application – or to the National Trust and English Heritage, because rumours do get around in the gardening world. I don't think I could ask them for a reference, either,' I added wryly.

'Maybe not,' she agreed. 'But I expect some of the people you've been gardening for in France would be happy to write you references.'

I'd spent the last five years moving around the surprisingly large circle of expat château owners, working for little more than pocket money and board and lodging, returning to my family at the Château du Monde from time to time.

Once I'd begun to feel safe, I'd found the life fun, but it meant I had little savings, and the small and decrepit old Citroën 2CV I'd arrived in was my only asset, unless you counted fluent, but Lancashire-inflected, French and a large collection of battered old books on gardening in that language, which I'd picked up along the way.

'I seem to have lost my ambition to work my way up the gardening hierarchy of any big organization,' I said, turning it over in my mind. 'I think a job on a private estate with a cottage thrown in, something like that, would be perfect.'

'You can stay with me while you look.'

It was a kind offer, but her end-terrace cottage was so tiny and full of animals that staying there wasn't going to be practical for more than a couple of days.

'Thanks, Treena, that would be lovely, but I think it would be best if I could have something lined up before I got back,' I said. 'I've got my BSc Honours in horticulture, so that and a few references from people over here should do it.'

'There are always copies of the *Lady* magazine in our waiting room at Happy Pets. They used to carry a lot of adverts for jobs like that with accommodation thrown in, so I'll scour the recent issues,' she offered.

'As long as the work involves gardening, I'm not fussy,' I assured her. 'I can even do some handyman stuff, after helping renovate all these old French houses.'

'Handywoman,' she corrected. 'But I know it's the gardening you love best – never happier than when you're grubbing about in compost and mulch.'

I grinned. 'There are a couple of job sites online I can look at, too, but I know I'm going to be back at the bottom of the ladder and starting again on a low wage.'

Aunt Em had given me her old laptop the year before and, though temperamental to turn on, was OK once it got going, apart from an anxious whirring noise from time to time. It was nice to be connected to the internet again, even if I was avoiding social media like the plague.

'Well, at least this time there won't be any snakes to bar the way back up the ladder,' Treena pointed out. 'Right, I'd better go now – email you later if I spot anything that sounds good.'

'Yes, I'd better go, too,' I said, as Jean, the elderly and irascible gardener, appeared from the greenhouse and began gesticulating at me in his own imperative manner. He had come with the château I was currently working at and had a bad temper and a face that looked the way Gérard Depardieu's would if it had been briskly clapped between the two big wooden butter paddles that hung in what had once been the dairy.

That was something I'd have quite liked to have done to him myself . . .

2

Back to the Future

I leaned over the ferry rail and watched Calais dissolve into the grey early morning gloom, while the cold salt air scoured out my lungs in what I hoped was a healthy way. The last French seagull, hunched on a nearby hatch, ceased to eye me malevolently and, with a Gallic-sounding screech, took off for home.

I wondered if seagulls had foreign accents. Though unless someone learned to speak Seagull, perhaps we'd never know.

I groped in my pocket for my mobile, meaning to call Treena and tell her I was on the way, then remembered that my cheap pay-as-you-go phone had met a watery end in the lily pond at the Château du Monde and even sealing it in a bag of rice hadn't revived it. I was the kiss of death to phones.

Unsurprisingly, given the chill, I had the deck to myself, but soon I'd have to go in search of warmth and hot coffee. I spared a thought for my poor little Citroën down in the creaking, oily-smelling hold. She was even more battered than she'd been when we'd made the journey in the opposite direction five years previously, so even if she got loose and skated around the hold like a dodgem, you wouldn't really notice any new bumps and scratches. I'd had a door panel and the bonnet replaced with parts from a scrapped white model, and perhaps when I could afford it I'd have the whole car resprayed in one colour. It might at least help to hold it together a little longer.

As the Runaway Bride, I'd travelled out on Treena's passport (just as well her photo had been taken when she was in her Goth phase, with dyed black hair and lots of heavy eye makeup), but I'd long since cancelled my own old passport which, for all I knew, was still locked away in Mike's safe, and got a new one, so I was returning as Marianne Ellwood.

Marnie: restored to myself again, and even if there were a few hidden scars, they were faded to the merest tracings of silver.

Since Treena's phone call, I'd applied for any job that sounded even remotely suitable. But unfortunately, it appeared that most of the situations with accommodation thrown in wanted a married couple, usually a gardener/housekeeper combo. I'd only had one positive reply and that was to an ad that Treena had happened to spot in her local paper.

Full-time gardener required to work at two adjoining country properties. Position includes small flat if required.

There had been a box number, to which I'd replied, and was astonished to discover that, by one of those weird coincidences that life sometimes throws our way, the advertiser lived in Jericho's End.

The letter offering me the position was stowed in the small, worn patchwork leather rucksack slung over my shoulder. I could feel it glowing brightly in there, like a promise.

The speed of the first response, and then the offer of the job following hard on the heels of my reply, made me suspect they'd had few, if any, applicants. The pay was low considering there were two gardens to look after, but then, the inclusion of the small flat clinched it for me.

I'd had a tussle with my conscience before accepting it for, after all, Mum *had* made me promise never to go to Jericho's End. Though, as Treena had pointed out when I discussed it with her, that was when she was very ill and probably confused. What danger could there possibly be in a small Lancashire village?

Aunt Em had thought it was because Mum's family had threatened to do horrible things to her if she ever showed her face in the village again, after she told them she was expecting me, but that was such an outdated attitude now and so long ago . . . I didn't suppose I'd get a welcome from whatever members of the Vane family still remained there, but there surely couldn't be any *danger*. In any case, I wasn't Marianne Vane any longer, but Marnie Ellwood, and there was no reason why they should ever know who I was.

I'd accepted the job offer and I was to start on Monday morning, or at least arrive then, which meant I could spend two nights with Treena and have a good catch-up first. Of course, I'd often seen her when she'd been over to visit the family, but the last – and only – time I'd stayed in her cottage in Great Mumming was when I was making my break for freedom.

I'd been a nervous wreck, illogically convinced that Mike would suddenly appear, even though Treena kept reminding me that, with a burst appendix and septic shock, he'd have been incapable of even rising from his hospital bed in Amsterdam, where he'd just arrived for a conference. He'd been complaining about abdominal pain and thought he was getting an ulcer, which just goes to show how good veterinary surgeons are at diagnosing their own ills.

I'd been afraid that he'd cancel the trip, because Treena and I had been counting on his absence for my Great Escape, so it was with huge relief that I saw his car emerge from the car park onto the road and vanish.

He'd been due back on the Monday, so the news of the appendix bursting, which came just as I was about to depart the flat for ever, was an unexpected bonus, though it had taken Treena, later, to make me see it that way without feeling guilty.

But I'd had my emotions twisted and pulled into such a complicated knot by then that it was to take five years of grubbing about in French soil to heal me.

I pushed away the memory of that fleeing and haunted version of myself and thought about the future instead. I was going to live in Jericho's End, the magical place of all Mum's childhood stories, including my favourite ones about the fairies, or little angels, as she insisted they were, that she'd seen by the waterfall at the top of the valley.

I smiled, thinking that it was probably the effect of flickering sunlight through leaves that had caused an imaginative child to conjure up something so fantastical, but I would search out the spot when I had time and think of her there.

The cold wind ruffled my short, dark curls – long gone was the Pre-Raphaelite mass of wavy black hair that Mike had so admired, for the moment the real Marnie had emerged from wherever she'd been hiding I'd ruthlessly purged myself of anything that reminded me of him.

One of the ways Mike had tried to exert control over me was by giving me clothes – short-skirted little suits, slinky dresses and ridiculous shoes with pointy toes and stiletto heels. Apart from not having pointy feet, there was no way I was tottering about on spikes, and I'd thrown them out of the window.

For a moment it had seemed likely that he would throw me out after them. I did wear the loathsome clothes at home, though – *Mike's* home, never mine.

I'd left every single thing he'd ever bought me behind and now my wardrobe was almost entirely utilitarian: dungarees and jeans, T-shirts and jumpers, anoraks and lace-up leather work boots.

I *love* dungarees, but ones made especially for me by Aunt Em, with a wide bib front and lots of pockets, because I've never found a pair of dungarees in a shop yet where the sides of the bib didn't hit the middle of my boobs dead centre, which is neither comfortable, nor a good look if you actually *have* a bosom. It's the same with most aprons, come to think of it, because they usually have ridiculous little bib tops too . . . and don't get me *started* on women's shirts with breast pockets. I mean, show me any woman who puts stuff in a *breast* pocket? Clothes designers should take a sanity check before they're allowed near a sheet of pattern paper.

There had been no chance of my acquiring even the slightest touch of French chic during the last few years. I was a lost cause.

The ferry gave a sudden lurch, dragging back my thoughts to the present. It was plunging up and down in a way that I found exhilarating, but I was feeling chilly and searched out a sheltered spot behind a lifeboat, where I took out Ms E. Price-Jones's last missive to read again, even though I knew it pretty well by heart.

> My sister and I are so glad you have accepted the position! The pay is not munificent, I have to admit, but the accommodation, a small self-contained flat, is of course included. The flat is situated at one end of Lavender

Cottage, over the café-gallery, and comprises a bedroom, sitting room/kitchenette and the usual offices.

Your working hours will be divided between our small garden (largely given over to varieties of lavender, as you may have guessed!) and that of my nephew's house next door, Old Grace Hall, the two being conveniently linked by an old, but sadly neglected, rose garden.

The Grace Garden behind the Hall was originally set out in the seventeenth century as a walled apothecary garden and is currently being restored. I am sure you will find it most interesting.

There certainly sounded plenty to keep me occupied there, even without the vague mention later in the letter of 'occasional other duties as required . . .'

I hadn't heard of the Grace Garden, but found the whole idea of a walled apothecary garden enchanting. I'd once visited and been fascinated by the Chelsea Physic Garden in London. And I also loved roses, so the challenge of a neglected old rose garden made me itch to come to the rescue, secateurs in hand.

It all sounded like my idea of heaven . . .

I suddenly realized that either the wind had shifted, or the boat had changed direction, for a gust tried to tear the letter from my hands and I hastily stuffed it back into my rucksack and headed inside to thaw out over hot coffee and croissants.

My drive north from Dover seemed endless, though I didn't remember it taking so long when I was fleeing in the other direction.

I stopped often for coffee to keep me awake, and coffee had certainly improved in my absence, even in motorway service stations.

By the time I could finally abandon the M6 and head for the increasingly small roads that would take me to Great Mumming, I was very tired and having constantly to remind myself to drive on the left.

I felt an unwelcome pull of tension when I saw a sign for Merchester, and I wished Mike wasn't still so close, even if he had totally lost interest in me. I tried to banish a sudden mental image of him sitting like a squat spider in the middle of his dark web, waiting for me to twitch the edges.

He wouldn't even know I was in the area unless I bumped into him and I vowed to avoid Merchester like the plague.

It was All Fools' Day, but I'd been there and done that, and I'd never be anyone's fool again.

I got to Treena's tiny end-terrace cottage on the very edge of the small town and, dazed by exhaustion but happy to be there, was borne indoors on a wave of warmth and dogs, fed supper and then fell into bed and instant oblivion.

3

Unlocked

I woke very early, with the panicked feeling that I didn't know where I was – but then, I'd often had that during the last few years, due to moving around so much.

Then I registered the familiar shape of Mum's small, scroll-backed antique chair, upholstered in rubbed gold velvet, and it came back to me: I was in Treena's spare room, into which had been wedged a narrow bed, a tiny chest of drawers with a mirror on top and a stack of boxes and bundles under a bright throw, which contained all the things Treena had been storing for me all this time.

The door opened slightly and Treena peeped cautiously round it, then, when she saw I was awake, came and deposited a mug of coffee on the bedside table.

'I didn't want to wake you, but I'm just off for a ride and I'll be back in a couple of hours. I'll take the dogs with me. The cats have eaten; don't let them tell you any different.'

'OK, have a lovely ride. I feel wide awake now, so I'll get up.'

'Water's hot for a shower, and help yourself to breakfast,' she said, and vanished, though I could hear her boots on the stairs and then her voice talking to the animals, before the front door shut behind her.

I propped myself up with the pillows behind me and then lay there, thinking that the room looked just the same as it had five years ago, when I'd arrived in the dead of night (later than expected, since I'd discovered Mike had locked me into the flat and taken my keys with him, so I'd had to call a twenty-four-hour locksmith to release me), with a car haphazardly stuffed with my belongings and the irrational feeling that Mike might have divined what I was doing, miraculously risen from his hospital bed, and would suddenly appear at any moment, possibly in a puff of sulphur-yellow smoke.

Treena had orchestrated my escape. I'd tried to distance myself from her after Mike's threats to blacken her professional name if I left him with her help, but it hadn't been any use: I'd found her one day standing by my unmistakable old 2CV in the car park of the garden I worked at, when I was heading home after work. She'd demanded to know why I wasn't answering her texts and emails and she wasn't in the least impressed when I told her about Mike's threats.

After that, it was easy enough to snatch brief meetings while I was still working. Things only got tricky later. But by then we had hammered out my exit strategy and were all set for the weekend Mike would be away at the conference in Amsterdam. We'd thought we'd only have the weekend and I'd have to cram all kinds of things into the Saturday, like seeing the solicitor Treena had lined up for me, before I vanished to France, but his being so ill gave us a little extra time.

On the Monday morning I posted a letter to him addressed to the flat, saying I'd left him and to contact me via my solicitor, and also sent a copy to the hospital in Amsterdam, for good measure, though I didn't think it would help speed his recovery. By late morning I was on my way to catch the ferry to France and the Château du Monde.

Most of my belongings stayed at Treena's cottage. I took my working clothes and some jeans and jumpers, a pre-Mike long washed-denim skirt and old, comfortable ballet flats and a good, warm, loose wool jacket in a cheery bright red that Aunt Em had once bought me. That was pretty well it, apart from my leather rucksack.

I certainly wasn't taking my laptop and phone. Mike had given me those and I'd eventually realized he was using them to snoop on me. Or so he thought. He never knew about the mobile phone I kept sealed in a waterproof bag in one of the plant pots on the flat's balcony, *or* that I had an emergency set of car keys hidden under the bumper – for of course my car keys had been on the ring with the door key he'd taken with him.

There were a lot of things he hadn't known about me, but he'd been so sure when he went away that weekend that he finally had me exactly where he wanted me.

It all felt like a bad nightmare now, the kind that gave me flashbacks I could have done without.

I got up and showered and then went down to the warm kitchen to forage for breakfast. The two Border collies had gone with Treena, but two of the sedately middle-aged cats kept me company while the other, a three-legged and slightly cross-eyed Siamese, was quite shy.

After I'd washed down toast and marmalade with two more mugs of coffee, I thought I might as well make a start on sorting out the stack of belongings in my bedroom and seeing what I could fit in my car around the stuff I'd brought from France.

I'd been surprised at how much I'd accumulated. There weren't a lot more clothes, but I'd filled two stacking boxes with old French cookery and gardening books and several old gardening tools I'd picked up along the way. There was also the last-minute find at a junk market of a pair of enormous old butter paddles . . . I was armed and dangerous.

I'd left most of this stuff in the car last night, just bringing in the rucksack and a slightly moth-eaten carpet bag I'd found in the Château du Monde attic. Just to be sure there weren't any ravenous inhabitants remaining, we'd wrapped it in plastic and left it in one of the big freezers for twenty-four hours, which Aunt Em reckoned would finish off any lingering moth grubs, so I had the most chilled luggage ever.

I was filling what space there was in the car with the nearest boxes and bundles – some mine, some things of Mum's that Aunt Em had packed up for me after her death – when Treena returned. She put the dogs in the house and then came back to watch me. Her cheeks were glowing and she smelled pleasantly of horses.

'It looks like one of those 3-D jigsaw puzzles,' she said, as I attempted to slide the wooden butter paddles between the back of the passenger seat and a battered tin trunk. 'What *are* those things?'

'Butter paddles, but much bigger than usual. Em reckons the dairymaid who swung these must have been Amazonian.'

'I expect you'll find a hundred and one uses for them,' she said, as I closed the door cautiously. The car didn't explode, scattering belongings in all directions, as I'd half feared.

'I've made a small hole in the stuff you've been storing for me, but I'll try and do something about the rest as soon as I can. It's been taking up space in your cottage for way too long.'

'Oh, no problem,' she said, looking slightly surprised. She was very laid-back, as were all the Ellwoods. 'I'd forgotten about it – I mean, it's just there, in nobody's way.'

She went to change and then we walked into Great

Mumming and had a pub lunch with her old college friend and partner at Happy Pets, Sam, and his wife, Karen, who was a doctor. They were fascinated by my nomadic life in France, moving from one crumbling château to the next, nominally gardening, but in reality also picking up other skills, from French cookery of the more hearty peasant type, to plumbing, plastering and wallpapering.

As I described the funnier episodes and recalled how, on warm summer evenings, the château owners and the volunteer helpers would all gather together at trestle table in the garden to eat after a hard day's work, I could already see how these years would soon become fond memories, to look back on with pleasure.

During that time, I'd slowly unwound until the old Marnie blossomed forth once again, though with a few additional thorns, as I'd restored walled gardens, semi-wild kitchen plots, neglected formal parterres and even a maze. Reconnection to the earth had been what I'd needed and I'd made many new friends, though never anything more, because I was entirely done with love.

From time to time I'd gone back to the Château du Monde for a little holiday with the family, but the time there never turned out to be that, because I couldn't resist working in the World Map garden, which gave the château its name. The family had thrown themselves into upgrading and extending the campsite and the lake facilities, then opening a garden centre, before they'd sorted out the accommodation for themselves, and they were still working on making the place a comfortable home.

'I sometimes wish I'd moved to France with them,' Treena said. 'But then, like you, Marnie, living in France was never *my* dream and my roots are forever dug into west Lancashire.'

We gave the dogs a quick walk when we got back and then

a tidal wave of tiredness washed over me and I zonked out on my bed before dinner under a coverlet of cats.

The remains of a pot of spaghetti Bolognese lay on the table along with an open bottle of prosecco, a scene almost exactly like the last evening I'd spent here before I'd set off for France.

Treena had obviously been thinking along the same lines, for she said now, 'You were still terrified Mike might somehow appear and drag you home, that last night before you left for France, do you remember? I had to put through a call to his hospital in Amsterdam before you were convinced he was still there.'

'I know, and in retrospect it still seems incredible that I let him get such a hold on me . . . but I think you have to be in that kind of relationship to understand it fully: how slowly it sucks you in before it even dawns on you what's happening.'

'Yes, it took me a long time to work out what he was doing and he had most people fooled into thinking he adored you and was so worried about your mental health, especially after you lost the baby.'

I shivered. I'd got pregnant after my pills had mysteriously 'vanished' and before I could replace them, but I'd hardly realized I was expecting before I'd lost the baby.

'I think the worst thing he ever said to me was that I couldn't even carry out the one function most women managed without any problem – have a baby.'

'He truly deserved a burst appendix and septicaemia,' Treena said. 'God moves in mysterious ways – and it was certainly a godsend for us that he was ill the exact same weekend we'd arranged everything for your escape.'

I smiled through a blur of sudden tears. 'Yes. It was ages before he got home and could start trying to find me.'

'He rang me when he got back to the flat and found you gone,' Treena said, to my surprise. 'I didn't tell you at the time in case it worried you. At first he tried to charm me into telling him where you were, and then, when I wasn't having any of his fake concern about you, he moved on to the threats. But I told him I was recording the conversation and if he tried to blackmail me I'd hand it to the police. That stopped him in his tracks and he rang off.'

'I should think it did,' I agreed. '*Were* you recording it?'

She grinned. 'No, but he didn't know that.'

'You said you thought he'd got someone watching you for a while, presumably to see if you led him to where I was hiding.'

'Yes, and it sounded like the same man Mum and Dad said turned up at the château, asking nosy questions, but of course by then you'd long since moved on and the trail was cold.'

'The fact that I left him a letter asking him to contact my solicitor to discuss a divorce must have given him a hint I wasn't coming back,' I said drily.

'I expect so, but it wasn't until he wanted to remarry that he actually did,' Treena said. 'Lucky for you – but not for her.'

'No . . .' I agreed. 'But perhaps things will be different.'

'Perhaps,' she said, though not sounding convinced, and then tipped the last of the prosecco into our glasses. She passed mine over and raised her own in a toast.

'Here's to your new, unfettered and free life in Jericho's End!'

We clinked glasses.

'Jericho's End is an odd name for a village, isn't it?' I said. 'Wasn't there a Jericho in the Bible, where the walls fell down when someone blew a trumpet?'

'Yes, so there was, but you should be safe unless anyone starts up a brass band,' Treena grinned. Then she added, 'It's just like old times, having you here. I wish you could stay a few days more.'

'I do, too, but they seemed very keen on my starting work as soon as possible. And actually, I can't wait to see this magical village that Mum used to tell me stories about. I'm just afraid the reality won't live up to them!'

'Haven't you even looked at the place on Google Maps yet?' she asked. 'That gives you a good idea of the layout and you can move around the village as if you're wearing an invisibility cloak.'

'No . . . I don't quite know why, but I sort of want it all to unfold in front of me when I arrive, not sneak about the place first, via the internet.'

'You're weird,' she said, but in a kind way.

'Don't forget, I couldn't afford a laptop for ages until Aunt Em gave me her old one. I had to rely on occasional access to the internet on someone else's, and my phones are always the cheapest and most basic ones I can find.'

'That old laptop of Mum's is so ancient, it belongs in a museum. Does it even work?'

'If I turn it on and off a few times and the wind's in the right direction, then it usually does. It's started making an ominous whining noise, though.'

'I'm just about to buy a new laptop, so you can have my old one,' she offered. 'It works fine; I just fancied the new model. I'll clean my stuff off it for you, ready for next time you come over.'

'Thank you, that would be great,' I said. 'I must buy a new phone, too. I dropped the previous pay-as-you-go one in a lily pond.'

'Why not sign up with my mobile phone provider? It's a rolling thing: you pay every month and you can cancel any time. It's cheap, too, and if we do it now on the laptop, the sim will arrive in a day or two. You don't have to hide behind a disposable phone any longer.'

I thought that seemed a good idea and it took no time to sort out. I refused her offer to get Jericho's End up on the screen while we were at it, though.

'No, I'll wait and see it for real,' I said. 'At least I did look for the road to it from Great Mumming on an old UK car atlas I found under the passenger seat, and it isn't that far away as the crow flies. Have *you* been there?'

'Yes, a few times, but only to a biggish house called Risings up on the left of the road before you get into the village proper. The owner's an overbearing woman with two Pekes that she's convinced have delicate constitutions. There's no reason why she shouldn't bring them to the surgery in Great Mumming, but I make her pay through the nose for dragging me all the way out there for every upset stomach.'

'Weren't you curious enough to drive into the village for a look?' I asked.

'No, I always seem to be rushed for time. I know it's supposed to be a beauty spot with waterfalls and stuff,' she said vaguely. 'But I will come and visit once you've settled in and . . . well, actually, I know someone who will be working there from Easter right over the summer, so I expect I'll be popping in occasionally to see how he's getting on, too.'

She looked faintly self-conscious and I gazed at her in surprise.

'A boyfriend?'

'No,' she said quickly. 'Just – someone I met a few months ago. A friend. He's an archaeologist and he's got funding for a dig at Jericho's End. There's some kind of small monastic ruin near the river on the village outskirts, more or less opposite Risings. It's never been properly excavated.'

'A small monastic ruin doesn't sound very exciting.'

'To Luke, lumps of mud and random bits of burned bone seem to provide endless excitement.'

Treena had always insisted that she was never going to get married, or live with anyone. She liked her independence and her own way of doing things too much, and had her animals for company. Seeing what happened to me had probably reinforced that determination.

But now I wondered if there was a softening around the edges . . . though there certainly wasn't around mine. Once bitten, more than twice shy. Forever shy.

We'd both turn thirty-six this year – we'd been born within a week of each other, and in fact it was at the antenatal clinic that our mothers met and became such close friends. Treena and I had always had joint birthday parties, twins of a kind.

I tactfully changed the subject. 'This Ms E. Price-Jones sounds very kind in her letters, and there's a sister, too. They're expecting me about ten tomorrow and I'm to go into the café, Ice Cream and Angels, which is at one end of Lavender Cottage. She sent me a little map on the back of the last letter, but it was in pencil so I've only just noticed.'

'Strange name for a café,' Treena commented.

'Yes . . . and oddly enough, "ice-cream and angels" was the last thing Mum ever said.'

I'd never told even Treena that before. Now I'd remembered I felt doubly excited. First Jericho's End and now the name of the café were connecting my new life with Mum in a way I couldn't wait to discover. I hadn't forgotten Mum's warning, but I felt there were answers waiting for me.

'Really?' she said. 'Then I think that's a good omen, don't you?'

4

Going to Jericho

Treena was to set out early for Happy Pets in the morning, since she was taking the first drop-in session. Over breakfast she presented me with a large-scale Ordnance Survey map of the Thorstane and Jericho's End area.

'The turn to the village is easy to miss if you haven't got sat nav.'

'I sneer in the face of sat nav,' I said, larding butter onto toast and adding some of last year's bramble jam. 'After all, when I went to France I only had an ordinary car atlas and a load of Post-it notes with road numbers written on them stuck along the dashboard – not to mention having to drive on the wrong side of the road – and I found the Château du Monde OK.'

Not that I actually remembered much of that nightmare flight to safety, with the imaginary hounds of hell on my trail in defiance of all common sense and reason.

'Didn't you circle Paris twice before you found the right road south?'

'You know very well that's just a family joke,' I said with dignity, though the other one they told – about my having inadvertently bought a supply of high-salt-content mineral water when I stopped for petrol and arriving with a raging thirst – wasn't.

Treena gave me a spare key to the cottage and left, taking the dogs with her, and saying she couldn't wait to hear how I got on and I must email her later.

I still felt slightly spaced out and as if this wasn't all really happening, but I spread out the map on the kitchen table, pushed away the cat that immediately came and sat on it, and studied the lie of the land.

From Great Mumming, which was an attractive small market town, I needed to take the road that ran vaguely eastward towards the large village of Thorstane, which was up on the edge of the moors.

The tiny village of Jericho's End looked very close to Thorstane on the map, but the turn to it onto a single-track lane came miles before you would expect it to, due to it forming a long, narrow 'V' with the main road.

It wound its way up a blind-ended valley that looked more like a ravine towards the top, where the road petered out and was replaced by a zigzag of dotted lines. There appeared to be only the one decent road in and out, which made it quite off the beaten track.

Only visitors looking for scenery or, possibly, fairies would have any reason to go there and neither of those had ever been interests of Mike's. To him, a village was something you ran through and I assumed he was still running – did runners go on for ever? He must be the wrong side of forty-six now.

I shivered. I might be free and in what passed for my right mind, but I still never wanted to hear his voice, or come suddenly face to face with him again . . . though now I was also so filled with anger at what he'd tried to make me become that I only hoped those butter paddles *were* handy if he ever turned up.

I grinned to myself, picturing that, but I didn't suppose I'd have the paddles to hand even if he did appear, because people would think I was a little strange if I took to carrying them about with me.

I looked at the clock and decided it was time to make a move.

As a concession to this first meeting with my new employers, I'd applied eyeliner and a smudge of ruby lip gloss, brushed my hair so that it curled neatly behind my ears, and I was wearing what now served as my special occasion outfit: a dungaree-style denim dress (made by Aunt Em, of course, so with a decently wide top), worn over a long-sleeved black T-shirt and with black and white striped leggings and clumpy Doc Marten boots patterned with bright butterflies. I slung my carpet bag and rucksack into the car, along with the cherry-red wool jacket, said goodbye to the cats and set off.

I found the right road out of town – it was past a place making huge terracotta garden pots that Treena had told me about – and soon the houses petered out, ending in a glimpse through trees of a large Victorian house that seemed to be some kind of private school. Then the road began a slow climb upwards through farmland.

It was a changeable early April morning and a brisk, chill breeze tried to insinuate its chilly fingers through the edges of the car's fabric roof. Small white bunny-tail clouds were rolling across a baby-blue sky and all looked clean, well scoured and fresh – entirely suitable for the new start I was about to make. I felt nervous, of course, but also excited, both at the prospect of helping restore the old lavender, rose and apothecary gardens, and of having a place, however small, to call my own.

The last few years I'd felt akin to something between tumbleweed and one of those plants with aerial roots that seemingly suck nutrients from thin air.

Then, too, I hoped I might in some way find and reconnect with my mother here in the valley she'd loved . . . though not, perhaps, with the family who'd inspired her with such fear she had warned me never to go there.

I assumed I still *had* Vane relatives at the farm, maybe even grandparents, though perhaps not, since they'd be in their nineties by now. But Mum had had an elder brother who might have family of his own, and I'd probably be able to take a sneaky look at them without their ever suspecting who I was.

The car wheezed slightly as the road grew steeper and the cows in the fields on either side gave way to sheep.

I began to keep a sharp lookout for the turn, and there, round the next bend, it suddenly appeared.

A tall signpost was planted in the long grass of the right-hand verge, with one arm pointing in the direction of a gap in the hedge.

Three other signs of differing sizes, shapes and colours had been nailed to the post, so that it looked like a strange totem pole. I paused next to it as I turned in, to read them. They advertised, from top to bottom:

The Devil's Cauldron Inn
Risings B&B
Fairy Falls

Nearby, in a niche clipped into the hawthorn hedge, was one of those brown Ancient Monument signs, looking as if it was trying to disassociate itself from the rest.

If it hadn't been for the signs I'd have thought the road was a farm track, but it immediately opened up into a passing place, which evidently also did service for a bus stop, improbable as that idea seemed. The thought of coming windscreen-to-windscreen with a bus round one of the bends in the narrow road was scary and I wasn't the kind of driver able to whizz backwards nonchalantly for miles.

Thankfully, I met no other vehicles at all, and the tall hedges soon gave way to drystone walls, lichen-patched in sulphur yellow and a slightly snotty green, over which I could see fields descending to a lazy, meandering river a long way below. The hillside rose steeply up to my left, the hardy-looking sheep wrenching tufts of grass with determined jerks of their heads.

My destination remained hidden until I rounded another bend and saw the centre of the village laid out below me, like a haphazard Toytown. I spotted a blue Parking sign as I swooped down the steep hill and I turned in, coming to a halt on a stretch of rough gravel.

I needed a breathing space before carrying on . . . not to mention an attempt to unclench my hands from the steering wheel.

This seemed to be the parking area for the Ancient Monument, a fenced enclosure in which all I could see was mysteriously hummocked grass, with a closed gate and a shuttered entrance hut.

A small stone building nearby proclaimed itself a public convenience, though inconveniently locked up with a huge chain and padlock, and the couple of other cars parked there were empty and haphazardly positioned, as if washed in by the tide and stranded.

On the other side of the road, some way up the hill, was a large house that I thought must be Risings, the place Treena was often called out to, with the overbearing owner and the spoilt Pekes.

A plump, bearded elderly man in a bright red bobble hat now emerged from the small lodge at the large house's gates and hobbled over the road and past my car, giving me a hard stare as he went. He slowly unpadlocked the toilet block, then did the same for the gate to the ancient monument, before fetching from the hut an armful of those wooden bat things with laminated information sheets stuck to them, which he deposited in a kind of wooden bucket on a post.

That seemed to be the extent of his caretaking duties, for, with another suspicious glare in my direction, he returned to his lodge and shut the door.

I got out, pulling on my red wool jacket against the icy breeze, and looked down at Jericho's End. There was a straggle of small cottages edging the lane past the lodge, ending in a large building that was unmistakably the pub. The road went past it and vanished upwards round a sharp turn, but opposite the pub was a small, humpbacked bridge that led to my destination. I could see the sparkle of water as it cascaded underneath into a pool far below and, on the other side of the river, a group of buildings clustered around a small green, including an improbable black and white Tudor building like an overgrown cottage from a fairy tale, which I guessed to be Old Grace Hall. The long, low stone shape set with a typically large café window near the bridge must be my destination.

It was time to go.

'You can drive over the bridge and park by the Green. Come into the café, which opens at ten, and you will find me there,' Ms E. Price-Jones had written.

The bridge was *very* narrow, but had embrasures on either side into which pedestrians could press themselves to escape any traffic. I came to a halt opposite the café, between a lime-green Beetle and a white van so bashed and battered that it looked as if it was made from a crumpled piece of dirty paper.

As I reached for the door handle, a movement out of the corner of my eye stopped me dead. A thin, wiry man was just turning into a gateway beyond the Tudor house and glanced back with an oddly furtive air as he did so.

My heart thudded to a stop for a moment and then restarted: it wasn't Mike, unless he'd taken to dyeing his hair bright red. I would have to stop seeing bogeymen around every corner.

Getting out and pulling my jacket around me, I headed across the road, noticing for the first time a large entrance turnstile between the café and the bridge, with wrought ironwork over it, proclaiming it to be the entrance to the River Walk and Fairy Falls.

The café window was set into one end of Lavender Cottage and bore a sign over it:

Ice Cream and Angels
Café-Gallery

The scalloped edge of a striped awning showed beneath it, where it had been folded back against the wall in a protective housing. In summer, it must pleasantly shade the small paved area in front of it, where a few white-painted wrought-iron tables and chairs were now stacked together. A grassy bank dividing it from the road was decorated with an ancient ice-cream vendor's tricycle, the box in front planted up with variegated ivy and spring bulbs.

It had been brightly painted and the gilded lettering on it advertised Verdi's Ice Cream.

It was all very picturesque, but a sharp cold spatter of rain hit me and I ran for the café door.

There was a heavenly chiming as I went in, appropriate for somewhere called Ice Cream and Angels, and I found myself in a surprisingly large, white-painted room, with a tiled floor like a chessboard and light wooden chairs and tables. Hung along one wall were large oil paintings, their subjects hard to make out at a glance.

The only customers were a middle-aged couple dressed for the ascent of Everest, in parkas, knitted hats, rucksacks, boots and sticks, who got up and left as I went in, bidding me good morning as they passed.

'Dear me! Perhaps I should have offered to find them a Sherpa for the ascent of the Fairy Falls,' said a small, elderly lady sardonically as she appeared from behind the counter at the far end of the café. She had turquoise hair cut in a sleek pageboy bob, lively dark eyes and a puckish grin.

'They'll probably go out by the turnstile at the top of the falls and hike up to Thorstane,' suggested a young man who had been half hidden by a huge and ancient stainless-steel coffee machine.

The woman lost interest in the hikers and advanced on me, holding out a thin hand encrusted with huge semi-precious stone rings. 'I am sure you must be Marianne Ellwood. Welcome, my dear!'

I shook the hand gingerly and it rattled metallically.

'I'm Elfrida Price-Jones, but do call me Elf – everyone does.'

'Thank you, and you must call me Marnie,' I told her.

'Short and sweet,' she approved. 'And this is Charlie Posset, whose family have the pub on the other side of the bridge, the Devil's Cauldron – they're distantly related through my mother's side. Such a *lot* of it in small villages like this,' she added, and Charlie grinned.

He was a very engaging-looking youth, with a wide mouth, a mop of indeterminate brown hair and freckles.

'I'm finishing off my gap year by helping in the café,' he said. 'The lure of all the ice-cream I could eat was too much for me.'

'I'm not surprised,' I said.

'Marnie's the new gardener,' Elf explained to Charlie. 'I told you she was coming, didn't I?'

'Yes, but not that she was arriving today.'

'Didn't I?' she said vaguely. 'Never mind, she's here now. Come along, Marnie, let's sit in the window with a nice hot cup of coffee and get acquainted. Frothy or espresso?'

'Er . . . frothy, please,' I said, but turned down the offer of ice-cream.

Charlie produced two cups of frothy coffee from the hissing stainless-steel monster, and it must have had plenty of caffeine content, because I felt myself perking up after only a couple of sips.

'Hear that noise?' asked Elf.

I nodded; I had become aware of a faint grinding and rumbling somewhere in the background.

'That's one of the original electric ice-cream-making machines in the back room – you need to keep using them constantly or they seize up,' she said, unpeeling a mini biscotti from its wrapper and dunking it into her coffee. 'I even sometimes use the original patented Victorian devices, where everything is done by hand. You can see some of the photographs and original adverts for Agnes Marshall's Ice Cave, and Ice-cream and Water-Ice making tubs on the wall.'

I'd noticed the wall opposite the paintings was decorated

with posters and photos, as well as being set with a stable door that had the top ajar, which presumably led into the adjoining Lavender Cottage.

'The Verdis opened a teashop here selling ices in late Victorian times, you know. They were of Italian descent and my mum was the last of the family.'

'Oh, really?' I said, interested. It seemed rather exotic for a little village up a dead-end valley and I'd had no idea ice-cream making was flourishing that early.

'Jericho's End was in its heyday of popularity with the Victorian daytrippers then, and they say it was the first ice-cream parlour in the north of England, but I don't know . . .'

She broke off as the small, battered white van that had been parked in front of my car drove slowly past, emitting a bronchial rattling noise, and the pale face of the red-haired man I'd glimpsed earlier scowled at us through the open window.

'Dear me – I wonder what he wanted? I suppose he's been up to the Hall, trying to make trouble again.'

Elf, seeing my blank expression, explained, 'He's one of the Vanes, a local farming family, but he set himself up as a self-employed gardener/handyman, though he's a poor hand at both. And almost as dour and unpleasant as his father,' she added. 'He helped in the Grace Garden one day a week for my late brother-in-law, but when my nephew inherited, last year, he let him go. Lazy and couldn't tell a lupin from a foxglove.'

'Did you say his name was Vane?' I asked, most of what she'd said washing over me, as I wondered if this was some relative of mine. If so, I can't say I'd really liked the look of him.

'Yes, Wayne Vane.' She giggled at my expression. 'His parents christened him Esau, but from a child he insisted on being called Wayne. Personally, I think he'd have been better sticking to the original.'

'You're right,' I agreed. 'Esau Vane has an unusual ring to it, but Wayne Vane just sounds a bit silly.'

'Anyway, that's neither here nor there,' Elf said a little more briskly, turning back from the window, where the last trace of blue exhaust hung in the air.

'What were we saying before? Oh yes – ice-cream. I'm making lemon today. Of course, our bestseller is my lavender and rose, but I like to ring the changes. Your wages may not be munificent, Marnie, but you may eat all the ice-cream you want, like Charlie. There is a little fridge-freezer in your flat, so you can keep some to hand, too.'

'Thank you,' I said, 'that sounds lovely.'

'We call the place a café-gallery now, but basically we're still an ice-cream parlour and, apart from tea and coffee, only serve ice-cream, sorbets and my home-made lemonade, ginger or nettle beers.'

'I didn't know you *could* make nettle beer,' I said, surprised.

'Oh, yes, it's quite delicious, but you must pick the young tender tips of the nettles. When the time is right and the fancy takes me, I brew up a fresh batch, or a jug of lemonade in what I call my stillroom in the cottage, which is through that door over there.'

So I'd been right about the stable door leading into the cottage itself.

'Lavender Cottage was originally a row of three and the Verdi family crammed themselves into the upstairs and back of this one. Father bought the other two when he came here to live, between the wars, and knocked them into one. Then when he married Gina Verdi, he had the doors put through into this one, too, and it's very convenient now that I have taken on the running of the café, because I can keep an eye on things from my own kitchen if I want to.'

My head was starting to spin a bit with all this information, and we hadn't even got on to the subject of my work yet! But she was twittering blithely on.

'My sister Myfanwy is a painter, like my father was, so we use the café to hang some of her works, though of course she sells mainly through London galleries – she's quite well known.'

The name Myfanwy Price-Jones did sound familiar, now I came to think about it, though I didn't know a lot about art. I looked at the dark serried ranks of oil paintings on the white-washed wall. Now my eyes had adjusted to the interior light, I could see that they were semi-abstract works that seemed to depict cascades of water, fern and rocks and the flickering suggestion of something winged and slightly humanoid . . .

'Myfanwy – we always call her Myfy' – she pronounced it My-fee, not Miffy, like the rabbit – 'looks after the garden, too, but she doesn't have a lot of time to spare. We had a much older sister, Morwenna, who married the last owner of Old Grace Hall. The two gardens are linked because our families are.'

I expect I was staring at her blankly by now, because she put down her empty cup and patted one of my hands with a clashing of metal and clinking of pigeon-egg-sized stones.

'Never mind trying to take it all in now, Marnie, because it's going to be terribly confusing for a day or two, until you've met everyone and got your bearings. I expect you'd like to see your little flat and then bring your things in and settle in before lunch, wouldn't you?'

'Yes . . . but we haven't yet discussed the work and—'

'Oh, time enough for that over lunch,' she said. 'Come on!'

She left Charlie in charge and took me through to a cavernous back room, where the ice-cream chugged away to itself, and on through a kind of scullery to a small hallway.

'There's the back door, which you can use to come and go, though there are keys to the café door on the ring I'll give you, too.'

She opened another door I'd thought was a cupboard and revealed a boxed-in flight of steep steps.

'These are the original stairs, and private to your flat because we have our own in Lavender Cottage. Up we go!' she added gaily, and led the way up to a small landing. 'There's the connecting door to the cottage – so we've put a bolt on your side, so you can make the flat quite separate – and this,' she announced, throwing open the door on the other side, 'is your new home!'

The large, light living room had a kitchen/diner area at one end. The floor was dark, varnished wood, scattered with brightly patterned rugs.

'We used it as a guest suite originally, then had it done over like this when Mum needed a full-time nurse towards the end. It's quite basic, I know, but I hope you'll find it comfortable.'

'Oh, I think it's lovely,' I said. There was a long, low squishy sofa in a faded linen cover, a sheepskin rug before a fake electric log-burner and a wicker basket chair with buttoned cushions. The bedroom just had room for a white-painted high metal bed, a small bamboo table next to it, a chest of drawers and a narrow wardrobe. A tiny shower room opened off it.

'I *love* it,' I said warmly.

'I'm so glad, though I'm afraid we only have electric night-storage heaters in the cottage, which aren't terribly efficient, but you have the little electric stove too, and we have open fires and log-burners in the cottage, so the whole building keeps very cosy.'

'I've been living in a series of more or less ruined French

châteaux for the last few years, so to me it's positively luxurious,' I assured her.

'Sounds fascinating and you must tell us all about it,' she said, with one of her bright-eyed looks. 'Now, I'll mind the café while Charlie helps you to bring your things in and then we'll leave you to settle in. You can come down for lunch in the cottage at about twelve thirty – come through from the café – and I'll introduce you to my sister then. She can tell you all about the gardens.'

'I'm afraid my car is very full of boxes,' I said. 'My sister in Great Mumming, who I stayed with over the weekend, has been storing a lot of things for me while I was away and I thought I'd bring some of them with me to sort out, if you don't mind.'

'Not at all – that seems very sensible.'

She took over the counter and Charlie soon had the contents of my car transferred to the flat and everything stacked in a corner of the living room. Then he hurtled precipitously back down the stairs to take over again from Elf and I was alone.

Faintly, through the floorboards, came the silvery celestial chime of the café doorbell – not noisy or disturbing at all but just gently welcoming.

5

Men Are from Mars

When I'd closed the door to the stairs behind Charlie I explored my little domain, which was simple, but just right. I thought there must originally have been two or three small rooms, which had been knocked into one to create the large living and kitchen area, and I'd certainly have plenty of space to bring over the rest of the things I'd stored at Treena's and sort them out at my leisure. Assuming I *had* any leisure, that is, for I had no idea so far what my hours and days might be.

But Mum's velvet-covered chair would look perfect by the hearth, and the small white bookshelf with my childhood favourites in it would fit against the wall next to it.

Someone – probably Elf – had thoughtfully stocked the fridge with milk, eggs, butter and cheese, and there was a fresh loaf of bread, a jar of honey and canisters of teabags and coffee. I loved good coffee and had a cafetière and a couple of bags of my favourite ground coffee in my luggage, but I made a cup of instant while I began to unpack my bags: my working clothes first, which was most of my wardrobe, my coats on the rack on the landing, with my boots and wellingtons underneath.

Then the box of favourite kitchen utensils, including my

cafetière and a tea strainer in the shape of a slightly squat Eiffel Tower.

That would do for now: I'd enjoy arranging everything else later, putting my collection of French cookery and gardening books on the empty shelves and making a little display of the bits of old Quimper pottery I'd picked up at markets.

Already the flat looked like home, not just a temporary resting place. In fact, the moment I'd set foot in Jericho's End, it had felt strangely welcoming, soft wings of familiarity folding around me.

Mum had said it was a special place and she was right – I knew already that I could bloom again here and reconnect, quite literally, with my native soil.

Perhaps I'd also be able to reconnect with Mum on some level? There were special places she'd mentioned in her stories, especially up by the Fairy Falls, even if there did seem to be some difference of opinion about the nature of their winged and elusive inhabitants. But they had been angels to Mum . . . and, I suspected, going by the paintings downstairs and the name of the café-gallery, to the as-yet unknown Myfanwy Price-Jones, too.

The sisters must be older than Mum would have been by now, but they surely had known her – and she had known the ice-cream parlour. It was an odd thought, a ripple in the fabric of time.

When I went downstairs to the café, Charlie was patiently explaining to a young family that no, they didn't sell Coca-Cola or Dr Pepper, or anything like that, just home-made soft drinks. They seemed to be finding this concept difficult to grasp. He winked at me as I went past, then turned a serious, helpful expression back on his customers and said, 'No, we don't sell anything in bottles or cans that you can take away, just in glasses, to drink here . . .'

I tapped at the stable door, which was now closed, turned the handle and went in, finding myself on the threshold of a warm, large kitchen of the old-fashioned country variety, with an Aga, a long pine table with bunches of herbs and lavender hanging from a rack over it, shelves of jars and bottles . . . and an *extremely* large and hairy marmalade cat, staring at me from narrowed green eyes.

'Do come in, Marnie,' invited Elf, who was assembling what looked like Welsh rarebit at one end of the table. I hoped it was, because I'm very partial to it and it's one of those things that doesn't work properly with French cheese.

The cat also seemed keen on the idea, going by the way it switched its bright green glare back to the table.

'This is my sister Myfanwy.' Elf gestured with the butter knife at a tall woman, who was standing by a glowing electric grill, watching cheese melt. 'Myfy, Marnie Ellwood.'

Myfanwy Price-Jones was a slender woman, perhaps in her mid-sixties, but it was hard to tell, because her face was unlined, even though her hair was purest shining silver and hung straight and loose to her waist. She had a long, dreamy face, a little like Virginia Woolf, but the same bright dark eyes as her sister. She was dressed in a bohemian fashion I rather liked, in a knee-length pink kurta tunic embroidered in a rainbow of colours, worn over black harem trousers. Round her neck hung two pairs of glasses on pearl chains and a long string of chunky oval amber beads. Her feet were bare.

'Pleased,' she said, a smile lifting one corner of her mouth attractively and taking away the slightly melancholy cast of countenance. 'Marnie? Such a nice name – from the Hitchcock film, perhaps?'

'It's Marianne really, but Marnie was as close as I could get to it when I was a little girl.'

'Well, Marnie, God knows we're glad to see you, because we certainly need some extra help with the gardening,' she said frankly. 'Especially our nephew, Edward, who's hoping to restore enough of the Grace Garden to open it to the paying public at Easter, and he can't do that single-handedly.'

'Edward – we call him Ned – is *sort of* our nephew, because his great-uncle Theo married our elder sister, Morwenna,' explained Elf helpfully. 'But he and Wen have both gone now and Ned's inherited Old Grace Hall and the very overgrown gardens.'

Myfy deftly removed two slices of toast from the grill onto a plate and replaced them with the ones passed to her by Elf.

'Do sit down and start your lunch,' urged Elf, sliding the plate in front of an empty chair. 'Welsh rarebit is one of those things you have to cook in relays, like omelettes. Mine's next and then these last two are for Myfy, so dig in while it's hot.'

I sat down and did, feeling slightly self-conscious. The cat, who was sitting bolt upright on the next chair, switched its attention to me and said something imperative.

'Ignore Caspar: he's on a special diet and isn't allowed any,' Myfy said. 'We got him from a cat rescue place a couple of weeks ago, so we're only just getting used to his little ways, and vice versa.'

'I don't think he's really taken to us yet,' Elf said. 'We took pity on him when we saw him there, because he seemed such a quiet, elderly cat, who just wanted somewhere warm and quiet to spend his last few years in.'

'Early days yet,' Myfy said, 'but it looks like he might wear us down and see us out.'

Caspar said something that sounded like, 'Too right!' and

then laid a large furry paw on my knee for a moment, to remind me he was there and hungry.

'He's very big,' I commented.

'He's supposed to be half Maine Coon, and they can be enormous,' said Myfy. 'Funny, he didn't look that big in the cat place.'

Elf took the next slices of toast when they were ready and sat down opposite to me.

'Myfy wasn't quite right about Ned having to restore the garden single-handedly, because he has Jekyll and Hyde to help him, though they aren't really up to the heavier work any more, especially James, with his rheumatism.'

'Jekyll . . . and Hyde?' I repeated, tentatively.

'Family joke,' Myfy explained. 'James Hyde and his sister, Gertrude, are twins, and when she married a man called Steve Jekyll, it was irresistible, though not entirely accurate as they're both lovely and neither at all a monster.'

'And Gertrude Jekyll is a very suitable name for a gardener, too,' Elf put in. 'There was that famous one.'

'Right,' I said resignedly, because it didn't look as if I'd escaped the tyranny of an entrenched ancient gardener even here – in fact, there were two of them and they'd probably look on me as someone who could do all the heavy digging. This nephew probably wasn't so young, either.

'Until recently, I've managed to keep more or less on top of our garden, which isn't huge, and mostly lavender,' said Myfy, 'but there are a few rosemary bushes that have got well out of hand and gone woody, and the Rambling Rector rose at the far end is trying to take over the world.'

'They can be very aggressive,' I said. 'Lovely rose, though.'

'I don't expect it will take you long to get the upper hand of it,' she said optimistically. 'And then, of course, you can spend most of your time next door. We don't mind how you arrange your hours.'

'Ye-es,' I said, and then added tentatively, 'What exactly *are* my hours . . . and days?'

'Oh, didn't I say?' exclaimed Elf. 'Silly me! We thought perhaps half past eight till five, with tea breaks, of course, and an hour for lunch. Tuesday will be your day off, since it's the closing day for the café and the River Walk – we sell the tokens for the turnstile to that in the café. When the Grace Garden opens to the public, it will have the same closing day, to fit in.'

'And, of course, you get Sundays off,' said Myfy, 'unless you arrange with Ned to work extra hours in the Grace Garden from Easter.'

'We all gather together here at about seven on Sundays for dinner, so we do hope you'll join us,' urged Elf, hospitably.

'How lovely,' I said non-committally, wondering exactly *who* this 'all' were who gathered for Sunday dinner. Were there more Lavender Cottage residents I hadn't met yet, or did they just mean the nephew?

'Myfy, you can tell Marnie about the River Walk when you show her round the gardens after lunch,' Elf went on.

'OK,' her sister said amiably.

I had finished my rarebit by the time Myfy was just sitting down to hers, but once she'd caught up, we all had ginger and honey ice-cream . . . except Caspar, who had now somehow managed to drape his front half over my knees and was snoring and drooling onto my best denim dress. He must have been at least four feet from nose to tail, the biggest cat outside a zoo I'd ever met. I decided to let him carry on.

'Ginger ice-cream is a good choice to follow the robust flavour of Welsh rarebit,' said Elf. 'Though it's not as good as the lavender and rose.'

'And you make all of it yourself?'

'Yes, though Charlie's sister, Daisy, who is sixteen, loves to help me. She seems to have inherited the Verdi gene for ice-cream making! Although I make some in the old machines in the café, as you saw earlier, I also use the room next door to this one, where I have a more modern ice-cream maker and huge freezer,' said Elf. 'Myfy will show you when she takes you round.'

'Yes, we'll go out through the house and my studio at the back,' Myfy agreed.

Elf made coffee and told Myfy how I'd been moving around various French châteaux for the last few years.

'It's been fun and given me lots of varied experience, but I felt I wanted to settle down over here now, and with the accommodation included, this is perfect for me,' I explained.

'Well, we hope you'll be very happy with us,' said Elf. 'I had a feeling you were going to fit in the moment I saw you,' she added. 'There was something sort of instantly familiar about you.'

'Yes, I felt that too,' agreed Myfy. 'But you've never been here before, have you?'

I shook my head, wondering what about me could have given that impression. They must have known Mum, but I didn't resemble her very much.

Elf went into the café to relieve Charlie so he could have his lunch and I cautiously extricated myself from under the cat and stood up, somewhat hairier than before.

Caspar sat up to watch as Myfy pulled on a pair of wellingtons without bothering with socks, shrugged into a long black woollen coat with brightly coloured tassels hanging from a pointed hood and led the way through Lavender Cottage.

She opened the door onto Elf's ice-cream-making room a crack and prevented Caspar's attempt to squeeze through with her foot.

'No cats allowed in there. Same in the ice-cream parlour, though luckily he doesn't seem to have thought of jumping up onto the stable door when the top's open,' she said, closing the door again. 'Dogs are allowed on the patio, of course, if their owners are well behaved.'

She gave that tilted smile again and carried on along an inner hall, past the foot of a wide, polished wooden staircase and several closed doors, merely saying, 'Small parlour . . . formal dining room – we tend to eat in the kitchen mostly – and here's the living room.'

She did open the door this time, revealing a huge, airy room obviously created out of several smaller ones. There were wooden floors, over which lay faded, but beautiful, old carpets, and a log-burning stove on a stone slab hearth.

She didn't pause, but clumped across the floor in her wellies and led the way into a studio that had been built out at the back and had French doors leading to the garden, pausing only to shut a very miffed Caspar in the living room.

'He has to stay in at the moment, till we feel he knows it's home and won't wander off,' she explained. 'I do let him in here when I'm working, though.'

'It's a great studio space,' I said, looking round.

'It was Father's – and now it's mine,' said Myfy, striding past a large, empty easel and stepping out of the French doors onto a small patio.

It was crazy paving, like the path that wandered off in a meandering fashion through huge hummocked beds of lavender and some rampant rosemary.

'Elf manages the café and does most of the cooking, and I take on the gardening, when I have time from my painting,' Myfy explained. 'Mum loved lavender and so do I. I've got as many different varieties as I can cram in – Hidcote, Munstead,

Miss Katherine . . .' she murmured dreamily. 'And the white varieties, Edelweiss, Nana Alba and Arctic Snow.'

'I'm not so familiar with the white kinds and, of course, I've been looking after mainly French varieties, lately.'

'Fathead,' she said, still in the same dreamy tone, and I stared at her.

'Not perhaps so hardy as the others, but pretty, so I'm trying it,' she added, to my relief.

'I see what you mean about the rosemary. It's got way too big for its boots and gone woody.'

'It certainly has, and it'll be a tough job getting it out, I'm afraid. It was Elf's idea to put some among the lavender, but I don't think it's working out.'

'I'll soon have it out and then you'll be able to replace it with more lavender,' I said cheerfully.

We were well down the garden now and I could see a trellis overburdened with thick, thorny stems. They reached out across the arch dividing the lavender garden from the rest, ready to snare the unwary.

'The Rambling Rector, I assume?'

'Got it in one,' said Myfy. 'I put it in to cover the trellis, but I hadn't quite realized how fast growing and *thorny* it was. I expect I should have radically pruned it back every year.'

'I'll tame it,' I promised. 'It needs a good cut back now, while it's still early in the year, then an eye keeping on it.'

Avoiding the grabbing, spiky stems of the Rambling Rector, I ducked through the arch and discovered beyond it a rectangle of paving, surrounded by a border of shrubs including several mahonia bushes. In the centre stood a neat row of three white beehives.

'Who's the beekeeper?'

'Elf. She's a member of the Thorstane Bee Group, though

there's not a lot to do with them at this time of year. Some die off, including the old queens, and the rest are either asleep or stay near the hive.'

'I'm afraid I know nothing about beekeeping,' I confessed.

'Nor I. I like bees, but I haven't time to mess about with them. I paint and garden and that's it. And Jacob says he's allergic to them, but I think that's just cowardice.'

'Jacob?' I asked at the mention of a new name.

'My husband. He lives in a converted barn up a track next to the Village Hut at the end of the Green. I mostly stay here in Lavender Cottage. We find it works better like that, with separate studio spaces.'

'Oh?' I said, interested by this revelation. *I* certainly never wanted another husband, but if you had to have one, then keeping him in a separate house seemed like a good idea to me.

'That door in the wall over there is our private entrance to the River Walk. I'll show you that later because we'd better go straight to the Grace Garden now. I told my nephew I'd bring you over and introduce you after lunch and he'll be wondering where we've got to.'

She strode back up the lavender garden and then opened a gate in the tall brick wall by the greenhouse.

'This is a short cut through the old rose garden, though I'm afraid it's now more of a big Brer Rabbit briar patch, with a path through the middle.'

You could say that again. The beautiful old herringbone brick path that ran across it, the mellow colours lit by a stray finger of sunlight, was flanked on either side by a hugely overgrown and impenetrable tangle worthy of Sleeping Beauty's bower.

'I hope you've got a good pair of secateurs,' I said.

'I'm sure Ned has, and luckily, this belongs to Old Grace Hall so it's his problem. The door into our garden was put in when Wen – my sister Morwenna – married Theo, so we could come and go easily. Wen was much older than me – we three sisters were well spread out in age, as if Mum and Father were trying to have one child for each decade.'

We skirted a small pond in the centre, in which the giant, ghostly shapes of fish glimmered under waterlily pads, and she opened another gate in the even higher old brick wall on that side.

'Here we are – the Grace Garden!'

As I passed her and took in the sheer scale of what I was looking at, I stopped dead on the gravel path and my jaw dropped.

'Good heavens, it's *huge*!' I exclaimed incredulously, gazing round.

'These houses were all built on a small plateau, which narrows towards the river, so the Hall has a lot more flat land,' Myfy said, but I was still dumbstruck.

A path to my right led off along the wall, behind a tall bed of trees and shrubs, while another, wider one ran straight ahead. To my left were lower beds, hedged in lavender and with lawned borders and walkways.

The tops of the high, mellow, old brick walls defined the giant square of the garden, but it was impossible to see the whole of it from where we were – there were too many tall shrubs and trees for that and also, unlike most walled gardens I'd ever seen, it was not flat but seemed to gently rise up towards the middle.

I longed to go and explore it . . . but I became aware that Myfy was talking again.

'Wen and Theo weren't much interested in gardening and it didn't help that the lower half was given over to vegetable growing during the war, though there was already a vegetable plot on the other side of the wall. Ned says there's a huge amount of work to do, to restore it to what it once was.'

'But how exciting, to be part of that!' I said.

Myfy gave her tilted smile. 'Well, I'm glad you think so! Ned did say the late seventeenth-century layout of the main paths is still the same – he found a plan.'

I thought he would need a plan, if he was to restore it all to what it once was, after years of neglect, though so far as I could see, the beds closest to us were in fairly good order and, surprisingly, there were even little painted plant name tags on spikes in front of some of the nearby shrubs . . . quince, elderberry and an Alchemist rose.

That last one seemed very appropriate. I wondered what was in the middle of the garden and, entirely forgetting the purpose I was there for, was about to go and find out, when Myfy summoned my attention back again.

'Now where *is* everyone?' she said. 'Perhaps we'd better go through into the courtyard and—'

But at that moment there came the scrunch of heavy footsteps on the gravel path along the wall behind us and she exclaimed, 'Ah, Ned – there you are! I've brought our new gardener to meet you, as I promised.'

I tore my attention from the tantalizing prospect before me and turned round, expecting to see the middle-aged, wax-jacketed and corduroy-clad man of my imaginings.

Instead, to my complete astonishment, I found myself staring up at a giant of a man of much my own age, clad in muddy jeans and a disreputable old blue sweater. His mane of tawny hair was rumpled and needed cutting, and framed a leonine face, with a long, wide, blunt nose and fair, bushy eyebrows over amber-brown eyes. They widened as he stared at me and recognition dawned.

'*Ned?* Ned Mars!' I exclaimed, astounded.

6

Thorny Paths

My immediate reaction, after that of astonishment, was one of pleased surprise, because Ned had been part of my happiest years, spent at Honeywood Horticultural College.

Ned, however, didn't seem to feel the same way, because his open face assumed a strangely shuttered and wary expression.

'It's me – Marnie Ellwood,' I said brightly, in case he'd got sudden-onset mid-thirties amnesia. 'I was in the year below you at Honeywood.'

He'd been specializing in garden design for his final year, but when he was talent-spotted after taking part in a TV documentary, *Gardeners of the Future*, his life had taken a different turn – right into TV stardom.

I'd made a brief and unwilling appearance in that documentary too, trenching for asparagus, but I'd done my best to keep my back turned to the camera as I shovelled.

While these memories galloped through my head, Ned's oddly wary look didn't lift, but he said, finally, 'Yes, of course I remember you. You were a friend of Sammie Nelson, weren't you?'

This was obviously not a recommendation and I recalled

that he'd briefly gone out with Sammie, before she'd suddenly dumped him in favour of a fling with the documentary presenter, a well-known gardening personality about twice her age.

'We weren't really friends, she was just in my year,' I said. 'We all tended to hang out in the pub together anyway, didn't we, because it was the only one for miles? I haven't seen or heard from her since she left without doing her degree year.'

In fact, she'd left very suddenly, the minute she'd finished her exams at the end of the second year and rumour had it that she'd shacked up with that presenter.

Ned made a non-committal grunt and said, 'You look . . . different.'

'Well, I'm older, thinner and my hair is short,' I said, slightly tartly, though I didn't think I'd changed that much. And neither had he physically, except that his broad-shouldered frame had filled out with a lot more muscle. No, the difference lay in his expression.

Everyone at college had liked tall, gangling, good-natured, easy-going Ned Mars . . . and so had the TV viewers, right from the first airing of his series, *This Small Plot*. When I left for France it had still been running and was as popular as ever, though I hadn't watched it for ages, since Mike had been jealous when he found out I'd known Ned.

But that was an entirely different Ned, for this one very evidently wasn't pleased to see me. And now I began to wish he *had* been the middle-aged, balding and rather stolid stranger I'd expected. I'd *so* wanted a whole fresh new start, leaving the past behind me, and now I suspected I wasn't going to get it.

Myfy appeared to have missed the uneasy undercurrents, for she exclaimed delightedly, 'You were students together? What a coincidence! And now you'll be working together on the Grace Garden, too!'

'Well, as to that—' he began and then broke off, bushy fair eyebrows twitched together in a frown as he stared at me.

Something in his voice and the lack of enthusiasm finally got through to Myfy and she gave him a sharp look.

'I heard on the gardening grapevine that you'd been doing well with the Heritage Homes Trust . . . until you left suddenly, a few years back,' Ned said to me, meaningfully.

My heart sank. Just what, exactly, had he heard?

'I resigned from the Heritage Homes Trust over five years ago and went abroad,' I said shortly.

'Marnie's been living in France for the last few years, Ned,' Myfy told him, puzzled.

'Yes, my adoptive family bought an old château. I've been based with them, but helping other expat château owners restore their gardens. I moved around a lot . . . but then I found I wanted to come home again. This job presented the perfect chance to move back to England.'

'Right . . . And you had no idea I was here?' He was eyeing me narrowly now.

'No, why on earth should I know you had any connection with the place? The last I heard of you, you were living near London and doing endless series of *This Small Plot*.'

I frowned, thinking about that. 'I wouldn't have thought you could still do that, if you're based all the way up here, now, but—'

I broke off abruptly, because I'd obviously said something very wrong. His face darkened like a threatening thunderstorm and for a moment I wished I had those butter paddles handy.

'That's not a problem any longer,' he snapped, and then, turning to Myfy, said ominously, 'Could I have a private word?'

'Well . . . of course,' she said, looking taken aback. 'Now?'

'Yes.'

'Right . . .' she said, then smiled at me, reassuringly. 'You will excuse us for a moment, Marnie, won't you? Perhaps you'd like to wait for me in the old rose garden?'

'Of course,' I replied, feeling a sick hollowness inside. Ned must know – or *think* he knew – how I came to leave my last HHT job. Word of that unhinged email of resignation sent by Mike, pretending to be me, with its many and varied accusations against my former boss and colleagues, must have leaked out. And once Ned had told Myfy about it, I supposed that would be the end of this job, too, before it had even begun.

There was a curved marble bench next to the pool and I sat on it, heedless of moss and damp. Under the waterlilies and shifting reflections of scudding white clouds, the gold and red koi circled like strange dreams in the darkness.

Myfy, looking troubled, walked slowly through the gate from the Grace Garden, closing it behind her, before coming to sit next to me.

I looked at her numbly, waiting for the axe to fall, but instead she gave me one of her tilted smiles and said, 'Ned had to go back to his office in the courtyard – he moved his garden design business, Little Edens, here last year.'

'But he didn't want to talk to me anyway, did he? He wasn't pleased to see me, let alone employ me.'

'The trouble is, he'd heard some odd rumours about how you came to leave your last job,' she said. 'But you can't depend on gossip, as he should know very well by now. Anyway, Elf is the fey one in the family and never misjudges a character, and she told me you were a good person who has had a difficult past and needs the healing powers of the valley as much as poor Ned does, but in a different way.'

'She did? And . . . Ned does, too?' I said, tentatively.

She nodded. 'I'd no idea you'd known Ned as students, of course, and then, living abroad, you probably entirely missed all the scandal.'

This all sounded very mysterious.

'But you see, poor old Ned has had a hard time, which is why he's so prickly. I'll tell you all about it on the way up the River Walk.'

She got up, dusting off the seat of her billowing black coat, and I followed her into the Lavender Cottage garden and under the overgrown thorny rose arch past the beehives.

As we reached a kind of wooden sentry hut by the back gate, she said, 'We did tell you that one of your duties would be to go right up the River Walk to the falls at closing time every day, to pick up any litter and check for damage and stray visitors, didn't we?'

'Not that I recall,' I said, still wondering if it was all academic anyway, and I'd still actually have a job by the end of this little talk. And what on earth was this scandal involving Ned that had so changed him and made him need healing? It sounded very unlike the Ned I remembered.

Myfy opened the hut and took out a stick with a pointed metal end, which she handed to me, and a large brown paper rubbish sack from a folded pile on a shelf.

'The shutter over the entrance turnstile is always pulled down and locked at four, when Elf or one of the staff has emptied the box of tokens,' she explained. 'Then someone has to walk all the way up to the top of the falls, which we started doing regularly after the time we found a poor Swedish tourist with a broken ankle near the waterfall, who'd been there the whole night and was quite demented, poor thing.'

I felt a little demented myself by this point, with so many

unanswered questions whirling about like dark bats in my belfry.

'Of course, you don't need to do it on Tuesdays, when we are all closed, or Sundays – someone else will do it that day.'

We passed through the gate, which she locked carefully behind us, and picked our way down a narrow path that wound through gorse and rocks, until we came out on a wide gravelled path by the riverbank.

We turned upstream, away from the turnstile, and began to walk up the valley. The river burbled, rushed and babbled over its stony bed and I could hear a blackbird singing and the distant plaintive bleat of a sheep.

The path was quite wide and easy here, skirting boulders, rocky outcrops and large, gnarled tree roots.

'As well as checking for injured visitors, you need to keep an eye out for any damage to the path and handrails,' Myfy said instructively. 'On the way back, you empty the two rubbish bins into the sack and collect any litter thoughtless visitors have dropped.'

My spirits rose slightly: it wasn't exactly sounding as if I'd been fired before I started . . . or not by Myfy, at any rate. I feared that convincing Ned might be altogether a harder task.

'The first stretch of the River Walk, about half a mile, is quite easy going, as you see. There are one or two little bridges across more difficult stretches further on, put in by the Victorian owners before the Verdis took over, when they turned it into a daytripper's beauty spot.'

It would not exactly be an onerous task to walk up the little valley every afternoon . . . though possibly it wouldn't be so pleasant in bad weather.

Myfy might have read my mind because she said, 'If it's bucketing down with rain or blowing a gale then no one in their right mind would climb the waterfall path up to the top, so you can just do a visual check from the viewing platform at the bottom.'

There had been no sign of any visitors, within earshot or otherwise, to prevent Myfy explaining what had happened to Ned, and I was just wondering if she had forgotten, when she said, with a sigh: 'I'd better put you in the picture about what happened at the beginning of last year, so you can understand Ned's attitude earlier. Poor boy,' she added, though Ned was most definitely *not* a boy, but a large, angry and seemingly troubled man.

'When I went to France five years ago he was still a TV celebrity and *This Small Plot* must have been on about its millionth series,' I said. 'I . . . I'd lost touch with most of my old friends by then, though.'

'It was a dreadful scandal, in all the papers over here, but I don't suppose those in France even covered it,' Myfy said. 'And really, it wasn't much more than a seven-day wonder, even if it did have a long-term effect on Ned.'

Now I was really intrigued to know what on earth Ned had got himself into, but when she began by saying that it was all caused by the unreasonable jealousy of his girlfriend at the time, it all began to sound horribly familiar . . .

'She began constantly accusing him of seeing other women, which he wasn't. Finally he felt he couldn't take any more and ended the relationship.'

'I'm not surprised, because an unreasonably jealous partner is hell,' I said with complete empathy. 'But if he was innocent of any affair, then I don't see where the scandal comes in and—'

'Why it should affect him so much that he threw in his career and came up here to hide away?' she finished for me.

'It's because it was all so public. His ex-girlfriend, Lois, sold a story to one of the tabloids – all made up, of course, there wasn't a word of truth in it. They called him a Love Rat.'

She mouthed the words as if they tasted rancid.

'It appeared that she'd not only been checking his phone but she'd actually hired a private eye to spy on him. A paper published a picture of Ned and Penny Sinclair, his director, embracing outside the hotel they were all staying at, under the caption "Love Rat TV Gardening Guru and his Director".'

'People do hug each other all the time, and I don't suppose if they'd been having an affair, they'd had done it in front of a hotel, presumably with the rest of the team around?'

'No, and the real explanation was that Penny and her husband couldn't have children, so had been trying to adopt for ages, and she'd just had a call telling her they'd been approved to adopt a baby boy. They'd almost given up hope, it's such a long process. Ned knew about it and was just delighted for them.'

'How horrible that that wonderful moment should have been misinterpreted like that,' I said. 'Didn't they check the story first, before they printed it?'

'It appears not – and of course, Penny and her husband immediately refuted it, because they were afraid it might affect the adoption . . . though luckily not, in the end. The paper had to print an apology, of course, but by then another piece about Ned had appeared in a gossip column. The source was by that student he mentioned.'

'Who, Sammie Nelson?'

'That's the one, and it was a ridiculous story, short on facts but full of unsavoury innuendo about how, when they were students and going out together, he'd callously dumped her when he was offered the chance to present a TV series.'

I stopped and stared at her. 'I do remember them going out together briefly – and she made all the running. Then when that documentary was being filmed at the college, she dropped *him* like a hot potato, because she got off with the presenter!'

'Yes, that's what Ned said,' Myfy agreed.

'Rumour was that she'd moved in with this man at the end of term. Certainly, she never came back for her final year. And then Ned was headhunted by a totally different TV company for his own series,' I said.

'So it transpired, but it's surprising how many people want to believe horrible things, isn't it? Mud does seem to stick, too, and the TV company hung fire on commissioning the next series of *This Small Plot*. Poor Ned just suddenly felt he'd had enough of people looking at him strangely and thinking the worst. He was totally disillusioned, not to mention having had enough of living near London and all the travelling about, so he came back here. It's been his home base for years anyway, since his parents were killed in a car crash, and it did mean that he was there for Theo in his last weeks. They were very close.'

'I would have thought the programme was so popular that, once the truth was out, they'd try to persuade Ned to go back.'

'They might have done, but he doesn't want to resume his old life. It was all such a shock to him that people could believe in all those lies. Now he's inherited Old Grace Hall, he intends to make his life here, restoring the apothecary garden and opening it to the public. He still takes occasional garden design commissions. He likes the challenge of small ones, like in the TV programmes, and it's amazing what he can do with them.'

'He was always brilliant at garden design,' I agreed, as we carried on up the path, turning over what I'd been told in my head. Ned had always been surprisingly sensitive under that rugged exterior and it didn't really surprise me that he'd retired here to lick his wounds . . . and then decided to stay for ever. Who, on inheriting such a magical garden, wouldn't have?

'I understand now where he's coming from,' I said. 'No doubt he's heard about a resignation letter to HHT, purportedly written by me, and he thinks I might be emotionally unstable and cause more trouble and possibly scandal for him?'

'Yes, I'm afraid so. His recent experience has naturally made him overcautious.'

Welcome to the club, I thought, slightly bitterly.

'Well, he needn't have any concerns because I didn't actually write that resignation letter,' I told her, wondering how much to explain and deciding on as little as possible. 'I had a jealous and controlling husband when I was working for the Heritage Homes Trust and while I was off work, ill, he sent the resignation from my email account, and then he emailed them as himself, telling them I'd had a nervous breakdown and not to worry about anything I'd said in the letter.'

'I . . . see,' Myfy said, and I knew she realized there were great chunks of this story I was editing out, but didn't probe.

'By the time I was well enough to pick up my emails and find their acceptance of my resignation, the damage had been done. They didn't believe me when I tried to explain.'

'And that's when you went to France?'

'Yes, and then divorced my husband as soon as he agreed to it.'

'He doesn't sound a great loss,' Myfy said drily. 'But with that experience behind you, you'll understand how Ned is feeling.'

'I do, but *he* must understand that all I want now is to settle into a gardening job and a quiet life, doing what I love best. I'll work hard, take orders and enjoy helping to restore the gardens . . . if I'm allowed.'

'Fair enough,' she said. 'I think I'm a good judge of character and I believe you. Your job with us at Lavender Cottage is secure – and perhaps, if I have a little word with Ned . . . ?'

'I think it might be better if *I* do that,' I said. 'I hope he believes me and gives me a chance, otherwise this wonderful opportunity will be only half a job.'

'I'm sure he will,' Myfy assured me. 'He's still that same kind, generous and outgoing person underneath, he's just warier these days.'

'Aren't we all,' I said, thinking that the past was a burden you might think you'd put down and left behind but, like Terry Pratchett's Luggage, it kept jumping up and running after you.

The path had been growing steadily narrower and steeper as the valley closed in and we now had to pick our way round outcrops of rock and clumps of gorse.

To our right, the drystone wall that seemed to hold back the steep and wooded hillside had drawn closer.

'I have no idea when, or how, they built the old walls that enclose our bit of land along the river,' Myfy said, pausing to unhook a fold of her coat from a snatching branch of gorse. 'But perhaps there weren't the trees there before and it was sheep grazing.'

'You do see walls on steep, rocky mountainsides that make you wonder the same thing,' I agreed.

The valley now felt more like a ravine and the water, constrained in a deep channel, louder.

We had already crossed two small iron bridges over difficult areas and now the path took us onto a metal walkway that actually projected from a stone outcrop over the water, which felt perilous . . .

'Iron. Victorian, like the turnstiles and bridges – they made these things to last, so long as you look after them, of course,' Myfy called back over her shoulder. The bright tassels on her hood and the back of her coat swung out as she turned a corner and I followed, to find myself standing on a viewing platform below a thundering cascade of water that seemed to spring directly out of the rock face high above us.

'The Fairy Falls,' Myfy said, with a somewhat ironic inflection and we stood at the edge, looking up, the dark trees crowding down close on either side of the river and shutting out much of the light, so that it seemed a very mysterious and dark spot.

Spray dampened my face and my head was filled with the rushing of water, which sounded like beating wings . . .

7

Flights of Fancy

Eventually I pulled myself together and found Myfy looking at me in amusement. 'There's something about waterfalls that draws in and mesmerizes us all,' she said. 'This one has more legends around it than most, though. Some of it's on the information board over there.'

I went over to look at the brightly painted board, which had a map of the falls with bubbles here and there, containing nuggets of old legends and information. There were also little ambiguous winged creatures near the top of the waterfall, which I thought were probably Myfy's work.

Myfy, who'd followed me over, confirmed this. 'I did the artwork and Elf wrote the info. She's extremely interested in old legends and folk history and has had lots of articles published.'

She named a few esoteric-sounding magazines I'd never heard of and then added, 'She's written a book about the history of Jericho's End, too, which was published recently.'

'That sounds interesting,' I said, thinking I'd google it later . . . among other things. I hoped Aunt Em's ancient laptop was going to be up to that evening's research.

'Right, on we go,' Myfy said briskly. 'From here, the path is unmade and much more difficult, since it's quite a climb, too. Although the sign warns visitors, they still attempt it wearing silly footwear. Elf's forever treating people for sprained ankles and cuts and bruises – she did a first-aid course, but as far as I'm concerned, if they're daft enough to go up there wearing flipflops or stiletto heels, they can deal with the consequences themselves.'

By now, I'd realized that Myfy, despite her long, dreamy and melancholy face, was a much tougher cookie than she had appeared at first glance.

'I suppose most people now have a mobile phone and can ring for help,' I suggested.

'Not right up here they can't, with the trees and the sides of the valley closing in like cliffs. You have to get much further down towards the turnstile before you can get any kind of signal.'

Myfy headed up the steep track like a mountain goat, but I followed more slowly, picking my way between huge rounded boulders and jagged, mossy rock outcrops. The waterfall thundered down on our left and we were close enough to feel the spray blown in our faces and the roaring in our ears. The valley was now little more than a cleft in the rocks, the branches of the trees interlacing high overhead.

Only shafts of light filtered through, mysteriously illuminating what felt oddly like an ancient and magical landscape. I had a feeling that something awaited me around every bend . . .

A final scramble up a series of rocky outcrops brought us out onto a wide ledge, bordered by an iron rail, next to the point where the river gushed from the rocks.

We were so much higher now and there were stunted

trees – oak and ash and hawthorn – springing from impossible crevices. Some kind of ferny plant framed the mouth of the river, like a deep green moustache.

One beam of light illuminated a rainbow dancing above the falls . . . and then I caught a fluttering movement out of the corner of my eye, though when I turned there was nothing there . . . except a faint sound of melodic voices and laughter, half heard and then suddenly turned off, like a radio.

I found Myfy looking at me strangely. 'You can feel it, too, can't you? Not everyone can and most of those who do are children. But there's old magic here.'

'Hence the name Fairy Falls, though you did say at lunch that some people thought they were angels rather than fairies.'

Like Mum, I thought; she certainly had.

'The old name was the Angel Falls,' Myfy said. 'The Victorians renamed it when Jericho's End became a renowned beauty spot – they seemed totally soppy about fairies. Then, of course, there was all that Cottingley Fairy business later on, between the wars. Do you know about that?'

'You mean those two young girls who fooled everyone with their fairy photographs? I've seen a film about it. They even got Sir Arthur Conan Doyle to believe the photographs were real, didn't they?'

'Silly man,' she observed. 'But then, we so often see what we most want to, don't we?'

'True.'

'Anyway, it rather debased the whole idea of fairies, except as some twee legend to attract tourists, and no one living in Jericho's End wants to publicize what's really here . . .'

She paused, her long, melancholy face going dreamy again, literally away with the fairies – or, more likely, the angels.

'The legends about fairies living in the valley do pre-date the sixteenth century, when a local child swore she'd seen an angel by the falls, just like the one in the window in St Gabriel's, the old church on the edge of Thorstane. The window is a very early one, well worth seeing,' she added.

'I'd love to go to look,' I said. 'Is that when the falls became known locally as the Angel Falls?'

'That's right. You can find it on very old maps. The child's story was widely believed. At one time, there used to be an annual procession up here to bless the valley, but Elf thinks that might just have been a new spin on some kind of annual pagan fertility rite that has since died out.'

'It's all very fascinating,' I said. 'I did feel for a moment there was *something* other-worldly up here . . . very odd.'

'As children, we were often aware of a winged presence, or heard something, when we came up here, but whatever they are, I've come to believe that angels and fairies are one and the same thing. So did Mum – she saw them when she was a little girl, too.'

'So most of the actual sightings have been by children?'

'That's right, though some continue to see them when they grow up. There's an early Victorian story about a teenage girl who came up here with friends and vanished entirely, a bit like *Picnic at Hanging Rock*. But Elf never found any evidence for that, so she left it out of the book.'

'Do *you* still see them – whatever they are?' I asked curiously.

'I know they're here,' she said ambiguously. 'They inspired my paintings and I think they're why the valley is such a healing place.'

'What was the café-gallery called, before it was Ice Cream and Angels?'

'Just Verdi's. Joseph and Maria Verdi moved here from London in the late nineteenth century and began selling ice-cream and water ices. Mum was Gina Verdi, the last of this branch of the family.'

I took a last, long look round.

It wasn't eerie, or threatening, it just felt as if there was another dimension close by, through the thinnest of invisible walls. Perhaps you needed the eyes of a child to see through that.

Mum had told me she'd once seen what she'd described as a cloud of small, glowing angels . . . I'd love to see those. Suddenly I really wanted to tell Myfy about Mum, but firmly quashed the impulse: it wouldn't be a good idea to reveal the Vane connection when the family were so obviously disliked. Besides, I'd already had to divulge something from my past I'd rather have kept to myself, so this new life wasn't proving to be quite the clean slate I'd hoped it would be.

'Right, now we go up again,' Myfy announced, heading away from the falls and up a rough-hewn flight of steps, which had another of the iron handrails, set into the rock and heavily painted against the damp air.

Eventually, we emerged onto a flattish area above the falls, with patches of bare rock showing through wiry grass. A dry-stone wall stopped the curious from plummeting over the edge, though it was more probably put there to protect sheep.

The path ended at a small turnstile set into a more substantial and taller wall and through it was a narrow, rutted farm track.

'Isn't this another Victorian turnstile, like the ones at the entrance? Did the early visitors come all the way up here?'

'Quite a lot of them did, including many women – the long skirts didn't seem to hinder them when they really wanted to do something. We won't go through the turnstile now, because it's one way only and we'd have to walk back down the road through the village. The track joins it near a small terrace of cottages called, appropriately, Angel Row.'

'When I arrived in the café this morning there were some hikers who I think Charlie said were coming up this way and then on to Thorstane,' I remembered. It was starting to feel like a very long time since I'd arrived!

'Probably. They can pick up the back road to Thorstane just beyond Angel Row. Not that it's much of a road, once you get out of the village,' she added.

'It did look tricky on the Ordnance Survey map. Zigzag and very steep.'

'It is: hairpin bends, with deep ditches on one side and a drop on the other. It's mainly used by farm and forestry vehicles – and hikers. It's the shortest way to walk from Jericho's End to Thorstane, if you have the stamina for it, and it brings you out by St Gabriel's, which is really our village church.'

'Has there never been a church in Jericho's End itself?'

'I suppose the monks who tried to settle in the valley had some kind of chapel, but they moved on after only a couple of years. So no, not unless you count the Brethren, a strict religious sect who sometimes used to hold meetings in the Red Barn at Cross Ways Farm. They've now died out with the last generation, which is hardly surprising, since they seemed to combine a sort of Amish lack of comfort with a belief that salvation could only be gained by the extreme oppression of women.'

'That doesn't sound much fun,' I said, though it *did* sound like the kind of family Mum came from.

'The Strange Brethren, they called themselves, and the

Vane family from Cross Ways Farm were in the thick of it, hellfire and brimstone, women the original sinners and the cause of every evil,' she said with a wry smile. 'That kind of sect.'

The Vane family were sounding ever more unattractive and I felt no desire now to confess I was related to them. Wayne had hardly seemed a sterling modern-day example, either.

'The St Gabriel's parishioners, unless they were from the top end of the village, tended to take the footpath that starts near the gates of Risings and skirts the edge of Brow Farm. Bier Way, it's called.'

'Beer way?' I echoed, puzzled. 'It goes to a pub?'

She gave her tilted smile. 'No, *bier*.' She spelled it out. 'It's because coffins were often carried up it to the church.'

'Cheery.'

She considered this. 'Perhaps not in winter, but in spring and summer, I think taking your last journey through the fields and meadows, carried by your friends and family, doesn't sound too bad.'

'No, you're right,' I agreed.

We retraced our steps down the path by the waterfall, catching glimpses of the viewing platform below as the path twisted and turned, so I could see why that poor tourist had found herself stuck here overnight.

All the same, I longed to come back there alone, with no possibility of anyone else about. When I asked Myfy, it seemed that I was welcome to walk there in my free time whenever I wished.

'I'm very glad you're going to be doing the check on the walk every day, too,' she added. 'I quite often forget the time and then it doesn't get done, unless Charlie or his sister, Daisy, are about.'

'The café seems to have a lot of staff,' I commented.

'Not really, it's usually just Elf. Charlie's been helping out a lot, because of being on his gap year, and Daisy is still at school and only works in the café on Saturdays and in the holidays when they're busy.'

We met no one at all on the way back and we'd picked up little litter, other than the inevitable plastic water bottles and one crisp packet that had obviously been blowing about the village for a few days before capture.

Locking the gate to Lavender Cottage carefully behind her, Myfy said, 'The recycling bins are near the back door, if there's anything that can go in them, but I'll sort that today. Tomorrow, of course, is Tuesday, when the café's closed, so you can spend your first day off settling in and then start work officially on Wednesday morning.'

'Yes . . . but I'd better tackle Ned first thing tomorrow, before I do anything else,' I said grimly.

'I suppose you had better,' she agreed. 'He's usually in his office in the courtyard at the top end of the Grace Garden from about eight thirty, unless he's gardening. I'm sure everything will be all right, though, Marnie. He's desperate for help to restore the garden, and he's trying to renovate the Old Hall too, when he has any time. Poor Theo didn't have a lot of money and an old period place like that drains your resources alarmingly, even if it isn't very big.'

'Ned has a lot on his hands, then,' I said, because five peripatetic years in France, spent living in old and dilapidated houses, had taught me quite a bit about the subject.

'If he says he doesn't want to employ me, are you still sure you want me to work for you and live in the flat?' I asked tentatively. 'It would be only half the job and all the benefit of the accommodation.'

'Oh, yes, that's not in question. We're very happy to have you. And I'm sure Ned, now he's had time to think about what I said to him earlier, will be ready to listen to you.'

'If he doesn't, then perhaps I can get some daily gardening locally instead, because your garden won't be a full-time job. Then you can pay me part-time wages.'

'Wayne Vane gardens locally, but he's neither good nor reliable. But it shouldn't come to that. Ned would be crazy to turn you down, and you're *very* cheap.'

I grinned. 'Fully qualified, very experienced in all aspects of gardening and economically priced,' I agreed. I still wasn't quite sure how I was going to persuade Ned that I had never written that unhinged resignation email, but I'd give it my best shot.

'I'll see Ned first thing, then I need to go to Great Mumming. I've been storing some of my and my late mother's things at my sister's house – I mentioned she was a vet at a practice there, didn't I? Elf said it was fine for me to bring them back with me to sort out in the flat.'

'Good idea, and I expect you'll find you can get rid of a lot of it. Very cathartic, disposing of old possessions.'

'Yes, I think you're probably right,' I agreed. I'd already found purging myself of everything that reminded me of Mike pretty therapeutic.

I parted with Myfy at the back door, where I could see that the lights were still on in the café kitchen. She told me that Elf and Charlie would be cleaning down the café – they liked to give it an extra deep clean on Monday evenings – but since it had been a quiet day they'd probably already nearly finished.

It was getting on for five by then and I felt ravenous, so back in my flat I made myself dinner from the ingredients in the fridge, and finished with some honeycomb crunch ice-cream from a box I found in the freezer. It was delicious.

The little flat was quiet and warm, though I switched on the flickering flame effect of the electric log-burner for cosiness and settled down at the table with the temperamental laptop.

It eventually consented to turn on and I emailed Treena to say that I'd be in Great Mumming next day to pick up more of my things, and was she free to meet me for lunch, in which case I could tell her all about my arrival in Jericho's End then.

An email pinged back almost straight away, suggesting we could eat lunch at the cottage and then she'd help me load the car.

I had so much to tell her tomorrow – and I'd have even more after I'd seen Ned in the morning!

After that, I made a cup of coffee and began to trace the downfall of Ned Mars via the internet. I had a faint suspicion Myfy might have left out a couple of details. Perhaps, although this allegation of an affair had been untrue, he had previously been unfaithful, giving his girlfriend grounds for jealousy? That didn't sound like the Ned I knew, but I suppose he could have changed in the years since I'd known him.

It was easy enough to track the story back to the original Sunday tabloid article, which was full of innuendo and short on facts, but much as Myfy had said. There was plenty of speculation and a lot of social media slurry, then the paper printed a retraction and apology in the following week's issue. I suspect there had been a threat of legal proceedings from Ned's director and her husband. It would all probably have died down after that, had Sammie Nelson not stuck her oar in by selling that nasty little piece to a gossip column. After reading it, I could only suppose she must have done it for money, whipping up something out of nothing. The word 'paydirt' sprang to mind and it certainly left a nasty taste in my mouth. There seems to be an art to implying things, without coming out and saying them in a legally actionable way.

Anyway, I just couldn't believe they'd printed this stuff, because it left their readers with the impression that Ned had not only dropped Sammie from his life when fame beckoned, but she had been pregnant at the time – plus, worst of all, they hinted he'd been violent to her!

My memories definitely didn't include any of Ned getting her pregnant, socking her in the eye and then dumping her and I'd have been prepared to go into a court and swear it! All the students in my year would know the truth of what happened and the whole class was there when Sammie gave herself that black eye, by standing on the end of a rake. I even remembered Sammie joking at the time that it looked as if Ned had been beating her up, except everyone knew he was so soft he wouldn't even hurt a fly.

But then, since it was all only implied, I don't suppose Ned could have sued them for slander, or libel or whichever it was.

It all died down fairly quickly, but so many people are ready to believe anything they read, especially on Twitter.

I felt profoundly sorry for Ned, who hadn't deserved any of this. He'd been so popular too, since he was very open and good-natured, with a genuine enthusiasm for gardening.

I could see that clearing his name, and proving it was all untrue, was one thing, but the taint lingered and I understood why he felt he had had enough and retreated to Jericho's End.

The jealous vindictiveness of Ned's ex-partner had disturbing echoes of Mike's behaviour towards me. He'd certainly blackened my name with the Heritage Homes Trust . . . and now it seemed with everyone else on the gardening grapevine.

There *had* been a new series of *This Small Plot*, though with a different garden designer presenting it every week, but the ratings had sunk like a stone and, though it was still going, it was now put out on daytime TV.

I was sorry for Ned, and understood what he'd gone through, but still, it rather irked me that while I'd immediately felt he was innocent of any wrongdoing meriting what had happened to him, he hadn't seemed to have had the same faith in me. But I suppose while I knew for a fact that Sammie's allegations were all untrue, Ned only had his recollections of me to go on. How much would I have to tell him about my relationship with Mike, which wasn't something I was exactly proud of, before he believed me? *If* he did, of course. I wasn't looking forward to the interview.

I switched off the laptop, the internet connection vanishing with a grateful whine, and got ready for bed.

I was just about to get under that inviting duvet after my long day when I heard a sort of scratching noise from the direction of the landing and went to investigate: if that was a mouse, then Elf and Myfy had serious problems.

But when I switched on the landing light the scratching stopped and was replaced by a sudden loud meowing that came from the other side of the door to Lavender Cottage.

Then there was a thud and the handle on my side moved, though of course it didn't open, because the bolt was across.

Caspar! I stood undecidedly as the yowl and the thud came again – and after a moment, I cautiously slid the bolt back and the door banged against my legs as a huge marmalade shape barged through.

'Come in, why don't you?' I said sarcastically, then turned to see if the rumpus had woken anyone in the cottage: but the landing beyond the door stretched away into quiet darkness.

'Pfft!' Caspar said disagreeably, disappearing into my living room, where I found him making himself comfortable on the sofa.

'Look,' I said, 'you can't stay here! I mean, I haven't got a cat tray or anything, and anyway, you aren't my cat. Where do you usually sleep?'

He narrowed his eyes at me. I determinedly picked him up and he made himself totally limp and twice as heavy as you'd expect. Then he twisted and leaped down, this time heading for the bedroom. He did turn back once and look at me.

His expression said he wasn't going anywhere without a fight. I hesitated, then opened the door onto my small landing a fraction, and then the one through into Lavender Cottage. I thought he might get bored and go back where he belonged or, if not, and nature called, find his way back to his usual haunts.

Five minutes after I'd got into bed and put out my light, a huge and heavy shape thumped down next to me.

I didn't know cats snored. He sounded like one of those hubble-bubble pipes, but without any Eastern promise.

8
Poison

Apart from the fact that there was a large dent on the duvet and a generous sprinkling of long marmalade hairs, I might have thought Caspar's visit the previous night was just a dream, brought on by tiredness and tension and, perhaps, the need for company.

It was still very early. I'd drawn back the curtains last night and through the window I could see an expanse of dusky, duck-egg-blue sky, warmed by a faint and spreading amber glow. It looked like it might be a brighter and less changeable day.

I got dressed and then looked for Caspar, but he'd vanished back into his own part of the cottage again and someone had closed the door. I didn't bolt it again: there didn't seem much point if Elf and Myfy weren't bothered about locking it from their side, which showed a surprising trust in a total stranger, especially since I assumed Myfy had shared what she'd learned about my resignation from the Heritage Homes Trust with her sister.

I was sure Myfy had believed my version, but Ned might be a different prospect.

In my cafetière I made some of the coffee I'd brought with

me, though it tasted quite different here, probably due to the water, which had a distinctly peaty tang. Perhaps it would turn my insides to leather over time, like Tollund Man and all those other people they'd found buried in bogs. I expected I'd get used to the taste in time, though.

My breakfast while in France (unless one of my employers had had a visitor bearing a gift of British streaky bacon and chunky marmalade) had usually been a croissant and a couple of big cups of coffee, so it felt luxurious to be spreading butter and jam (a jar of home-made strawberry, which proclaimed itself on the handwritten label to be of Elf's making) onto wholemeal toast.

To have a day off before I'd even started seemed a trifle odd . . . but then, if I couldn't sort things out with Ned, I'd only have half a job at most, and half a salary to go with it, unless I could get other gardening work locally. But there was no point worrying about that until I'd bearded the lion in his den.

I'd put on my best jeans and a cotton jersey tunic in a dark shade of turquoise, patterned with green willow leaves, a bit William Morris. I added dark grey eyeliner and ruby-tinted lip balm, brushed out the tangles in my hair and examined myself in the full-length mirror set in a bleached wooden frame, which was fixed to the wall at the end of the landing. I thought I looked entirely sane and sensible: nothing there to frighten Ned.

It was now after eight, so I went downstairs, where there was no sound beyond the scullery door, and let myself out into the cottage garden.

It was a still, clear morning, though up in the trees a wood pigeon was giving it some welly.

The rambling crazy-paving path was damp with dew and

the overgrown lavender and rosemary bushes sprinkled me with water as I brushed against them – they were more than ready for a good pruning.

I couldn't see much beyond the high stone walls except trees, but I could just hear the sound of water rushing under the nearby humpbacked bridge and thundering down into the pool below, the Devil's Cauldron, that Elf had told me had given its name to the pub.

I inhaled deeply as I walked slowly down the path: the air was cold and crisp and smelled of leaf mould as rich and delicious as plum cake.

Further along, the spiders had spread great jewelled webs between the bushes and from both sides of the steep, wooded valley more wood pigeons had woken and joined in with the first. Small, pale beams of sunshine lightly gilded the top of the greenhouse and, despite my mission, my heart suddenly lifted and I felt again a connection with this enchanting valley, and that I had come home.

'Into each life, a little sunshine must fall,' I said aloud, changing the trite saying to suit myself, since I'd already had the rain, not to mention the thunder, lightning and hailstones. Then I selected the rose garden key from the big ring, which Myfy had helpfully labelled.

I made straight for the gate to the Grace Garden on the other side of the pond: I might love old roses, but this was no time to linger, though as I skirted the dark pool, my weird imagination provided me with the image of a hand rising from the depths, brandishing aloft, Excalibur-like, a gilded garden rake.

That would certainly bring in the paying visitors! I was grinning as I left the overgrown and gloomy tunnel of roses for the light and tranquillity of the apothecary garden.

The early sun was burnishing the ancient bricks of the high, sheltering walls, and this time I noticed at the further end of the garden to my left, beyond the low beds bordered by hedges of lavender, what looked like a tall, black, metal cage.

This was intriguing, but then, so was the whole garden, because from this point I couldn't really see much of it, what with the rising ground and the specimen trees and banks of tall shrubs.

It seemed entirely deserted, except for a pheasant, who was ambling aimlessly away down the path directly ahead of me, in the manner of his kind, and though I knew I should head to the path to the right, behind the Alchemist rose, where the entrance to the courtyard apparently lay, I instead impulsively followed the pheasant.

My path joined a wider one that curved away on either side, seeming to circle the central beds, which I now saw were planted with mid-height herbs and shrubs. I began to note the signs of recent activity – the paths all newly gravelled and neatly edged, to trace the pattern of what was once there. But there was also evidence of years of neglect.

If the lower half of the garden had been totally let go, then it would take a lot of effort to restore it to what it once was – the repository of healing and useful plants, gathered together in one place: the so-called apothecary or physic garden. A little Eden . . . which reminded me of my purpose.

Instead of going in search of the heart of the garden, I took the next right turn that skirted the tall bed of trees and shrubs and went through the wide arch at the top of it, into a paved courtyard. A sign on one of the buildings opposite proclaimed:

Little Edens Garden Design
Small Plots, Big Ideas

The pheasant, who must have followed me in, had now been joined by a slightly bedraggled-looking peacock and his mate, but I barely took them in, for my attention was all focused on the task ahead.

A glimmer of light shone through the slatted blinds over the windows, so I knew Ned was there, and I knocked firmly on the door. And of course, the moment I'd done it, the short, carefully prepared and entirely reasonable explanation of how I'd come to leave my Heritage Homes Trust job flew straight out of my head like a flock of startled starlings and scattered to the four winds.

That was a pity, because it had to be admitted that my naturally slightly acerbic tongue had sharpened somewhat over the last few years, so that I wasn't always able to stop the slings and arrows of outrageous comment from shooting forth at entirely the wrong moment.

Without the script to stick to, I'd have to try to curb that a bit so I came across as sensible, quiet, totally non-neurotic and unthreatening.

Added to that, I needed to keep a lid on the bubble of resentment that I felt that he'd accepted the gossip he'd heard about me at face value, while he, as much as anyone, should know not to believe everything he heard.

I mean, it might have been a long time ago since we'd been students at Honeywood Horticultural College, but *I* hadn't forgotten what *he* was like: that we'd laughed together, exchanged heated opinions on gardening matters in the pub over pints of Gillyflower's Best Bitter and both been in the same team at the end-of-term quiz, winning the coveted Honeywood Cup and a set of chocolate gardening tools. I'd got the trowel.

These things ought to have lingered in his memory, as they had in mine. He should have known me better.

I remembered now how amused he'd been when, after offering him the chance to front his own TV series, having spotted him in that documentary, the company had approached me to be one of the team, and I'd turned it down flat.

Ned had known how much I'd hated being in that documentary and, naturally, I'd got snappy when the director kept insisting I turn round and face the cameras . . . and even gave me *lines* to say.

But evidently the viewers had liked that and the clincher had been the bit where they'd asked Ned to call me over while I was trying to finish weeding the rockery and I told him to get lost in no uncertain terms, not realizing it was caught on camera. They kept it in, and it went down a storm.

Sammie Nelson had been furious when they offered the job to me and not her, after all her efforts with the presenter, though, of course, *he* wasn't with the company making the new series, so she was out of luck there.

Yes, I thought bitterly as I stood on the doorstep, Ned *should* have known me better than to believe the rumours – and at that moment, the door swung open.

The old, gangling, good-natured student Ned I'd been remembering morphed into the current version: nearly six and a half feet of ruggedly attractive, broad-shouldered and well-muscled masculinity, wearing slightly muddy jeans, a blue checked lumberjack shirt and a deeply distrustful expression.

He didn't look as if he'd spent the intervening years just drawing up garden designs and fronting a TV series, but from what I remembered of the programmes, he'd mucked right in with the heavy work alongside his team.

His light amber-brown eyes widened and grew wary when he saw me and he took an involuntary step backwards, which

I have to say I found irritating. Presumably he'd forgotten his crucifix and bulbs of garlic.

However, I managed to smile and say in a voice of sweet reason, 'Good morning, Ned. I thought we'd better have a chat. Do you want to come out, or shall I come in?'

But when he hesitated, my resolutions crumbled and I snapped impatiently, 'You can leave the door open so you can scream for help, if you want to.'

'I'd forgotten that sharp tongue of yours,' Ned said, reluctantly drawing back to let me pass.

'You seem to have forgotten pretty much *everything* about me, though I haven't forgotten what you were like,' I said, finding myself in a light space with a drawing desk and tables at one end, with tall baskets of rolled plans and a whole back wall of white-painted corkboard. It appeared to be covered in photographs of projects, plants and what looked like a blown-up photo of an old plan of the apothecary garden . . . And there *was* a wide circular path around the central beds, as I'd suspected, with narrower straight ones radiating out from it to the four corners. There seemed to be another, smaller circular bed right in the middle of the garden, that I hadn't been able to see and—

Ned's voice stopped me in my tracks as I moved towards the plan.

'College was a long time ago and we're different people now,' he said, going to an area at the other end of the long room that looked designed for customers, with a minimalist sofa and chairs arranged round a coffee table, and switching on a kettle.

'Leopards may grow older, but I don't think they change their spots,' I said, but he didn't seem to hear that.

'Coffee?' he snapped.

'Coffee, hemlock, whatever's on offer,' I agreed, seating myself on one of the angular chairs. The seat seemed to hang from the frame and swung as I sat down, which was a little disconcerting, but it was surprisingly comfortable.

He was taking his time over the coffee mugs, back turned to me, so I thought I might as well begin what I had to say.

'Yes, college *was* a long time ago and we didn't keep in touch – plus, I've been living in France lately, so I had no idea what happened to you last year, until Myfy told me,' I said. 'But *I* immediately realized that the Ned Mars I'd known wouldn't have behaved like that, even before I'd googled it and seen all the details – and although I never liked Sammie Nelson, I'd never have thought she'd turn out to be such a lying cow!' I added. 'But *you* seemed quite willing to believe any vile tale about *me*.'

He finally turned from the kettle, teaspoon in hand, and stared down at me, frowning. 'But I was told by someone who actually saw your resignation email that it was totally . . .'

'Unhinged?' I suggested helpfully. 'A long, rambling list of deeply detrimental statements about my boss and colleagues? Yes, I know – *I've* seen it, too. But I neither wrote it nor sent it.'

'But he said you'd been off work – and everyone understood that it had affected you badly, once your husband had explained it.'

I felt myself go white: this was ripping old wounds apart with a vengeance. The pregnancy, unplanned and initially unwanted, had been quickly followed by a traumatic miscarriage and my being rushed into hospital . . .

'Tongues *have* been busy,' I said, when I could control my voice. 'Yes, I had an early, but bad, miscarriage and was off work for a month recovering, but I had no intention of resigning . . . or not in a way that would slam the door in my face for future jobs,' I said, because when Treena and I drew up my original escape plan, I was to email HHT and tell them I'd been called away urgently to France because of family illness. Then, after that, resign on the grounds that I would be absent for some months.

'I loved my job and was in line for promotion – and I can guess who told you the sorry tale and then got that promotion himself.'

He looked thoughtfully at me, as if actually seeing me properly for the first time, then carried two mugs of coffee over and set them on the table, before sitting down opposite.

'I did think at the time he shouldn't be spreading the story about like that, but he had seen the letter you say you didn't write, so perhaps you'd better explain a bit more. I mean, maybe you wrote it while you were ill and don't remember?'

'I lost a baby, not my mind,' I snapped. 'And I suppose I will have to explain a bit more, though I'm only asking you to employ me as a gardener on a pittance, not take out adoption papers.'

Given what I'd read in the papers online about the scandal nearly scuppering his director's adoption proceedings, that was perhaps an unfortunate turn of phrase and he scowled at me.

'I'd forgotten there was always a certain unripe fruit tartness about your conversation and you don't seem to have mellowed.'

'Well, dig a bit deeper and you might remember that I was about as down to earth as it was possible to be without growing roots,' I advised him, then took an unwary sip of coffee. My taste buds immediately shrivelled and died and my throat tried to close up.

He was looking at me curiously. 'What's the matter?'

'Your coffee is *disgusting*,' I said, when I'd mastered the urge to spit it out, which would not have quite set the tone for the rest of the conversation, besides leaving a horrible stain on the rush matting.

'Don't hold back from politeness, will you?' Ned said, sarcastically.

'Sorry, but I've been used to something a bit better than cheap instant. I think this one must have been brushed up off the factory floor.'

'I didn't think it was that bad,' he said defensively. 'But I'm thinking of getting a coffee maker for the office. It would be nice for the clients.'

'I'm only surprised you have any, if you give them this muck.'

'I don't have that many these days . . . but then, I haven't been advertising for customers, since I moved here. But I do need some income coming in until the garden opens to the public and starts to pay its way.'

'I'd get a cafetière or filter jug,' I suggested. 'That way you can put the grounds on the compost heap.'

'I'll think about it, but my coffee-making facilities aren't really what's on my mind at the moment.'

'No, I don't suppose they are. You want me to convince you that if you employ me, there aren't going to be yet more scandals hitting the headlines,' I said bluntly.

'That's about it,' he agreed. 'I've left all the media stuff behind me, so I'm not in the public eye any more, and that's the way I want it to stay. I'm making a new life here – it's always been home to me and a refuge when I needed it.'

'With no serpents in Little Eden,' I agreed. 'And I'm certainly not that serpent, because *I* hoped Jericho's End would be *my* refuge too, where I could literally get back to my roots and start over again, among people who didn't know anything about my past.'

'And then we came face to face,' he said. 'It's a small world.'

'It is, and now I'm going to have to drag the past up again, which is the last thing I wanted to do, and tell you about my marriage.'

'I assume you aren't married now? Elf seemed to think you were single when she told me she'd offered the job to someone.'

'Not any longer. It was a brief marriage – little more than a year – and I'd have left sooner, except for the unexpected pregnancy and the miscarriage. It was a difficult relationship, because he was jealous and controlling. That kind of thing is talked about more these days and called coercive control. But he picked the wrong victim in me.'

I gave a bitter smile. 'He was never quite sure he had me completely under his thumb, until I let him think the fight had gone out of me, those last couple of weeks. But I was just biding my time.'

I paused, but Ned said nothing, just sipped his disgusting coffee. I supposed he was used to it.

'As soon as I was well enough, Treena – who is my adoptive sister, as well as best friend – helped me get free and over to France. I went to stay with my family first, then moved around their circle of friends after that, even when Mike – my ex – gave up trying to find me.'

'He *did* try?'

'Oh, yes, and attempted to convince my family I didn't know what I was doing and needed him. He was good at that kind of thing and had already managed to come between me and my family once – and my friends. But they weren't buying his lies this time. I kept in contact with my solicitor over here, though, and eventually Mike agreed to a divorce because he wanted to remarry. That was when I finally thought it was safe to come back again.'

'I'm so sorry. I know how horrible jealousy in a relationship can be, especially when it's totally unfounded,' Ned said sincerely. 'And I'm sorry about the miscarriage, too.'

'It was totally the wrong time – just when I was about to leave Mike – but I did want the baby when I found out, even if it complicated things. Mike was delighted, of course – he never wanted me to work, but stay at home, where he could keep track of me. But after I lost the baby and was so out of it in hospital, he sent that resignation email in my name.'

When I had opened my inbox for the first time and found an email from the HHT accepting my resignation, I have to admit I'd doubted my own sanity for a moment, but I wasn't about to tell Ned that. I'd tracked the resignation email down in my Sent box and another Mike had sent, telling them I'd had a nervous breakdown and to take no notice of anything odd I might have said in my resignation.

Ned, however, seemed still to have some reservations, but be unsure how to frame them. 'Right . . . And I mean, you *are* sure you didn't write that email and forgot?'

'No, of course I didn't and, what's more, the day it was sent I was in hospital, having the contents of my womb scraped out, which was as much fun as it sounds.'

That was brutal, but then, so had my miscarriage been.

He winced. 'I'm so sorry and . . . I think I do believe you and that you haven't made all that up.'

'Thanks very much,' I said drily. 'Anyway, once I'd recovered, Treena and I decided to put my escape plan into operation and at the first opportunity . . .'

'You did a bunk?'

'Yes, it seemed the only way out at the time. Mike had done a good job of convincing everyone he was the perfect husband, coping with a neurotic wife and isolating me. If your partner was jealous too, you should know how things get twisted and people are ready to believe stupid lies about you, even when they've known you for years.'

'That's true. And I apologize for not realizing you would never cast yourself as a neurotic victim. You really haven't changed much at all.'

'You should have seen me just after I reached France. I was a nervous wreck! But once I had time to get things back into perspective, I was fine.' I paused. 'My aims in life are totally different now. I've no ambition to be head gardener at a stately home, which would probably mostly involve doing paperwork anyway. What I love is the physical connection with the soil and the seasons and new life. I like getting my hands dirty and I'm not afraid of hard work. Other than that, I want peace, quiet and somewhere to live.'

'There's a lot of peace, quiet and hard work here, that's for sure. When I inherited Old Grace Hall, I decided my mission in life was to restore the apothecary garden to what it once was. But I love the house, too. It's in need of a lot of work, and there isn't much money. I need to get visitors into the garden and keep on my design work . . . but at the moment, there are only two very elderly part-time gardeners to help me. There was an occasional jobbing gardener, but he wasn't reliable.'

Wayne Vane, I supposed. Revealing my connection with that family really would send my stock dropping like a stone down a well!

I said briskly, 'Which is where the idea to share a gardener with Elf and Myfy comes in – I'm cheap, hardworking and on the spot, even if not cheerful,' I said. 'I'm fascinated by the apothecary garden and dying to sort out that jungle of rose briars, too.'

Ned grinned suddenly, which took years off him, and said,

holding out his hand, 'Yes, I think you *are* exactly what I need, Marnie Ellwood. Pax?'

'Pax,' I agreed, taking his hand. His strong fingers closed warmly around mine for a moment and then let go.

'Right, that's settled, then,' I said, more briskly, getting up. 'I'll have to go now, because I've got loads of things to organize in Great Mumming and I won't get the chance again till next week. But I'll come here first thing in the morning and then make a start on the Lavender Cottage garden later. I have to go up the River Walk after four every day, anyway.'

'OK and then I can show you round the garden and fill you in on our plans,' he agreed, following me to the door. 'I'll introduce you to James and Gertie then, too.'

'I'm looking forward to it,' I lied, though it would at least be a nice change to have elderly gardeners barking commands at me in English instead of French.

The pheasant had vanished, but the peacock was now squatting on the wall and his lost-soul wail followed me all the way back through the gardens.

9

Hot Beds

I didn't go back to the flat, since I had with me the small rucksack which did duty as a handbag. I skirted round the end of Lavender Cottage and drove off over the humpbacked bridge. There were few people about and luckily I met no other traffic on the narrow lane to the main road. This time, opposite the layby near the end of it with the bus stop, I noticed a sign for Cross Ways Farm . . .

I was in Great Mumming before ten and, feeling a little jangled by my talk with Ned and having to drag up the past again, I had coffee and a giant apple and custard Danish pastry in a teashop in the market square, where I'd parked. The coffee was good and I felt better for the sugar rush, even if a bit sticky.

I needed to stock up my larder with a few basics that had become indispensable to me since I moved to France. I'd learned to cook quite a lot of French recipes, though mostly not Cordon Bleu. I was more of a bean-rich cassoulet kind of girl than a Boeuf Bourguignon one. Just as well, because I wouldn't be able to whip up anything lavish in the kitchenette of the flat, with its mini oven/grill, microwave and two hotplates.

I'd checked my list of things to do while eating the last of the pastry and the first stop was to pop in and see my solicitor, to thank her for all she'd done for me in the last few years and give her my new address, which Elf had included in her email after I'd accepted the job: The Flat, 1 Lavender Row, Jericho's End. I'd email her with my mobile phone number once the SIM card arrived, which it might have done today. It would be odd to have a permanent mobile phone number again.

I'd written it all down in case she wasn't free, but luckily she had ten minutes before her next client and we could have a chat.

After that I tackled the banking situation. I'd closed my account before I left for France, giving most of what was in it to Treena, so she could pay any solicitor's bills that came up.

There hadn't been a huge amount in my bank account, since I'd been transferring most of my wages into Mike's, to help with the household bills, while he was supposed to be paying money into a building society account ready for when we bought our first house together.

But that was the past, and another country, one I didn't want to revisit. I decided to open a Post Office bank account instead.

That settled, I went to the supermarket and bought a basic and rugged phone, nothing fancy, and a cheap digital watch. I was just as deadly to watches as I was to phones, maybe even more so, forever dropping them into things, or plunging my arms deep into wet earth or leaf mould before remembering I was wearing one.

I drove the short distance to Treena's cottage in sunshine, my spirits lifting a little. She'd said she would bring lunch, and I'd bought two gigantic cream horns for afterwards, the kind with buttery crisp flaky pastry cones, filled with thick cream and delicious dark jam at the bottom, a cornucopia of confectionary decadence. We both had a sweet tooth and I hadn't eaten one of those for *years*.

When I'd bought them, that weird kink in my imagination had shown me another of those odd little visions (just as well Ned didn't know about those . . .), in which I was wearing one on each side of my head, like Brunhilde in a horned helmet, only stickier.

Flaky.

Treena had only just arrived when I got there and was unwrapping two traditional Lancashire hotpot pies in foil cases, fresh from the bakery oven.

We ate them while they were still hot, peppery and delicious, watched avidly by all the animals, then guzzled the cream horns, too (I didn't confess to my earlier giant Danish pastry; it seemed a Miss Piggyness too far), before settling down with a pot of Earl Grey to sort out the laptop and phone.

Treena had transferred everything she wanted from her old laptop to the new and cleaned her stuff off it.

My SIM card had arrived too, so after that we unpacked my new phone.

'I didn't know they still made phones that basic,' she said disparagingly.

'It's all I need, and I've got the laptop now for anything else,' I said, watching her deft fingers inserting the new SIM card. 'It'll be great to have a permanent phone number again.'

I'd been a bit paranoid about changing numbers with my phones, but there was no way Mike could find this one out, even if he wanted to. And I certainly wasn't ever going on social media again. It made me too easy to track down.

'And I suppose I'll have to try and get my poor old car through the MOT soon,' I sighed.

'There's a small garage in one of the backstreets here that's reasonable and they don't give you that "Oh God, there's a woman in my workshop" look when you go in.'

'The good thing about 2CVs is there isn't very much that can go wrong, and if bits drop off, you can stick another one on. Though I don't suppose there are many as old as mine over here.'

'Probably not outside a museum, anyway,' Treena said, pouring us both another cup of tea.

While we drank it, I told her all about my arrival in Jericho's End, the Misses Price-Jones – or Mrs, in Myfanwy's case – my glimpse of Wayne Vane (over whose name we both giggled), who was probably a cousin, and then, finally, my surprise discovery that Ned Mars, with whom I'd been at college, was the owner of the Grace Garden, where I was to spend the majority of my working hours.

'Elf hadn't mentioned the name of their new shared gardener to Ned, so he was totally taken aback, too, when he saw me, and *not* in a good way.'

'I'd no idea you were at college with Ned Mars,' she said. 'He's that tall, fairish bloke who presents a TV gardening series, *This Small Plot*, isn't he?'

'He *was*,' I agreed, surprised she knew even that much because, despite growing up in a green-fingered, garden-centre-owning, plant-obsessed family, Treena remained totally uninterested in anything except animals. It had always been that way, while I, merely the adopted daughter, was a bark chip off the Ellwood block.

'I was at Honeywood Horticultural College with him, though he was a year ahead of me. But although it's affiliated to a university, Honeywood's such a small college out in the sticks that we all knew each other. There was only one pub within walking distance, so that helped, too.'

Treena had been at a different university, training to be a veterinary surgeon, at the same time, so she'd never visited it.

'But if you were students together, why wouldn't he be pleased to see you, even if it was a surprise?'

'Well, for a start, he'd heard about that resignation letter I'd supposedly sent to the Heritage Homes Trust, with the allegations of inappropriate behaviour against several staff members, and he thought I'd create another scandal when he'd just been embroiled in one himself.'

She frowned in an effort of recollection. 'That does ring a bell. There was some kind of scandal about him early last year, but I can't remember what it was.'

'"LOVE RAT TV GARDENER CAUGHT OUT IN HOT BED",' I suggested helpfully. 'That was the gossip column headline.'

Her eyes widened. 'Yes, that's it. Hadn't he been having an affair with the married director on his gardening show?'

'Except that he hadn't. The whole thing was all in the mind of his jealous ex, and there was a perfectly good explanation for that picture they printed of him in a clinch with his director.'

Then I told her everything I'd gleaned from my Google search and what Myfy had told me.

'Of course, they had to print a retraction and an apology in the next issue, but by then the damage had been done – and it was compounded by another student from Honeywood selling a trumped-up sensational titbit to a gossip column. Ned's quite sensitive under his rugged exterior and the lies had a terrible effect on him.'

'But half the male so-called "personalities" on TV really are love rats, aren't they?' Treena pointed out. 'I wouldn't have thought it would harm his career, once the dust had settled, even if it had been true.'

'It was more like mud settling, than dust. One minute everyone loved him, because he was so open and enthusiastic and *nice*, and then the next, they were willing to believe sordid stories and say vile things on social media. His image was well and truly tarnished and the TV company got cold feet about the next series, even though the tabloids retracted the main story. When there was some talk of getting different garden designers in for each episode in future, he just quit and went back to Jericho's End, to put it all behind him and start a new life. And then, of course, *I* arrived on the scene!'

'Wanting to put your *own* past behind you and start a new life where no one knew you,' she said. 'It's odd how things work out.'

'It certainly is. I'd no idea he had any connection with Jericho's End when we were students, but he must already have been living at Old Grace Hall by then. Myfy told me his parents were killed in a car crash when he was in his teens, and he made his home with his great-uncle Theo. And now he's inherited.'

'And Mum and Dad had adopted you by then, too, so you were Marnie Ellwood, not Vane.'

'It's not that uncommon a name, so I don't expect he'd have made any connection with the Vane family at Jericho's End – who sound ghastly, by the way, so I think I'm going to keep that connection *totally* secret!'

'To go back to the scandal thing, surely if he was innocent, then everyone would soon move on to the next bit of salacious gossip about someone else? He only had to sit it out.'

'Perhaps it dragged on longer than it should because of that nasty bit Sammie Nelson sold to the gossip columnist.'

'She must be a total cow,' Treena said.

'Yeah – I never liked her, though I wouldn't have thought

she'd do something that unpleasant. The journalist wrote the article so cleverly, though, that there was nothing you could pin down, just innuendo and suggestion. Sammie was in my year,' I added, 'but she wasn't interested in having female friends.'

'Oh, that kind,' Treena said. 'And everything she hinted about in that article was untrue?'

'Absolutely. But there are always people willing to believe the worst, aren't there?'

'I suppose so. Perhaps it isn't surprising that Ned wanted to hide himself away.'

'Like me – though luckily for him, he had somewhere lovely to do it in. Old Grace Hall is the most amazing Tudor house, like an overgrown fairy-tale cottage. And now he can get his teeth into the wonderful project of restoring a walled apothecary garden and opening it to the public,' I enthused. 'That's where I come in. Oh, and there's a horribly overgrown rose garden, too. I'm dying to hack my way into that and see what's there!'

'It sounds like your idea of heaven,' Treena said, amused. 'If he'll let you help him, that is?'

'He can't really afford not to, because he's trying to restore it all on a shoestring and they're getting me dirt cheap. Anyway, I've had the whole thing out with him this morning and put him straight about that damned resignation email! I had to tell him a little bit about Mike, which I really didn't want to do, in order to convince him I wasn't likely to cause trouble in future.'

'I should think not!' she said indignantly.

'Myfy and Elf had already told him they were certain I was a good person, which might have helped . . . and, of course, once I knew what had happened to him last year, I sort of understood why he was petrified I might start throwing accusations about. But I think we're OK now. At least he's employing me, and I mean to prove I'm both sane and hardworking.'

'You can always set him on to me, if you think he has any doubts,' Treena suggested. 'I'll put him right!'

And if he made her *really* angry, he might just find himself microchipped and neutered, too, I thought, amused.

'I'm really looking forward to learning about the apothecary garden. I saw what looked like a blown-up photo of the original plan on his office wall, and as well as being huge, it's very unusual for the late seventeenth century. I'm longing to get my secateurs into that rose garden, too!'

She laughed. 'I think it sounds like your idea of heaven, rather than mine!'

'Definitely. I know it's going to be hard work, but fun! Ned's going to show me round the garden tomorrow morning, and I can hardly wait. The Lavender Cottage side of things won't take me long, once I've given everything a good pruning, probably an hour or so a week in the afternoon, just before I go up the River Walk.'

'River Walk?' she echoed.

I told her about this unexpected addition to my duties and added, 'You'll have to come and see it all – and the Grace Garden, when it opens at Easter.'

'I'll let you settle in first, unless I'm called out to Risings to see those spoilt Pekes again. And then, Luke is starting his dig at the monastic ruins on the Tuesday after Easter, so I expect I'll be popping in to see what's happening there, too.'

'It should be fascinating,' I said tactfully, though I didn't think Treena had much more interest in old walls and post holes than she had in gardening.

She helped me to carry down the last of the stored things from the spare bedroom and we managed to fit them into the car. There was the little chair and the tiny white-painted bookcase to get in somehow. In the end I had to pile things high, with a travel rug tucked over it all, and leave the roof down, so it was going to be a chilly drive back.

'It's amazing what you can get in a Citroën 2CV,' Treena said. 'You'd think it was made of elastic.'

'It's a Tardis.' I wished, though, that I could put a giant luggage strap around it, in case it sprang open like a suitcase with a broken lock.

Treena checked her watch. 'I'm doing evening surgery, then it's my turn to be on twenty-four-hour emergency call. I'll take the dogs for a good run now, before I go back. Do you want to come?'

'I think I'd better take all this stuff back and unload it,' I said. 'I might have time for a little walk round the village after that, to stretch my legs.'

'OK. And let me know how things are going. See you soon.'

We hugged and I drove off, full of hotpot and cream horn and a faint and probably entirely unfounded stirring of optimism.

10

Cat Flap

It was mid-afternoon when I bumped and rattled my overstuffed car across the humpbacked bridge and parked outside the café. It was a pity it was their closing day, because Charlie would have made short work of carrying everything up to the flat.

I had a key to the café door, but didn't somehow like to use it and instead began to haul everything round to the back door. It took me about a dozen trips, and the chair, with its elegantly scrolled and padded back, was the last thing. The heap sitting on the crazy-paving terrace looked like a slightly dubious garage sale, with odds and ends sticking up out of boxes and strange bundles tied with string.

I sat on the chair for a minute to recover, before going upstairs to open all the doors and deposit the first box in the corner of the living room with those already there.

When I got down again the French window to Myfy's studio further along opened and she stepped out, followed by a tall, hawk-nosed and handsome man. His silver hair was as long as Myfy's, but caught back in a thick plait and he was dressed from head to foot in black.

Myfy was wearing a knee-length patchwork and beaded

tunic over harem trousers, and a black cloak was draped over her shoulders. Together, they looked as if they'd stepped out of a slightly dark fairy tale, or a mythical kingdom.

Catching sight of me, they came over and Myfy introduced the tall man as her husband, Jacob Springer.

'He's an artist too, did I say? Or perhaps more of a sculptor, really, since he mainly constructs three-dimensional moving things.'

'I'm a kinetic artist,' he said, shaking hands.

'Right . . .' I said uncertainly, thinking that would be one to google on the new laptop.

'Let me give you a hand, if you're taking all this lot up to the flat,' he offered.

'It's the last of the things I had stored with my sister, Treena, in Great Mumming, Myfy,' I explained. 'You did say you didn't mind if I brought it here to sort.'

'No, of course not,' she said, as Jacob, without another word, seized the chair and bore it upwards.

'I'd let him get on with it,' she advised, when I made to follow with a box. 'He's very strong and it won't take him a minute. I've seen Ned, by the way,' she added, 'and I'm so happy everything's been resolved. You can both put the past behind you now, can't you? There's so much to do and I'm sure you'll enjoy working in the Grace Garden.'

'I'm fascinated by it and dying to know all about Ned's plans to restore it,' I agreed. 'And I'll soon have *your* garden tidied, too. It's just got away from you a bit.'

'Or quite a lot. My gardening is rather spasmodic – the painting comes first.'

As Myfy'd said, Jacob had everything up to the flat in no time. The last thing to go was the small white-painted bookcase. Then he ran lightly down the steps and smiled.

'There – I've stacked it all in the living room.'

'Thank you so much,' I said gratefully. 'It would have taken me ages to do it on my own.'

'Not at all. I could hear that insane cat on the other side of the door to the cottage, Myfy,' he added. 'I think it was swearing and the door handle kept rattling.'

'I found the door to the landing was open first thing this morning,' said Myfy, 'and shut it again. Was he bothering you last night, Marnie?'

'I went to bed late and heard him trying to get in,' I said, 'and I thought he might disturb you, so I opened it. And then I decided I'd better leave the door ajar in case he needed his litter tray, or anything.'

'He must have taken a fancy to you, which is more than he seems to have done to us!' she said.

'I don't know, but I don't mind him coming into the flat, if you don't object to the door on the landing staying open.'

'Not at all, but if he's going to make a habit of it, maybe Jacob should put a cat flap in the door instead, so you can shut it and have a bit of privacy.'

'A *big* cat flap,' agreed Jacob. 'I'll get one. You wanted me to make a wall-mounted pigeonhole for Marnie's post at the bottom of the stairs anyway, didn't you?'

'But won't a big cat flap spoil the door?' I asked. I mean, Caspar was practically the size of a tiger.

'It's not one of the original old ones. Father had it put there when we knocked through to the flat, so it doesn't matter,' Myfy said.

Jacob wrapped her in her cloak. 'You mustn't get cold, my darling,' he said. 'There's still a chill in the air.'

They smiled fondly at each other and I felt as if I was intruding on a private moment.

Then Myfy turned to me and said: 'Well, we'll leave you to it – we're going out to see friends.'

They went off, Jacob's arm around Myfy's shoulders, and I climbed the stairs and made some coffee, contemplating the now much larger mountain of stuff to be sorted. I suspected an awful lot of it would be heading for the bin, the recycling or the charity shops. I'd make a start that evening. But first of all, I needed to stretch my legs and get some fresh air.

Outside, the sun had vanished and dark lavender-grey clouds had begun to gather. It was colder, too, and although I could see one or two cars and several people on the main street, there was no one on my side of the river.

I could imagine that on hot days there would be tourists all over the Green, though, picnicking and eating ice-cream, or rattling through the turnstile to the River Walk and the Fairy Falls.

I paused to look at the Victorian turnstile, which was practically a work of art, heavily embossed with leafy foliage and clearly built to last for ever. It was painted a dark royal blue and freshly gilded on the lettering and embellishments.

A more modern metal shutter had been pulled down over the entrance side and secured with a large padlock.

There was a public viewing point between the high wall around the turnstile and the bridge and I stood there for a few moments, watching the dark water slide by in a deep channel before cascading down into the pool on the other side.

Water, especially any kind of waterfall, is always magical and mesmerizing, but eventually I tore myself away and headed for the bridge.

There was someone standing in the embrasure at the highest point, a man with his back to me, leaning over to drop pebbles into the Devil's Cauldron.

He straightened and turned as I approached and I recognized the wiry figure of Wayne Vane, his hair, the colour of scraped carrots, blown into elf locks around a freckled face that should have been pleasant, but was instead lit with a kind of smouldering malevolence that took me aback.

For a moment, I wondered if he could know who I was – though why that should make him angry, I had no idea – but from what Elf and Myfy had said, he didn't sound a pleasant character, so perhaps he just hated everyone.

I quickened my pace and would have gone past with just a nod of the head, if he hadn't stepped directly into my path.

His head lowered like that of an angry bull and he said, in a voice that grated like a rusty gate, 'I want a word with you!'

'Me?' I said, startled.

'Yes. You're the new gardener they've taken on at the Hall, aren't you?'

'Well, yes, though I'll be dividing my time between there and Lavender Cottage.'

His face twisted spitefully. 'Gardener? New slave, more like, but you'll soon find out. They work you to the bone for a pittance and then begrudge you a bit of fruit or veg to take home. I was giving Ned one day a week, but he fired me. Doesn't need me, now he's got you on the cheap, but I could tell you a few things about that Ned Mars . . .'

'Do you know, I'd so much rather you didn't, thanks,' I said crisply and, sidestepping neatly round him, walked quickly over the bridge and turned right up the hill. I could feel his eyes on my back, but there was no sound of pursuing footsteps.

I quickened my pace anyway. On this side of the road there was a narrow pavement and then the drystone wall dividing me from the steep wooded drop to the river, which was a long way below. All the buildings seemed to be clustered on the other side, backed up against a steep rock face.

I glanced back and, to my relief, Wayne hadn't followed me, but was making off in the other direction, towards the car park by the ruins. I wondered if he'd left his van there, or was heading back to Cross Ways Farm on foot . . . if he still lived there, with the rest of the Vanes. Mum had said she had an older brother and various uncles and cousins living nearby and they were all very clannish, though, of course, a lot of time had passed since then and things could have changed. Myfy had said that that strangely repressive religious sect her parents had belonged to, the Strange Brethren, had died out . . .

I walked on, feeling thoroughly unsettled, both by having come face to face for the first time with someone actually related to me, but more particularly by his attitude. He seemed to have a grudge against Ned, that was for sure, and now that I had, in his eyes, taken his job, that appeared to extend to me, too.

The road rounded a bend and I could see the rest of the village, a couple of shops of some kind, cottages, and what looked like guesthouses, but I decided to look at those on the way back.

To my right, the valley quickly narrowed into what was practically a ravine and it was a long, long drop to the river. At first I caught occasional glimpses of it through gaps in the trees, but it was soon hidden.

As the gradient of the hill grew ever steeper, the last cottages slowly petered out, until I came to a point where a farm track led off to my right, with a sign for Angel Row and Spout Farm, so I knew I must be above the falls, near the top turnstile.

The well-made road through the village now quite suddenly turned into a rougher-surfaced single-track one, snaking sharply up into dark woodland.

I examined a thicket of signs on the other side of the road, which were clearly intended to discourage any adventurous or unwary motorists from attempting to get to Thorstane that way. They proclaimed:

Single track road
Steep hill
Hairpin bends
Beware falling rocks!
Unsuitable for large vehicles

If that didn't put them off, the immediate deterioration in the road surface and a severe pocking of potholes probably would.

According to the signpost, Thorstane was amazingly close . . . or it was if you were a crow. Then I remembered the map and the way the lane to Jericho's End by which I'd arrived had formed a narrow V with the main one up to Thorstane, so the top of the village couldn't be that far from the outskirts.

As I stood there, a young rabbit skittered out of the bushes and, on seeing me, ran back again, and distant wood pigeons started up their throaty, repetitive song.

The light was now fading and the occasional large splodge of cold rain hit my head, or smartly slapped a leaf. Time to return, though now on the side of civilization, even if it did seem to be precariously clinging to a rock face.

Then it occurred to me that the houses had most probably been built with stone hacked out of that very rock face, which is why they looked as if they'd grown there.

There were little rows of terraced cottages, interspersed with foursquare detached houses, like the ones in a child's picture book. Several had the shut-up look of out-of-season holiday lets and, as I got further down, I came to a couple of more substantial Victorian or Edwardian guesthouses, also closed, and a row of three shops in what the sign proclaimed to be The Old Stables.

The art and craft gallery wasn't open, and the paintings in the window were not of Myfy's calibre, but the type of views that can only be described as competent wallpaper.

Next to it was a small gift shop, where there were actually customers – a youngish couple and a little girl, who seemed to be selecting a pair of fairy wings from a display.

In fact, the whole shop was awash with angel- and fairy-inspired souvenirs and gifts of every conceivable type, and some I never would have thought of. On the whole, the fairies seemed to be winning out over the angels.

I wandered down the display of fairy figurines, picked up a fat little hardback book from a stack on a shelf and found it was the one Myfy had told me about that her sister had written. Embossed on the cover were the words:

A Short History of the Village of Jericho's End
Elfrida Price-Jones

I flicked through it, finding a whole section of fascinating old black-and-white photographs of the village, the falls and local characters. The list of contents looked interesting, too, so I bought it . . . and then, at the till, succumbed to an impulse buy: one of those small crystal stars, made to hang in a window and cast a rainbow prism over your world. A lucky star.

The last shop in the row and the largest was the village store, Toller's, set out like a mini-supermarket and selling a wide range of goods, from a well-stocked deli counter to a good selection of fresh fruit and vegetables, cakes, bread, sandwiches and hot pasties and pies . . . except that this late in the day, the locusts had already cleaned the place out and the cabinets had been cleaned, ready for tomorrow. It obviously catered for everyone: staples for the villagers, food for hungry hikers, snacks and drinks for the daytrippers and more exotic items for the holiday cottage contingent.

I bought a couple of bags of jelly babies – one of my weaknesses – a block of mature Cheddar, a small jar of pickled onions, some tomatoes and a pot of Marmite, and went out again, my little rucksack now bulging.

I rounded the bend in the road and there was the bridge again, happily now a Wayne-free zone, with the pub sitting opposite.

It had a porch supported by wooden pillars and the main part of the building looked ancient, though you could see where there had been later extensions in both directions. A painted board fixed next to the porch advertised coffee and bar snacks . . . though perhaps not at that moment, for the door was firmly shut.

On the far side was a restaurant with its own entrance, the windows overlooking a cobbled yard and outbuildings. Inside were lights and signs of activity, even if it wasn't yet open.

Darkness was falling over the valley now that the sun had sunk below the surrounding hills, and I decided the delights of the ancient ruins could wait for another day, especially since Wayne had vanished in that direction and I didn't much fancy running into him again, should he be still roaming in the gloaming.

Returning over the bridge was a little like stepping back in time, with the half-moon of the Green, the intricate black and white Tudor façade of Old Grace Hall and the long, low shape of Lavender Cottage. Though the café, with the ice-cream vendor's tricycle parked outside it, was a bit out of step.

I wandered across the grass to peer through the pointed iron rails on the wall that prevented the unwary from the dangerous drop down to the river below and then crossed to look at the Village Hall – or Hut, as my employers had called it. I thought it might have started out as a hut, but was now much more substantial.

By the gate there was one of those notice boards behind glass, and peering closely I discovered that the Friends of Jericho's End met every Tuesday evening at seven, new members always welcome. They would be holding an Easter egg hunt in the garden (by which I supposed they meant the enclosed stretch of turf with a few bushes that surrounded the Hut) on the morning of Easter Sunday, to be opened by the vicar of St Gabriel's, the Reverend Jojo Micklejohn.

There were also various adverts for the amenities of the village, like the general store and the pub, which had a quiz night on Fridays. There was a bus timetable, too. The only bus stop was in the car park by the monastic ruins and it left on weekdays for Great Mumming at nine thirty and returned, having first gone up to Thorstane and back, at four thirty. If those times and days didn't suit, you could whistle.

There was a card in one corner with a Thorstane taxi number, which I should think got a lot of use.

I was glad I had my little car, even though it was pretty much held together by string and hope.

Between the Village Hut and Old Grace Hall was the entrance to some old outbuildings, probably the original barn and stables for the house.

There was warm light behind the mullioned windows of the Hall, the gleaming white door flanked by neatly dug borders planted with spring bulbs.

It was all very pretty, but I didn't linger, in case Ned was indoors and caught me goggling at his house.

Next came a tangle of dense black briars behind a short stretch of wall dividing the Hall from Lavender Cottage and I thought the rose garden must be wedge-shaped, for it was much wider by the fish pond. I wondered how far back it went . . . and itched to get my hands on some secateurs and find out.

There were more neat beds in front of Lavender Cottage, which I remembered were the special domain of James Hyde, the ancient gardener I hadn't yet met and would do my best not to cross. There was work enough, without adding extra.

All was quiet as I opened the door to the flat, which already felt familiar and welcoming: a haven, where I could settle happily into my new life.

If it was proving impossible to excise completely from my mind what had happened during my brief marriage, at least here I could finish the healing process . . . and, as they say, what doesn't kill you makes you stronger.

There might still be a few bumps along the way, even though I'd ironed out the situation with Ned. Wayne Vane could well be one of them.

I had dinner, followed by a dessert of jelly babies and an apple, then put the TV on low for company, while I made a start on the Matterhorn of possessions in the corner.

First, the low velvet chair, which went by the fireplace, with the small, white-painted bookcase next to it. Then I unrolled a rag rug that had been carefully layered with lavender bags and stored in a flat-topped wooden box, which became my new coffee table.

I was just filling the bookcase with the Beatrix Potters and Enid Blytons of my childhood, when I was interrupted by the imperative summons of Caspar, who had decided to join me.

He watched from the sofa as I finished filling the bookcase with more battered old favourites, but soon the busy day began to catch up with me and, after propping the landing door ajar for Caspar, should he need to make an exit, I retired to bed with Elf's book. There was a good bedside lamp and I settled down, or I did once Caspar had stopped trampling across me with his great, hairy feet.

A Short History of the Village of Jericho's End
Elfrida Price-Jones

Table of Contents

Chapter 7: The Jericho's End Group
The flourishing artists' colony between the wars.
Chapter 8: Jericho's End Today
The post-war decline in visitors and the slow climb back to the popular tourist destination that it is today, with a map of the various interesting points and amenities.
Chapter 9: Then and Now
A collection of old and new photographs.

My eyelids were growing heavy at this point, but I turned over the page and read on.

Introduction

In this short book I have endeavoured to describe the varied fortunes of this small and out-of-the way village – even the Black Death gave it a miss – which later came to attract artists, writers and all those who love the beauty of natural form and the magnetic and enthralling power of water cascading from rocky outcrops and rushing forward towards the valley . . .

Even had I not been so sleepy by now, Elf's writing style was a bit on the soporific side and the words began to dance in front of my eyes. I put the book on the bedside table, turned out the light, and Caspar stretched out luxuriously beside me and then relaxed with a long, contented sigh.

11

Wheels within Wheels

Caspar was still there when I woke, but once I got up he leaped off the bed and headed for the door to Lavender Cottage, so I closed it after him.

I wondered if Jacob really *did* intend installing a giant cat flap in the door.

Dawn was a tinge of rose in a dark lilac-grey sky, but it soon grew light and promised to be a crisp but sunny day.

After breakfast I dressed for work, in warm layers under a padded waxed cotton gilet of great age, which some visitor had left behind at one of the châteaux I'd worked at and never reclaimed.

You'd be surprised at the odd things you find in lost property boxes.

My anorak was stuffed into the rucksack, along with a bottle of water, and then I was ready to go.

I went into the café first, even though it was too early to expect anyone to be there, but I thought perhaps if Myfy or Elf was in their kitchen I could have a quick word.

The top half of the stable door was ajar, though, and Myfy

must have heard my boots on the floor, because she looked over it.

'Morning,' she said. 'Would you like some breakfast? We're having porridge and toast.'

'Oh, no, thank you, I've had mine,' I said. 'I just came to say that I was going over to the Hall this morning, but I'll make a start on your garden some time this afternoon, before I check the River Walk. Is that all right?'

'Yes, fine,' said Elf, popping up next to her sister in a way that started to remind me of an old-fashioned Punch and Judy show I'd seen on the TV. We just needed a dog, a policeman and a string of sausages.

'You and Ned just arrange it how you want to,' Myfy told me. 'His need is greater than ours.'

'I can't wait to start on the rose garden – but I'll see what he wants me to do first.'

'I don't remember a time when you could get down any of the paths in the rose garden,' said Myfy. 'So good luck with that.'

'You might find Caspar out there,' Elf suggested. 'He had his breakfast early and then we thought we'd try letting him out for the first time, so we hope he'll come back again.'

Myfy said, 'But he's microchipped, if he wanders off.'

'I'll keep an eye out for him,' I promised.

But it was Ned I found first, sitting on the marble bench in the rose garden, tossing food to the koi, whose great red-gold and silver shapes emerged from the murky depths like ghosts, swirled, mouths opening and shutting, then slowly sank back into the darkness again.

'I wondered who fed those,' I said, closing the gate behind me and going to sit on the end of the bench, leaving a respectable distance between us.

'My uncle Theo looked after them and the peacocks – he used to sit here for hours on warm days – but unfortunately he wasn't much of a gardener.'

'Sounds like Treena, my sister. Her family had a garden centre and nursery, but all she ever cared about was animals and birds. She's a vet now, in Great Mumming.'

He was still looking down at the pool, where a last koi surfaced, then vanished, leaving a spreading circle of ripples, so I could safely study his face for a moment. It was intended by nature to be open and good-humoured, with those lean cheeks bracketing a long, straight mouth that could quirk upwards at the corners in amusement. But now, even in repose, it wore a reserved, wary expression that wasn't natural to it . . . and maybe my arrival was the cause?

I looked away and found the surface of the water smooth again . . . and there were our reflections, side by side: my heart-shaped face, with wings of black hair springing from either side of my forehead and eyes darkened by the shadows, so that I looked like a little goblin, green jerkin and all, next to his tall fairness.

I turned quickly and saw that the peacock was strutting through the open gate to the Grace Garden, followed by his drabber and more homely mate.

'Lancelot and Guinevere,' Ned said, seeing where I was looking.

'Really? That's a coincidence,' I said, and told him about imagining a hand and arm appearing from the middle of the pond, Excalibur fashion, brandishing a gilded rake.

That surprised a grin out of him that made him look much more like his old self. 'You're crazy! Though of course, if we could get it to make a regular appearance, it would certainly draw in the visitors.'

He stood up suddenly, giving me a half-smile that told me he didn't *entirely* yet trust me, but wanted to, and this time I didn't feel angry. In fact, it was sort of endearing, like a badly treated dog trying to wag its tail. That image made me grin back, which unfortunately seemed to unnerve him.

'Right, I'd better give you a quick tour of the garden and then start you off on something – though God knows, there's enough to do to keep ten full-time gardeners busy for a year and I've been managing with Gertie and James, and Wayne one day a week, till I fired him.'

'Well, now you've got me too, and I'm not afraid of hard work – in fact, I can't wait to start,' I said, then paused before adding, 'Actually, I had a brief encounter with Wayne yesterday afternoon on the bridge and he wasn't very pleasant.'

I gave him the gist of what Wayne had said and Ned ran a hand through his tawny hair, so that it stood up on end like a ruffled eagle's crest, and sighed. 'I'm sorry about that. He's got a bit of a grudge about my firing him, but he wasn't only useless, he took things.'

'He *did* say something about you begrudging him a few vegetables to take home.'

'He helped himself to a lot more than that. The odd bit of produce for his own family wouldn't have mattered, but he was taking tons of stuff and selling it. Gert was livid; the vegetable and fruit gardens are her preserve. Then I caught him red-handed one day, sneaking out with most of the early potatoes and a brand-new hoe, and that was it. Other things had gone missing too – more garden tools and a tenner from James's jacket, when it was hung up on a spade handle, but we just hadn't caught him at it. He denied it, of course.'

'I suppose he would, but you can't really talk your way out of a sack of new potatoes and a hoe, can you?'

'No, especially since he was actually carrying them out to his van when I accosted him. Anyway, nothing went missing on days when he wasn't there, so unless the peacocks had turned light-fingered, it had to be him.'

'He must have known that made him the obvious suspect, but I suppose it was better just to let him go quietly than make a fuss about it?'

'Except he's *not* going quietly. He came round here on Monday, blustering and threatening – said if I didn't give him redundancy pay, he'd take me to an employment tribunal!'

'Could he do that?'

'Not really. He's self-employed and he always wanted to be paid in cash, so I reckon he wasn't declaring all his income. He shut up and went away when I suggested HMRC might be interested in investigating his tax returns.'

'Checkmate!' I said.

'I hope so, and that that's the end of it, but if he bothers you again, let me know and I'll deal with him,' he said grimly.

'OK,' I agreed, then changed the subject. 'Myfy told me that James won't let anyone help him with the front borders, so I won't touch those.'

'Much better not. They're his pride and joy, though his taste in spring and summer bedding plants is a bit garish, to say the least. Still, he helps out with the rest of the gardening when his rheumatism will let him and he's going to man the ticket office when we open to the public.'

'What about Gertie?'

'She's quite spry, but her real love is the vegetable garden and the greenhouses, which are outside the Grace Garden itself, through a gate at the bottom. I'll show you in a bit, but first, perhaps we'd better go to the office, where you can see a blown-up photo of the original plan.'

He strode off through the gate and took the path past the Alchemist rose to the arched entrance, trailing me and the peacocks behind him.

Last time I'd visited the courtyard I'd been too focused on the coming interview with Ned to take in what was there, so this time I stared around curiously. It was a large, rectangular cobbled yard, the brick walls a little lower than those around the garden. Straight ahead was another arch, this one with a closed gate, which must lead to Old Grace Hall, for I could see the twisty chimney-pots and roof above it.

To my right, Ned's office and a long building with a sign on the door proclaiming it to be 'The Potting Shed, Private', stood at right angles to each other.

There were more buildings against the wall on the other side and a smaller gate, presumably the visitors' entrance. But there was no time to linger, for Ned had already thrown open the door of his office and vanished inside. I hurried after him, closing the door on the peacocks.

'Here we are,' said Ned, when I joined him in front of the corkboard wall. 'The original plan of the apothecary garden, begun in the late seventeenth century.'

I moved closer. 'I spotted this yesterday and thought that's what it might be. You're very lucky to have it!'

I studied the unusual layout, with a large circle within the square and a criss-cross of paths to the four corners.

'I know I'm lucky to have it – and it's a very early example of an apothecary or physic garden, especially so far out of London. I suppose I'd better give you a potted family history, so you can understand the context.'

I dragged my gaze away from the plan with an effort and said, 'Go on then, I'm listening.'

'The Grace family were local minor gentry – Grace was a

corruption of a Norman name – and as the family fortunes flourished, due to a tendency to marry money, they remodelled the original house that was here into the Tudor one you see now.'

'I'm sure this flat area must have been inviting for building on, but how did they get across the river, before the bridge was built?' I asked curiously.

'There was an earlier one of slabs on stone piers. You can just see the remains of it above the present bridge, where the channel narrows.'

'I wouldn't have fancied that on a dark night, with the Devil's Cauldron waiting below!'

'Nor me,' he agreed. 'Anyway, a bit later on, the then Grace heir excelled himself by marrying into the minor nobility, to a Miss Lordly, and the family decided this house wasn't good enough any more and built Risings Manor on the hill opposite. That was when they changed their name to Lordly-Grace, too.'

'How very pretentious! What happened to *this* house?'

'They sold it to a Grace cousin called Nathaniel, a rollicking Elizabethan character, somewhere between an adventurer and a pirate – the distinction was a bit hazy back then. He'd made enough out of it to buy the Hall, marry and settle down here. And this is the point where it gets interesting, Marnie, because one of *his* descendants married a Tradescant, which is where the beginning of the Grace Garden lies.'

'Not one of the famous London plant-collecting Tradescant family?'

'The very same, and she too had a fascination with plants and their medicinal and culinary uses. Not long after the marriage, the walled garden that already existed here was enlarged and the plan drawn up.'

'She must have been a girl after my own heart!'

'She was certainly interesting. Uncle Theo found several of her letters about plants to and from her relatives in London, together with the garden plan, in a chest full of family documents. She corresponded with other keen gardeners up and down the country, too, and often exchanged seeds and cuttings. It gives us an idea of what she was growing here, though of course there were already herbals in print, like Culpeper's, listing hundreds of plants and their uses.'

'It's wonderful to still have all that original material, though,' I said. 'It'll really interest the visitors.'

'I've put a bit about it in the garden guide we're going to sell, but I might eventually have room to make a display of facsimiles of the plan and letters, and perhaps some antique garden implements,' he said. 'There's an old outbuilding adjoining the other side of the wall from the shop, so it might be possible to knock through into that to create the space. But that'll have to be later.'

'You've got a shop?'

'The other end of the ticket office. It's not ready yet, though. We'll have to get a shift on with it, because Easter's at the end of next week.'

He turned back to the plan on the wall and said, 'So, that's how the garden came about. The circular layout is unusual for the time, though not unique.'

'Yes, that's what I thought, and I noticed it wasn't flat, either – it seems to rise towards the middle.'

'Only a bit, but the mid-level planting in the central beds makes it look higher. It slopes down slightly to a little sunken round herb garden in the middle, with an old sundial.'

His fingers traced the outlines of the quartered mid-level beds. 'We're trying to plant these up mainly with things that would have been there before, but this one at the lower end of the garden was the area flattened and used for vegetable growing during the war. It's just an overgrown mess at the moment and I haven't quite decided what to do with it.'

'And then there are two more tall beds beyond it, at the bottom of the garden, matching the ones at this end?' I guessed.

'Yes, and low beds on either side of the central circle.'

'I think I'll grasp the layout a lot better when I actually walk around it,' I hinted, but first he insisted on showing me, with printed transparent overlays, the later tweaks and changes that generations of Graces had made to the original.

'And I've added a couple of new features of my own,' he said, indicating the right-hand corner at the further end of the garden with one long finger. 'This is a boggy area where a spring rises, so I'm turning it into a wetland habitat with a wooden walkway . . . and in the corner opposite is the Poison Garden.'

'Poison Garden?' I echoed.

'You'll see – come on, I'll give you a guided tour all to yourself. It'll be good practice for when we open.'

We took the wide gravel path between two beds of trees and large shrubs towards the heart of the garden, crossing the circular path on the way. I had to admit, it all made much more sense, now I'd seen the plan.

'Last year I began by restoring all the original paths and a few later ones that led to seating areas among the mid-level herb beds . . . or what will *be* the mid-level herb beds, when I've finished replanting them.'

'You've made a good start,' I said as we walked down the gentle slope to a shallow, sunken garden.

'Hyssop, herb of grace, valerian, common Solomon's seal, chamomile, feverfew . . .' he said, like an incantation. 'So many herbs, so little time!'

The small herb garden right in the middle looked in good order, though, with brick paths radiating out from the sundial.

'The pointer on that sundial is a sailing ship – that's unusual,' I said. 'It looks very old.'

'It is, and the ship is a galleon.' He looked down at the herbs, all low-growing kinds, like thyme, mint and marjoram, and said: 'Luckily, Gertie likes this small herb garden so she's kept it in good order . . . and James has maintained and renewed the dwarf lavender hedges around the side beds, even if he's ignored the overgrown beds themselves! Really, those two are a law unto themselves.'

'You said they were part time – what hours do they work now?'

'I *pay* them from twelve till four at the moment . . . but they appear and disappear at will, any time between about ten and five. That'll have to change a bit when we open to the public, though.'

I expect Ned, being tall, had a view out of the sunken garden in all directions, but I could see only the lower end, the great segment of hummocky grass and weeds that Ned had mentioned.

'That's where you said they put the vegetable plot during the war, isn't it?'

'Yes. According to some old photos, they were in long, narrow beds with grass paths between,' Ned said. 'I've wondered about keeping that layout, though with something other than vegetables in the beds, of course.'

'I think that would be a great idea, and the grass edging and paths will tie in with those of the two side beds, won't they?'

'Yes, though without the lavender borders,' he agreed, leading the way out of the far side of the sunken area and heading for the bottom right-hand corner. 'My new wetland and water feature is this way.'

He'd narrowed the low bed on this side to make more room for his new project.

'The spring always came up in the corner, but it's been left to go boggy. I'm channelling the stream, so it'll run through a marshy area and down a small waterfall, into this pond I've dug out. The runoff will go through an old drainage culvert under the wall.'

It was certainly a boggy mess at the moment, but either Ned or a giant mole had been busy excavating a large hole. On the far side, against the wall, were steps up to a platform.

'Marshy plants, like marshmallow and mullein are going to love that top part. What are you going to put in your pond?'

'I thought blue water iris and maybe katniss – arrowhead – in the shallows.'

'And what about watercress?' I suggested. 'What's going up on that round platform over there?'

'A domed wooden gazebo – I've got it, I just need to put it together. It'll be the one place where you'll be able to see most of the garden. I've got a small bridge to go over the stream, too.'

'Sounds lovely,' I said, even if I couldn't quite imagine what it would look like yet.

He might have guessed what I was thinking, because he said, 'Take it from me, it will be. And now for my other new feature, the Poison Garden.'

We walked along the circular path past more tall shrubs and trees, and he pointed out the small gateway to the vegetable garden but said I could see that another time.

The black metal structure that I'd spotted earlier now came fully into view: a tall, wrought-iron fence, curved inwards like claws and set with a very Gothic-looking gate, shut off this corner.

'I thought it might be better to collect the more dangerous plants in one section, behind a fence, to stop the visitors killing themselves. Though some of the other plants won't do them a lot of good if they touch them, or try and sneak cuttings, despite the warning signs,' he said. 'That Irish yew at the back was already here, so it seemed the perfect spot.'

He'd obviously devoted quite a lot of time to planting up this part. There was another tall black metal structure in the middle.

'That fence is like a cage, keeping everything from escaping,' I said. 'And actually, there seems to be a cage within the cage.'

'The railings give the right impression, especially now I've got James to paint them black. They came from a architectural antiques place in a village not far away, and that really is a cage in the middle of the Poison Garden – a Victorian aviary, with a rosary pea in it.'

I stared at him. 'But those are *hugely* poisonous – deadly!'

'I know, that's why it's in a cage in a cage, and the gate locked. Later on, I'll take small groups round it occasionally, and I'll look after this part of the garden myself.'

'You're welcome to it,' I said.

'You don't mean that – I've got a brugmansia – angel's trumpet – that's already six feet tall, and lots more interesting things, like deadly nightshade, foxglove, rat's bane and hemlock. I think I might put some mandrake in there, too, because its history is really interesting,' he enthused.

'I can hardly wait to see it,' I said, though since I'd never seen an actual rosary pea or an angel's trumpet, I was only half-joking.

'Of course, some of the things in there, like foxgloves, you can find anywhere,' he said. 'Amazing how many ordinary garden plants are quite poisonous.'

'I know, like laburnum, which just looks so pretty.'

'I pinched the Poison Garden idea from Alnwick Castle, though mine's a lot smaller, of course.'

I could see the Poison Garden was Ned's baby, just as much as the vegetable garden and the borders were Gertie and James's.

We began to retrace our steps towards the courtyard, along the circular path and past the wide, low bed on that side.

'I'm obviously promoting the garden as a work in progress, but I thought that would be a draw – I've ordered information boards to put up round the garden, explaining what we're doing in each area, and leaflets to give out with the tickets if they don't want to spend the money on the glossy brochure.'

'I think you're right: seeing the restoration in progress will be a big attraction.'

I stopped and turned for another look as we reached the archway again.

'What with the war and lack of manpower, I can see why the garden has got into such a state, Ned,' I said. 'Especially if there wasn't much money. It needs an awful lot of work to bring it back to what it should be, though.'

'I think Uncle Theo just let it go after my aunt Wen died.'

'It's still a magical garden,' I said encouragingly. 'It'll really come alive this year, you'll see!'

'You don't feel . . . daunted by it?' he asked, looking down at me seriously.

'No, of course I don't! It'll be a wonderful challenge and I'm so lucky to be part of restoring it to its former glory.'

'It'll be good to have someone enthusiastic to help me,' he

said, and then gave me the first really warm and genuine smile I'd seen since I'd arrived.

I smiled happily back but his quickly disappeared before he said, 'OK, enough messing about, Ellwood – time to get to work.'

He'd always called me Ellwood at college, when he wanted to wind me up, especially when we were filming that stupid documentary, and I felt he really was beginning to relax his guard and accept me back as a friend again.

Or maybe, in our mutual enthusiasm, he'd just forgotten to be cautious . . .

12

Bed of Thorns

Whichever way it was, I did feel we'd made progress and, as we headed back into the office, Ned seemed to have forgotten we were going to get straight to work, and, instead, put the kettle on.

'You aren't making coffee, are you?' I asked.

He looked at me in amusement. 'I went straight out and bought one of those cafetière things after your comments about my instant coffee. I got a bag of ground Java, too.'

'Your visiting clients will love you for it, and be able to leave the office without wanting to throw up.'

'I don't think it was that bad before!'

'You have to be joking. That, or your taste buds have withered and fallen off.'

I made sure he was spooning a generous amount of coffee into his new cafetière, before wandering off to stare at the original garden plan again.

Over coffee, we talked about the Chelsea Physic Garden, which we'd both visited.

'Of course, the climate must be totally different up here,' I said.

'We do tend to be a few weeks behind – which is actually

quite good, as far as the rose garden is concerned, because we *could* still get it all radically pruned back now. I was going to leave it till next year, but it would add a bit extra to the Grace Garden experience.'

'Was the rose garden created at the same time as the rest?'

'No, it's a lot later, early Regency. That triangle of land between this garden and the cottages used to be where the pigs and hens were kept, until they were cleared out to make way for the roses.'

'I wonder if any of the Regency roses are still there, Ned? There have been some amazing survivals from even earlier,' I said eagerly. 'I expect new ones were added later, anyway – the Victorians were gaga about them – so it'll be fun finding out what's there.'

'Perhaps we'll go for it, then, and you can make a start there,' he suggested. 'James isn't a rose man and, anyway, his rheumatism is pretty bad sometimes. Gertie would much rather nurture the rhubarb with her hoard of well-rotted manure, until it's so big it takes over its bed.'

'You have rhubarb in the apothecary garden?'

'It's in one of the central mid-level beds. It has lots of medicinal properties, as well as the more culinary uses – and wine. Gertie does all sorts of things, though. She's been great at propagating plants and cuttings and growing things from seed, ready to go into the garden this year. Luckily, I still have lots of friends who've been sending them to me, once they found out what I was doing.'

'That must be saving quite a bit of money.'

'It is, though with some slower-growing shrubs and trees, I buy the biggest I can afford, for instant effect. Gertie's planning to sell the excess herbs in the shop when we open.'

'Great idea,' I said. 'People love going home with plants.

Just make sure none of them are baby rosary pea vines,' I said, and he grinned.

'I want our visitors to come back again, not turn their toes up.'

I drained my coffee and said, 'If you definitely want me to start on the rose garden, there's no time like the present.'

'OK, I'll give you a key to the Potting Shed and show you where everything is kept. Keep an eye open for Victorian metal plant tags in the beds, while you're working. We've found quite a lot in the walled garden, so you might find some for the roses, too. We're replacing them with temporary plastic ones, so they can be restored and put back, so if you do come across any, leave them in the Potting Shed, for James.'

'OK,' I agreed, though I thought it might be some time before I could even *see* any of the beds, under that mass of tangled thorny branches. 'Did you say you were going to be opening the garden to the public every afternoon except Tuesdays?'

'Yes, twelve till four. There'll be an opening ceremony on Good Friday and then, we're off. It means we'll be doing a lot of our work under the eyes of the visitors.'

'I got used to that, working for the Heritage Homes Trust,' I said unthinkingly, and saw a wary shadow cross his face that showed he still had some lingering doubts about me.

But all he said was, 'I'm charging them four pounds a head, so I hope they'll feel they're getting their money's worth. When Uncle Theo used to open it a couple of afternoons a week in summer, it was a pound, which was barely worth the effort.'

'I think they'll all be riveted by what you're doing and happy to contribute to saving such a wonderful garden. Have you got a website?'

'Yes, and it's up and running, so I can keep updating what we're doing and our future plans.'

'Good, and I think I'd develop that museum area sooner rather than later. Shops can be *very* lucrative, if you stock the right things.'

'I have to prioritize, because there isn't much money. I'm spending what I made from the sale of my house and it's stretched as it is,' he said, and I thought he must have stretched it quite a bit to create his Poison Garden and wetland area.

The Potting Shed proved to be as big as his office, a long, low building that served several purposes. The end near the door was set out like a mini staffroom, with chairs, a little stove, a kettle and a fridge.

Beyond this were long wooden workbenches, with racks of tools and shelves of packets, tins and jam jars full of odds and ends, then at the further end were the garden tools, a couple of wheelbarrows and a big heap of those woven green garden waste bags.

'We'll have to keep the door locked all the time when we open, because people are so nosy, even when there's a "Private" sign on the door. Gertie and James like to have their lunch in here and I sometimes join them . . . but if I forget, Gert brings something over to the office, or wherever I am in the garden. I suppose we'll need to rearrange things a bit when we're open, though. I'll need someone to take over from James on the ticket hatch while he has lunch or a break.'

'More expense?'

'Yes, but necessary, and I've got someone in mind who might do a few hours when needed – Gertie's husband, Steve. I'll see.'

He showed me some of the spiked metal plant markers James was treating for rust, before repainting, then found me long leather gauntlets and two different sizes of secateurs, though probably a machete would be more use in the first instance. He put them in a wheelbarrow and topped them with several of the green bags.

'There we are: all ready to go,' he said. 'Bring the tools back here at the end of the working day, but leave any bags of cuttings and I'll take them away later.'

He looked at his watch. 'Both Gertie and James are much later than usual today, but you can meet them in a bit. In fact, if they need you to help with anything heavy, they'll come and find you anyway, once they know you're here.'

'Oh, I'm used to being bossed about by elderly gardeners,' I said resignedly. 'Do you have a cunning plan for how you'd like me to deal with the rose garden, or shall I just go for it?'

'Well, I know it's wedge-shaped – a narrow triangle – so it'll be much wider near the back. I assume the brick path goes right around it – there seems to be the start of two paths at either end of the fish pond. The top part is much smaller and narrows towards the road, but Wen told me once that she could *just* remember being able to walk around it and that there was a small marble bench at the top.'

'How about if I simply clear a way round all the paths first, for access, before tackling the actual rose beds?' I suggested. 'That way, we'll have an idea of what's there, too, and maybe I'll have spotted some helpful plant markers.'

'OK,' he agreed rather grudgingly, as if he'd have liked to order me to do something else, just to assert his authority, if mine hadn't been such a sensible suggestion. He said nothing more as I trundled my barrow past him and out of the Potting Shed.

'What are *you* going to do?' I asked him as he locked the door behind us.

'Me?' He seemed surprised to be asked. 'I'm going to put in some time on my pond – I want to get the liner in soon and finish any hard landscaping – and then I've got a commission for a garden design to make a start on.'

I thought there was a good chance he'd be so engrossed in his pond that he'd entirely forget the garden design, though at least that was something that could be done in the evenings.

I parked my wheelbarrow by the fish pond and contemplated my task. I could see the entrances to the paths, two on each side of the pond, now I knew they were there, but they vanished after about a foot into an almost impenetrable-looking thicket of entwined thorny branches. I wondered if I might indeed find Sleeping Beauty in there, but not the Beast, because Wayne was already perfectly cast for the role.

I decided to begin with the bigger task and hack my way to the back of the garden – Marnie of the Jungle.

Time flies when you're enjoying yourself.

I started on the path nearest the gate to Lavender Cottage, not pruning carefully, which would come later, just clearing a way through.

The old, handmade bricks of the path were laid in a herringbone pattern and slippery with algae and moss. Under their heavy mulch of dead leaves, I'd discovered the beds had been edged with those wavy-topped terracotta border tiles, probably a late-Victorian addition.

I'd filled several of the huge garden bags and was making good progress up one side of the path – though perhaps a machete really *might* have been better for the first cut – when Ned's deep voice somewhere behind me startled me so much I dropped the large secateurs. I'd been totally off in a world of my own.

'Marnie, where are you?' he repeated, and I turned to find

him standing at the entrance to the path, a huge, dark, but unthreatening shape against the light.

'Wow! I really didn't think you'd have got more than a few feet in by now, though I suppose you have actually been at it for quite a while,' he said. 'Did you have some lunch?'

'No! Is it that late already?'

'It's well past one.' He walked cautiously towards me, ducking where tall brambles reached out overhead. 'This path is really slippery.'

'I know, it needs the moss scraping off and then, once the light can get to it, it should all dry off.'

'The public won't be coming down here until it's safe, anyway. I'll rope it off, so they can only walk around the fish pond, and goggle at you while you're working.'

'I think watching me lop briars might soon pall,' I said.

'I'd better order another information board for in here, though there isn't a lot to say about it yet.'

'You were right about the old metal plant tags – I've spotted a few at the front of the beds already.'

I took my long gauntlets off and pushed my hair behind my ears.

'I'd really like to completely clear each bed and properly prune the roses as I get to them,' I confessed. 'I think we'll find some interesting old varieties in here. But I'll resist until I've cut a way round the paths.'

'If we have the tags, we should be able to replace any roses that have died off, though they might have changed names over the years.'

'That tag over there is for an Eglantine Briar . . . which I think is a Regency name. But the tags are Victorian, aren't they?' I said. 'The name had probably changed by then, so that's odd.'

'Perhaps they found the original planting list,' he said. 'I haven't come across it, but the family papers are well and truly jumbled up, so it might be in there somewhere.'

'It would be handy,' I agreed. 'But it'll be a while before we can put in replacement roses anyway, because even once I've cleared the beds, we'll need to feed them up with a good rich mulch.'

It sounded like I was going to cook them a big dinner, rather than provide a lovely thick layer of well-rotted manure, if I could find some.

Ned dragged the bag of clippings I'd just filled back to join the others near the gate to the Grace Garden, while I started filling a new one, but after a few minutes he took the larger pair of secateurs from the barrow and began clipping away the higher branches that tangled over my head and made the paths such a tunnel.

'Yer office phone's been ringing off the hook this last half-hour, lad,' said a dour voice behind us. 'Gert and me could hear it from the shed while we were having a bite and a brew.'

'Oh – thanks, James,' Ned said guiltily. He patted his pocket. 'I think I must have left my mobile there, too . . . and I only came to make sure Marnie'd had some lunch. Marnie, this is James Hyde,' he added.

'Hi,' I said, to the somewhat wizened and bent elderly man, who was actually smaller than me and wearing a red knitted bobble hat and an indescribably filthy overcoat, which seemed to be minus its buttons, for it had been tied round his waist with a bit of frayed rope.

His rheumy pale grey eyes examined me, then looked at the path I'd cleared and seemed to arrive at some measure of approval.

'Pleased, I'm sure,' he said. 'And Gertie says if you've not had a bite yet, there's a cuppa and a spare cheese and pickle sandwich going.'

'I meant to pop back to the flat for something – I'll have to get more organized,' I said. 'But I got carried away.'

'Looks like it,' he said. 'Ned, hadn't you better go and see who's been ringing you? It might be a job.'

'I suppose I had better get back to the office,' he said reluctantly.

'And I'd be very glad of that sandwich,' I said to James, so we returned to the Potting Shed, to be greeted by Gertie, who was boiling up a kettle over the paraffin stove.

Despite their being twins, Gertie didn't resemble her brother in the least, being tall, raw-boned and sturdy. Her iron-grey hair was cropped and her unadorned complexion sallow, seamed and rayed into sun-lines around her eyes.

Ned left us to it and we all bonded over stewed tea, the spare doorstep sandwich and slabs of lardy cake, which was apparently Gert's speciality and fuel of choice. It was just as well I was burning off so many calories.

The boundaries were set and I made it clear I had no intention of encroaching on James's preserve of the bedding out front, or Gertie's vegetable garden domain, beyond the wall at the bottom of the Grace Garden.

'And I can manage the herb beds round that sundial on my own, too – been doing it all my life,' she said. 'But then, you'll have more than enough work, helping Ned with the rest of it.'

'He seems to want me to sort out the rose garden first, while it's still early in the year, and I love roses, so I don't mind. But if you need me to help with anything else, just shout.'

'I'll mostly be manning the ticket office when we open at Easter,' James said. 'And the bit of a shop, too, I suppose.'

'Ned's got great plans for getting the visitors in and parting them from their brass,' Gertie agreed. 'I wouldn't have thought they'd pay much to see a half-overgrown garden, but he says watching the restoration is a selling point.'

'I think he's right. He's got several information boards coming too, hasn't he?'

'New plant labelling, information everywhere, a leaflet with a map of the garden – that'll be free, but there'll be a glossy brochure, too,' said James.

'And now the visitors will be able see the rose garden being cleared. Ned said I'd already got further than he expected in one morning.'

'*And* part of the afternoon,' Gertie pointed out.

'Yes, and I'd better get back to it now,' I said, getting up and thanking them for the food.

'No problem, I always bring enough for a coachload,' Gertie said. 'Ned would forget if I didn't put food under his nose and there's no point in you bringing any, when there's extra going spare here.'

'That's very kind of you,' I said. 'But can I put something in the kitty, towards that and tea and stuff?'

That offer went down well, so at least I'd be contributing to the daily feast.

Ned had said he'd remove the bags of clippings, but I thought he had enough to do, so I asked James where they should go and he said to take them down through the gate at the bottom of the walled garden, where they had a bark chipper, several compost heaps and a bonfire, and he'd sort them out when he got round to it.

So I dragged the ones I'd already filled down there and left them by the outer wall, scuffing away the tracks I'd left on the gravel paths as I went back. I'd at least got a glimpse of Gert's veg plot and rows of fruit bushes, plus the front of a very large greenhouse against the garden wall.

I returned to hacking my path through the roses, though the next time I looked at my watch, which felt like five minutes later, it was just before four, so I had to dash off to put away my tools before I set out for the River Walk.

As I followed the path down the lavender garden to the sentry hut to collect my bag and spiked stick, I felt guilty that I hadn't yet made a start on tidying it up – for after all, Elf and Myfy were the ones letting me live in their flat and paying part of my wages! But the Grace Garden was opening next week and there wasn't a moment to lose there.

It was well after four by then, so presumably the entrance gate would be locked, though when I came out onto the River Walk I could see a few visitors making their way towards the exit.

I spotted one or two bits of rubbish on the way up – why will people throw things away like that, especially when there are litter bins? What are they thinking? Or maybe, since most of it seemed to be bags of gummy bears and the like, sugar rots your brain to the point where you *can't* think.

There were a couple of the inevitable plastic water bottles too, with the little sippy teat tops, because obviously adults can't drink out of ordinary bottles without tipping water down their fronts.

It's a strange world.

The sun was getting low now and intermittently disappeared behind lilac-grey clouds and, as the valley narrowed, it seemed to get quieter and quieter, until it was just me and the birds singing.

I climbed the waterfall path and stopped to look at the river emerging in a rush from the rock face, the sun, now out again, filtering magically through the trees.

There was the entrance to the cave, or crevice, half-hidden by the falls, which Myfy'd said had a legend about it: an ancient warrior had been laid to rest in there with his treasure – though looking at the ledge below it, I'd be surprised if anything other than a goat could get along there.

I remembered there was a chapter on treasure in Elf's book, so perhaps I'd skip to that one. The subject would be interesting, even if Elf's writing style wasn't.

The water and the flickering light might be magical, but this time I didn't feel the presence of anyone – or anything – else. It was just . . . tranquil.

My mother must often have stood on this very spot, which was a strange but oddly comforting thought.

After a bit, I finished the climb up to the top turnstile, finding nothing more than an empty drinks can, placed carefully in the middle of a large slab of grey stone. I added that to my collection and then went down again and back to the turnstile, emptying the bins on the way.

As I sorted it into the various recycling containers behind the café, I felt physically weary, but *very* happy: this had to be the most perfect job ever!

Ned was already relaxing his guard and soon he'd realize that all I wanted was to work hard and help him attain his goal of making the Grace Garden a thing of beauty and wonder. A miniature Chelsea Physic Garden, in fact, but with added roses and extra poison.

The rubbish sorted, I took stock of the lavender garden – and thought I'd get up extra early tomorrow and put in an hour on it, before going over to Ned's. While I was still pondering what there was to do, Elf popped out of the back door and handed me a cone of ice-cream.

'Lemon, very refreshing,' she said. 'We'd just about finished cleaning down for the day and there was just a little bit of this one left in a tub, so we've all had a cone.'

'Lovely,' I said gratefully, making short work of it.

'You're not going to do any more today, are you?' she asked. 'Ned came in earlier and he said you'd already made a huge clearance in the rose garden.'

'Did he?' I said, pleased. 'It's the tip of the iceberg, but I'm dying to find out what roses are in there.'

'I can see it's your idea of fun,' she said, smiling.

'It is, but I did mean to start on your garden before I checked the River Walk today,' I confessed. 'Then I forgot the time. I'll have a go first thing in the morning, instead.'

'Oh, not to worry, I'm sure you'll soon get it into shape and there isn't any rush.'

A giant marmalade-coloured creature suddenly shoved its way through the nearest clumps of lavender and came to twine itself sinuously around my legs.

'Caspar!' Elf cried. 'Myfanwy said she'd let you out for the first time earlier, but she hadn't seen you since. Where have you been?'

Caspar told her, but unfortunately neither of us spoke Cat. Then he said something directly to Elf and headed for the back door.

'I think he wants his dinner,' I suggested.

'I suspect you're right – though he isn't supposed to go into the café. Still, I don't suppose it matters when we're shut and at least he's come back!'

She followed him through the hall and into the scullery.

Straight away I spotted a large white-painted cubbyhole for my post hanging on the wall, lettered over the top with 'The Flat'.

That had to be Jacob's work, and upstairs I found he'd installed a giant cat flap into the door on the landing, too.

I left the door unbolted but shut, and waited to see what Caspar would make of it if he came over again, which I already suspected was going to become a habit.

A long hot shower relaxed my muscles and removed the bits of leaf and debris from my hair. Then, after dinner, I settled down with my coffee and Elf's book to read the chapter on Lost Treasure.

> There often are legends about gold hoards being hidden near water – and of course, back in the mists of time, people did deposit valuable items as tribute in marshes and pools.
>
> Anything put in the cave by the Fairy Falls – more of a narrow fissure in the rock – would have had to be placed there during a severe drought, since it is usually at least partly covered by the cascade, as is the ledge leading to it. But of course, it is an apocryphal treasure.
>
> There is another hoard of treasure reputed to be hidden in the valley, too: Nathaniel Grace, the buccaneering ancestor of the present owner of Old Grace Hall, was known to have seized much gold and valuable jewels from Spanish ships, some of which, of course, he presented to Good Queen Bess, with whom he was a favourite. He certainly had enough left to purchase Old Grace Hall from his cousins when he retired from seafaring and married. He is, though, said to have concealed his greatest treasure somewhere on his property.

> The oldest part of the house has several times been searched, but to no avail, so I suspect that this treasure is just as much a tale as the other!

I suspected she was right about both of them, but part of you always wants to believe in this kind of thing, like the Loch Ness Monster and Yetis!

I heard a bumping noise and, putting the book aside, went out onto the landing, where Caspar was headbutting his new cat flap, before cautiously squeezing through. He had a lot of thick fur, so it can't have been as difficult as he made it look.

He went to bed first, highly miffed because I refused to share my cup of cocoa and two Jaffa Cakes with him, but I soon joined him, pushing him over to one side to make room, and then quickly fell asleep to the sound of his bubbling snores.

13

Follow the Yellow Brick Road

I woke very early, to find a very hairy face pressed in between my chin and neck. When I moved, Caspar rolled onto his back and stretched luxuriously, then lay there like a giant stuffed toy, big feet in the air.

The sky was still a magical dusky, duck-egg blue and I could see the bright pinprick of a star. I *love* stars; they always make me feel hopeful. I'd hung the crystal one I'd bought in the village in my bedroom window, though I expected that, apart from my day off, I'd rarely be in the flat to see the sun cast prisms from it across the white duvet and walls.

I went through the living room to the front windows, where dawn was a thin hammered silver line behind the hills on the other side of the valley, above Risings.

I heard Caspar land on the floorboards with a heavy thud and then he padded past me and I followed him into the hall in time to see him cautiously headbutt the cat flap, before squeezing through it, in that oddly ectoplasmic way cats have, as if they could just simply materialize somewhere else if they really put their minds to it.

I felt fine this morning; I mean, I'd been doing hard

physical work for years, so it wasn't exactly a novelty. But I was full of energy and anticipation for the job ahead – to reveal the secrets of the rose garden! And who doesn't love a secret – or *almost* secret – garden?

I warmed up a *pain au chocolat* from the freezer – old habits die hard – and had two cups of coffee. Then I was good to go, intending to make a start on Elf and Myfy's garden.

All was silent from the direction of the café when I went down and let myself out into a diamond-encrusted world of webs and shadows, where the birds had struck up an enthusiastic dawn chorus.

I found all the tools in a small shed by the greenhouse and filled a wooden trug with everything I thought I'd need. They had a few of those big, woven green garden bags, too.

I began to tidy the overgrown shapes of the lavender bushes into neat mounds, like little islands, working my way along the meandering crazy-paving path. There were three woody rosemary bushes that would have to come out, but since they'd take a lot of digging and hacking to get the roots up, I left them for later.

There was the over-rampant Rambling Rector, too. He ought to be firmly dealt with, but I'd borrow the long leather gauntlets from next door before I tackled that.

After an hour or so, the sun was fully up and I cleaned and put away the tools in the shed, then went through to the Grace Garden, where no one was to be seen, if you didn't count the peacocks, though the lights in the office were already on, so Ned must have been in there, working.

In my rucksack I now had keys to the Potting Shed and Grace Garden, as well as the big ring of keys for Lavender Cottage and the River Walk, so I jangled like a gaoler when I walked.

I'd left the heavy gauntlets and other tools from yesterday together and someone had replenished the big stack of empty garden bags. I helped myself to some plastic plant markers from a box on the end of one of the workbenches, then dumped everything into the small green wheelbarrow I'd used yesterday, which I'd already started to think of as my own, as you do.

I was more organized this morning and had a small notebook and pen in my dungaree pocket, so I could jot down any details I noticed about the roses as I went. I'd even remembered to put my new phone in a zipped pocket in my gilet, so it wouldn't fall out into the nearest bucket of water or the pond and die a watery death, like most of my previous ones.

I assumed Ned had already fed the fish, since they weren't hanging about in a crowd at the surface, looking like hungry teenagers, but were just a glimmer in the depths. He must have made as early a start as I had.

I started by collecting the two or three old metal plant markers I'd noticed in the beds next to the bit of path I'd cleared and replacing them with plastic ones. The roses all seemed to be old, unfamiliar varieties so far, so it was just as well they had the tags, because it's often nigh on impossible to guess what a rose is until it flowers, and even then it can be hard.

Then I took up where I'd left off yesterday. I'd uncovered the path for quite a long way, but since I was heading along one side of the wider end of the wedge, I probably had at least as far to go again.

In my head I was now Dora the Explorer, hacking my way through to goodness knows what, turning a dank, overgrown tunnel back into a light-pervaded pathway.

I had to be careful, because some of the thorns on the branches were huge and vicious, though most were small and less likely to pierce through my clothing.

After a while I found I was singing 'Follow the Yellow Brick Road' as I worked, though now the parts I'd revealed yesterday were cleaned off a bit, the path wasn't so much yellow as a beautiful patchwork in shades of old rose pink and orange.

I'd filled four large bags and was going for the fifth, when that familiar deep voice suddenly broke into my song.

'I've brought you a cup of coffee, Dorothy, but no oil for the Tin Man.'

I turned and there was Ned, holding one of those bamboo travel beakers with a lid.

I straightened, tossed a long and viciously barbed stem into the bag and said, gratefully, 'Oh, thanks, I could really do with that! I must remember to start bringing a flask with me as well as my water bottle.'

'It's nearly eleven and I saw you heading here hours ago, so I thought you'd lost track of time again.'

'I had, but that's very easy to do. I'm determined to get all the way to the back wall today, and then I assume the path just goes up the other side to the pond again.'

'I think so,' Ned agreed.

I took the lid off the cup and a lovely aroma met my nostrils.

'I think that Java stuff woke me up this morning,' Ned said. 'I had a really good idea for the design for an awkward-shaped garden first thing, soon after I'd had some.'

'I thought you must be working on a design when I saw the lights were on in the office.'

'I was, but since then I've been digging out the pond area in the Grace Garden a bit more. Gert's been helping me. James is sanding and painting plant tags, so I'll take these new ones you've found back with me.'

He rubbed the dirt off one and said, '"Double White"? That could be almost anything.'

'The ones I've found so far sound like the old names, but we'll see what they're like when they flower.'

'I've ordered that extra sign, explaining what we're doing in here, though it'll probably arrive after the others do. But I've got plenty of those moveable rope-and-post barriers to put across the paths we don't want the visitors to go down. In here, we'll confine them round the fish pond for the present. They can watch you vanishing into the brambles from there.'

'I don't mind an audience. One or two of the châteaux where I worked had gardens open to the public, as is the one at my family's house. It's called the Château du Monde because it has one of those gardens with the beds laid out to represent various parts of the world.'

'I'd like to see that.'

'It had got a bit overgrown, and there were some inappropriate additions, but Aunt Em's got it looking wonderful now.'

Ned collected up the old metal markers and I followed him with my coffee back to the marble seat by the pond, which had now acquired a cat.

'Hello, Caspar,' I said.

'Pfut!' he replied, pulling a face at me that I couldn't interpret, before going back to staring down at the moving shapes beneath the water.

'I hope he doesn't try to catch the fish,' I said worriedly.

'He doesn't seem to be thinking that way, just mesmerized by the movement. We'll have to see. If he does start trying to catch them I'll have to put something over the pond, which would be a pity.'

I drained the last of the coffee and handed it back with thanks.

'Gertie says she's got a sandwich for your lunch, and to go over when you want it.'

'She's very kind, but I don't want her to feel she *has* to feed me lunch every day,' I said. 'I was going to go back to the flat for something.'

'Gert feeds us all: you'll just have to accept it, or you'll hurt her feelings. I have a greaseproof paper bag sitting on my desk as we speak and there's a plastic box with a buttered cherry scone and a slab of lardy cake, too.'

'Just as well we're burning off so many calories, if lardy cake is on the menu every day,' I said.

'You sometimes get a bit of carrot cake, or fruitcake, but that one's a staple, because it's her husband, Steve's, favourite.'

'Do they live nearby?'

'Just up the road in the lodge at the gates of Risings. Steve was left it by Edwin Lordly-Grace, the father-in-law of Audrey, probably to spite her, because they never got on,' Ned said. 'Steve used to be their gardener, but he retired as soon as he got the lodge and Wayne is doing it now – or pretending to do it, unless Audrey's gimlet eye is actually upon him.'

It was a great pity, I thought, that the first of my Vane relatives I'd come across should be the shifty and work-shy Wayne.

'Steve's taken on a couple of small part-time jobs. He opens the gate to the ruins every day and looks after the public toilet block in the car park there, too.'

'I think I saw him the day I arrived, when I stopped for a few minutes in the car park. Treena told me there's going to be an archaeological dig there after Easter, run by one of her friends.'

'I heard about that. Jericho's End is such a small place, anything is big news! The site has never been dug before, but I can't imagine it being very interesting, because the monastery was abandoned only a couple of years after it was founded. Elf says the river flooded the water meadows right up to it for two years running and so the monks moved on and joined a more established priory somewhere else. I don't know how she knows that, though – perhaps they took their records with them?'

'Oh, well, archaeologists seem happy with very little, don't they?' I said.

'Steve looks after the Village Hut, too, and he's a leading light in the Christmas panto every year,' Ned said. 'That's organized by the Friends of Jericho's End, and I bet they try to rope *you* into it.'

'I shouldn't think so. I've only been here five minutes,' I said. 'Did you mention Steve might be helping with the tickets when you open?'

'I hope so. He's coming over to talk about it later. He's older than Gert and doesn't want to work in the garden, but he'd be happy to help out with the tickets and the shop, if he can fit it round his other jobs. James will need a break, and though Gertie could fill in, I need all the gardening help I can get.'

'It sounds like a good idea to me,' I said, getting up and dislodging Caspar, who had somehow managed to drape himself across my legs without my noticing it. I was now covered in marmalade cat hair.

'I'll carry on for a bit before I have lunch,' I said. 'I think there might be a marble statue, or something like that, at the far end of the path. I can *just* make out something white between the branches.'

'Let's have a look,' he said, and when he had, agreed. 'I think you're right! Go carefully, won't you. I'd better get back to what I was doing. I left Gert to it.'

He dragged off the full garden bags with him and I got on with my pruning, though he must have brought the empty ones back, because when I finally stopped, due to the howling wolves of hunger prowling round my stomach, they were heaped on the path behind me.

For such a big man, he moved very quietly.

Some time had passed and, as I headed for my sandwich in the Potting Shed, I spotted Ned going into his office with James and another elderly man, whom I thought I recognized from the day I arrived and now knew to be Steve.

I found a note on the table in the shed that said, 'Ham and mustard sandwiches in fridge and buttered scones: help yourself, we've had ours. Gert.'

I did, after scrubbing my hands in the chipped sink in the staff toilet, a grandiose name for an ancient Victorian loo that lurked behind a blue-painted door on the other side of the yard. The identical one next to it was for visitors, so I hoped there were some urgent plans being put into place for upgrading those facilities!

I fed the inner woman, who was very grateful for it, then rushed back to work, because that glimpsed glimmer of white at the end of the rose garden was tantalizing me. Unfortunately, I *still* hadn't got near enough to make out what it was before I had to put away my tools and dash off to do the River Walk again.

It was already after four when I set out and I was still hot, dirty and sweaty, so hoped I wouldn't meet any visitors on the way. But, of course, as Sod's Law has it, I did meet several of them making their way back to the entrance.

They greeted me warily, probably because, with my grubby and dishevelled appearance and the bag and stick, they thought I was a tramp.

There was no one near the waterfall. I left the bag and stick behind a boulder near the viewing place, while I climbed up to the top, without seeing anyone . . . or *anything*. When I descended, though, and approached the mouth of the falls again, I did catch a momentary flicker of movement and felt some kind of presence . . . but the mind plays strange tricks.

I didn't linger, but collected my stick and bag and headed straight back. I was ready for a hot shower and a substantial dinner.

Treena would want an update later too, and I should let the family know how I was getting on. I had so much to tell them about the garden!

Treena was much more likely to be interested in the cat.

14

Pure Folly

A loud flapping noise woke me early on the Friday morning, bringing vague thoughts that some large bird had got into the flat, but then I relaxed as I realized it was only Caspar, making a speedy exit through the cat flap.

Last night he'd appeared earlier than before, right after I – and presumably *he* – had dined, in my case off macaroni cheese followed by a yoghurt.

Although I'd unpacked and arranged my entire Agatha Christie collection and other cosy crime favourites on the vacant shelves along one wall, besides having bought the latest Clara Mayhem Doome novel in Great Mumming, I'd instead found myself taking another lucky dip into Elf's book.

Her style might be a bit soporific, but some of the chapters sounded fascinating. I was sure the rise of a 'strange religious sect' in Chapter One would be about the Strange Brethren. Mum's parents must have been part of the last generation to belong to it . . .

I skipped the first part of the chapter, about the beginnings of Jericho's End, and skimmed the bit about the monastic settlement, which was much as Ned had described it, and then finally arrived at the Brethren.

And really, after reading a description of their beliefs – mainly that we were all doomed, but some, i.e. women, were more doomed than others – it seemed amazing that the Brethren had gone on for so long!

The Vanes had been a prominent local family in the sect and, after the Thorstane meeting house was closed, my grandfather had continued to hold meetings to a rapidly dwindling congregation, in one of the barns at Cross Ways Farm, until his death.

Poor Mum, what a childhood that must have been! Except, of course, when she slipped off to her favourite places in the valley, or escaped to school. It would have been a revelation when she went off to train as a nurse and entered into a whole new world she could only have dreamed of before.

Thinking about Mum had made me cry a little: she had been so bright, kind and sweet-natured, yet with an inner strength and toughness. And being so tall and Titian-haired, she'd had an imposing physical presence, too.

Caspar, seeming to divine that I needed comfort, had decided to climb onto my lap – or place the half of him that fitted onto my lap – and face-bump me.

I closed the book in order to stroke him, which met with his approval, and decided that at the first opportunity I'd try to discover a little more about the current members of the Vane family at Cross Ways Farm. Perhaps some of them weren't as awful as Wayne. But still, they hadn't sounded like the kind of family I'd want to claim kinship with, and it certainly wouldn't go down well with Ned if he found out about them, just when I hoped we might be becoming friends again.

*

I spent another early morning hour on the Lavender Cottage garden, cutting back the first of the three overgrown and woody rosemary bushes.

The last thick branches I removed as near to the ground as possible, using a handsaw of my own – one of those things like a giant penknife, with a tough, serrated blade. I'd made good progress and was just starting to dig around the roots to loosen them when Elf appeared, bearing a steaming beaker of frothy coffee and a large biscotti.

'I saw you from the kitchen window – I got up early to make a new batch of ice-cream – mint with dark chocolate chips. But we really don't expect *you* to start work this early, Marnie! You mustn't overdo it.'

I took the cup and dipped the biscotti into it. 'Lovely – thank you! And I *wanted* to make another early start on the rosemary, because I keep losing track of time in the rose garden. The best kind of job is the one you'd do for love, even if you didn't get paid for it, isn't it?'

'Very true – which is why I'm up with the larks, making ice-cream, and Myfy and Jacob so often vanish into their studios and forget to come out for food.'

I looked down at the half-exposed root ball of the rosemary and said, 'I've nearly finished with this one now, but I'll ask Ned if I can borrow one of the pickaxes from the Potting Shed for the other two. I've seen a couple of them in there and it would make it easier.'

'No rush,' she said, taking the empty cup.

'No, but I'm looking forward to having this garden trim again. I'll have a go at the Rambling Rector at the first opportunity, too! It won't take much effort to keep it all in hand after that.'

'Myfy will be delighted to have more places to put new

lavender,' Elf said. 'She did her best with the gardening, but only when her Muse hadn't claimed her. Or Jacob,' she added.

'I'd better just finish off here and then I can start on the roses, again,' I said, seizing the spade and driving it deep beneath the root ball. Then I stood on the edge and up rose the dense mass, with a wrenching noise. I tossed it into one of the green bags.

'You're a lot stronger than you look,' Elf said thoughtfully.

'Muscles of steel, after everything I've been doing the last few years,' I said. 'But what I did just now was more technique.' I shoved the hand tools into the trug and prepared to put everything away in the shed.

'I must fetch my flask of coffee from the flat, but I don't seem to need to take packed lunches,' I said, and told Elf about Gertie's insisting on sharing her sandwiches and cake.

Elf laughed. 'Gertie feeds everyone. I'd just go with it! She used to take in lunch for Ned's great-uncle Theo, too – and he always came here for dinner with us every Sunday as well. We're hoping you'll join us this Sunday. It's such fun, having a crowd round the table.'

'It's very kind of you . . .' I began, but she seemed to assume it was a given, because she beamed at me.

'Don't forget it's quiz night every Friday at the pub, dear,' she reminded me. 'You must walk across with us – scampi and chips in a basket, very retro, and then the quiz.'

'I'm not sure I—'

'Oh, you *must* come, Marnie! Everyone goes. You'll meet lots of the locals all at once, so it'll be very useful.'

I hesitated, long habit making me feel uneasy at the thought of mixing with a lot of people, but there was no need to live as a recluse any more – and probably hadn't been for several years. The phone lines weren't going to be hot between Jericho's End and Merchester, telling Mike I'd been sighted!

'That would be fun, thank you,' I said resolutely. I was going to meet all the locals at some time in the near future, anyway. It was not the sort of place where you could avoid it, even if you wanted to. I might as well, as Elf said, meet most of them at once.

'Half past six – come through to the kitchen when you're ready and we'll walk over together. Jacob usually comes, too; he's great at quizzes. And my friend Gerald will be there.'

With that, she returned to the cottage, bearing the empty cup, and I finished clearing up, then popped upstairs to fetch my rucksack.

I was eager to get back to the path clearing, because yesterday I was sure I'd been close to that tantalizing glimpse of white and was longing to know if it was a statue, or some other garden feature.

And I was close, because in no time, I'd broken through into a small, circular space that would have been open to the air had the roses not almost roofed it over.

Trails of ivy covered the ground where a path must once have circled an elegant white marble urn on a pedestal.

It wasn't this that stopped my breath, however, but the small building so incongruously set against the back wall of the garden. Enshrouded in the thorny stems of a climbing rose was a tiny, open-fronted and pillared Grecian temple, in the same white marble as the urn.

The steps up to it were mossy and the columns streaked with green slime. But it was *perfect.* I felt as explorers must have done in the jungles of South America, when they suddenly realized that the green-shrouded shapes around them were ancient buildings.

Inside, I could see there was a bench along the back, but no Sleeping Beauty reclined there, unless of the spidery variety.

I was so excited by my discovery that when I'd cleared enough of the encroaching growth to see it properly, I went and fetched Ned, who was equally amazed.

'I'd absolutely no idea that was there. I've never seen or heard any mention of it!' he said, untangling a rose briar from his tawny hair, having not ducked low enough through the opening from the path I'd made.

'Even with all the rose beds trimmed back, I don't think you'll be able to see it, or the urn, from the other end of the path: the central beds will be in the way,' I said.

Ned began pulling away huge swathes of ivy that were creeping from the circle of the path round the urn and up the steps, and flung them aside in a heap.

'The urn's very Grecian,' he said, dragging more ivy from the plinth. 'It would look pretty, set with trailing flowering plants . . .'

But I was still riveted by the folly. 'I think that rose was intentionally trained up one side of the temple. I've no idea what it is . . . It's been squeezed by that huge bush behind it, but it's alive and I'll give it a good cut back and feed and see if it recovers.'

I longed to start on that then and there, but with a sigh I said, 'I suppose I'd better clear the other side of the path back to the pond first, though.'

'It would make access easier,' Ned agreed. 'When you've done that, I'll be able to wash down all that marble. I've got one of those wheeled pressure water barrels I can bring in. If the green marks are stubborn, there's probably some kind of special solution I can get, but hopefully, water will do it.'

'I should think so, with maybe a bit of scrubbing,' I agreed. 'Perhaps you should install a standpipe in the rose garden at some point. I can see you have them in the Grace Garden.'

'Yes, not so many, but there's a system of pipes and sprinklers I've put in that I can move about as needed.'

I turned to look back at the temple. 'It's going to look beautiful in summer and it'll be a perfect spot to sit and admire the roses.'

'You don't think it has a touch of the mausoleum about it?' he asked, tentatively.

'No, it only looks gloomy because of all those branches closing in on either side and shutting out the light,' I said firmly. 'It's a fairy-tale thing, perfect. This is going to enchant the visitors when they see it.'

When he'd gone, dragging two bags of ivy behind him, I began jungle-hacking my way down the path on the other side of the garden, rather faster this time. I don't know if that was impatience to get it done, so I could uncover the temple, or just my technique getting into its stride, but I made good progress.

At some point either Ned or Gertie must have come round the path behind me, because several full bags of clippings vanished from the clearing round the urn and a heap of empty ones had taken their place.

About half past one, James came to have a look at my discovery.

'Gert's already seen it,' he said.

'Oh, was it Gertie who took the full bags away? That was kind.'

'It was, and she says you've just got time to come and eat something before Elf gets here.'

'What's *Elf* coming for?'

'She's going to teach me how to use the new electric till in the ticket office, isn't she?' he said, as if this should have been blindingly obvious. 'And Steve, too, because he's going to spell me in there. Ned said you and Gertie ought to know how to do it too, just in case.'

'I'm the kiss of death to most electronic machinery,' I said, putting down my secateurs and taking off the long leather gauntlets. I felt reluctant to leave the garden, but then I was ravenous!

'So, what do you think about the folly I found?'

'It's a bit fancy for my taste and sitting on cold stone gives you piles,' he observed, dourly, and stumped off again.

I don't think he has a romantic soul.

In the Potting Shed was Gertie, who poured me a cup of tea and said she was off to join Ned, James and Steve in the ticket office, because Elf would be arriving any minute, and I was to join them as soon as I'd eaten.

So I wolfed down a sandwich – corned beef and bright yellow piccalilli – before following her.

The ticket office hatch was set in the end of a long outbuilding abutting the wall, next to the visitors' gate.

There was a door to the courtyard, which stood open, and I followed the sound of voices inside and found myself in a long, narrow room with whitewashed walls.

The overhead lights looked newly installed and wooden shelves and racks stood ready to receive the contents of the boxes piled against one wall.

James was sitting behind a wooden counter in front of the closed hatch, with a new and shiny electric till in front of him. An open box of garden leaflets stood at the other end, as well as a small wire rack of faded and elderly-looking postcards, presumably relics of the occasional opening days of previous summers.

He was arguing with Ned, who was saying, in the voice of

sorely tried sweet reason, 'No, we can't sell these old postcards, even at reduced prices, James. But I've ordered new ones. They should be here any day.'

'It's a waste of money, just to throw them out,' James said stubbornly.

Ned ran his hands through his mane of tawny hair and said, resignedly, 'Well, if it'll make you happy, you can put them in a box marked "Old Stock" and sell them for ten pence each, or something.'

James brightened and said, 'Right you are, then.'

The portly elderly man I'd seen the previous day, with a round, rosy face, bunchy cheeks and a white beard, suddenly bobbed up from behind the counter, a dusty box in his hands. He could have been Father Christmas, but I'd guessed he was Gertie's husband even before she introduced us.

'Steve, this is Marnie, the new gardener.'

'How do?' he said, which didn't really seem to need an answer.

'What's in the box?' asked Gertie.

'Old rolls of entrance tickets, but I think the mice have been at them.'

'Some of them might be all right,' began James, but Ned firmly removed the box outside and came back, rubbing the dust off his hands.

'What are you going to sell in the shop?' I asked Gertie.

'Well . . . this rack is for packets of seeds . . . and then there'll be gardening books on this shelf,' she began.

'And all kinds of Grace Garden tat, like rulers and rubbers and mugs and stuff,' said Ned. 'I thought we'd start out small and see what sells. And I've only just realized we're opening a *week* today!'

'That's plenty of time for everything you *need* to do,' said

Elf calmly, arriving just in time to hear this despairing exclamation. 'Once I've shown you how the till works, a couple of hours of setting up the shop and price ticketing the stock, and it will be ready for opening. What more must be done to get the garden ready to open on Good Friday?'

'Loads of things!' said Ned. 'All the information boards probably won't arrive until early next week and they'll need putting up. Then the paths and areas not open to the public need roping off . . . a good tidy up and the paths raking . . . and more information added to the website.' He searched his pockets. 'There's more. I've got an urgent to-do list here somewhere.'

'All those are minor things,' Elf said comfortably. 'Now, gather round and I'll explain the till. It's dead simple.'

She demonstrated and then everyone had a go, though I was the only one who repeatedly jammed it. The instructions on inserting a new paper till roll were also beyond my understanding.

James and Steve didn't have any problem with any of it, and nor did Gertie, when her mind could be dragged away from pondering what cuttings and plants in her greenhouse were surplus to requirements and could be sold in the shop.

'I think we'll only put Marnie on the till if some plague wipes out the rest of us,' Ned said drily. 'Now, James is used to putting the float in the till and then cashing up when we close, from previous open days. There will, I hope, be a lot more money than before, so at the end of the day, Steve or James can print out the till roll, put in the float again and bring the rest to the office.'

'I'll show Steve all that as we go,' James said.

'Good, and I should think when it's fairly quiet, one person could sell the tickets and handle the shop, but you and James can work it to suit yourselves. I know you'll have to dash out from time to time, Steve, to open or close the Village Hut, or to your other jobs.'

'They don't take up much time and I can always clean the Hut first thing in the mornings and the conveniences in the car park after the garden's shut.'

'Fine,' Ned said. He'd found a little notebook now and was scribbling in it.

'Did you order paper bags?' Gertie asked suddenly.

'Yes, brown paper ones, but also some inexpensive cotton totes printed on the side with a design Myfy did for me: a circle of flowers and foliage with little angel or fairy faces peeping out and "Grace Garden" written across the middle. They're supposed to arrive tomorrow.'

'They sound lovely,' I said. It all seemed like a good start, but quite low key, as if Ned was unsure how many people would actually turn up to visit a partly restored old herb garden, but I thought he'd be surprised. People would go a long way to look at an unusual garden, and this was certainly that. Then during the school holidays and the tourist season a lot of visitors to the valley would visit it just because it was another thing to do. He could well soon find himself radically expanding the stock of the shop, if he wanted to make more money.

And I'd have to train him not to call the souvenirs 'tat'!

'There'll be a glossy guidebook,' Ned said. 'I'll have to update it regularly, as parts of the garden are restored. The rose garden will have to be included in the next one – it's amazing how much difference you've made to it already, Marnie. You're a one-woman powerhouse.'

'The thought of cleaning up the temple folly certainly

speeded up the path clearing today,' I said. 'And I keep wondering what other varieties of roses we'll find in the beds when I start actually working on them.'

I remembered the latest metal tags I'd found and fished them out of the big pocket inside my anorak, along with a generous amount of ripe leaf mould.

'You give those to me,' James said, taking them. 'They'll come up a treat, like the others.'

'How much are you charging people to come in?' asked Steve. 'It used to be a pound on open days, didn't it?'

'Four quid,' said James. 'But concessions for geriatrics like us, and the disabled.'

'Who are you calling a geriatric?' demanded Gertie. 'I'm in my prime.'

I grinned, but Ned's mind was on more serious matters. 'Maybe when people know how much it costs to get in, they won't bother,' he said gloomily.

'I really don't think so, Ned,' I assured him. 'In fact, if you put out a collecting box asking for donations towards the restoration, people would put in loads of money. Most of them really will be interested in what you're doing here.'

He brightened up. 'I did wonder about having a "Become a Friend of the Grace Garden" page on the website, with an annual subscription that gives Friends unlimited free access. There could be newsletters and special events later.'

'Great idea,' I enthused. 'You'll probably get people volunteering to help in the garden, too.'

'If their services are free, that would be really useful,' he said.

Gert said she was going back to the greenhouse, but Ned could shout when he wanted her help spreading the liner in the pond, while Steve and James elected to unpack the stock and play with the sticky price-labelling gun.

I returned to my beds of thorns, where there was no feline presence, not even a furry Cheshire Cat grin hanging in the air.

Once Ned had lined the pond, he couldn't resist the lure of the rose garden either and, leaving Gertie starting to line up some pots of damp-loving plants ready to go into the top marshy area, he appeared with gauntlets and secateurs of his own, and started cutting back the blocked path from the pond end, working even faster than I was.

I had to dash off to check the River Walk, which was obviously going to regularly punctuate my afternoon activities, but I dashed straight back again and, by then he'd made such inroads that after only a few minutes we met in the middle.

'Livingstone, I presume?' he said.

'Since I'm sweating cobs and filthy, I'm certainly no Sleeping Beauty,' I said. 'But I'm glad we've cleared all the way round.'

'So am I, and I think that's more than enough for one day,' he said. 'I'll take all the tools back and clear up, if you want to get off.'

'No, I'll help you, because I want to borrow a pickaxe from the Potting Shed, if you don't mind,' I told him. 'I need to take out two rosemary bushes with really deep roots and it'll loosen them more easily.'

'Do you know how to use a pickaxe?'

'I certainly do!'

'Help yourself, then,' he said. So I did, choosing the smaller of the two . . . and then, suddenly, I remembered the quiz night and dashed off for a quick shower, and change of clothes.

As I trotted through the lavender garden, Caspar appeared from the bushes and ran after me, making complicated spluttering noises.

I was starting to suspect he might be Russian.

15

Back to Black

My chosen outfit for the evening was black jeans, black T-shirt, black sweatshirt and my best Doc Marten boots. The effect was lightened slightly by ruby lip gloss and the butterflies decorating the boots, which was just as well, because otherwise the patrons of the Devil's Cauldron might have thought the Grim Reaper had popped in for a quick pint.

Elf was waiting for me in the café, in which one dim light burned behind the counter. Sounds of feline indignation came from the other side of the closed stable door to the cottage kitchen.

'Myfy will be out in a minute,' she said. 'Caspar didn't seem to like the new flavour of cat food and is demanding something else.'

'Yes, I can hear him,' I agreed with a grin.

Elf was also wearing black, though her tunic was alleviated by a large and chunky necklace of turquoise beads, which matched her hair, and her spike-heeled boots added about three inches to her height.

I admired her beads while she put on a silver quilted coat and she told me she'd bought the necklace in Mexico some years ago, when on holiday with her friend Gerald.

'We always have our annual holiday together and like to go somewhere new each time. We wanted to see Machu Picchu, and we decided it would be much better to do it before we got any older, because of the altitude. We didn't want to pop our clogs there, however spectacular it was.'

'I suppose the same went for Everest?' I joked, but she replied quite seriously.

'Oh, that had no appeal – so many people queue all the way up the mountain when the weather's good, and there are squalid camps and litter. I'm told it really isn't a magical experience at all, now. But we might try Tibet,' she added, as if it was a new kind of tea, possibly one with added yak milk and butter.

'Where are you going this year?'

'Just Iceland, because our *big* one next year will be an extensive tour of China, including the Great Wall and the Terracotta Army.'

Myfy slid through the stable door at this point, fending off Caspar's attempt to follow her with her foot, and closed it.

'Elf does more globetrotting than Michael Palin,' she said, catching the last sentence.

'I don't think he does so much now,' said Elf.

'Aren't you tempted to go, too?' I asked Myfy.

'No, I got the travel bug out of my system when I was fresh out of art college. Backpacked with friends, had a wonderful time and came back with a head full of ideas. I'd posted sketchbooks back every time I came to somewhere you could post anything from, too. But nothing was quite like Jericho's End and the waterfalls.'

'You picked Jacob up in Morocco,' pointed out her sister, as if he was the ultimate souvenir.

'I didn't pick him up – we'd already met in London. It was more that we gravitated together and then, somehow, had difficulty with the idea of parting.'

'You manage to part on almost a daily basis now,' Elf said.

'Having separate houses so near each other doesn't count, and you need a little space to be truly creative,' Myfy said serenely. 'You and Gerald only live together when you're on holiday.'

'But *we're* just best friends.'

'Yeah, with perks,' Myfy said rudely.

I expected Treena and I would still be engaging in this sort of sisterly bickering when we were in our sixties . . . and beyond.

Myfy was already cloaked and booted and we let ourselves out to the sound of celestial chiming.

The night was quite quiet, just the occasional vroom of a car in the lane, the faraway hoot of an early owl out hunting and the thunder of water under the bridge. Elf and Myfy were still gently arguing, though this time the subject seemed to be some weird kind of clock that had vanished from the dining room.

'It hasn't been stolen, Jacob's simply borrowed it – he's interested in the idea of a mechanism utilizing big metal ball bearings and gravity.'

'That clock is very unusual and valuable,' Elf pointed out. 'He isn't going to take it apart, is he?'

Myfy didn't answer directly, but instead said, 'It'll be more valuable if it works, and Jacob will put it back together when he's had a good look.'

'Huh!' said Elf.

'Jacob's very interested in ways of making kinetic sculptures that rely on natural forces, or by turning a handle – or any other method of ecologically sustainable movement,' Myfy explained to me.

'That sounds fascinating,' I said, thinking I really must get round to looking up kinetic art.

'I'll take you up to the barn one of these days. There are several wind- or water-driven installations around it, as well as quite a lot of smaller pieces in the barn itself. In fact, it's quite a job for anyone to get his works away from Jacob to exhibit or sell. He'd like to keep them all.'

'I'd love to see them,' I said.

We were over the bridge now and the pub on the other side of the road was brightly lit, several cars parked in the courtyard at the side, in front of the restaurant windows.

'The Possets have a good thing going with the new restaurant and bar, even when it isn't tourist season,' Elf said. 'But we go in through the old front door to the lounge with the other locals – it's cosier.'

The large room was already well filled. It had a low ceiling and was furnished with long, dark wooden tables and padded benches along the walls, with smaller ones scattered seemingly randomly in the central space. Another room must open off it at the back, for from somewhere in that direction came the sound of darts hitting a board and loud male voices.

Standing at the bar was a familiar tall and wide-shouldered figure, the top of his tawny head almost touching the thick dark beam above him.

Ned hadn't said he'd be there, but on the other hand, I hadn't asked. But I suppose even if he had been shunning the outside world, he'd be happy enough to socialize in this safe, familiar one, where everyone knew him and would judge him on what they knew, rather than what they read.

'Hi,' he said, turning and catching sight of us. 'Gerald and Jacob are already here saving seats, and they've got your drinks in,' he said to Elf and Myfy. 'Let me get you one, Marnie – what would you like?'

'I'll get my own, thanks,' I said. 'I don't want to get sucked into buying rounds for everyone. It would be a bit out of my budget.'

'Oh, come on, Ellwood! I think I could buy you one drink, without you feeling a crushing sense of obligation to buy everyone else one later,' he said, and Charlie, who was standing on the other side of the bar, grinned.

'What'll it be?' he asked me.

'A half of bitter shandy, please,' I said, giving in.

'They only have Gillyflower's Best Bitter here and it's sacrilege to put lemonade in that,' objected Ned.

'Well, that's what I like,' I said. 'We used to drink Gillyflower's at that pub near college, didn't we?'

'We did, but I don't remember you adulterating it with lemonade back then.'

'The customer is always right,' Charlie said. 'One bitter shandy coming up.'

'We can order food in a minute, but it's scampi or sausage and chips in a basket, so it doesn't take long to decide what to eat.'

We carried our drinks over to one of the long tables in the darkest corner, where I was introduced to Gerald, who was a slightly Mr Pickwickian man, portly and rubicund, and with twinkling grey eyes behind round rimless glasses. He didn't look like my idea of an intrepid world traveller . . . but then, now I came to think of it, neither did the birdlike Elf.

I slid onto the bench seat next to her and Ned sat on the chair opposite.

While I sipped my shandy, I looked around at the rapidly filling tables, spotting several people I knew, like Gertie and Steve, at a table with James, and several others who looked vaguely familiar.

Elf decided to point out some of the more notable locals: 'That's the Tollers over there, Stacy and Cal, who have the general shop. Their two eldest are in that group of young people near the bar . . . and then Charlie's parents will be around somewhere, probably in the restaurant lounge at the moment. Charlie looks just like his dad, so you can't miss him, but Katy's really fair. Odd, because she's the one distantly related to the Verdi family. There's an older son, Harry, who is a chef, but he's off working on a world cruise liner . . .'

'Don't baffle the poor girl with a list of who's who and how we're all related; just let her find out in her own good time,' said Myfanwy.

'But it's all very interesting,' protested Elf. 'The original Victorian Verdis had about a dozen children and they married into the local families, like the Tollers and Possets. You get the dark Italian looks popping up all over the place. Myfy and I both have dark eyes, but Myfy had the lovely raven hair, too.'

'It's equally beautiful now,' Jacob said. 'Like a cascade of pearls.' He and Myfy exchanged one of their intimate smiles.

'My father was Italian, but my mother English,' I said.

'That accounts for your rather unusual and pretty combination of dark hair and warm complexion, with light blue-grey eyes,' Gerald said kindly.

Food had been ordered and it did indeed arrive in retro plastic baskets, but was simple and good: chunky home-made chips and crispy scampi.

Gerald was eating sausages, which he told me were excellent and that the organic pork came from the pig farm at Cross Ways Farm.

'That's the Vanes' farm, isn't it?' I said, even though I knew very well that it was.

'That's right. The Vanes turned to pig farming in a big way. Old Saul may be the most surly, ill-tempered man in the valley, but he certainly knows his pigs, and his eldest son, Samuel, is a chip off the old block.'

'Wayne's the oddball one,' Elf said. 'Didn't want to work on the farm, doesn't seem to want to do anything much to earn a living. Then there was that big family fuss when he got a Thorstane girl into trouble a few years ago and refused to marry her.'

'At least that's one local family you're not related to,' I said.

'Oh, but actually there *is* an extremely distant link – not to us, but to Ned,' Elf said, to my surprise. 'It's in my book. A Vane servant girl ran off with one of the Lordly-Grace sons, came back pregnant and somehow ended up married to Richard Grace, a widower who lived at the Hall. He adopted the boy and Ned is descended from that line.'

Ned made a face. 'I'm more of a Lordly-Grace descendant, then, though it was such a very long time ago, I think we can forget all about it.'

I fell silent, thinking this revelation over, because . . . well, I must be extremely distantly related both to the Lordly-Graces and Ned, through my Vane ancestry!

I'd have to read the story in the book and find out more.

I'd finished my food and someone had put another drink in front of me, without asking. My tired muscles were relaxing in the warmth and I felt a bit sleepy, despite the hubbub.

A last group of people came in. I recognized the owner of the gift shop and Ned said one of the others was from Brow Farm on the hill behind Risings.

Then Ned looked at his watch and said the quiz would start any minute.

'And here's Cress,' said Elf, as a tall, lanky girl in waxed jacket, riding breeches and paddock boots came in and stood looking vaguely round. She had the face of a not unattractive, but slightly worried, bloodhound, and her mouse-brown hair was in a long plait that hung over one shoulder like an unravelling bell rope.

Gerald stood up, waved and beckoned, and her expression

brightened as she waved back. She got herself a drink and then made her way over and took the last seat, on the end of the bench next to me and directly opposite Ned. In fact, her surprisingly lovely big grey eyes were fixed on him with a sort of doglike devotion.

'Hi, Cress,' he said, casually. 'This is Marnie Ellwood, the new gardener I'm sharing with Elf and Myfy. Marnie, meet Cressida Lordly-Grace from Risings, allegedly our remote relative by the backstairs.'

Cress looked faintly surprised and he added, 'We've just been talking about the ancient family scandal. Elf's put it in her book.'

'Oh, right,' Cress said vaguely. 'I knew the family had a big bust-up over it with the Grace cousins at the Hall in the early nineteenth century.'

'Yes, that's why the two families ignored each other until recently,' Myfy said.

'But it's so silly to carry on with that sort of thing,' said Cress. 'We're all friends now.'

'Audrey, Cress's mother, doesn't exactly mix with the rest of us peasants,' Ned said, when she'd gone to the bar to get crisps, which seemed to be all the dinner she intended eating.

'No, Audrey's always been snobby,' Myfy agreed, then explained to me, 'Her late father-in-law left the property to Cress, but Audrey carries on as if she owns it.'

'The old man left the lodge to Steve just to spite her,' Elf said. 'The only reason he let her carry on living there after his son died was because he loved Cress.'

'There wasn't much money, though, so that's why they're having to run Risings as a B&B,' Ned explained.

'Or Cress is. Audrey still has her pretensions,' Elf said. 'Cress and some daily help run the B&B, but her main passion is horses and she does some teaching at a riding school over near Great Mumming, when she can get away.'

'She keeps two horses at Brow Farm, too,' Jacob said. 'I like the piebald with the wall eye best.'

'Only because he looks so odd,' Myfy said. 'He has a pink floppy lower lip, too, and grins a lot.'

'Can horses grin?' asked Gerald.

'Rags does,' she said.

'Cress would get on well with my sister, Treena,' I said. 'Her horse is at livery near Great Mumming and she spends all the time she can spare with her.'

'They might already have met, because it could be the same stables.'

'Maybe,' I said, as Cress returned with four packets of crisps and a bag of peanuts. Her horses would probably be able to use her as a salt lick by the end of the evening.

'Gerald teaches music at Gobelins, a small private school,' Elf said.

'I'm sort of semi-retired, so a few hours here and there suit me very well,' he told me.

Charlie and a young girl so like him she must be his sister, Daisy, brought round pads of paper and pens for each table and there was a bit of moving chairs about and regrouping in the room, which was now crowded. Through a gap at the far end of the bar I could glimpse the new lounge and the restaurant, and that looked busy, too. For a pub up a dead-end lane off a minor road, it was surprising how popular the place was!

But on this side, everyone seemed to be local and when we'd sorted ourselves out a bit, the quiz began.

The questions were read out by an elderly man, who I was

told was Frank Toller, Charlie's grandfather, and were very wide-ranging.

I'd only done gardening quizzes before, and that was when I was a student, but we seemed to have a wide range of general knowledge on our table, apart from TV soaps. Between them, Gerald and Jacob answered the music questions, from pop and rock to classical, and Ned proved to be hot on history and general knowledge. My input was confined to nature and an obscure question on Agatha Christie.

Ned looked at me with a raised eyebrow and I whispered: 'Cosy crime fan.'

In any small intervals of silence, the *tock, tock* of darts hitting a board came from the out-of-sight area at the back and occasionally the players would emerge to order in another round of drinks. One of them was Wayne Vane, I saw. He didn't look around, though, just shambled up to the bar and then straight back again.

We came second in the quiz, narrowly beaten by the next table. Apparently Stacy Toller was an ace at quizzes and had appeared on *Mastermind*.

The prizes were not extravagant – the winning table got a free round of drinks and the booby prize winners a bag of pork scratchings apiece.

'We just do it for the fun, really,' Ned said. He looked much more relaxed this evening than I'd seen him since I'd arrived, as if he might actually remember what fun was, if he gave it a bit more thought.

After the quiz the room began slowly to thin out and the talk at our table became more general. Ned told the others about the marble folly I'd uncovered, and how there were Victorian metal rose-name tags, some of which seemed to have the old Regency names on them, and then Ned and I fell into a discussion about whether it was better to try to find and replace the old varieties where they'd died, or put in newer ones, a topic that we, at least, found engrossing.

'I think we should restock with what was there originally, if we can,' I said. 'But you could put lots more roses into the Grace Garden, because apothecary gardens always had them, didn't they?'

Cress, who I rather liked for her gentle air of melancholy, like a human Eeyore, listened to our talk about roses and then said she'd like to pop in and see the little temple we'd found.

'Gertie asked me to bring her some more manure, anyway,' she added.

'Gertie has a huge hoard of well-rotted manure round the back of the vegetable garden,' Ned told me. 'But she'll have to part with some for the roses.'

'I do like gardens, even if we've had to turf most of ours over to make it easier to keep up,' Cress said. 'We don't have very extensive grounds now anyway, Marnie. We used to own most of the valley, but we had a gambling Lordly-Grace back in the nineteenth century and that's when most of it was sold off.'

'Wayne still does your gardening, doesn't he?' asked Elf, and Cress's face clouded.

'After a fashion, but Mummy has to constantly keep an eye on him and all he does, really, is drive the mower over the lawns and run a brush cutter across the shrubs. We do have a few tubs and pots about, to brighten the place up, and Steve kindly looks after those, when Mummy's out playing bridge.'

I hadn't realized people still played bridge, or had bridge parties . . . in fact, I had only the vaguest idea of what bridge was – some kind of card game.

'I'm going to order some huge pots for the less hardy trees

and shrubs I want to put into the garden. I'd like an oleander, for a start,' Ned said. 'A friend of mine in Great Mumming makes the giant traditional pots, Marnie. His firm's called Terrapotter.'

Recollection stirred. 'Oh, yes, I noticed it when I was driving past. Treena told me about it, too. What else are you going to put in the pots?'

'Citrus trees in some, and I've got a few more ideas.'

'Gert says you need a heated greenhouse, one you can put your coconuts in,' I told him.

'I'm not thinking of having coconuts; that was just a very Gertie joke.'

'But you could squeeze one into the courtyard, couldn't you? There's room along the archway wall.'

He considered this. 'It wouldn't be huge, but I suppose it could be quite tall . . . I don't know, I'll think about it. And it will have to wait until we've got the rest of the Grace Garden under control.'

By now, it was just me, Ned and Cress sitting at the table, for the others had either gone home, or to talk to friends. In fact, now I looked around, there were very few people left and it was a lot later than I'd thought.

But it was nice to be sitting in an English country pub, in good company, which Ned was – when he wasn't remembering to be wary of me, though that seemed to have almost worn off – and Cress, too, who seemed to be interested in everything, like an eager puppy. It reminded me of happy evenings spent at the pub near Honeywood Horticultural College when we were students, unwinding at the end of a strenuous day. Looking up, I thought Ned had the same thought, because he gave me a friendly, uncomplicated smile, as though he was really seeing me clearly for the first time since those long-ago days.

16

Heartfelt

Our gazes met . . . and held, as I remembered a time when life seemed like an open garden, in which you could sow anything you wanted to, and nothing was complicated . . .

But then the moment was broken by Cress's phone ringing loudly, or rather, *neighing* loudly. I didn't even know you could get that as a ringtone! Maybe I could have Caspar snoring as mine. Not, of course, that anyone much was likely to ring me, since I'd shared my new number with only my employers, Treena, the family and my solicitor.

Cress listened to her caller gloomily and then clicked off the phone and got up, shrugging into her waxed jacket, which had seen better days, most of them while being worn by someone much larger.

'Have to go. Apparently Mummy's in a flap,' she said in her posh but gloomy deepish voice. 'A family had booked to stay tonight and didn't turn up, so we thought they weren't coming. But now they've arrived – they got lost and then stopped somewhere for dinner. The beds are made up anyway, but I need to go and book them in.'

When she'd loped off, I said, 'She's very nice – I like her.'

'Yes, so do I – and she leads a dog's life with that mother of hers. Cress adores Risings, even though it has no architectural merit whatsoever that I can see, but there's no money, hence the bed and breakfast. Audrey shuts herself away in a separate wing and pretends it isn't happening.'

'That's not very helpful,' I said. 'I told you my sister, Treena, is a vet, didn't I? And she's often called out to Risings to look at the two Pekes, though it's always something like indigestion.'

Two Pekes – Twin Peaks, said the random weird voice in my head, but I kept that one firmly to myself.

'I can imagine Audrey would call her out at great expense, rather than take the dogs to the surgery,' Ned said. 'Cress's father died when she was a baby, but her grandfather adored her and he scraped up enough money to send her to some posh boarding school or other, where you could take your own pony with you. But then the money ran out and she came home. She did take her British Horse Society teaching qualifications, though, and gives advanced riding lessons – once she's cooked breakfast for any visitors.'

'I must ask Treena if her horse is at livery at the same stables and she knows her.'

'Cress likes to keep hers handy, at the farm behind Risings, so she can slip out for a ride as often as possible. They don't do lunches or evening meals at Risings, but people can eat here, or at one of the guesthouses up the road. The village starts to come alive from Easter, when the schools break up, in fact, any minute now—' He broke off and suddenly looked anguished, then ran his long fingers through his mane of hair. 'Oh God, we open the garden a week today!'

'Yes, I know, you said so earlier.'

A middle-aged couple, who had just wandered in, spotted him and did a double take. I suppose he's used to people knowing him from the telly . . . and all that publicity. They didn't come over, though, just sat in a distant corner and pretended they weren't looking at him. Luckily, he didn't seem to notice.

Quite suddenly voices were raised in argument from the darts room and Mr Posset came out from behind the bar in a purposeful way and stood in the entrance, looking at the players.

We heard him say: 'What's all this? I'll have no arguing and tempers in my pub – and no, I don't want to know if anyone was cheating at darts. Wayne, if you use that sort of language again, out you go!'

Wayne came pushing rudely past him, shrugging into a leather jacket. 'I'm off to Thorstane, anyway. The beer's better at the Pike and so's the company.'

He slouched out and, as he passed, cast us a dark look, as if his behaviour was *our* fault.

'The local bad boy,' said Ned. 'None of the Vanes from Cross Ways are exactly a bundle of joy, but at least they're mostly hard-working and honest. It's odd to think that the Graces – and the Lordly-Graces – are even remotely related to them.'

'I must read that chapter in Elf's book,' I said, thinking that it was even more important that I keep my much closer relationship to the Vanes a secret.

I wondered how many generations ago this elopement had taken place and, suddenly, I *really* wanted to go home and read that story!

'I suppose I should be heading back,' I told Ned.

'Stay and have one last drink with me first,' he urged. 'The great thing about going out in Jericho's End is that no one cares if I was on the telly or not, or thinks I did any of the stuff in the papers . . . possibly excepting Wayne.'

I sincerely hoped he didn't spot the couple at the corner

table, who were still covertly watching him, as if they expected him to stand up and perform magic tricks any second.

'I'm just Ned Mars from the Hall, who they've known for ever – even before my parents were killed, because I spent most of the school holidays here.'

'When the garden opens, there's bound to be some publicity and your name will be linked with it,' I felt compelled to warn him. 'I expect it's already on the website?'

He grimaced. 'Yes, and I expect there will be some curiosity seekers who come to goggle at me, not the garden, but there were lots of lovely people who supported me and didn't believe any of that muck the tabloids raked together, and they'll probably be interested in what I'm doing now.'

'I should use *any* publicity to increase visitor numbers, since it's bound to happen anyway,' I suggested. 'Eventually it'll all be forgotten and only genuine people, interested in gardens, and holidaymakers doing the rounds of the local attractions, will visit.'

'It wasn't possible to hide totally anyway, because my name was still on my Little Edens website. But I'm going to stay out of camera shot as much as I can.'

'Me, too. You might recall I never wanted to be on camera in the old days at Honeywood and I *certainly* don't now.'

He grinned. 'You were the most reluctant extra ever in that documentary! But are you still camera shy, or are you afraid your ex will spot you? Didn't you tell me he'd married again?'

'Yes, and I'm sure he's long since lost any interest in knowing where I am. It's just that, however illogical it might be, I'd prefer that he didn't know.'

'I can understand that,' he said, and somehow, over another drink, we found ourselves opening up to each other about our past experiences with unreasonably jealous and controlling partners.

I told him how ashamed I'd felt that I, an independent – not to say spiky and determined – character, came to be sucked into a coercive relationship because I'd only gradually realized what was happening.

'At first – well, I thought we were in love and it took time to build a relationship. And it did, but not the sort of relationship I'd had in mind,' I said. 'He managed to alienate me from my friends and even from my family for a time – except Treena. And she discovered his first wife had killed herself and left a note blaming him.'

'I can understand why it took a while to wake up to what was happening,' he said, 'because my relationship with Lois started out fine, but she slowly got more and more jealous, so that I couldn't even speak to another woman without Lois making a scene. If I even showed the slightest sign I was enjoying myself at a party or something like that, she'd say she felt ill and insist we go home.'

He looked sombrely down at his glass, remembering. 'And when I was off on location for the series with the team, she was constantly ringing and trying to check up on me. She kept threatening if I broke up with her she'd kill herself.'

'Mike didn't do that, though he was perpetually ringing me at work, too, or just turning up and getting in the way. He threatened to blacken Treena's professional reputation if I left him, too. But those threats your partner made to harm herself must have made it really difficult. And then she set that private eye on you.'

'Not to mention the press, as a grand finale,' he said drily. 'In retrospect, *I* feel stupid for letting it go on so long, too.'

'Hindsight is a wonderful thing,' I agreed, 'but at least we've learned our lesson. We both realized we needed to go back to our roots and start again.'

'True, and since we're both gardeners, quite literally back to our roots!' he said. 'Here's to us!'

We clinked glasses and his amber eyes were warm and friendly again, so that I was sure any last lingering doubt about me had long since vanished.

But deep inside, a little worm of guilt squirmed because there was something about me that, if he knew, might well bring back that look of mistrust . . .

I squashed it down: why should he ever find out? Why should *anyone* know?

We walked back over the bridge to the now familiar sound of the water rushing through its narrow channel and then cascading down into the pool.

Other than the occasional slam of a car door and an engine being started, or the distant plaintive bleat of a sheep, all was quiet. The sudden, silent, ghostly white swoop of a huge owl nearly sent me over the parapet, though, and Ned grabbed my arm.

'Is that a lucky sign?' I asked, slightly shakily.

'I expect so. It's lucky for you you didn't go over.'

We parted in front of the café – asking him back for coffee might have sent him all the wrong messages, and undermined our newly forged relationship – and besides, I really wanted to read that chapter on the Lordly-Grace family scandal!

Ned strode off towards the Hall and I went round through the side gate to the back door and let myself in.

I discovered Caspar in the flat, curled up on Mum's little

velvet chair, and he gave me a look and said: 'Szkyckitpfit?' Or something like that. It was clearly the cat equivalent of 'What time of night do you call this?'

Before I went to bed I read all of that chapter, and the story was a familiarly Victorian melodrama of the 'out into the cold, cold, snow and never darken my door again' type.

Only this one happened to be true. It had all taken place during the early eighteen hundreds, when Lizzie Vane, youngest of a large family at Cross Ways Farm, went into service at Risings, as a sort of companion/maid to the daughter, Susanna, who had taken a fancy to her. Susanna had two older brothers and when Lizzie was almost sixteen, she ran away with the younger one, Neville, when he returned to his regiment, which was stationed near York. Neville's regiment was then almost immediately posted to Portugal, where he was killed in battle towards the end of that year, leaving Lizzie expecting a baby and with no means of providing for herself and her child.

In desperation she'd returned to her family, who, being Strange Brethren, had turned her away and she'd had no other choice but to go to Risings. There, the master of the house, Horace Lordly-Grace, also would have had her thrown out into the snow, but his distant cousin, Richard Grace, happened to be dining there that night and, taking pity on her, had her taken to his home, Old Grace Hall. This sad story had a happier outcome than most Victorian morality tales, though, for Richard eventually married Lizzie and adopted the boy she bore as his heir. And he and Lizzie not only shared a love of the apothecary garden, but transformed the land between that and the row of cottages next to it into a rose garden.

That was interesting: my distant ancestor had not only loved the apothecary garden, but been instrumental in creating the rose garden I was working in now! I felt an unexpected sense of connection with her.

The family breach caused by this marriage appeared to have gone on for a very long time. In fact, it had sounded as if Audrey Lordly-Grace was still carrying it on.

I didn't feel any sense of connection or affinity with her at all. She sounded very disagreeable.

I rang Treena after I'd read the story to tell her about it, and that I'd had a heart-to-heart with Ned that evening in the pub.

'It sounds as if you understand each other now,' she said. 'There's nothing like shared misfortune to bring people together.'

'Don't be daft,' I said. Then I asked her if she knew Cress, which she did, because Cress *did* teach at the same livery/riding school as where Treena kept Zephyr. But since Cress hadn't been around at Risings when Treena had been out to look at her mother's Pekingese, she hadn't made the connection.

I'd slept surprisingly well after this, which might have had something to do with all that bitter shandy and also, perhaps, the cathartic effect of baring my soul to Ned . . .

But somehow, in the light of morning, that made me feel a little shy about seeing him again. Confessions and soul baring often do have that effect, and perhaps he felt the same, because I didn't see him all morning.

I began the day by removing the second rosemary bush, making short work of the root ball with the pickaxe.

I was just about to go into the rose garden after I had disposed of its remains when Myfy wandered round the end of the cottage, wrapped in her tasselled coat and a dreamy air.

'Good morning!' she said, with her tilted smile. 'I was up at Jacob's but I woke early feeling wonderfully inspired, so I've come back. And you must have been up even earlier!' she added, looking at the freshly dug earth where the rosemary had been.

'I wanted to get this bush out, then there's only one more, which I'll do tomorrow.'

'I'll have three new places to plant more lavender,' she said happily. 'I must look for some new ones.'

'I hope to prune the rambling rose at the bottom of the garden later today. It really needs doing now. I got a bit carried away when I found that little folly in the rose garden, or I'd have done it earlier.' I sighed. 'I *love* clearing the rose garden, but I'm equally longing to help Ned with the apothecary garden, too. It's like having a wonderful box of chocolates and not knowing which one to eat first.'

'I suppose it must be. I expect Ned feels the same way.'

'He does, and though he needs my help with the rest of it, he decided he wanted me to clear the rose garden first. Still, now you can get round the paths, it's just down to a major pruning back and then enriching the beds. Oh, and there's that smaller area at the top of the garden to tidy up, too. I'd forgotten that.'

But Myfy's mind had clearly slipped back to whatever inspiration had struck her this morning and her dark eyes were looking at something that only she could see. With a vague smile, she strode off towards the door into her studio, coloured tassels swinging, and vanished inside.

I spent the rest of the morning working in the rose garden, finding a few more metal plant tags along the way. I have to admit, I cleared away the ivy and encroaching branches from around the folly first, so it was all ready for Ned to clean up.

I sat on the rather green bench at the back of the little temple to drink my flask of coffee and contemplate the urn on its pedestal.

It was amazing how much work I'd managed in so short a space of time, though it had to be said that when Ned had helped it had all gone about four times as fast. But then, he was about four times as big as me.

Caspar appeared from one of the newly cleared paths, stared at me, then pulled a silent face and padded off back the way he'd come. He, like Ned, mustn't have been feeling sociable this morning.

I got up after a bit and went to look at the other, much smaller but equally overgrown, end of the garden. When I'd walked along the road past it on the day I arrived, all I'd been able to see above the short stretch of railing-topped wall, was another thicket of thorns.

About one o'clock I went over to the Potting Shed for lunch and found Gertie and James there, finishing theirs, along with Steve, who'd been helping James clean up plant tags. I added my latest haul to that of the apothecary garden.

Gertie told me Ned had had to go out earlier, but was now in his office, so maybe I'd been mistaken and he hadn't been avoiding me after all.

'Cress brought me some manure down, so I've started a new heap. But I can let you have some of my well-rotted stuff when you're ready for it,' she said, as if promising me a high treat.

'That'll do them old roses a power of good,' agreed James, which it certainly would: air and light and space to breathe and a good manure mulch equalled rose bliss.

Ned must have escaped from his office while I was eating, because I discovered him cleaning the folly when I got back. He had the pressure barrel of water he'd mentioned, plus buckets, squeegees and scrubbing brushes for the places where the slime resisted.

He was already damp and faintly green, and too engrossed in

his task to be self-conscious about last night's heart-to-heart, even if he felt it. He immediately sent me back to fetch the step-ladder, so he could reach to scrub the pediment, and when Steve, driven by curiosity, returned with me to have a look, he ended up spending the next hour scrubbing the urn and its pedestal.

When Steve had gone and the temple and urn had been rendered spotlessly white, and ourselves a dirty greenish colour, Ned and I admired our handiwork . . . and then I suddenly glanced at my watch which, despite its dampness, was still working.

'Look at the time! I meant to give that Rambling Rector in the cottage garden a radical pruning before I went to check the River Walk, but I've only got time to change into something dry now, so I'll have to do it afterwards.'

'You get off, then. We've finished here for the day so I'll put the tools away.'

'Great,' I said gratefully, 'and I only have one rosemary bush to get out of Myfanwy's garden in the morning and then I'll return that pickaxe I borrowed.'

'No rush,' I heard him say, but by then I was dashing off to render myself less like a slime monster before my walk up to the falls. Which was just as well, because there were a lot more people about than before, though all on their way back down towards the gate.

My haul was three of the ubiquitous plastic water bottles, a couple of crushed cans, the wrapper off a sandwich and a pair of stiletto shoes in a bin, with the heel snapped off one of them. I hoped the owner had carried something more suitable for walking with her.

I didn't dawdle, since I was determined to cut back that rose, and there would be plenty of time another day to sit by the falls and think, or dream, or commune with the angels/fairies, or whatever. And possibly, with Mum.

17

Well Trained

To my surprise, when I got back to the Lavender Cottage garden I found Ned there, hacking back the Rambling Rector in a no-nonsense manner.

When I thanked him, he said, 'I thought it wouldn't take long with two of us and I do feel my side of the gardening has monopolized most of your time so far.'

'It looks much better already, and at least I can now walk under the archway without having my hair raked by brambles.'

He'd thoughtfully brought the long gauntlets and secateurs I'd been using, as well as his own, so after I'd disposed of the rubbish and the stilettos (there is no special recycling box for dead shoes), I set to work at the other end of the trellis.

We always seemed fated to meet in the middle of everything we do together, but this took a lot less time than the rose garden path. We'd finished and were admiring our handiwork, when Elf called us from the back door with a loud, '*Coo-ee!*' which was something I'd thought they only said in Australia.

'Spotted you from the window,' she said, when we reached her. 'And I thought you'd be ready for a cold drink – and perhaps to try my new ice-cream.'

We went through the scullery into the café kitchen, where the glad sight of two large glasses of home-made lemonade greeted us. My throat felt as if it was lined with bark.

'Charlie's finished the cleaning and has gone home; he's such a hard worker, that boy.'

'I might be able to give Charlie a bit of work in the garden, if he's got time to spare,' Ned suggested. 'I know he's not a gardener, but a bit of muscle is always useful.'

'Good idea, though he'll be volunteering at that archaeological dig up at the ruins right after Easter so—'

She broke off what she was saying and instead gazed in a horrified way at the window behind us. When we turned, we saw a large, marmalade-coloured face pressed against the glass, green eyes glittering and pulling the cat version of that figure in Munch's painting *The Scream*.

'It's only Caspar,' I said. 'I expect he wondered where we'd gone, but he'll go round the proper way when he wants his dinner.'

'Did Marnie tell you our rescue cat has fallen in love with her?' Elf asked Ned. 'Jacob had to put a cat flap in the landing door, so he could come and go into her flat. We just see him for meals, really.'

'It's nice having him for company in the evenings,' I said, 'but I feel he's using you like a hotel, popping back for food and comfort breaks!'

'We don't mind, so long as he's settled and happy. And Myfy says he does spend a lot of time in the studio when she's painting, watching her. Jacob put a bigger cat flap in the back door, too, so Caspar can now come and go anywhere in Lavender Cottage as he pleases – except in the café, of course.'

'Caspar seems well on the way to having you all trained,'

Ned said, smiling. 'Now, what's this new flavour of ice-cream?'

'Oh, yes – I kept two little pots aside for you to try when I was putting the rest away in the big freezer,' Elf said, fetching them and getting out teaspoons. 'See if you can tell me what it is?'

'Lime?' suggested Ned and I said, 'Lemon?' at exactly the same moment.

'Both right. I thought I'd try lemon and lime together. I think I've got the sugar content right . . . not too sweet, so it will be very refreshing in summer.'

'It's lovely,' I said, finishing the rest of mine.

'I must remember to keep aside small boxes of ice-cream for you to put in your freezer, Marnie,' she said kindly. 'And I'll bring you some more over soon, Ned.'

I thanked her: a free supply of delicious home-made ice-cream is not a usual perk of a gardening job.

Elf said she hoped I wasn't finding the work of looking after two gardens too hard and I assured her it wasn't.

'In fact, I wish the days were longer!'

'But aren't you exhausted? I know for a fact that you've been up at daybreak for the last two days, working in our garden!'

'Oh, no, I'm used to hard outdoor work and anyway, in my book, gardening counts as fun.'

'Mine too,' Ned said, and then described how we'd cleaned up the folly and pruned back mega amounts of overgrown rose brambles together.

'Even Gertie's now enthused to the point where she's voluntarily offering barrowloads of her best, well-rotted manure to mulch the rose beds.'

'I want to get the rose garden to a state where I can leave it and go and help Ned with the water feature and wetland area,' I said.

'Yes, I could do with another pair of hands to help finish the hard landscaping in that corner. Then we can plant it up. I've ordered a lot of plants from a specialist nursery and Gert's been growing others from seed.'

'Yes, she said she'd been planting up a few of them,' I agreed.

'I ought to get back to the office and tweak the website a bit more,' Ned said, though leaning back in his chair with a refill of lemonade, as if he was there for the long haul. 'And I realized earlier that I should already have distributed the leaflets about the garden all over the district . . . just one more thing to fit in before we open!'

'When did you say the information boards were coming?' I asked.

'First thing Monday, so I'll have to fix those up.'

'It's going to be hectic till opening day, I can see,' Elf said, 'but once Easter weekend and all the fuss of the opening is over, things will quieten down until summer and give you a chance to get into the swing of being open.'

'I hope we're in the swing of a lot of visitors at four pounds a pop,' he said. 'Otherwise, we're sunk.'

'You'll probably have loads of tourists coming over from Starstone Edge when the holiday season gets underway,' Elf said. 'Did I say Clara rang to confirm what time you want her on Friday for the opening ceremony? I told her to get here for eleven and I'd give her coffee first: was that OK?'

'Yes, fine,' he said, then explained to me: 'The garden will be officially opened by one of our local celebs, Clara Mayhem Doome. She's an epigrapher, but you probably know her for her crime novels.'

'Gosh, yes, I've got most of them! Treena used to bring them out for me when I was in France and I bought the latest one on Tuesday.'

'Her husband's the poet Henry Doome, but he's not so keen on crowds, so I don't know if he will come with her,' Elf said. 'But our beekeeping friend, Tottie, probably will.'

I must have looked at sea, because Ned said, 'Starstone Edge is a valley high up on the moors, a few miles above Thorstane, though most of it was flooded to make a reservoir. Clara, her husband and a mixed bag of family and friends all live in the Red House, part of the hamlet that escaped the drowning.'

'Yes, and now in summer there's lots of holidaymakers and sailing on the lake and that kind of thing,' Elf said. 'One of the Doomes has opened up the old manor house as a very expensive wedding reception venue.'

'The weather can be really bad there over winter, but then there's a bit of a population explosion from late spring to early autumn, so any businesses have to make their money then,' Ned said.

'You can take some of your garden leaflets over there – and there are lots more places you can leave them.' Elf began to count on her fingers: 'There's the Pike with Two Heads, the cracker factory on the other side of Great Mumming . . . the ghost trail and the Roman Bath up in Halfhidden . . . and there are a couple of big houses further afield that are open to the public, like Rufford Old Hall, near Ormskirk.'

'I'd better quickly draw up a list,' Ned said. 'It's not something I can put off until we've opened.'

'Like expanding the shop – I think that really would make a lot of money and you did say there was an outbuilding on the other side of the wall that you might possibly be able to knock through into. I'd like to see that,' I said.

'I think the money would be better spent on the garden for the time being,' he said dubiously. 'But I'll be about all day tomorrow, if you want to come over and look at it.'

'I could do, in the morning, but I think my sister's coming over later in the day,' I said. 'I'd like to have another walk round the Grace Garden anyway and see what you've been doing.'

'Well, don't let Ned rope you into working on your day off,' Elf said. 'You need a rest.'

'You're right, Elf. Marnie's already working more hours than she's being paid for and she's only been here five minutes.'

'But we're all – Gertie, James and me – working more hours than we're paid for, because we enjoy what we're doing,' I said. 'If you want me to work on Sundays too, I will.'

'You're a glutton for punishment,' Elf said, but she was smiling. 'I hope you'll join us for Sunday dinner tomorrow evening? It's an open invitation, because of course sometimes you might want to go off for the day, but Jacob and Ned usually come, and Gerald.'

'Roast beef and Yorkshire pudding,' Ned said reminiscently. He didn't seem surprised I'd been invited to join them for dinner, but then, I expect he knew how hospitable they were.

'Sometimes it's roast chicken instead,' Elf pointed out.

'I'd love to, thank you,' I agreed, capitulating, and Elf beamed.

Ned got up, stretching, his head almost touching the ceiling. 'Well, I'd better get back to the office for a bit, even though I don't want to. See you in the morning, Ellwood.'

When he'd gone, Elf looked at me. 'Why does he call you by your surname, Marnie?'

'It's just . . . sort of a running joke from when we were students.'

'Well, as long as you don't mind.'

And I didn't – in fact, I'd welcomed it as a sign that we were resuming our old friendship.

*

Treena had sent me a message saying she was definitely coming over to Jericho's End tomorrow, when Luke wanted to do a little initial surveying at the ruins, so I was really looking forward to showing her where I now lived and worked.

Caspar and I had a quiet night in, snuggled on the sofa, while I read a bit more of Elf's book. I'd missed a couple of pages at the end of the Lost Treasure chapter, about a miser who was supposed to have buried a wonderful hoard of gold in his garden, but it was never discovered . . . until more recently a rotted wooden box was found hidden in the beams of an old outbuilding. It contained a few halfpennies and a small leather bag of silver sixpences. The place had promptly been rechristened Sixpenny Cottage, which was an improvement on the original Scrogg's End.

I can't say I found that story very riveting and when I moved on to 'Gentlemen and Buccaneers', Elf's writing style caused my eyelids to droop, even when reading about the excitingly swashbuckling Nathaniel Grace. I gave up and swapped Elf's book for the new Clara Mayhem Doome novel.

That kept me wide awake for longer than I'd intended. Caspar had to be very insistent before I finally put it down and went to bed.

It might be Sunday, but I rose with the lark anyway and hacked up that last overgrown and woody rosemary bush. It put up a struggle, but once it was out and the hole filled and dug over, the garden looked a lot better: I could trim the remaining lavender into neat shapes at my leisure – or Myfy might feel the urge to do some clipping – and it would all now be a doddle to keep under control.

When I went back up to the flat to change out of my working clothes, Caspar was still asleep on my bed, in the exact position he'd been in when I went out: on his back, four big furry paws in the air and a blissful expression on his wide face. He didn't stir while I was changing into clean dungarees and a long-sleeved T-shirt in a nice shade of smoky blue that I knew did things for my eyes.

My hair was getting a bit long, but at least, being naturally curly, all I had to do was run a brush through it and shove it behind my ears: Marnie the Human Mop.

I breakfasted on the last of the *pain au chocolat* and about a gallon of good coffee, neither of which appealed to Caspar when he finally made his appearance, so he made a noisy exit through the cat flap to search for a better class of catering.

Before I went out I remembered to search for my phone, which eventually I found zipped into a gilet pocket. Then I managed to drop it on the floor, but luckily it still worked, and I pushed it well down into my dungaree pocket before heading for the Grace Garden.

It was still very early and I'd have plenty of time to discuss the possible extension and improvements to the shop before I was to meet Treena, even after a leisurely diversion to look around the apothecary garden on my own.

I knew Gertie and James wouldn't be in today, since this was the last Sunday they'd have free before the gardens opened to the public. That meant I'd have the walled garden to myself before Ned was likely to make an appearance.

I resisted the urge to detour and admire the clean marble folly again, but instead went straight through past the pond, where the koi were circling hungrily, and into the Grace Garden, empty of all creatures great and small, even peacocks.

I'd totally grasped the original layout from the old plan in Ned's office – the small sunken circular herb bed and sundial at its heart, then an outer circular path, flanked on either side with low beds edged in lavender. The tall beds at top and bottom of the garden and the four paths leading from the circular one to the corners . . . they all balanced and formed a pleasing pattern in my head.

But then, there were the small changes generations of Graces had made to the design, the years of neglect and then Ned's more recent innovations.

I wandered around for a bit, finding that some of the smaller paths in the mid-level beds led to gravel circles with stone seats that would be hidden when the plants grew taller.

Down in the sunken garden, Gertie had kept the thyme, chives, mint, marjoram and other lower-growing herbs neat in their brick-edged beds, radiating out from the old sundial – and it did look *very* old indeed.

The galleon pointer was in full sail and round the edge of the dial words had been engraved, though the archaic script was hard to make out. But it was quite poetical really, when I'd grasped that they'd written 'f' where they'd meant 's'.

'*The sun is my treasure, it measures the hours in bars of gold.*'

I wondered if it had been put there by the buccaneering Grace, Nathaniel? I thought it might, though then it would pre-date the apothecary garden and I wasn't sure what was here before.

I took another path out, past beds planted with the sturdy stems of lovage and fennel . . . and the rhubarb Ned had mentioned, heading for his mud hollow in the bottom right-hand corner.

Last time I'd seen it, it had looked a bit like a muddy building site, but he'd certainly put in a lot of work since then and most of the hard landscaping was finished.

The spring by the back wall was now channelled down a small waterfall of old, lichen-spotted boulders, to the new small pool, now lined and the edges landscaped to look natural. It just wanted planting up – and then water creatures of all kinds would discover it and even, perhaps, dragonflies.

I remembered there was to be a small wooden bridge across the stream, just above the pool, which would lead to a gazebo, but only the foundations were there, waiting for the structures. I could imagine it, though . . .

By the back wall were barberry bushes around the marshy area, where flags marked the path of the wooden walkway, still to be laid.

I thought Ned had done very well to get it to this stage so soon, especially now I knew that he'd spent last year re-gravelling the paths, reinstating the lawn borders in the side beds, replanting most of the segments of the mid-level beds and, of course, creating the entire Poison Garden.

I walked past that on my way back to the courtyard, but didn't turn off for a better look: I could wait for my guided tour, when Ned felt the need to enthuse about his collection to someone who knew what he was talking about.

But I still wasn't going anywhere near that rosary pea vine.

18

Slightly Gnawed

Ned was in the courtyard, sitting on the steps up to the office and feeding the peacocks handfuls of something from a small blue bucket. The gate to the house had been left ajar, giving a tantalizing glimpse of a small stretch of lawn and a terrace, then the house with its gleaming mullioned windows, intricately patterned black and white walls and, to the right, the side of a newer wing in white stucco, somewhat in need of a new coat of paint.

He looked up. 'I spotted you making down the garden when I went to feed the fish, but I thought you'd like to explore it on your own this time.'

'Yes, it was nice to just wander and take it all in,' I agreed. 'The Victorians seemed to have had a mania for marking everything in the garden with those metal tags, didn't they? They must come in handy: you can see what goes where, even when the beds are currently empty.'

'Yes, they've been useful, though when they dug up that large area during the war, the old tags that were there were just dumped in one of the outbuildings. Now I'm going to reinstate the vegetable-plot-style beds, with lawn pathways between, I'll replant some of them.'

'It was lucky you found them, and anything you can't fit in the new beds will probably find a place somewhere else,' I suggested. 'Was it the late Victorians who put all those little paths into the mid-level beds, leading to the round seating areas?'

'Yes. They're also responsible for replacing some interesting old plants with newer, showier, but entirely useless things too,' he said. 'I don't mind new varieties of plants, because gardens should evolve, but if they don't have culinary or medicinal uses, they've had to come out.'

'Or deadly ones,' I pointed out.

'I've got a few more things coming for the Poison Garden,' he admitted. 'But lots more for the wetland area.'

He went to put the plastic bucket back in the Potting Shed. When he returned, I said, 'Gert's right, you could fit a small greenhouse on this side of the wall to the garden. A tallish one, where you could overwinter those less hardy plants in terracotta pots you were telling me about.'

'Maybe later. For now I can always wrap anything delicate in fleece over winter,' he said. 'Come on, let's look at that outbuilding and see just how feasible knocking through into the current shop would be.'

He unlocked the visitors' gate and we went out onto the path that led up to the road. Over a low stone wall on the other side of it was the cluster of barns and outbuildings I'd seen on my walk around the Green, but there was a gate to them here, too.

The path at this end widened slightly into a small yard just in front of the old building that we'd come to see.

It was definitely a lot bigger than the shop. There were two windows, obscured by dirt, and a wooden door that looked as if something had been chewing the bottom.

'When Nathaniel Grace bought the original house it wasn't

very grand, so there's no big carriage house, just an old barn and a couple of stables,' Ned said.

'Good heavens – where am I to keep my barouche and four matched grey horses, then?' I demanded, and he grinned.

'No idea, but you can park your car in the yard over there, if you want to, like Elf. And Jacob keeps his old Land Rover in the barn in winter when the track to his house is too difficult.'

'Jacob's house is a converted barn, isn't it? Why is there a barn up there, in the woods, where it's so steep?'

'It wasn't always wooded. They used to run sheep on it, I think. Maybe it was something to do with that . . . I don't know. The track does carry on past it, because there's a farm just over the ridge. You can hike up to the top of the woods and then along until you come out above the Fairy Falls eventually. It's quite a trek.'

'I might try that one day off, when I'm feeling energetic,' I said, then turned to look at the building we'd come to see, with its squat and slightly belligerent air.

'I don't know what its original purpose was. It might have started out as a feed store or tackroom or something,' Ned suggested, pushing open the gnawed door with a creak onto a gloom only slightly alleviated by the brownish light coming through the century of cobwebs and encrusted filth on the windows.

'That doorway is quite wide, so they might have kept animals in here,' I said.

'Maybe, but going by the workbenches and that rusty vice, it's been used as a workshop fairly recently.'

'Recently as in about seventy years ago?'

I'd followed him in and stood in the middle of what I was already thinking of as the Grace Garden Shop and Visitor

Centre. 'This has lots of possibilities,' I told him encouragingly, even if most of them were currently large, black and had lots of legs.

Luckily, I'm not in the least afraid of spiders, or other creepy-crawlies, most of which are very helpful to gardeners, and even those that aren't, like Cabbage White caterpillars, provide a tasty meal for the birds.

'This is a good, big space,' I said approvingly, then spotted something. 'It looks as if there might originally have been a door through into the other side.' I went over to examine the wall more closely.

'Oh, yes, I'd forgotten. I spotted that from the other side when we were painting the shop walls. It looks like there was an opening through, then they filled it in when the lintel above it cracked.'

'I don't know how you managed to forget that, because it will make it much easier for us! It'll just need much more support,' I told him. 'Apart from that, it looks in better shape inside than you'd expect, from the state of that door.'

'I have no idea what they might have kept in here that could chew through thick wood,' he said, eyeing it.

'Maybe one of your madder ancestors?' I suggested, and he gave me a look.

'I really don't see why you shouldn't knock through the wall to the shop, with suitable supports put in, and that would more than double the current space, Ned.'

'I think it would be quite a big job,' he said dubiously. 'Expensive.'

'I'm sure any builder worth his salt could do it in no time,' I said. 'Ideally, the visitors should exit through the shop, so they'd have to walk past loads of lovely shopping opportunities on the way . . .'

'I'm still not sure it would make enough to justify all the outlay converting it.'

'Trust me, it will,' I said confidently. 'You'll need to make the door from the courtyard wheelchair accessible with a short ramp, and then you can solve the loo situation, by having an easy access one at the back of this new part.'

'Which loo situation?' he demanded.

'You have one outside loo for visitors and one for staff – that's not going to cut the mustard when you have loads of visitors, some of them disabled, or needing baby-changing facilities.'

'Baby-changing facilities?' He looked horrified.

'Don't worry, there can be a flap-down baby-changing table in the new toilet cubicle, so it's multi-functional.'

'Oh . . . great,' he muttered, looking worried. 'Planning permission . . . and plumbing . . .' He ran his hands through his hair in a distracted way.

'The current loos must be on the other side of the wall at the far end, so there shouldn't be any difficulties with the plumbing. And you aren't building a new shop, just extending into another area of it,' I said reassuringly. 'If the loo is at the end of this new part, perhaps divided by a stud wall, then the museum section can be in front of it . . . with more displays of things for sale nearer the exit door.'

'We had to take the flags up in the shop and put a damp-proof membrane down before we re-layed them,' Ned said. 'We'd have to do the same in here.'

'We might be able to save money by doing some of the decorating ourselves. I can do plastering, rough or otherwise, so you needn't pay for that.'

'Really?' he asked sceptically.

'I have all kinds of odd skills, from helping to renovate all those châteaux,' I reminded him. 'You can't sit about in the evenings watching people working around you.'

'I suppose not,' he agreed.

'I do think it will pay dividends in the long run, Ned, and sometimes you have to set a sprat to catch a mackerel.'

That was one of Aunt Em's sayings.

'You said you'd like to display the original garden plans and some of the old photos and documents here, for the visitors to see.'

'True, and I do have several things we've found in the outhouses, like old gardening tools and blown-glass forcing jars, which would make a good display,' he said, warming slightly to the idea. 'I've still got more boxes of old papers and photos to sort through, if I ever have any time.'

'Perfect: photos of the garden and house, past and present, a pamphlet about the history of the family and the garden . . . Elf could write that, and visitors will love to learn about the buccaneering Grace. I'm sure he had that sundial made now I've seen it closer. That's a very Tudor galleon and the writing's old and funny.'

'You're probably right. I think it was on the lawn behind the house originally, but was moved to its present spot later.'

'So, *are* you going to add converting this building to your plans – maybe get someone to do an estimate?' I demanded.

'I'll think about it,' he said, and led the way back into the cobbled courtyard, locking the gate behind us.

'Meanwhile, you need one of those big collecting boxes so people can donate towards the restoration of the garden.'

'So you said . . . Seems a cheek when they've just paid four quid to look at it.'

'There are a lot of garden lovers out there,' I said, and then checked my watch and realized how long I must have spent pottering about with Ned.

'Look at the time! I'll have to go,' I said. 'Treena came over this morning with her friend Luke, the archaeologist in charge of that dig.'

'You'd better get off, then,' he said, and I thought he sounded slightly disappointed. Probably he'd hoped to rope me in for a bit of extra work, as Elf had warned me.

'Treena's meeting me at the bridge. She's never been further into Jericho's End than Risings, when she's been called out to see the Pekingese, so it's time she did. I thought we'd go up the River Walk and—'

My phone buzzed, cutting me off, and I fished it out of my pocket. 'On my way, Treena!' I said hastily. 'Two minutes.'

I looked up. 'Have to dash. Treena's already waiting for me.'

Something about his expression – I don't know, perhaps I imagined a faint wistfulness had replaced the disappointment – made me add, 'Luke's meeting us for lunch at the pub – join us if you're free?'

I didn't wait for an answer; I was already heading for the gate to the rose garden. I nearly dropped the phone again, trying to shove it in my pocket as I ran past the koi pond, another watery phone death narrowly averted, though maybe it would have lasted long enough for the fish to call their friends.

I wonder what fish would talk about to each other. Maybe the huge, orange, hairy creature that sat on the edge of the pool watching them, with a kind of detached, languid interest, and who barely glanced at me as I hurtled past.

Treena was standing in the embrasure on the upstream side of the bridge, leaning over the wide stone wall to watch the water slide deeply and quickly underneath.

'You couldn't play Pooh Sticks here,' I said when I joined

her. 'They'd get smashed to bits in the Devil's Cauldron on the other side.'

'So would anyone who fell in,' she said, with a shiver. 'I wonder if anyone ever has?'

'I expect people do fall in the river further upstream from time to time, but there are lots of big flat rocks sticking out into the water, so they probably get out again. Come on, let's go and have a cup of coffee in my flat – unless you'd prefer the café?'

'No, I want to see this flat of yours,' she said. 'I'm ready for a hot drink, too. Luke had me all over the site, holding the end of measuring tapes, or carrying things while he took pictures and dictated notes into his tablet. The wind really whips round you like liquid ice up there.'

'Very poetic,' I said. 'I'm looking forward to meeting Luke later and hearing all about it . . . And I mentioned to Ned that Luke would be in the pub with us later and he'd be welcome to join us if he wanted to. He's interested in the dig.'

'Yes, of course – and I'd like to meet him, too!'

We went round to the back door and had barely got up to the flat when the cat flap gave a huge rattle.

'That's Caspar, the cat the Price-Joneses have just taken on from a rescue centre. He's decided to spend most evenings with me, so they've put a cat flap in. I wonder how he knew we were here,' I added as he appeared. 'He was in the rose garden five minutes ago!'

Treena made much of him. 'He's a bit thin under all that fur, but seems in good condition.'

'They're trying to fatten him up a bit,' I said. 'He's half Maine Coon, but they have no idea what the other half is.'

'Whatever it was, the Maine Coon is winning out,' she said.

She admired my little domain and said it already looked

homely, what with mine and some of Mum's bits and pieces spread about. Then she picked up Elf's book and began glancing through it, while I made the coffee. Caspar lay over her knees like a slightly knobbly rug.

'This is quite interesting,' she said when I put the mugs and a packet of chocolate digestives down on the chest that did duty as a coffee table.

'It's Elf Price-Jones's book. I bought it in the village. Her style is a bit dull, but it's full of fascinating information. I mean, I've already found out that a distant Vane ancestor of mine ran off with a son of the Lordly-Graces, which makes me very distantly related to Ned.'

'Really? But everyone does seem to be distantly related to everyone else in these out-of-the-way villages,' she said. 'Though not usually, perhaps, the local bigwigs.'

'I suppose I'm also distantly related to the current Lordly-Graces, too – or Cress, at any rate. But still, it all happened *centuries* ago, so it's too remote a connection to count. Of course, no one, including Ned, has any idea I'm a Vane and I'm going to keep it that way. The Vanes are very disliked and sound unpleasant, even without the way they treated Mum. The only member of the family I've met is Wayne Vane and he was horrible – and possibly light-fingered.'

'Well, Mum was adamant you shouldn't approach the Vanes and make yourself known,' Treena said. 'And *your* mum didn't want you to even come here, so I think you're quite right to keep it quiet.'

Later, as we walked up to the Fairy Falls, I told her about the angels-versus-fairies arguments and how I felt sure, as Mum had done as a child, that there was *something* present up by the falls.

Treena is not at all imaginative and looked sceptical. This

being a Sunday and so near Easter, there were quite a lot of visitors about and, although it was beautiful up by the falls, it had none of the magic it so often held.

We went out of the top turnstile and down the village street, pausing for Treena to buy her own copy of Elf's book. The proprietor of the gift shop, who had been one of the quiz night regulars, greeted me in a friendly way and seemed to know all about me – or everything that was public knowledge, anyway. The whole village presumably does, by now.

He said the book had been selling well, but then his face clouded suddenly and he told us that someone had stolen a copy that morning and he had his suspicions about who it was.

'It seems an odd thing for anyone to take, really,' I said, thinking that even in small rural villages, you couldn't get away from shoplifting. It sounded, oddly, as though this was someone local and known to the shopkeeper . . .

19

Full House

Outside Toller's general store, we bumped into the tall, rangy figure of Cressida Lordly-Grace, dressed in what was probably her everyday garb of riding breeches, boots and waxed jacket.

'Hi, Cress,' said Treena. 'Marnie told me you lived in Jericho's End. I just never happened to bump into you when your mum called me out to see her dogs, so didn't make the connection.'

Cress looked faintly alarmed. 'She didn't mention there was anything wrong with Wu and Wang this morning – but I do keep telling her not to feed them cake and biscuits!'

'It's OK, I'm not here on an official call-out this time. I came over with a friend and thought I'd catch up with Marnie – she's my adopted sister, you know.'

'Oh, right,' Cress said, looking relieved, probably because she'd been worried about the expense of Treena's professional house calls. She looked interestedly at me. 'I didn't realize you were sisters. What a coincidence that I should know Treena.'

'It's a small world,' I agreed, though I hadn't realized quite *how* small, or how overlapping the coincidences were going to be, before I got the job here.

'Mummy's out of sherry, but so are Toller's, unfortunately,' Cress said, explaining her presence. 'I might be able to buy a bottle in the Devil's Cauldron, though.'

'We're on our way there for lunch,' I said. 'Treena's friend Luke is the archaeologist who's going to be in charge of the dig at the ruins after Easter and he's looking over the site, then joining us for lunch.'

'Would that be Luke Ridgeway?' Cress exclaimed. 'He rang me yesterday evening to ask if I could give him a room until they finish in September. Of course, I told him we're just a B&B and don't do lunches or evening meals, but he said that wasn't a problem.'

'He did mention he was going to look for somewhere to stay in the village,' Treena said. 'Risings will be very handy for the site, if you can take him.'

'I've said I will. It's a regular booking and he's going to pay weekly, up front,' she said cheerfully.

'Why don't you join us for lunch, too, Cress?' I suggested. 'Ned said he might come.'

She looked wistful. 'I wish I could, but I won't have time. I'll need to drop the sherry in for Mummy and then dash off to give an advanced dressage class at the riding school at two. But I have got time for a cup of coffee, first.'

'Won't you want anything to eat?' I asked. 'A quick sandwich?'

'No, we've got two lots of B&B guests and I find when I've cooked all those greasy breakfasts, I don't feel hungry for hours. Gosh, it's amazing how much food people can put away when they've paid for breakfast. They really want their money's worth!' she added. 'And Mrs Laidlaw, who takes over when I have to go to the riding school, was late . . . and then, to top it all, Mummy suddenly reminded me about her sherry, which she needs because a friend is coming over later. So it's all a bit of a scramble today.'

'Well, have a cup of coffee and chill for half an hour before you rush off,' Treena suggested.

We found Luke already there and Treena introduced him to me and to Cress, his future hostess.

He was like a taller, older version of Harry Potter, though with hazel eyes, instead of green, and an engagingly boyish smile.

He went to order our lunch and Cress's coffee, and she and Treena fell into horse talk, as was entirely inevitable.

Cress told her how she kept her own horses at Brow Farm behind the house, where she rented two paddocks and some stabling.

'It's very convenient, because I can slip out for a hack whenever I get the chance. There are some great rides locally,' she added. 'If I can't get up there, one of the boys from the farm sees to the horses for me.'

'It sounds a perfect arrangement. The riding school looks after Zephyr very well, but it's extremely expensive.'

'Well, there's room for a couple more horses with mine – you could move her up here,' suggested Cress.

Treena, turning this over in her mind, thought it might work out. 'It's not that much further than the livery stables from my cottage in Great Mumming, just in a different direction. I'll have a think about it.'

But at that moment Ned walked in, and Cress's eyes went unfocused.

I hadn't *really* thought he'd join us – it had been more likely that he would have started work in the garden and entirely lost sense of time passing – but, after nodding to a couple of acquaintances, he came over.

Cress patted her hair, which was today drawn back into a

messy pleat and, smiling eagerly, made room for him on the bench seat next to her.

I introduced Ned to Treena and then pointed out Luke, over at the bar, ordering food and he went to join him.

'I wish I *could* stay for lunch,' Cress said wistfully, looking after him, and Treena and I exchanged amused smiles. Ned seemed to come at least a close second to her horses in Cress's affections.

The two men were already talking ruins when they came back and seemed to be getting on like a house on fire. If Luke was aware of Ned's previous incarnation as a TV gardening personality, or all the scandal, it had clearly made no impression on him in the least.

Cress, once she'd drunk her coffee and purchased a bottle of sherry over the bar, reluctantly tore herself away just as our ploughman's lunches of Lancashire Crumbly cheese, fresh bread and pickles arrived.

While we ate, Luke told us that his dig would start on the Tuesday after Easter. 'I've taken a sabbatical from my university till September, got some funding, and most of the manpower will be students and local volunteers.'

'It's going to be handy for you, if you're staying at Risings,' Treena said.

'Yes, Cress seems nice and she said she did a good cooked breakfast that would set me up for the day. Then I'll probably eat in here most evenings.'

'Now I've met a few archaeologists, I can confidently predict you'll find most of them hanging out in the nearest pub after work finishes for the day,' Treena said drily.

'This dig's a bit off the beaten track, though,' Luke said. 'They may have to travel quite far every day and so want to get off home after work.'

'I often have a quick meal here in the evenings, when I can't be bothered cooking,' Ned admitted.

'I expect I'll see you here, then, and you'll have to come and see what we're finding when the dig gets going,' suggested Luke. 'The first few days we're mostly just rolling and stacking the turf and moving rocks.'

'I've walked round the site a few times,' Ned said, 'and I wouldn't have thought there was a lot to dig up.'

'I think it's more extensive than it looks. I've seen some aerial photographs of the area that showed more walls extending out.'

Luke was off again on his pet subject. Apparently, he hoped the site would have been a very early monastic settlement, even if it had been abandoned quickly.

'Depending on when that was, it might have been the result of Viking invasions into the area, though in west Lancashire, they mostly seemed to have come to settle and farm.'

'Elf – she's my great-aunt and a local historian – says their land was flooded by there being two successively rainy years, so they decided to join forces with one of the larger established monastic foundations further to the east,' Ned said.

The dig was starting to seem a little more interesting than the collection of not terribly inspiring hummocks and bits of wall that I'd seen from the car park, on the day I'd arrived.

'I'll come and have a look at what you've found, too, once you've got going a bit,' I said.

'Why not help with the dig?' Luke suggested eagerly.

'Because Marnie already spends all day digging, Luke,' Treena reminded him. 'She's a gardener!'

'I don't get a lot of time off,' I said, 'and being involved in restoring the Grace Gardens is enough for me.'

'Oh, yes – of course. Treena told me you were restoring a

historic apothecary garden,' Luke said to Ned. 'It's behind that interesting Tudor house over the bridge, isn't it?'

Ned nodded. 'Old Grace Hall. The garden was originally laid out in the late seventeenth century, but part of it was commandeered to grow fruit and vegetables during the war and it's been neglected ever since. The house, of course, is very much older. In fact, I'm told there was an even earlier building on the site and you can still see part of it incorporated in the later structure.'

'It sounds fascinating,' Treena said, and Ned suggested we all go back there for coffee and he would give us a quick guided tour of the interesting bits.

'Coffee?' I said dubiously, and he raised one fair eyebrow.

'Good coffee. I've got a machine now that does it all at the press of a button or two – foolproof.'

'You can't go that far wrong with a cafetière, like in the office,' I pointed out, but men do seem to like their gadgets, and the more complicated, the better.

Still, I'd been longing to see inside Old Grace Hall, without wanting to suggest he showed me alone, in case it brought back any lingering worries about my being dangerously neurotic. But there was safety in numbers, so here was my opportunity!

Ned put on the lights as soon as we entered the house, illuminating the long passage that opened before us, with doors off it on either side and a narrow, worn wooden staircase that vanished upwards into darkness.

'I hope you aren't going to be too disappointed with the interior,' Ned said, 'because most of it was remodelled in the thirties and forties. Several of the smaller rooms were knocked into one.'

'I suppose they could do that kind of thing with impunity before you had to get Listed Building permission,' Luke said.

'Yes, I think an Englishman's home was still his castle back then. The house isn't in too bad a shape structurally, but inside it's very shabby and needs some replastering, painting and decorating. I just don't have the time or the money to spare from the garden, right now.'

'Or the skill, when it comes to things like plastering,' I pointed out. I'd happily help him do things like that later, if he'd let me . . .

'The Hall appears to have started out as a much humbler dwelling, with a room on either side of a cross passage,' Ned said. 'One side was for the animals and the other, the family. It developed from that and was rebuilt later into the Tudor house you see now. There's a wing, added around the early eighteenth century, where the kitchen and dining room are now.'

Luke was looking with interest at some stones sticking out of the wall below the stairs, which he said looked like the remains of an earlier stone one. 'So it may have been bigger and perhaps fortified in its earlier incarnation,' he added.

Ned opened a door on the right to show us a parlour that had been knocked through all the way to the back of the house and made into a sort of library-cum-study. It was quite cosy, with a log-burner, a big desk, modern lamps and some squishy chairs.

Some of the upright beams from the dividing wall that had been removed had been left in place, presumably to support the upper structure, and both they and the beams of the ceiling were huge and had odd bits cut out of them.

'Family legend says that the beams are all from ships that have been broken up. The Grace family had shipping interests in the past, when it was built, even if they thought "trade" was a dirty word later.'

On the other side of the hall was another big room, with

long windows at the back onto the terrace, the walls painted a soft sage green, and the furnishings of a vintage gentlemen's club variety. It was all quite Agatha Christie; you could stage a nice murder in there.

'It must have been a warren before it was opened up a bit,' said Treena.

'The rooms between this part and the new wing still are, though the kitchen was modernized around the seventies and the electrics have been upgraded fairly recently.'

He didn't seem to mind Luke poking about and examining beams and exposed bits of wall, or the carving over the huge fireplace, which incorporated a galleon like the one on the sundial.

'I think that's the sign of Nathaniel Grace,' I suggested, and then told Treena and Luke that Ned had a buccaneering ancestor.

'He was one of those Elizabethan seafaring men who sailed close to being a pirate, but so long as he only attacked Spanish vessels and kept the Queen sweet with occasional gifts of looted jewellery, she turned a blind eye,' Ned said. 'He married and retired here – bought it from his cousin, after he'd moved his family to Risings.'

'And became the first of the Lordly-Graces,' I finished for him.

'I'm glad I bought a copy of the book. I'm looking forward to reading it,' Treena said.

'I read it when I went through the proofs for Elf,' Ned told us. 'There was a lot of detail about my family and the other local ones that I didn't know, though I was vaguely aware there was some slight link way back with the Vanes from Cross Ways Farm – and I'd much rather not have known about that.'

'The family scandal,' I said lightly, avoiding Treena's eye, and inside my dungaree pockets crossed my fingers in the hope he'd never find out I was a part of that clan.

'Still, it's so far back, it's negligible,' he said, dismissing it.

'I told you the story of the servant girl who eloped with the younger son of the Lordly-Graces,' I reminded Treena.

'And ended up married to my ancestor, Richard Grace,' agreed Ned. 'That caused a rift with the Lordly-Graces. Audrey Lordly-Grace, Cress's widowed mother, still likes to keep her distance.'

'She isn't very pleasant,' Treena said. 'Talks to me as if I'm her servant and then haggles over the bill.'

'She's like that with everyone she considers beneath her,' Ned said, and then added, since Luke was looking slightly alarmed, 'She lives at Risings, Luke, but she keeps herself to herself, so you probably won't cross paths with her.'

'From the sound of it, that suits me fine,' he said. 'Cress's nice, though, and I'm sure it'll be very comfortable. Better than trying to commute to and fro between here and Liverpool.'

'Do you want to see a bit more of the house?' asked Ned. 'Upstairs there's an amazing Victorian bathroom, though luckily there's also a very new one, put in when my uncle Theo got frail.'

We duly admired the Victorian bathroom, with its absolutely huge, claw-footed bath, but he didn't open all the bedroom doors, just showed us one that had an ancient dark four-poster bed, and another furnished with a complete Edwardian suite in maple.

'Furniture through the ages,' he said.

'I think old houses should reflect the generations that have lived in them, just like old gardens,' I said.

At the further end of the corridor, past the splendours of

Victorian plumbing, was a door to the new wing – so called – with the modern bathroom, and the bedroom that had been Ned's uncle's next to it. There were signs of occupation, so I think he'd taken it over.

A narrow, twisting staircase brought us out near the kitchen, which was a very big room with a somewhat schizophrenic air: what might have been the original Regency closed stove remained, with various bits of metalwork hanging next to it that were probably roasting spits, but looked like instruments of torture. But around the other sides of the room were cupboards and dressers and a range of more modern cabinets, with worktops in a horrid speckled granite finish.

There were some mod cons, though: a big fridge-freezer, a dishwasher and all the usual gadgets, including a gleaming new monster of a coffee machine.

I looked critically at it as he filled up the jug. 'I think that's overkill.'

But I accepted the coffee, which was good, and we sat in the kitchen to drink it. It was warm and cosy in there, probably due to the Aga that now sat next to the old stove.

'I could do with proper central heating,' Ned said. 'Uncle Theo had electric night storage heaters installed all over the house, but they only seem to take the chill off.'

'Something more ecologically friendly,' I suggested.

'I don't know what, but it'll have to wait till the garden is earning its keep, anyway,' he said, predictably.

'Unless you find this treasure that Nathaniel is supposed to have hidden,' I said with a grin.

'I'm sure that's just an old tale,' Ned said, smiling. 'The house has been remodelled so much since his time, and people must have searched for hidden places, so it would have turned up if it really existed.'

'These old stories get passed on like Chinese Whispers,' agreed Luke, 'changing with each retelling.'

'I have found a couple of treasures in an old chest in the library,' Ned said. 'The original plan of the apothecary garden, and some impressive documents, including Nathaniel's will. I expect there's still more to discover.'

'Well, if anything relates to the monastic ruin, let me know,' Luke said hopefully.

'You'd be better asking Cress, because any papers pre-Nathaniel probably went to Risings when the original family moved there.'

'I might do that,' he said. 'You never know.'

'At some point I'll go through all the papers,' Ned said. 'There's a large wooden box full as well as the chest – and one of the library window seats is full of old accounts books and paperwork, too. My uncle had a rummage about in everything, when he was thinking of writing a family history, so it's all very jumbled.'

I'd quite have liked a rummage in there myself: who knew what other garden-related treasures might lie within?

Luke looked at his watch and said perhaps he and Treena had better be heading back.

'I'm taking the evening surgery at the clinic,' Treena explained. 'I've got Good Friday off, so I can come to the opening of the garden, but then I'm on call for twenty-four hours over Easter Sunday.'

We donned our coats again in the hall, where we'd piled them onto an old oak settle, and Luke and Treena thanked Ned for letting them see the house.

'And me,' I said. 'I was expecting it to be in a much worse state than it is, but it only really needs some redecoration and a lot of TLC.'

'Shabby chic is in!' Treena said with a grin.

'See you later, Marnie,' Ned said to me, as I left with the other two, and for a minute I was flummoxed, until I remembered I'd said I'd go to the family Sunday dinner at Lavender Cottage that evening.

I said goodbye to Treena and Luke by the bridge. There were still lots of visitors about, mostly coming out of the River Walk, rather than going in, for it was less than an hour till closing time.

Several people were still sitting at the tables outside the café, too, despite the chilliness of the air, eating ice-cream and drinking coffee. The main road through the village looked quite busy, as well, which all gave me some idea of what the place would be like in summer!

Not, perhaps, quite the quiet little hideaway I'd originally envisaged.

At least today it wasn't me picking litter up on the River Walk, so I went back to the flat, where a familiar bubbling snore alerted me to the fact that Caspar was there, asleep on the sofa. He opened his eyes when I went in and changed the snore to a throaty purring noise.

I started sorting and unpacking some more of the things I'd brought over from Treena's and found my box of childhood treasures – a shell box from some long-ago seaside holiday, a packet of photographs of me growing up, taken by Mum, and one or two of us both together. She was tall and vibrantly glowing, Titian-haired and full of life. It was so cruel that it had been taken away from her in that way.

There were no pictures of her earlier than a few snaps taken when she was a student nurse, looking younger and more serious. There were pictures of me with Aunt Em and a baby Treena. They'd become fast friends at antenatal classes and

Aunt Em had looked after me with Treena when Mum had gone back to work. And then, once Mum was facing her final battle and knew she wasn't going to win it, they arranged between them that the Ellwoods should adopt me . . .

For the first few months after Mum died, I'd repaid them by being the teenager from hell. The hurt, angry child I'd been stayed hidden inside me long after, stirred up again when the family had moved to France, which had seemed like another abandonment, however illogical I knew that to be.

Then Mike had come along and so skilfully worked on and exploited that inner insecurity . . .

I shook off the past resolutely: understanding meant I could move on. I *had* moved on. I put the photos back in the envelope and into the chest I was using as a coffee table.

Then I found a few of Mum's ornaments in the next box, though she hadn't been one for clutter, and arranged them on top of the bookshelf.

Time had passed and at some point, unnoticed, Caspar had vanished. He was probably in the kitchen next door, eating his dinner . . . and now I was conscious that the celestial chimes of the café door had ceased to ring out a considerable time before, and when I looked out of the front window, no one was to be seen. It was time to freshen up and go next door for Sunday dinner. By then I was ravenous and looking forward to it.

20

By the Book

Dinner proved to be fun, with good food and interesting conversation, as you'd expect with such a mix of individual characters.

Jacob had returned the ball-bearing clock, now restored to working order, so Elf was appeased. She and Gerald had cooked the dinner between them, which they seemed to enjoy doing. Myfy wandered in late, with a smear of ochre paint on one cheekbone that no one mentioned. It sort of suited her, though after a while, Jacob went out and came back with a rag that smelled rather pleasantly of linseed oil and, without a word, tilted up her face and removed the daub gently, then kissed the place where it had been.

Jacob told Ned that now he'd seen the new waterfall feature in the Grace Garden, he was going to give him a small, kinetic installation that would look very well there.

'The power of the water will be enough to very slowly open and close small metal flowers among the rocks,' he said, illustrating what he meant on a Post-it note block he'd removed from one slightly saggy pocket.

'It's very *kind* of you,' began Ned, looking taken aback, 'but—'

'Now, don't try and tell me you're restoring the garden to the absolute original, because you know very well that the lay-out of the main paths is really the only *truly* original part of it,' Jacob said.

'Some of the planting will be original, too, where there are notes,' Ned said.

'But you're keeping some later additions and introducing new ones,' Myfy said. 'Even a garden must evolve and change to survive. Your new wetland area can only be enhanced by Jacob's sculpture.'

'I think it's a lovely idea,' I said. 'It'll give a magical quality to that corner and really intrigue the visitors.'

'When they spot it, because it will be quite subtle, the flow-ers small and of delicately coloured metal,' Jacob said dreamily. 'Trust me, it will look right, as if it's always been there.'

'I'd let him do it and then, if you don't like it, he can take it away again,' suggested Gerald practically.

'And sell it – he's very well known, you know,' Elf said to me. 'His works fetch a fortune.'

'The ones he'll part with, anyway,' said Myfanwy with a grin, and then, to me: 'You must go up and see all the water-powered sculptures around the barn, when you have time – Jacob won't mind.'

'If I'm working I won't even notice,' he agreed. 'And that clock has inspired a lot of ideas, so I think I'm going to be very busy for quite some time. I do prefer kinetic sculpture that relies on natural and renewable methods of movement.'

'I rely on a natural and renewable method of movement, too,' said Ned, then sighed. 'This will probably be the last relaxing moment I get for a long time. There's so much to do between now and Friday, when we open.'

'It'll get there,' Elf assured him. 'And I'm certain Friday will be pure fun! We'll all come, and our friends, and loads of villagers, and the vicar . . .'

'*And* someone from the local newspaper, who rang me just after you'd been down for a look round the garden this afternoon, Jacob,' Ned said, his face darkening slightly.

I suppose he was thinking that once the connection was made between him and the Grace Garden, there might be a bit more than local news coverage.

As for me, I'd be staying well out of any publicity, the incognito gardener in the background.

I told Myfy how much I liked her design for the tote bags and souvenirs in the shop and then said perhaps there should be a line of things particularly aimed at children, possibly using a ship logo – the galleon of the buccaneering Nathaniel.

'Something bold, but not Blue Peter,' I explained. 'We could put it on the donations box, too.'

'Which donations box?' asked Ned.

'The one I keep telling you to put on your to-do list,' I said patiently.

Back at the flat with Caspar, I made a cup of cocoa and read a little more of Elf's book – the account of that first little girl who'd seen the angel by the waterfall – but waves of sleep kept trying to crash over my head and in the end, I gave up and went to bed.

On the whole it had been a lovely day, with only that brief descent into sadness and regret while I was sorting those photographs, though even that had been cathartic: it showed me how I'd understood the past and learned from it.

I rose with the start of dawn, a silver-pink ripple along the hills, but not to work. Instead, I let myself out of the gate at the bottom of the garden and, as the light slowly grew brighter, headed upriver to the waterfall.

I thought of all the others over the centuries that had made their way up this path. Our human presence here inhabited not so much a fold, but a mere pucker in the fabric of time.

Up by the source of the falls, although I had that feeling that there might be another world close by, behind an invisible curtain, I had no sense that winged creatures of any kind kept me company, not even birds . . .

All was quiet, except for the sighing of the trees in the breeze.

It was a good moment for thinking things through and coming to terms with the past – and recognizing my hopes for the future. I realized then that I wanted always to be here, in Jericho's End, where I knew I belonged.

Back at the flat I had toast and honey, having finished the last of the *pain au chocolat*. I wondered if Toller's stocked them; I wouldn't put it past them.

Caspar wandered in from the bedroom while I was drinking my second cup of coffee, said something that sounded distinctly like, 'Where have you been?' and then exited in search of breakfast.

I'm sure Treena's cats never try to talk to her.

I left soon after, mentally gearing up to make an early onslaught on the narrow blunt tip of the rose garden, which I hadn't even touched yet. It couldn't extend very far, so I hoped at least to get the paths cleared all the way round today.

I was increasingly eager to get involved in the apothecary garden itself, now, but torn because a) I like to finish a job properly, once I start it, b) I love roses, and c) Ned was my boss and this is what he'd told me to do.

No one was about as I collected the tools I'd need from the

Potting Shed, though when I came out with them, Guinevere the peahen was squatting on the shop roof, like a drab and badly constructed tea cosy. Then, as I looked up at her, wondering where Lancelot had got to, I heard voices from beyond the entrance gate, which I now noticed was ajar.

Curiosity killed the cat and would probably be my downfall, too. I moved closer and unashamedly listened when I caught the unmistakable rumble of Ned's voice and the higher and indefinably shifty tones of Wayne Vane. He sounded as if he was trying to be ingratiating.

'I wasn't doing no harm, just looking for a bit of chain I remembered seeing in one of the stables. Thought it would do for the gate across the track up past Jacob's house. I was doing a spot of work on the hinges yesterday and the old chain's broke and the padlock hanging.'

'You were certainly having a good rummage round when I heard the barn door squeal and came out to see who was there,' Ned said.

'I'm interested in old buildings, aren't I?' Wayne said, sounding aggrieved. 'And I'd have OK'd it with you before I took this chain away.' Something clinked. 'I knew you was usually in that office of yours early.'

'Right,' Ned said disbelievingly. 'Well, you can take your bit of chain and get off my property. And don't let me . . .'

Whatever else he said, I didn't linger to hear, in case he came back and caught me listening. He didn't sound in too good a mood, so I removed myself and my tools to the rose garden.

Time passed and I'd soon cleared the short stretch of path to the outer wall. I guessed it just curved back to the pond on the other side of a central bed, but there was another small marble bench here, too, entwined with variegated ivy.

The bushes at this end were much less rampant and

overgrown, as if someone had paid them a little attention at some more recent point. Through a small gap behind the bench, I could see a bit of the wall, with railings set into it like a series of blunt and twisted pokers.

I leaned the rake against it, then after pulling off some of the ivy, sat on the marble seat to drink my flask of coffee.

A cheeky robin came and sat on the other end, but I hadn't got any crumbs to share.

When I'd finished the coffee I spotted the edge of a fallen metal name tag in the middle bed and retrieved it, brushing off the layer of leaf mould. 'The Apple Rose', it said, which wasn't a name I'd heard of, but it was certainly flourishing.

Then, as I began to turn back, I saw out of the corner of my eye a long-fingered, freckled hand reach through the railings and grasp the handle of the rake I'd leaned against the wall. With a certain fascination, I watched it slowly withdraw, pulling the rake with it, then stop when it finally occurred to the owner of the hand, as it already had to me, that the rake head would not fit between the rails.

A head bobbed up, the face with its slightly weaselly features familiar under a khaki forage cap, from which wisps of bright orange-red hair stuck out. I saw the shallow, pale blue eyes spot me and widen . . . and then, very, very slowly, the rake slid back down again.

Wayne brazened it out. 'Morning! Hard at it already?'

'Yes,' I said shortly. 'Did you want something?' *Other than my rake*, I added silently.

'No, just passing. I've been finishing a job off for the farm up the track by the Village Hut. Anyway,' he added cockily, 'it's a free country, ain't it?'

Wayne obviously considered everything in it to be free to him, that was for sure.

'How you getting on? Saw you and old Ned being chummy in the pub the other night, so he's probably going easy on you for now. But you watch your step. He's got previous form for dumping his women when he's had enough of them.'

I felt a flame of anger. 'I'm not interested in old gossip, I'm just here to do the gardening – and all those stupid stories about Ned were disproved. I'd advise *you* not to go spreading slander about him, or you might find yourself in trouble.'

'There's no need to get all uppity, when I was just dropping a hint in case you had any idea he meant something serious, like,' he said, digging himself further into his unsavoury little hole.

'Well, I haven't! Ned is just my employer – or one of them, because I'm working for Elf and Myfy, too. Excuse me,' I added brusquely, 'I want to get on with my work.'

I removed the rake from his reach, but he said quickly, in the ingratiating tone I'd heard him use to Ned earlier that day, 'No offence meant – and no rush to get on, is there? I'm interested in what you're doing with the garden. We're in the same line of business, aren't we?'

'After a fashion,' I agreed. 'You're a handyman, too, though, aren't you?'

'Gardening, mostly, but I'll turn my hand to anything for a bit of cash. It beats working with Dad and our Sam on the pig farm, that's for sure.'

'I've heard you have an organic pig farm,' I said, interested despite myself. 'Is Sam your brother?'

'Yeah, eldest. And the Vanes are noted for our pork,' he agreed. 'Dad works the farm with our Sam, but I had other ideas, didn't I?'

Getting no response to this he added, on a note of disgust, 'Pigs!' But whether this was meant for his family or the animals, I'd no idea.

'There's a few mentions of your family in a book about local history I bought the other day,' I said on impulse. 'They were members of a strict religious sect, weren't they?'

'Yeah, Strange Brethren, and our Dad's still pretty strange, if you ask me – him and some of his friends. All that old "hell and damnation" mumbo jumbo's pretty much died out, and a good thing, too.'

I thought he was right about that one.

'They even christened me Esau,' he said in an aggrieved voice, as if it was a personal insult, 'but I wasn't having that. Christened myself Wayne later, and no dunking in cold water to do it.'

For a second time, I thought Esau had an unusual distinction that the name Wayne lacked. But then, Wayne himself didn't have any unusual distinction.

'Someone already told me my family was in that book the old Price-Jones bat with the funny-coloured hair wrote.'

'Nature seems to have given *you* funny-coloured hair, too,' I said, for the wisps escaping from under his hat were so orange they almost fluoresced.

He frowned, puzzled, then said, 'Mine's natural, not dyed.' Then he gave me a closer scrutiny, as if really seeing me for the first time, which I didn't like in the least.

'You're so dark, you could be foreign. Where you from?'

'Merchester,' I said coldly. 'It's noted for the dark Latin good looks of its inhabitants.'

He gave me another baffled look and abandoned this tack. If there were any brains left in the Vane family, he hadn't inherited much of a share of them.

'I got a copy of that book, though I've not read all of it yet – I don't do much reading.'

'You astonish me.'

I remembered what the shopkeeper had said when Treena bought hers and was dying to ask him if he'd paid for his copy or not. I had to clamp my lips together.

'There's a whole chapter on treasure that's hidden in the valley, there for the taking, if you can find it,' he said with more enthusiasm. ' 'Course, everyone knows those daft tales about fairy gold hidden up by the waterfall, but maybe there's more to it.'

'There wasn't much more to the one about hidden gold at Sixpenny Cottage, though, was there? It was just a few silver sixpences and some old copper coins.'

'Well, more fool them for thinking an old skinflint living in a hovel up in the woods would have any gold to hide,' he said. 'But these days, with metal detectors, people are turning up good stuff all the time. Me and my mates have got them, but we haven't found much yet except rusty nails and the like. I might try those old ruins, before they start to dig it all up.'

'The monastic ruins?' I exclaimed, startled. 'I really wouldn't, because you'll be caught and prosecuted. Anyway, the monks moved to another monastery after only a couple of years, so they'll have taken anything of value with them.'

Wayne looked unconvinced, but said, 'That pirate that bought Old Grace Hall probably came back dripping with treasure.'

'I really don't think so,' I said dismissively. 'But I'm sure the house has been searched several times over the centuries since, so anything hidden there would have been found.'

'Unless he was cunning and it's out in the garden somewhere,' he suggested.

'Not in the Grace Garden, it isn't. That wasn't created until the seventeenth century and this rose garden was where they kept the hens and pigs till long after that.'

He looked first dampened and then wary as James suddenly came round the curve of the path.

'What are you doing skulking about there, young Wayne?' he demanded.

'Just talking to the new gardener, like. Warning her what a curmudgeonly old sod you are.'

'I'll have less of your sauce,' James told him angrily. 'Ned said he caught you messing about in the stables earlier.'

'I've already told Ned I was only looking for a bit of chain for a gate.'

'A likely story,' said James. 'I'd take yourself off, before Ned spots you.'

'I got a right to walk up a public road, haven't I?' Wayne said belligerently, but he slouched off, all the same.

'He's a bad lot,' said James. 'The Vanes are a dour and bad-tempered family, but at least most of the rest of them are honest and hardworking.'

'James!' came a bellow from the direction of the Grace Garden and he started. 'Forgot why I'd come for a minute! They just rang Ned's mobile to say they were delivering the signs, but they've brought a van too big to go over the bridge, even though he warned them about the access. They're unloading them on the other side, so we'll have to carry them from there.'

We all trooped out and over the bridge, and Charlie came out of the pub to lend a hand, too.

'If we don't hang about, we can move them across before the café gets busy and people start getting in the way,' Ned said. 'Let's stack them on the patio behind Lavender Cottage first – I'm sure Elf and Myfy won't mind – then we can take our time shifting them from there.'

So we did that, Charlie and Ned taking the bigger ones and James guarding the slowly diminishing heap by the bridge, as if afraid sign thieves would hurtle down the one-way road and steal them.

I had barely got back to the pruning when I was summoned yet again, this time to help carry in a plant delivery, though actually it wasn't just plants; there were small trees and shrubs, too. At least this time they'd arrived in an open-backed truck that had been able to be driven over the bridge and into the courtyard next to Old Grace Hall, where the contents were offloaded.

The plants now stood in a group on the cobblestones, like a lot of nervous sheep in a field, and all had to be carried across the path, through the visitors' gate and then on into the garden, where they were lined up on the paths near where they were destined to be dug in.

'We might as well have a bite of lunch and a brew, before we do anything else,' Gertie said as we walked back once we'd finished.

'If you don't mind, I think I'll take a sandwich back with me, so I can get on,' I said, so in the Potting Shed, Gert fished out a plastic box and shoved several sandwiches and a slab of foil-wrapped lardy cake in it.

That should keep me going for a bit, I thought, as I headed back.

It was some time later, and I'd hacked back quite a bit of the path down the other side of the giant central bed of Apple Rose, when Ned appeared, carrying a bucket of soapy water and a brush. He was wearing waders.

'I've been planting up the pond with the water plants that came,' he explained, seeing my quizzical look.

'You're the biggest garden gnome I've ever seen,' I said, and he grinned.

'Forgot my fishing rod. But while I was fairly waterproof I thought I might as well clean down this marble bench James told me you'd found.'

'Pity you didn't do it earlier, before I sat on it,' I said ungratefully. 'I've got a mossy green bottom.'

'If it's permanent, we could advertise you as a garden feature,' he suggested. 'Speaking of which, Wayne seems to be becoming a garden feature, too, though an unwelcome one,' he added. 'James said he found him talking to you over the wall, earlier.'

'Yes, and he'd have had the rake, too, if he wasn't too thick to realize the head of it wouldn't fit through the railings.'

'Nothing's safe,' he said. 'Did James tell you I found him in the stables very early this morning?'

I nodded. 'I suppose he was up to no good there, as well.'

'He had an excuse, but it wasn't a good one.' He looked at me, amber eyes serious. 'What was he saying to you earlier? I hope he wasn't making a nuisance of himself again?'

'Not really. He's got hold of a copy of Elf's book, because someone told him his family was mentioned in it, but he seemed more interested in the chapter about hidden treasure. He's got a metal detector. I must tell Treena to warn Luke, in case he tries to use it at the dig site.'

'He'll be sorry if he does, because Steve's sheepdog will bark his head off if he hears anything at night, and if he's let out, Wayne will be sporting a set of toothmarks up his legs for weeks.'

'He asked me if I thought your pirate ancestor had really hidden treasure here and I told him no, because if he had it would have been found.'

'He'd better not try digging up my garden!'

'He won't. I reminded him the Grace Garden wasn't there

until long after Nathaniel, so if there had been anything there before, it would have been found.'

Then something connected in my head and I said, 'That old sundial with the galleon in the middle – the words round the edge mention golden bars, though of course they meant sunshine. But perhaps someone reading that got the wrong idea and it started the rumour?'

'It's surprising how little it takes sometimes, so you could be right. But it's probably just wishful thinking – though I could really use a chestful of pirate treasure right now!'

He went to change, leaving a gleaming white bench and a trail of soapy water behind him. He and James were going to sort out all the new signs next and start putting them up.

Later, they came in and cemented one in the rose garden, while I was packing up my tools and gathering the full bags of prunings together: River Walk time, again.

'Just leave all that,' Ned said. 'We'll put it away. You've done enough for one day.'

'I am a bit stiff, but nothing a hot shower won't fix,' I agreed.

'Never mind, you've got all tomorrow to recover.'

I stared at him: 'You only have three more days before the garden opens! You can't possibly think I'm going to take all tomorrow off.'

'Nor Gert and me – and Steve says he'll be round when he can, between jobs.'

Ned looked taken aback. 'But—'

'Nor do we want paying. We're a team effort, aren't we, young Marnie?'

I liked being called 'young'; it reminded me that I still was. 'We certainly are,' I agreed.

'Well . . . thank you,' he said. 'Marnie, I could do with some help in the office first thing, if you wouldn't mind – and then perhaps we'd better finally go and distribute the leaflets everywhere we can think of. Or maybe Charlie could? His sister Daisy's taken over helping in the café now it's her school holidays and he said earlier he could give me a hand with anything I wanted doing, before he starts on that dig.'

'What about the expense?' I teased him.

'Charlie's coming cheap, as long as he gets cash in hand,' he said. 'I wonder what he's like at putting wooden walkways and bridges together?'

'They're all brought up on Lego; it'll be a doddle,' I told him.

21

Flower Power

For the next few days I knew I'd have to devote myself to the Grace Garden, so I spent a quiet early morning hour trimming the remaining lavender bushes into pleasant hummocks, ready for the new growth later in the year. One of the bushes had been half-pruned into a sort of Mohican, presumably by Myfy before inspiration made her wander off again.

Ned wasn't expecting me for a little while yet. He'd rung me briefly the previous night to make sure I really *did* want to work today. He'd had another word with Gertie, James and Steve, too, and in the end persuaded them to take the day off, in order to prepare themselves for a very busy two days getting the garden as ready as possible for the opening – and all the visitors we hoped would come over Easter weekend.

Of course, I'd given my new, permanent mobile number to Elf and Myfy as well as Ned, since they were my employers . . . though after the Paranoid Years it felt odd that anyone other than my family and my solicitor should know it.

Ned had suggested that I meet him at the office around nine, when Charlie was also calling in, because he and a friend were now going to distribute the garden leaflets all over the district, which was a much better idea than Ned doing it.

Charlie must have been early, because he was just leaving the office when I got there, carrying three boxes.

'Hi, Charlie,' I said. 'Are those the leaflets?'

'Yeah, and a list of places to leave them, though I've got a few ideas of my own, too,' he said slightly indistinctly, since he was pinning down the list on the top of the boxes with his chin, so it didn't blow away. 'I'm not coming back with any, that's for sure.'

He headed off towards the visitors' gate and I went into the office, where Ned was sitting at his desk in front of a laptop, looking slightly harassed.

'I hadn't realized Charlie had a car,' I said. 'That's handy.'

'If you can call it a car, though he swears it has a full MOT.' He looked at the screen again and sighed. 'I made the mistake of checking the website inbox and loads of people have been emailing me, mostly with questions.'

'What kind of questions? Interesting ones?'

'No, so far they're all stuff like what the opening times are, how much a ticket costs and how to find us – all the information they can already find under their noses on the website.'

'There's nowt so queer as folks,' I said, going and looking at the corkboard wall, which was now liberally covered on one side of the old garden plan with Ned's to-do lists, some marked *Urgent!* There was also a three-phase long-term plan.

He'd already ticked off one to-do list and right at the top of the next was, 'Lay wooden walkway around top marshy area, then plant up.'

'Jacob's here – he's down by the new water feature, fixing up his kinetic flower sculpture, or installation, or whatever he calls it,' he said rather morosely, swivelling round in his chair and watching me run my finger down the lists. 'Myfy spent last night up there, so she helped him carry it down. She said I should be honoured to have it.'

'So you should! It'll be a popular attraction and you'll probably get art lovers making a special trip to the garden to see it.'

But my finger had stopped at 'The Project – Phase 1: Marnie to complete the restoration and any necessary replanting in the rose garden and open paths to public.'

I read on, but Phases 2 and 3 didn't provide any surprises: the low beds with lavender borders to be dug over and replanted, more mid-height planting in three of the central mid-level segments within the circular walk, and the long strips of vegetable-style beds created, with lawn walkways in the fourth.

All the usual weeding, hoeing and watering was taken for granted, a bit like breathing.

'Feasibility of new visitor facilities, museum and shop area' was still stuck in Phase 3, though it did have a red ring drawn round it.

'I've been thinking about the loos,' I said thoughtfully.

'And a delightful thing to ponder over on a bright April morning,' he said sarcastically. 'Who could blame you?'

'Get lost, Mars. I'm the sarcastic one, remember?' I pointed out. 'It occurred to me that the current outside visitor toilet might be incorporated into the new part of the building later, so you accessed it from inside the shop. You'd just have to block up the outside door and turn everything around. The new door would be the disabled loo.'

'Oh – easy then! What about the staff one, don't you want to drag that into your expensive alterations, too?'

'No, because it's right on the end, so it can stay as it is, with the door onto the yard. I mean, if we're muddy, we won't have to traipse through the shop, which would be locked in the mornings anyway.'

'I suppose we could look into it – if knocking the two buildings into one is feasible, anyway.'

'Well then, get someone in to look at it and give you an estimate. We must have proper facilities for the visitors,' I said, abandoning the wall and going to fill and plug in the kettle. I spooned a generous amount of ground coffee into the large red cafetière.

'Help yourself,' he said, still being sarky. 'Eat my biscuits too – they're in that Dundee Cake tin.'

'I think *you* should eat some,' I told him. 'You're so grumpy this morning that your blood sugar must be rock bottom.'

'It's just . . . all the extra little things that need doing before we open that keep cropping up. And then as soon as I got in here this morning, the phone started ringing!'

'That's only to be expected, if the number is on the website.' I looked round. 'It's not ringing now . . . wherever it is.'

'Under the sofa cushions. I shouldn't have put that advert for the opening day in all the local papers. It wasn't so bad until they came out.'

'Yes, you should, if you *want* the garden to be a success.'

'One of the local papers is going to cover the opening event, which I suppose is good,' he admitted. 'But this morning, someone from regional TV rang me and wants to film me in the garden, telling them about what I'm recreating here,' he said, even more gloomily. 'The last place I ever wanted to be again was in front of the camera.'

'I expect it'll only be a tiny bit of a local interest feature in the programme, won't it?' I consoled him. 'They won't be interested in last year's something-and-nothing bit of scandal-mongering. That's old news.'

'Old news,' he repeated, then his narrow mouth quirked up at the corners into a smile. 'Thanks, Ellwood – I think that cuts my life crisis and meltdown to size.'

'Everything has its season. You're hoeing a different row now.'

'I suppose I'm being over-sensitive . . . *and* about the visitors to Jericho's End who want me to pose with them for selfies.'

'It's the new autograph and you're just a personality to be snapped with. I mean, they're not shouting, "Oh, look, there's the lecherous love rat, Ned Mars", are they?'

'Not that I've noticed recently,' he agreed gravely. He ran his hands through the tawny mane of hair in a familiar fashion. 'You're right, and most people already know where I live. I'm not hiding out. There was a small piece in the local papers when I inherited Old Grace Hall, about my moving my garden planning business here and how I was looking forward to the longer-term project of restoring the old apothecary garden. Nothing about the scandal.'

I remembered that couple who had stared at him in the pub last Friday evening . . . but they hadn't bothered him, just been excited to recognize someone fairly famous.

'I'm sure your novelty value has long since worn off, but even if you *were* a notorious philanderer, it would still bring the punters flocking to see you, as well as the garden, so it would be win-win.'

He winced slightly. 'When the garden's open, I'm hoping to spend most of my time down at the bottom of it, in the roped-off areas.'

'And I'll be making sure I'm well out of sight when there are any journalists or cameras about,' I told him. '*I* really am hiding out and I don't want anyone to know I'm here.'

'You're not still nervous about your ex finding you, are you?'

he asked curiously. 'I thought you said he stopped trying to track you down ages ago and found someone new.'

'N-oo . . .' I said slowly. 'I mean, I know he hasn't got any power over me now – and I can't understand how I ever let him have any – but he might think it was amusing to turn up, if he knew where I was. And I don't know how I'd feel, seeing him again.'

I gave a shiver, somewhere between irrational fear and anger.

Ned gave me a look I couldn't read, but didn't say anything.

'Butter paddles . . .' I murmured, following an inner train of thought.

'What?' he said, surprised.

'Oh, nothing,' I said quickly. 'Mike's not interested in old gardens – or any kind of garden – so as long as I keep my name and face out of the media, I'm safe enough. But Jericho's End hasn't turned out to be quite the quiet backwater to lose myself in that I hoped it would be.'

'That's true, but for a small village up a dead-end road, it has a lot going for it,' he said. 'Only in the middle of winter is it really quiet, especially if we get bad weather. The road in snows up, the bus is cancelled and Elf closes the café.'

By now he'd drunk the coffee I'd put in front of him and eaten two gingernut biscuits and a bourbon cream. He looked slightly less frazzled.

'What do you want me to do this morning?' I asked as the phone, muffled by the cushions, began to ring.

'If you could bear it, hold the fort in here for a couple of hours,' he said. 'Answer the website emails, open that stack of mail I haven't got round to, and put anything urgent in a heap. Then if you could answer the phone—'

'It sounds like a morning of unadulterated pleasure – *not*,' I said.

'I've made a list of some other things you might have time to do and here's a list of passwords and stuff you might need to know.'

'Not *another* list? You have been busy! But yes, I suppose I'll be your PA and secretary and dogsbody – just for today.'

'You get free run of the coffee and biscuit tin,' he offered.

'And what will *you* be doing?' I asked as he got up, stretched cautiously, like a cat in a slightly too small box, and put on the jacket that was hanging on the back of his office chair.

'I'm off to Great Mumming first, to get a master set of all the keys cut, to hang in the Potting Shed. We'll have to be much more careful to keep the gates to the private areas locked against the visitors, because there are always some unable to read the signs and I don't want them wandering round into the Lavender Cottage garden, or sneaking off to peer in the Hall windows.'

'Would people really do that?'

'You'd be surprised. Anyway, the master set of keys will be in the Potting Shed and we all have a key to that.'

'Good idea.' I didn't want to carry any more keys, because I already jangled like a gaoler when I walked, due to the bunch of Lavender Cottage ones, as well as those to the Grace Garden.

When he'd gone I did help myself to more coffee and then settled down in front of the laptop (feeling a warm glow of pleasure that he trusted me enough to give me his password) and replied to all the emails he'd mentioned, though I think they might have been breeding in the inbox since he last looked.

Ned had been right and most of them asked the questions the website had been set up to answer . . .

Duh.

But there was one from a married couple living locally, who described themselves as keen amateur gardeners, retired but very active, offering to work for nothing as volunteers. I noted down their names and email: this was the sort of help that would be invaluable!

After that, I gingerly replaced the phone on its rest, but it had rung itself into an exhausted silence.

I took the opportunity to work down Ned's list of people to ring, chasing up a missing signboard from the delivery, checking the consignment of glossy brochures was on its way, and one or two more tasks.

I'd only just ticked off the last thing on the list and replaced the receiver, when it rang and a posh, high-pitched, female voice asked whether entrance to the garden on Friday would be free to local residents.

'Local residents *are* free to walk in the garden any time – so long as they've paid their four pounds entry fee,' I said. I'd no idea what Ned's policy was going to be on this, but I didn't somehow take to that voice . . .

There was a splutteringly indignant noise and then a sharp-pitched yapping in the background.

'Do be quiet, Wu and Wang!' she exclaimed, covering the phone inadequately and I was suddenly sure this must be Audrey Lordly-Grace!

She came back on and said, 'Surely, at least on opening day, entry will be free?'

'No, though there *will* be free cold drinks and cake in the courtyard.'

Elf was going to provide a couple of large jugs of lemonade and Gertie was baking a huge lardy cake.

'All the details are on the website,' I said helpfully. 'You could become a Friend of the Grace Garden, though,' I suggested. 'For only twenty-five pounds, you get free entrance at all times and there's a special garden party in summer.'

I'd made all that up, too, but it was such a good idea I scribbled it down on the pad next to the phone.

She made another outraged squawk and I nearly said, 'Who's a pretty Polly, then?' but luckily, just as the words were beginning to slide out from between my clenched lips, she put the phone down on me.

I added 'Set up Friends of the Grace Garden on website' to Ned's urgent list.

He came back just as I'd finished doing that and must have detoured by way of the house, because he'd brushed his hair and changed the brown woolly jumper with holes in the elbows he'd worn earlier for one of a mossy colour and a less disreputable waxed jacket.

I told him what I'd done so far and asked him if he wanted me to put in the order he'd left for a lot of scented geranium plug plants.

'Only they might want to be paid up front.'

'I haven't dealt with them before, but they'll probably send an invoice,' he said. 'Apparently, it's the secret dream of James's heart to plant up that big stone water trough in the courtyard with scented geraniums. Gertie told me he'd been drooling over the catalogue for this specialist nursery for ages.'

'So, it's his secret obsession?'

'Not any longer. They've some really unusual new varieties. I doubt they're all going to be hardy, but nurturing them through the winter will give him something to occupy himself with, when things are quiet on the visitor front.' He grinned. 'We won't tell him – it can be a surprise!'

As we put the order through, I thought how kind he was

and that underneath his new wariness, he hadn't really changed much from the young student Ned I'd known: generous, thoughtful and warm-hearted.

As if to emphasize it, he'd brought me back a sandwich, too: smoked salmon and cream cheese on wholemeal bread – delicious.

'I wolfed mine down in the car park before I came back. I was ravenous,' he said, and just then his mobile rang and, when he'd answered it, he got up.

'Here we go. The TV people have arrived. I'll go and meet them.'

When he opened the door I could see that nature had helpfully set the scene for him: the sun had suddenly popped out from behind clouds, Lancelot had appeared in the archway to the garden, tail spread, and the birds began to sing sweetly, as if auditioning for a Disney film.

Ned returned looking more relaxed and said that once he'd started talking, he'd forgotten everything except what he was hoping to achieve in the Grace Garden, totally oblivious to the camera pointing at him.

This ability to lose himself in his genuine enthusiasm for gardening was what had made him such a natural on TV in the first place: he just forgot the cameras and the millions of viewers.

'Someone's coming back on Friday, but just to add some film of the actual opening – and Clara Mayhem Doome. She's a much bigger celebrity than I am,' he said.

I left him to it and popped out to the café for coffee and ice-cream with Treena, who had rung to say Audrey Lordly-Grace had called her out to the Pekes yet again, but she'd also seen Cress and had a quick look at the stables up the hill behind Risings and thought she might move Zephyr over at some point fairly soon.

'I felt guilty about charging so much for the call-out to the Pekes, now I know it's Cress's house and she's struggling to make a living from it.'

I told her about the phone call to the garden office and that I was sure it was Audrey Lordly-Grace. 'She was really indignant about having to pay four pounds like anyone else if she deigned to come and see the gardens, so she's obviously penny-pinching in other ways.'

'Since you heard her mention Wu and Wang, it has to be her,' Treena said, then sighed. 'They'd be much happier little dogs with less sugary biscuits and more walks. I keep telling her, but she doesn't listen.'

Treena couldn't stay long and when she'd gone I walked slowly back to the Grace Garden and followed the sound of voices borne to me on a brisk breeze.

Ned, Charlie and Jacob were grouped round the little waterfall that Ned had created above the new pond, watching small, iridescent metal flowers slowly opening and closing their petals amongst the mossy rocks and frondy ferns.

Jacob looked up and smiled. 'I had to go back to the barn and make a few small adjustments. But it's all working now.'

'It looks absolutely magical!' I told him.

'Yeah, it's fantastic,' Charlie said. 'Really cool.'

'You're both right,' Ned agreed, all doubts evidently vanished. 'It's so strange, but yet, it does look as if it somehow grew there.'

'It did, with a bit of help from Jacob,' I said.

22

Signs

When Jacob had gone, Charlie and I helped Ned with the next task on his endless to-do list, moving the remaining boxes of stock that had been stored in the office across to the shop.

Then we began to fill the empty spaces on the shelves and racks with books, souvenirs printed with Myfy's pretty design, packets of seeds and flower-printed trowels and forks.

True to his word, Charlie hadn't brought back any of our leaflets, but he did have a whole box full of other people's, pressed on him along the way. Some of them sounded really interesting, like the cracker factory on the other side of Great Mumming, which I remembered Ned mentioning once, too. I filled one of the clear plastic stands with those and stood it on a shelf near the entrance door. There was plenty of room, because the stock was a little sparse. I was going to have to take the situation in hand . . .

We carried out a tiered plant stand and set it in the courtyard by the door, ready for Gert's pots of herbs and other surplus plants. Then Ned said there was something in one of the old stables that might give her a bit of extra display room and he and Charlie went to find it. They came back with a funny old flat-topped barrow, with a painted iron frame and wheels.

'There we are,' Ned said, parking it next to the plant stand. 'Gertie can put some of the bigger pots on it; it's strong enough to take them.'

'Yes, and it's got character,' I agreed. 'Maybe a bit too much character? Would James remove the rust and give it a quick coat of paint?'

'It's just the sort of job he loves – providing we can get it into the back of the Potting Shed, where he can be cosy. But it's not much bigger than the barrows we keep in there.'

'Let's try it now,' suggested Charlie obligingly, and they squeaked and grated it over the cobbles and squeezed it through the door.

It might not be my idea of a high treat, but I was sure James would be delighted. *And* with his geraniums, when they arrived.

The others went off down the garden again, this time intending to put down the wooden walkway that would cross the top marshy area and perhaps, if there was time, the small bridge that was to go over the stream above the waterfall.

Apparently, everything was pre-cut and numbered, so I expected it really would be just like giant Lego to Charlie and they'd have it done in no time.

I left a space on a shelf for the glossy brochures, which were allegedly arriving the next day, and then I could do no more, so I went out, locking the door behind me.

I could hear the phone ringing away in the office again, but I felt I'd had enough of being a secretary and PA and went to join the others. By the time Charlie left late in the afternoon, the slats of the walkway had been screwed down into their supports and the bridge almost completed.

It wasn't really *worth* bridging a stream so narrow you could step across it without a stretch, but it looked pretty in a Monet's water garden kind of way and would lead people to the gazebo . . . when we'd put that together, too.

After finishing the bridge and exhausting his Sonic Screwdriver, Ned and I began sorting through the pots of damp-loving plants that lined the nearby gravel path – marshmallow, chervil, milk thistle, meadowsweet and more – and moving them into position before digging them in.

We worked in happy and mostly silent amity until the sun dipped below the encircling hills and, as Shakespeare didn't quite phrase it, all the birds bogged off back to the rooky woods for the night.

Ned's spade stopped moving suddenly and he exclaimed: 'It's Tuesday!'

'Is it really? You amaze me,' I said. 'You'll be telling me next that it's April.'

'No, I meant, if it's Tuesday, then it's the Friends of Jericho's End meeting in the Village Hut at seven.'

I checked my slightly earthy watch. 'You've still got enough time to clean yourself up and eat something, first.'

'I do if I get a bit of a shift on. You should come, too,' he suggested. 'I'm surprised Elf hasn't already roped you in.'

'I think she did mention the meetings, but I've only just got here, so I've hardly been absorbed into the community yet.'

'The quiz was a good start – everyone knows who you are now – and Elf's always looking for new blood.'

'So it's a society of vampires?'

'Ho, ho,' he said. 'Nothing so exciting. It's run by Elf and Gerald and they arrange the regular events, like the Annual Fête, the Christmas pantomime and the Easter egg hunt, which is the next thing coming up. There are occasional litter-picking days, too, when most of the village turns out.'

'That doesn't sound too taxing. What other things do they do there?' I asked, curiously.

'Well, there's the book group once a month, and occasional talks, and a jumble sale. Oh, and a mother and toddler group meets one morning a week.'

'I was wrong, it's a positive riot of dissipation. When do you have the Easter egg hunt?'

'Sunday morning at eleven, but the Easter Bunny goes out early and leaves chocolate eggs under all the bushes in the ground round the Hut. In fact, you can *be* the Easter Bunny, if you like.'

'No thank you, I've never fancied the floppy ears and fluffy tail look. Anyway, I'll be working.'

'It's a Sunday,' he pointed out. 'You don't have to.'

'Don't be daft. Like today, I'll be there whether you pay me or not. We'll need to do a lot of our work in the mornings in future, too, once we open to the public, won't we?'

'It would certainly be easier to trundle barrows up and down and that kind of thing without the visitors on the paths,' Ned agreed. 'And thanks – but I'll pay you for any overtime.'

'How about I give you my time free this Sunday and we see how busy the garden is and whether an extra pair of hands is needed?'

'OK – thanks. Though actually, it's amazing how much work you've already done. You just set to and get on with it, like I do, without being told. It's almost as good as having two of *me*.'

'Gee, thanks,' I said. 'Hadn't you better get going, if you don't want to miss the meeting?'

As we headed back to put our tools away, I asked curiously, 'Who else goes to these Friends meetings besides you, Elf and Gerald?'

'Sometimes Myfy and Jacob . . . and Gert, James and Steve, of course. The vicar, if she can make it . . .' He frowned. 'I've missed someone out . . . Oh, yes, Cress comes, too. The first Lordly-Grace to take any interest in village affairs for centuries.'

'That sounds almost irresistible, but I think I'll pass,' I told him.

But then, not five minutes later, Elf accosted me as I made for the stairs to the flat and, after thrusting a box of blueberry ice-cream into my still somewhat grubby hands, insisted I join them at the FOJE meeting that evening.

'We need more young blood.'

'Yes, Ned said much the same – but I'm not *that* young,' I protested, but she simply smiled and said she'd see me there at seven, and it would be fun.

And you know, it *was* fun, even if I did somehow find myself agreeing to don a fluffy all-in-one rabbit suit and hide the chocolate eggs on Sunday.

I woke next morning after a nightmare in which I was buried in a strangely warm avalanche, only to find Caspar lying on my chest with his head tucked under my chin. He is one heavy cat, but when I pushed him off, he seemed to take it as a gesture of affection and just lay there next to me with his paws in the air, purring loudly.

It was not quite light yet and I lay there thinking about yesterday and especially the Friends of Jericho's End meeting.

Cress had arrived last, flustered and apologizing. 'Mummy got terribly cross and upset while I was out at the riding school this afternoon! Wayne turned up unexpectedly and when Mummy went out to see what he was doing, he called her Auntie Audrey and was very familiar!'

'*Auntie Audrey?*' repeated Gerald, rather blankly.

'He said he'd been reading your book, Elf, and now he knew he was related to the Lordly-Graces. Of course, Mummy knows about that ancient scandal, but it was yonks ago and I mean, it's *history*! Of course, Mummy was furious and gave him a good telling-off *and* fired him, so now I'm going to have to persuade her to let him come back, because there isn't anyone else to do the garden.'

Her large and beautiful light grey eyes rested on me and she brightened. 'Unless you, Marnie, could—'

'Marnie's got her hands full with the Grace Garden already,' Ned interrupted firmly.

'It'll have to be Wayne again, then,' she said gloomily.

'Of course there is a whole chapter on the old scandal in the book,' Elf said. 'But I'd have thought the Vanes would have known all about it already.'

'I expect they expunged her name from the family Bible and never spoke of her again, after she ran off,' suggested Myfy. 'Wayne probably had no idea.'

'Have you read that bit, dear?' Elf asked me, and I nodded.

'Yes – the young Vane girl who was a servant at Risings running off with the younger son of the family.'

'Then being cast off by both her own family and the Lordly-Graces, when she came back pregnant after her lover was killed,' Myfy finished. 'Like a Victorian morality tale, though this one took place in the early Regency.'

'*And* had a happier ending, because Richard Grace took her in, then eventually married her and adopted the child, a boy, as his heir.'

'When you think that that makes the Vanes very distantly related to *me*, too, it sort of takes the edge off the romance,' said Ned.

'It's all too long ago to be worth bothering about,' Elf said. 'Now he's found out about it, Wayne's just making mischief, as usual.'

'He'd better not try calling me "Cousin Ned" or anything like that, or he'll be sorry,' he said grimly.

I thought it was a pity someone had told Wayne his family were mentioned in Elf's book. He'd seemed over-interested in the idea of hidden treasure, too.

But Cress was now asking us what charity the money raised by the Easter egg hunt would go to this year and we'd moved on.

And I *still* didn't know how I'd been roped in to don that damned bunny suit!

But I couldn't lie there in bed any longer, because it was now getting light and I wanted to make an early start on the top of the rose garden . . . though first, somehow, I found my feet taking me to the little folly, instead.

It was very pleasant, sitting on the steps with the early sunshine reaching in to run a Midas finger around the top of the marble urn. A blackbird was singing sweetly and a robin sat companionably on a nearby branch, watching me with bright, dark eyes that reminded me of Elf. I mentally gave it a turquoise wig, then grinned: I didn't think that one would make the cut for a Christmas card.

When I finally got up, my bottom somewhat chilled and numb from the marble step, and went to fetch my tools, I met Ned in the courtyard, firmly closing the office door behind him on a loudly ringing phone.

'*There* you are!' he said, as if I'd been having a long lie-in and it was now midday. 'James and Gert are already here.'

'They're in early,' I said and then added, pointedly, 'And so am I!'

But it went over his head, because he continued, 'James is in the Potting Shed, working on the new plant stand, and Gert said something about neglecting her vegetables and wanting to pot up more seedlings for the shop.'

'I can see you have your staff under firm control,' I said, and he gave me a blank look, before suddenly grinning.

'I've got something I want you to do before you get back to the roses,' he said. 'And when Charlie gets here I need him to help me put in the rest of the signboards.'

'I think you'll probably need a Private sign in front of the office, too,' I said. 'People are bound to try and look in.'

'Maybe I should have a row of pots along the front to keep them at a distance.'

'I suspect you've ordered enough scented geraniums to fill a hundred pots and several stone troughs, once James has potted them up and grown them on.'

'That'll take time, though. I need a quicker fix.'

'More of those stands with ropes hung between them, then?' I suggested.

'Good idea – we've got plenty of them. In fact, we could rope off the whole corner, from the end of my office to the other side of the Potting Shed door, because none of that is open to the public. We can add the potted plants to pretty it up later.'

The job Ned wanted me to do first was to put in more of the water-loving plants around the waterfall and in the bed on the far side of the stream above it.

When I'd run out of things to plant, Gertie, who was passing, roped me in to help her with the small central herb garden. She'd brought out some she'd been growing on and my task was to put them in the beds as directed: three kinds of thyme and several of mint, though we'd have to keep an eye on that, to make sure it didn't try to take over the whole garden.

It certainly seemed to be all hands on deck that morning, for when I finally made my escape, even Steve had arrived, presumably having opened up the monastic ruins and the convenient conveniences, and was doing a little desultory hoeing and weeding along the borders, where the first fresh weeds of the year were sticking their green fingers through the loam. Mind you, in the opinion of most gardeners, many of the things we were actually nurturing here were weeds – but then, as they say, a weed is just a plant in the wrong place.

I said as much later to Ned in the rose garden, when he came to see how I was doing.

'Elf told me last year that the best nettles for brewing her beer came from either side of the wall at the end of Gert's vegetable patch, so I told her I'd leave them there for her to pick. I should have some around the place anyway, even though I don't want them in the actual garden, because they do have some medicinal qualities.'

'I've heard of nettle tea,' I said, 'though I'm not sure what it does for you.'

'I'm starting to think I should have kept that rhubarb in the vegetable garden too, because whatever Gert is feeding it on, it's getting ginormous.'

It was easy to guess what was making it grow so much, because Gert had several ripe and fruity-smelling compost heaps at various stages, which she lavished with loving care.

'I could put in some different kinds of lavender,' Ned mused. 'That has lots of uses too, including protecting against the plague.'

'Do you get a lot of that in Jericho's End?'

'No, and the Black Death missed us out entirely,' he said. 'I'd better go back and see how Charlie's doing. We finished with the signboards and I left him in the barn, unpacking the pieces of the gazebo. We're not putting it up yet; I just needed to be sure it was all there.'

That sounded like more hours of harmless fun later on.

I returned to my endless rose pruning, trying to finish off the small top part of the garden.

The paths were nicely cleared, the roses neatly pruned of dead wood and leggy, unwanted suckers. I just needed to do a little more, then clean the beds so they could be fed and mulched.

There was a honeysuckle hidden behind the rose in the top corner, perhaps seeded from the one in the lavender garden, the stems twined around the railings: survival of the twistiest.

It was twisting round some of the nearest roses, too, but once I'd pruned those enough to get at it, I soon had it cut back to size. The flowers would be pretty, and the bees would like them, though they'd be permanently drunk on lavender and roses once everything started to bloom.

Charlie came to fetch me for a late lunch and we all ate sociably together in the Potting Shed, Ned and Charlie perching on one of the workbenches and me on an upturned wooden crate. Gertie had brought enough food for ten people as usual, but it seemed that Charlie had the sort of appetite that could hoover up any amount of sandwiches and rib-sticking lardy cake.

She said to him approvingly that he was a proper lad.

After the last of the treacly tea was drunk, plans were made for what was left of the afternoon.

Steve went off to clean up the Village Hut after the onslaught of that morning's mother and toddler session and Gert and Charlie intended digging in the last of the plant consignment. James was waiting for the undercoat to dry on the metal parts of the old garden barrow and said he was going round with the latest batch of refurbished metal plant tags and replacing the temporary plastic ones with them.

'Busy, busy, busy,' Ned said. 'And I'm off to Great Mumming to pick out half a dozen tree-sized pots at Terrapotter. It's a fascinating place, Marnie, and I'd suggest you came with me, but Lex – my friend who owns it – isn't there today and anyway, a good look round would take too long.'

'I'd need to be back in time to check the River Walk, anyway,' I said regretfully. 'I'd love to see it when there's more time, though.'

'Lex learned how to make those really huge terracotta pots abroad, after he left college, mostly in Greece,' Ned said. 'A friend helps him. It's a two-man job for the whoppers.'

'I should think it is,' I said.

'You'd like Lex. He's just married a portrait painter called Meg Harkness. Myfy says she's brilliant, but I haven't met her yet. I haven't been socializing that much outside the valley since I came back.'

'Will they have what you want in stock, or make them specially?' asked Charlie, interested.

'I rang Lex the other day and he said he had some that I might like in the storeroom – they make straight reproductions of early pots, and also ones that are in traditional shapes, but with a *very* untraditional twist. I quite fancy the idea of those in the Grace Garden – old and new combined in one pot.'

I wished more than ever that I could go and see Terrapotter, but duty called. I got off my box, my bottom probably neatly patterned by the slats. 'I'll get back to my roses. At this rate, we should be able to let the visitors loose in there in another couple of days.'

*

As I pruned, snipped and raked, I found myself singing an old song that Aunt Em often warbled as she worked in the World Garden at the Château du Monde, her own particular pet project. I think it was called 'An English Country Garden' and was all about the various kinds of flowers you'd once have found there. I couldn't remember all the words – I'd google it later . . .

'Hollyhocks and something else, something else and—'

I was still singing when Ned returned, though by then I had stopped work and was regarding my handiwork complacently: the rose beds in front of the walls were entirely pruned, the soil raked over, a tilted edging tile straightened and a hole dug, ready for a replacement rose. All it needed now (other than the mulch) were the original name tags putting back, and I expected the Name Tag Fairy would be along as soon as he'd finished them.

'Ah, my little songbird is still here,' said Ned, breaking into my reverie.

'Are you back already?' I demanded, surprised.

'It's gone four,' he pointed out. 'This all looks great. Are you still keeping that list of roses we need to source where they've given up the ghost?'

'Of course I am. I've got about half a dozen. There might be more later, but I want to give some of the ropy-looking ones a chance to bounce back. Roses are amazingly resilient sometimes.'

Then suddenly, what he'd said about the time struck me and I said, 'I must go and check the River Walk!'

'Leave the bags full of prunings and I'll take those down to the compost heap in the morning,' he said, and we walked back together to the Potting Shed to clean and put away the tools I'd been using.

Gertie and James were just leaving for home, though Charlie had dashed off earlier. But then, as Gertie said, he was only of use in a garden if there was someone there to tell him what to do.

'He doesn't know a dandelion from a dahlia, but he's cheerful and willing.'

'He seemed to like the Poison Corner,' I said. 'He calls it the Triangle of Death.'

'He's still such a boy,' she said indulgently.

I thought Ned might vanish into his office, but instead he ignored the eternally ringing phone and said he'd walk up the river with me.

'I need the exercise.'

'Gardeners get exercise all day,' I pointed out.

'You know what I mean – a good walk is different.'

I did know and, after collecting the stick and bag, we set off together. It was much later than usual and the last of the visitors had long since vanished. Dark shadows lay across the path like splashes of ink and, for once, I felt glad of the company.

23

Celestial

'You didn't mind my coming with you, did you?' Ned asked after a few minutes of silent walking.

'No, not at all, though I have been up to the falls at dawn when I *did* want to be alone. Anyway, I'd have told you straight out if I didn't want you to come.'

'So you would,' he agreed. 'Were you communing with the angels, or fairies, or whatever hangs out up here?'

His voice didn't sound teasing, but quite serious and then he added reminiscently, 'Dawn's a good time of day to do that – I often did when I was staying here with my uncle and aunt in the school holidays. Theo made me promise not to go near the edge, where the rock is slippery, but Aunt Wen just said that if something with wings tried to lure me through a door into the rock face, I should decline politely. I was pretty sure she was joking.'

'*Did* you ever see or hear anything . . . unusual, or hard to explain?'

He looked at me sideways, through those amber-brown lion's eyes. 'I sometimes *thought* I heard voices and faraway laughter. And once I was certain I'd caught sight of something . . .

winged.' He shrugged. 'When I looked properly, there was nothing there.'

'Yes, that's how I've felt too, and the impression of a presence and wings is very strong. It's nothing to do with birds, because they all seem to go still and silent when it happens. But you can't pin anything down; it could easily be imagination and the effect of light through the leaves and spray, couldn't it?'

'Quite possibly, but some places do have an aura about them, almost as if they were portals to another world, and this is one of them.'

'But if there *are* winged creatures,' I said, 'are they angels or fairies? I think Elf and Myfy are more of the angel persuasion.'

'Actually, they think fairies and angels are one and the same thing,' he said. 'Not the cutesy Cottingley type of fairy, but taller, feathery winged and looking like the angels flying about in the top of the stained-glass window in St Gabriel's church.'

'I really must see that when I have enough time. I should start making a list of all the things I want to do, if I ever have a day to myself. Perhaps the angels in the window impressed themselves on the imagination of that little girl in the old story, so that her imagination conjured up one here by the falls?'

'Or maybe she fell asleep and dreamed it all, but we'll never know. And the Victorians preferred their fairy folk dancing about, weaving flowers into crowns, or whatever harmless nonsense they could think of.'

'Some of the Victorian fairy books, especially the ones with the Rackham illustrations, were pretty scary, though,' I said doubtfully. 'Myfy's paintings in the café-gallery are a bit unsettling too, now I've had a closer look.'

'It's amazing how much you think you can see in her paintings that really isn't there at all,' he said. 'Much like the effect up here, by the falls.'

We'd lingered there a lot longer than I'd realized and when we set off back, it was hard to see any litter under the dark bushes, but I collected what I could.

Inside the gate to the lavender garden, Caspar was sitting by the sleeping beehives, waiting for us.

'Why aren't you in the kitchen, pestering Myfy or Elf for your dinner?' I asked him, and he made one of his enigmatic noises and ran off ahead of us up the crazy-paving path, his bushy tail up in the air.

'It must feel odd having a tail,' I mused, watching him. 'I mean, having to remember what to do with four legs must be hard enough, but then you have to think about what to do with your tail, too.'

'It must be odd to be Marnie Ellwood, even before she puts on her bunny tail,' he observed, taking the bag from me. 'You go in – you've done enough for the day – and I'll sort this rubbish out. I want to catch up in the office for a bit and then that's me for the day, too. Then there's only one more day before opening.'

'It'll all come together tomorrow,' I said encouragingly.

'I hope so. And since I seem to have been too preoccupied to buy supplies, I've now run out of anything interesting to eat, so I'll have to do a quick dash up to Toller's now, before they close. If you want me to fetch you anything, I can drop it off on my way back?'

On impulse, I said, 'I feel in need of good, solid carbs tonight, so I'm going to cook pasta – nothing fancy, just cheese and bottled tomatoes, a bit of garlic . . . And dessert will be either ice-cream or jelly babies. Why don't you join me?'

His lip twitched. 'The jelly babies make it sound almost irresistible.'

'I expect Caspar will have had his dinner and be back in the flat by the time it's cooked,' I said, as if offering a chaperon – and perhaps that was the clincher, because he agreed that pasta sounded just the thing *he* needed, too.

On Thursday I awoke filled with that feeling of unfounded optimism that often suddenly strikes me.

The previous night Ned and I had been relaxed and companionable over dinner, like the two old friends we were, despite our recent experiences having temporarily warped the picture.

We'd talked mostly about the garden, of course, our mutual obsession, and he showed me pictures on his phone of the pots he'd ordered from Terrapotter. They were huge and the shape reminded me of Ali Baba's jars, though there were swirls of applied seaweed fronds and barnacle-like decoration that made them look as if they'd just been dredged up from the Aegean Sea bed.

Four of them would be positioned on the circular path at the points where the diagonal ones met it, while the rest were to provide points of interest in the low beds at the side.

He said Lex Mariner would deliver them next week. 'I'll get some more later, when I've decided what I need: smaller ones on the path around the sunken herb bed, perhaps.'

'Good idea, because then you could move the mint into them, stopping it trying to escape from its bed and making room for other herbs,' I suggested.

'I think Gertie would like that idea, and I could use pots to hold a few more invasive things I'd like to have in the garden, but don't want to plant out.'

After we'd eaten Ned admired my collection of old French and English gardening books and also the butter paddles, which I'd arranged in a cross shape on top of one of the shelf units. He knew what they were, too, he'd just never seen any quite that size.

'And don't I remember you mentioning them before?' he asked, brows knitted over his long, blunt nose, so he looked like a very puzzled lion.

'I might have done,' I admitted. 'It's sort of a running theme in my imagination.' And I told him about Jean, the irascible old gardener at the last château I'd worked at, with the face like an elderly Gérard Depardieu that had been clapped between two large butter paddles – and how sometimes I'd have quite liked to have done that to him myself.

'I'll have to watch my step!' Ned said, but in a teasing way, not as if he thought I was barking. Though actually, a desire to slap people's heads between butter paddles might not be entirely a normal one.

I think I'd imagined there had been just a faint trace of hesitation before he'd accepted my invitation to dinner, because we'd put all that behind us now. Just as well, really, because Caspar was a useless chaperon. He was disgruntled because he wanted all my attention – preferably while lying across my lap.

Instead, I sat at the table for ages with Ned, then made coffee, before we looked up on the laptop the words to that 'English Country Garden' song that had lodged in my head.

When we found someone actually singing it on YouTube, Caspar gave up in disgust and went to sleep on my bed.

Ned didn't stay late, because it suddenly hit him again that the garden would be opening only the day after tomorrow! From being relaxed and chilled, the weight of the world instantly fell again across his (admittedly broad) shoulders.

But I was sure he'd feel better tomorrow. I gave him the remains of the bag of jelly babies we'd been sharing to take back with him, suggesting he save them for the morning, to keep his blood sugar high.

However, either he forgot to eat them, or it didn't work, because he was inclined to be a bit terse and bossy again next morning, handing out orders to his troops . . . or to me, Gertie and James, who were the only ones there that early. We all understood that it was just the pressure of the rapidly approaching opening day making him tense, though, and hoped the more laid-back and easy-going Ned would re-emerge after that.

My first job of the day was to clean off the brick paths in the rose garden, especially the one round the fish pond, using lots of water, a stiff yard brush and elbow grease, so I was hot and sweaty when I took the bucket and brush back. In my absence, the garden had turned into a hive of activity: the gravel paths were being raked by Charlie, the borders hoed by Steve, Ned was placing the freestanding posts and ropes at the side of the paths that would be closed off tomorrow and even Jacob was there, putting up the information board that had been missing from the original consignment.

In the courtyard, the freshly washed windows and paintwork of the outbuildings gleamed. James had finished the flat bed barrow and it now stood next to the display stand near the shop door, where Gertie was arranging on it the serried ranks of potted plants that would be for sale.

She'd stuck handwritten descriptions on the pots and was about to price-sticker them . . . when she and James had finished arguing about what price they should charge.

'Let's have a tea break and decide afterwards,' Gertie suggested, and I went to fill the kettle while she called the others.

Ned, who had a huge new list of things that had to be done

today, none of them tea breaks, didn't answer the summons, but Gertie made him come and have lunch with us later.

Steve had been sent to the Hut on an errand by Gertie and returned bearing a huge bundle of bunting, most of it printed with faded Union Jacks. It must have been left over from the Coronation, or something like that, though there were also a couple of long rolls of newer and brighter bunting made from cotton triangles in vivid colours.

'We keep it in the storage room at the Hut and use it for all the fêtes and celebrations,' Gert explained. 'It'll be just the thing in the courtyard to brighten it up for the ceremony.'

Ned was a bit dubious, but once it was draped around the courtyard and fluttering in the slight breeze, it did look very festive.

Steve and Ned moved two tall, thin, Italian cypress trees in pots to stand on either side of the archway leading into the garden and then stood back to admire the effect.

'I think . . . we're almost ready,' Ned said, sounding surprised. 'Or as ready as we'll ever be!'

He crossed something off the bottom of the list on his clipboard, probably: 'Move cypress trees'.

'Yes . . . unless I think of anything else. Elf and Myfy will bring Clara Mayhem Doome through to the office at about half past eleven tomorrow, so she's ready on the spot for the opening. James, we'd better put the float into the shop till before then and you can get yourself ready to open.'

'You've got the change all bagged up, so that won't take a mo,' James agreed. 'It's just putting it in the till and opening the ticket hatch.'

'Good – and I've put the boxes of glossy brochures, which have arrived at last, in the shop, so those need to go out on the shelves.'

'Then I open the gate at twelve,' Steve said.

'Yes, though there might be someone coming to film the opening ceremony and a local journalist or two, so you can let them in early.'

'Right you are,' said Steve.

'When everyone has gathered in the courtyard,' Ned said, 'Clara will come out of the office and say a few words, before cutting the ribbon and declaring the garden open.'

'Which ribbon?' I asked.

There was a small silence before Ned said: 'The one I haven't got. I knew I'd forgotten something! Where can I get several metres of wide ribbon before tomorrow? And how am I going to fix it up, ready to cut?'

'There's a lot more than that on the big spool of yellow satin ribbon left over from when I brightened up Widow Twankey's dress for last year's panto,' Gertie said. 'Don't you remember? We covered an old dress from the storage room in yellow ruffles.'

'It *was* fairly unforgettable,' Ned agreed. 'Especially since Jacob was wearing it. I didn't know there was any ribbon left, though.'

'Tons,' Gertie said, and Steve was sent back to the Hut to fetch it. It was a very lurid saffron colour, which would stand out well.

'You don't have to fix it to the wall, you can just tie it loosely round the tops of the cypress trees on either side,' Charlie suddenly suggested, so we tried that and it seemed to work well.

Ned wound it up again. 'I'd better put it in the office tonight, in case it rains and we can drape it across last thing tomorrow morning once Clara's arrived.'

'Then all we have to do is remember the big pair of scissors from your office,' I said. 'They're very shiny and new.'

'The forecast's good for the whole weekend, if they've got it right,' James said.

'That'll bring even more visitors out,' Charlie said. 'But I don't think you'll really need me any more after today, so I've promised to help out in the café over the weekend, and then that's it for work. I'll be a volunteer on the archaeological dig from Tuesday.'

'I think you'll find that's work, too – quite hard work,' Ned pointed out.

'Yes, but not paid,' Charlie said. 'Well, I'll get off now if you don't want me for anything else.'

'And I must go and check the River Walk,' I said. 'I'll come back afterwards, just to see if there's anything last minute that wants doing, though, Ned,' I promised, before I went.

But when I returned, he was alone in the courtyard, looking bemusedly at a metal sculpture of a galleon on a white wooden plinth.

'Where did that come from?' I asked, then guessed as I came nearer and realized that the effect of a ship in full sail had been cleverly constructed from bits of curved and wavy scrap metal, welded together. 'Did Jacob make it? It doesn't move, does it?'

'No, it's static and it is a present from Jacob and Myfy. They remembered you mentioning we could do with a donations box at Sunday dinner and Jacob whipped this one up out of bits of odds and ends he had lying about. There's a coin slot on top of the wooden base.'

There was, too, and a little door in the back for emptying out the loot.

'It's lovely. It just needs a sign on it to encourage people to put money in.'

And when I'd popped into the office and carefully lettered

'Captain Nathaniel Grace's Collecting Box: help restore the Grace Gardens' on a bit of card, we stuck that on and then carried the ship into the shop.

'The finishing touch,' I said as we placed it in the middle of the floor.

'Captain Nathaniel seems to be taking over – and he wasn't even the one who began the garden!' Ned said.

'I know, but his descendants did, and everyone loves a pirate, especially children. We should order that range of promotional items for the shop with the galleon logo on, now, too.'

'You're probably right,' Ned admitted, and ran a nervous, exhausted hand through his hair, which made it stick out even more. 'That damned phone's ringing again, but I'm not answering any more calls tonight.'

For the first time, he seemed to become aware of my slightly shattered and dishevelled appearance.

'Look, Marnie, we're both tired – why don't we meet in the pub in an hour and I'll buy you dinner, in return for last night?'

'Sounds good to me,' I agreed, and I thought that once he'd got some food and a couple of pints of Gillyflower's Best Bitter inside him, the old enthusiastic and optimistic Ned would probably re-emerge.

24

Fêted

I think the food and beer, over which we slumped in exhausted but not unamicable silence, followed by an early night, must have done the trick for both of us. Next morning I woke up full of bounce and, although naturally a little tense, Ned was much more his usual self again.

While he was pulling the rope barriers across the paths, I washed away a copious amount of peacock poop from right under the arch, where the ribbon was to be tied. It wouldn't exactly have created the look we wanted to achieve.

James, Gertie and Steve all arrived together later and had the shop ready to open long before the Clara Mayhem Doome party were escorted through the rose garden and up to the office by Myfy and Elf. At least I'd ensured they'd be offered decent coffee there!

Gerald and Jacob followed them, bearing the big, covered jugs of lemonade and paper cups, which they set on the small table to one side of the courtyard, next to Gert's lardy cake, while James looped the yellow ribbon across the archway.

I was interested by my first glimpse of Clara, who was a very tall, strongly built elderly woman, with a bold Roman nose, bright dark eyes and a lot of curling dark grey and silver hair. She was dressed in a long, quilted scarlet velvet coat that had a sort of Old Russian vibe going for it and her earrings were wooden matryoshka dolls. I'd seen photos of her on the book jackets, of course, but they didn't do the reality much justice – or reflect the impression that she was almost crackling with energy.

Gertie told me that the angular, middle-aged woman with short, pepper-and-salt hair who'd accompanied her was Tottie Gillyflower, last of the brewing family.

'Friend of Elf's and runs the Thorstane Bee Group,' she added.

When Steve opened the visitor gate briefly, to let in the TV cameraman and a businesslike-looking young woman who might as well have had 'Reporter' stamped on her forehead, I could see visitors queuing outside.

I moved back behind Gertie, out of sight of any filming. Gertie was humming that 'Tie a Yellow Ribbon Round the Ole Oak Tree' song, though in this case it wasn't a person coming back, but a garden.

The sun shone with surprising warmth, the ribbon and all the bunting fluttered gaily, the cameraman placed himself for a good angle and Steve came out of the shop and swung open the entrance gate.

A steady stream of people flowed past the ticket window, until the courtyard was almost full and Lancelot, over-excitedly displaying himself on the Potting Shed roof, had had his photograph taken a thousand times.

Then everyone fell quiet as Clara, escorted by Ned, came out of the office. A path cleared like magic in front of her and she made her way to the allotted spot at one side of the arch.

I was glad to see that Ned had remembered the large pair of

scissors, which he now handed to her, before making a short speech welcoming everyone and hoping they would be as interested in the ongoing restoration of this important apothecary garden as he was.

'Now, I'm delighted to hand over to the renowned epigrapher and crime novelist, Clara Mayhem Doome,' he finished, and there was a lot of enthusiastic clapping.

'Our big local celebrity,' whispered Myfy in my ear, making me start, since I hadn't noticed her come up behind me. 'Opens everything within about a twenty-mile radius, so we all know her.'

Clara beamed at the audience, showing a lot of strong white teeth.

'This is a fascinating project and I hope you'll all continue to support it, by visiting again to see the progress they've made – *I* certainly will,' she said. Then, turning slightly so that the cameraman got a full view of her profile with that strong Roman nose, she added: 'It gives me great pleasure to declare the Grace Garden open.'

She snipped the yellow satin with a satisfying scrunch and stepped back as everyone clapped again.

Then there was a general surge forward through the arch into the garden – except for the journalist, who made a beeline for Clara.

The cameraman seemed to have vanished the moment he'd filmed the opening ceremony, which was a relief. Mind you, I thought they probably wouldn't use any of the footage they'd shot in the garden at all if something more important or interesting turned up. It was very much in the nature of a quirky filler.

A few bold autograph seekers presented themselves, too, but were elbowed out of the way by a woman with an enormous bust atop a thin body and skinny legs under a too-short skirt. When she reached the front, she held out her hand.

'We meet again, Professor Mayhem Doome,' she said with an ingratiating social smile. 'I'm Audrey Lordly-Grace, you know?' Clara looked blankly at her and she added, 'Surely you remember me? We met last year, when you opened the new community centre in Great Mumming and—'

'Oh, did we?' Clara said vaguely. 'Is attending openings your hobby?'

'My *hobby*? No, of course not! I—'

But at this point, the impatient queue of fans behind her, some of whom had brought copies of Clara's latest novel for her to sign, jostled her out of the way.

She stood undecidedly on the edge of the group, looking disgruntled and affronted, then finally turned and tottered off through the arch on stilt-like stiletto heels. The gravel wouldn't do them a lot of good.

I'd spotted Treena and Luke during the speech, as well as lots of other familiar faces from the village. Cress had been there too, though she hadn't waited for her mother, but instead vanished with the rest of the crowd into the garden.

'A good turnout,' said Tottie Gillyflower to Ned.

'Yes, and they're still coming in,' he agreed.

'Of course they are, it's going to be a *huge* success,' Clara said, disposing of the last book offered to her with a flourish and handing it back. 'There we are, duty done and now you can show me round this garden of yours, Ned. Henry is going to slip in quietly later for a look – you know how he hates crowds.'

I supposed she meant her famous poet husband, Henry Doome. The local community seemed rife with celebrities – real ones, who'd actually done something meaningful, not TV reality show stars.

We were all still gathered around her, but now suddenly recalled where we should be and the group broke up. Elf went back to the café and Gert into the garden to keep, as she explained, an eye on what the visitors were up to.

'You can't trust any gardeners among them. It'll be out with the snippers and a plastic bag and away with a cutting or even a small plant, if you don't watch them,' she said darkly.

Lacking their audience, Lancelot and Guinevere jumped down from the roof and followed the official party into the garden, while I removed the pieces of yellow ribbon, coiled it up and put it in the Potting Shed. Then I took James and Steve a cup of tea each and found that, oddly, some people had made a beeline for the plants for sale before even seeing the garden, and their selections were being put to one side by Steve, for collection as they left.

James and Steve were glad of the tea and said they'd take it in turns to go and have a sandwich later, unless it was too busy, in which case one of them would fetch some over.

'I'm going to take mine with me now. I thought I'd go and have a good session on the roses in the central beds at the back of the garden. They're the last ones that need pruning, really; most of the rest are done. Then just a few beds to rake and we can feed and mulch.'

'If that's going to be with Gert's special five-year-rotted manure compost, maybe do it on a day we're closed,' suggested James.

But before I went back to work, I simply couldn't resist a quick walk round the garden to see how it was all going, which seemed to be very well. Groups of people were reading the information boards or wandering round the paths, Jacob's flowers were drawing a crowd of fascinated visitors and Gertie was near the Poison Garden, keeping an eye on one or two small children whose parents barely seemed in control of them, despite the warnings on the leaflet they'd been given, the information board in front of them and the skull and crossbones on the gate.

'Some of these parents are so daft, we might need a moat full of piranhas round the Poison Garden, too,' Gert muttered darkly to me, as I passed.

Over the usually quiet garden hung a bee-like buzz of conversation and although it still felt magical, like all walled gardens, it had lost its air of secrecy.

Ned, who was taking Clara round, was waving his arms about excitedly and his amber eyes were glowing as he enthused about his plans for the garden. I'm sure he had, as usual, entirely forgotten who he was talking to.

I bumped into Treena and Cress as I finally headed back and Cress asked me slightly despairingly if I'd seen her mother in the courtyard.

'She would insist on going to talk to Professor Mayhem Doome, so I slipped away.'

'Does she like gardens?' I asked.

Cress sighed. 'No, but she insisted on coming, because she wanted to invite the Doomes to dinner, or bridge . . . or really, anything at all they'd agree to come to. She'd like to be in their circle, though they're not remotely on the same wavelength.'

'I think she *was* trying to talk to Clara, but got elbowed out by the autograph hunters,' I said.

'Yes, we did see her after that and she was very cross about it. She also said the gravel had ruined her heels and she was going home.'

Cress turned and smiled at a man who was standing nearby and introduced him to me as Roddy Lightower. He looked a few years older than Cress, but was handsome in a thin-faced, horsy kind of way. I could see he would appeal to her.

'Roddy, this is the new gardener, Marnie Ellwood. Roddy and I used to know each other as children; we rode our ponies together,' Cress said, faintly pink and glowing. 'He's taken early retirement and bought a house on the other side of Thorstane – and he's going to volunteer to help in the garden.'

'Great,' I said. 'There's a married couple who emailed about volunteering too, so the more the merrier. I expect they're here somewhere.'

'I won't be up to hard manual work,' Roddy explained apologetically, 'but I'm a historian and a keen gardener, so perhaps I could be a guide and take tours around, something like that.'

'That would be great, because Ned's really the only one who can do it at the moment and he'd rather garden,' I said.

'What about yourself?' he asked.

'Oh, I'd hate it. I'm just a gardener.'

'Well, I'd enjoy it and I could do office work too, anything like that.'

'You know, you really are *exactly* what Ned needs,' I told him.

From the way Cress was looking at him, he might be exactly what she needed, too. Ned had a rival for her affections!

'I'll try to have a word with him before I go,' Roddy said. 'I'm hoping Cress will have enough time to spare to join me for a late bread and cheese lunch at the pub.'

Cress went even pinker, if possible, and said she'd love to. Treena and I looked at each other, and she winked.

'I should really go home and smooth Mummy down a bit. She ran into Wayne and his father right after she'd tried to speak to Professor Mayhem Doome, so that didn't help, after he cheeked her the other day.'

'Wayne and his father are here?' I exclaimed.

'Yes – it surprised me that they'd paid to see the garden. I mean, Wayne used to work here and Saul's not one to part with his money for something like this.'

'That *is* odd,' Treena said. 'Perhaps curiosity was just too much for them.'

I didn't much feel like another one-to-one with Wayne, though a glimpse of his father would be interesting . . . my uncle.

But I was sure I'd have other opportunities, so when Luke appeared and it looked like the four of them were heading to the pub together, I left them and went back to the Potting Shed for my tools.

A working gardener is just so much wallpaper to visitors, as I'd learned while working for the Heritage Homes Trust, so I wasn't surprised no one took any notice of me as I unhooked the rope on one side of the path by the pond in the rose garden, pushed the barrow through and turned to replace it.

'There she is, Dad!' said the all-too-familiar voice of Wayne Vane. '*That's* the girl I was telling you about.'

Lizzie

I was born at Cross Ways Farm, on the furthest outskirts of the village of Jericho's End, in 1794, the last of twelve children and, as such, neither welcomed nor wanted.

Being small and puny, I was considered by my father to be the weakest of the litter, besides having committed the sin of being female. I suspect he would have preferred to drown me in a bucket of water soon after birth, like an unwanted kitten, but since he was an Elder in that strict religious sect called the Strange Brethren, who believed in completely immersing a baby in a deep font of icy water at baptism, I expect he thought this would carry me off, without his assistance.

I was given the name of Elizabeth, though always known as Lizzie. Since our farm was situated some way outside the village, I had no playmates among the local children – indeed, I had little idea of play, for my father considered that the Devil would find occupation for idle hands, so that toil from dawn to dusk was the only way to avert this.

One of the main tenets of the Brethren's faith seemed to be that all ills stemmed from the Daughters of Eve and thus her female descendants should be made to suffer for it in perpetuity.

Unlike my tall, strapping and red-haired siblings, I remained small and delicate, and my hair a dark chestnut colour. I had been so confidently expected to rid the world of my presence due to some illness before I reached my fifth birthday that I think it came as a surprise to everyone to find me still there. However, I survived and, being deemed fit for nothing else, almost as soon as I could walk was given charge of feeding the hens and collecting the eggs.

25

Relatively Speaking

The man who had walked into the rose garden with Wayne was not unhandsome, if you liked the elderly St John the Baptist look. As well as the head of a slightly mad prophet, he had a huge barrel of a torso and very short legs. He somehow reminded me of the Minotaur in the maze, possibly because there was something bullish about his stance as he drew closer and then stood, looking me over.

I took an involuntary step back, behind the frail barrier of the twisted rope.

'Dunno why you wanted to see her, anyway, Dad,' said Wayne, hovering at his elbow. 'I know I said she looked kind of familiar, but foreign with it, so I'd have remembered her if I'd seen her before, wouldn't I?'

'You shut your mouth, boy,' Saul Vane growled menacingly, like the teddy bear from hell. Wayne flinched, as if his father might actually smite him one, but Saul's attention was now all on me and my throat went dry.

Could he possibly have even the faintest suspicion of my identity? But if not, why this interest in me?

I didn't see how he *could* know and, though I knew him to

be Mum's older brother, I felt no sense of connection between us, any more than I did with Wayne. They were an alien species and it was hard to accept that my vibrant, clever and lovely mother was related to them.

Not, of course, that I was expecting instant rapport, after the way they had disowned Mum.

'What's your name, lass?' Saul barked at me.

'I told you, Dad, it's Marnie—' began Wayne.

'Shut it,' his father said succinctly and Wayne backed away.

'It's Marianne Ellwood, and you must be Wayne's father, Saul Vane,' I said, facing up to him. 'People have told me about you.'

'What they been saying?' he snapped out.

'That you breed the best pigs in the county,' I said.

He gave me another long, cold, searching look from grey-blue eyes that were the same colour as mine, though without the dark-ringed iris. 'That I do – and built the organic pig side of the farm up from nowt to what it is today.'

'Brilliant,' I said, trying to infuse some enthusiasm into my voice, but thinking it was all getting a bit too *Cold Comfort Farm* and, any moment now, he'd tell me he'd been scranletting his mangelwurzels, or something.

'Yes, *pigs*,' he said, with a depth of meaning I couldn't understand. 'You'd best bear that in mind, if you were thinking of coming calling.'

Wayne was looking as baffled as I felt – and I *still* wasn't sure if Saul was always like this, or really did have some suspicion about who I was, despite my being so dark and looking nothing like a Vane. He'd certainly had some reason for searching me out . . .

The crazy voice in my head chose this moment to start singing 'There is nothing like a Vane' to the tune of a song from an old musical.

'Well, it's been lovely chatting to you, but I must get back to work,' I said, summoning a brisk smile and starting to turn away.

'Not before you tell me, lass—' Saul began, his hand reaching out as if he meant to grip my arm and keep me there, except by then I'd grabbed the wheelbarrow handles and was off.

I heard Wayne say timidly, 'Best come away, Dad. There's people looking at us,' and I glanced over my shoulder, half-expecting Saul to have followed me, but he was still standing there, staring.

Then, in a low, carrying hiss that raised the hairs on the back of my neck, he said, 'You stay away from me and mine, if you know what's good for you.'

He stomped off, his son hurrying in his wake.

I escaped round the corner, out of sight of visitors, and sat on the marble bench in the temple, feeling shaky.

I went over everything he'd said and it seemed clear that something Wayne had told him had made him suspect who I was – but he couldn't know for *sure*. That warning must have been to prevent me from attempting to claim any relationship to him, if he was right. Not that anyone in their right mind would want to, of course.

But then, suddenly, an alternative and almost as disagreeable explanation for the scene struck me: Wayne had obviously talked about me a lot, so what if his father thought he was romantically interested in me and I'd encouraged him, because I knew he was the son of a wealthy pig farmer?

That scenario would fit his warnings, just as well as the other did – or perhaps, I thought, hopefully, he carried on like that all the time, especially to foreign-looking interlopers?

But whichever it was, he'd warned me off, so that was presumably the end of it. I began to feel a little calmer, and after a while I unwrapped the sandwiches and got my flask of coffee out of my rucksack.

I could hear the voices of the visitors from the other side of the big central rose bed – 'Great Maiden's Blush', according to its tag. Life was going on as if that disturbing little scene had never taken place.

I put away my flask and carried on preparing the beds for the mulching, until everything in the garden was rosy again.

When I took my barrow back to the Potting Shed later, I found Gert on her way out, but she changed her mind and came in with me for another cuppa.

'Only just had a bite to eat. We've been taking it in turns, so there's always a couple of people in the garden or shop,' she explained.

'You should have fetched me, so I could spell one of you.'

'That's all right, we managed fine, and after today I expect it'll all quieten down and be more steady, like.'

'It all seems to be going very well, though, doesn't it?' I said. 'It was practically standing room only in the garden just after we opened, and I see there are still visitors coming in.'

'It's what Ned needs, I understand that, but I like my garden to myself, really.'

'I know what you mean,' I said sympathetically, 'but you can always escape into the vegetable patch and the greenhouses on quieter days, can't you? I've worked in gardens open to the public before and the visitors don't seem to see the staff, so they don't get in the way of the work.'

'Ned said the same,' she admitted grudgingly. 'He says after this weekend me, you and him can carry on much as usual and leave the shop to Steve and James to sort between them. They're happy as pigs in muck, those two, playing shop.'

The pig reference was unfortunate, since it reminded me of Saul Vane. I told her that I'd run into him and Wayne in the rose garden and he'd ranted on a bit at me, then asked her, was he quite sane?

'He's surly and not much liked, is Saul, but shrewd as they come with the pig farming,' she said judiciously. 'He doesn't like foreigners and he's a bit too ready to tell anyone who looks as if they're enjoying themselves that they're sinners heading for hell. He found a courting couple on his land last summer,' she added. 'Backpackers, they were. He set the dogs on them and they're vicious brutes, those dogs, so there was quite a fuss about it.'

'He sounds delightful! I think I'll give Cross Ways Farm a wide berth,' I said, then changed the subject. 'Ned will *have* to give guided tours of the garden. When he was showing Clara round, loads of other visitors were hanging on every word.'

'I don't know . . . He says he's had enough of that kind of thing and just wants to work in the garden now,' she said doubtfully.

'I realize he doesn't want to be in the limelight any more, but once he gets going, he forgets he has an audience, he's so enthusiastic.'

Then I remembered Cress's friend Roddy Lightower, and told her about him and his offer to work in the garden as a volunteer. 'He sounded perfect, because he can take on a lot of the things Ned doesn't want to do, like the guided tours and office work.'

'A few volunteers would be a godsend,' Gertie agreed. 'There was a couple I was talking to who wanted to help in the garden, too. They're going to come back another day and I'll show them the vegetable patch then.'

I didn't think her vegetable patch was that high on Ned's list of things he'd like more help with, but I smiled encouragingly and said many hands made light work, and if they were free, that was even better.

'James heard someone asking Ned about a garden design, too,' Gertie said. 'So maybe he'll get more of those and he can go and hide in his office in the afternoons, when it all gets too much for him.'

She gave a grin and went off again, and I finished my tea and a large chunk of Bakewell tart (the lardy cake put out for the visitors had vanished down to the last crumb and the empty plate stood on the end of the nearest workbench), and went back to work, this time to tie up that honeysuckle I'd found and a vigorous rambling rose near the little temple.

And this time, no one took a bit of notice of me.

I still felt uneasy about my encounter with Saul Vane.

Ned and I were back on the old terms of trust and friendship, so what would he think if he found out I'd kept something like that a secret from him?

I really, *really* didn't want him to find out . . .

It was after four when I went back to the courtyard to put my tools away before setting off for the River Walk. The last stragglers were coming out of the shop, past the depleted plant stands, clutching their purchases. Steve was waiting by the gate to let them out and then lock it behind them.

And it must have been an equally busy day for the River Walk, for the litter bins were full to overflowing and my haul from under the bushes, or stuffed behind rocks, was three plastic bottles, two cans and a pair of socks, one with a large hole in it.

The last, faint echoes of chattering holidaymakers, screaming children and crying babies seemed still to linger and the only atmosphere detectable up by the falls was one of hope that silence and peace would fall upon it some time soon, if it held its breath . . .

The litter picking and sorting had taken longer than usual, and by the time I'd returned to the Grace Garden, the shop had been cashed up and closed and Ned was just returning from a circuit of the garden.

Apparently even in the Grace Garden itself, one or two chocolate bar wrappers had been planted among the herbs and an empty Coke bottle placed on the sundial.

Perhaps someone had given it a libation?

Everyone except Ned had long since gone and I accepted his suggestion that we have a cup of coffee in the office, because he was obviously dying to go over the whole afternoon in exhaustive detail.

But it was good to sit down for a bit and chill after the eventful day. I assured him everything had gone wonderfully well and we discussed the volunteers. Roddy had talked to him and, as I had expected, Ned was delighted at the prospect of unloading most of the jobs he didn't like onto him.

'And he's an old friend of Cress's, so I know he's OK,' he added. 'She was so pleased to see him again, she could hardly take her eyes off him!'

I had wondered if Ned was aware of Cress's blind adoration. I knew he was fond of her, but he didn't seem to mind her sudden switch of affections in the least!

'Well,' he said finally, putting down his cup, 'there's nothing more to do tonight, except feed the peacocks and the fish, so you get off now, Marnie, and I'll see you later at the pub for the quiz.'

I stared at him. 'It's *Good Friday* – they won't hold the quiz tonight, will they? Won't they be too busy?'

'They will be busy, but most of the visitors will be in the new bar, or the restaurant.'

'But . . . won't everyone be too tired to go, anyway? Elf must have been rushed off her feet in the café, too, and Gert, James and Steve must be exhausted!'

'Oh, I doubt it,' he said, surprised. 'In fact, Elf said earlier that she'd see me there. Cress has a full house of B&B guests, but they all arrived yesterday, so she'll be able to come. Her old nanny usually holds the fort in the evenings when she's out, anyway.'

'She has an old nanny?'

'The madwoman in the attic; every home should have one,' he said with a grin. 'She was Audrey's nanny, really, I think, and she's ancient, but she keeps a beady eye on things and rings Cress if anything crops up. The pub's only minutes from Risings, after all.'

With a mother like Audrey and a house full of guests, Cress was probably keen to sneak away whenever she could and I hoped she'd managed to have a nice, quiet lunch earlier, with Roddy, Treena and Luke.

Ned had been quite right: everyone seemed to be there for the quiz just as usual and, if many of us were tired, there was also a buzz of satisfaction that the café and garden, the pub, the guesthouses and the shops were doing such good business.

I'm not entirely sure we were all awake enough at our table to concentrate on the quiz, though, because we came third, and even that by the skin of our teeth.

Cress hadn't joined us this evening, but was sitting in a far corner at a small table with Roddy and, so far as I could see, took no part in the quiz at all . . .

Relaxed by a couple of halves of bitter shandy and a basket of scampi and chips, I'd almost managed to forget that strange little scene with Saul and Wayne, when the latter came into the bar, so late I was just thinking of going back to my flat and a peeved cat.

He looked his usual slightly shifty self, but grubbier, as if he'd been working since I saw him earlier. He cast one furtive glance in our direction, then took his pint of beer round the corner into the darts room, leaving me feeling unsettled all over again.

I walked back in the cool darkness with Ned, Myfy and Jacob.

Jacob was quiet – he'd spent most of the evening scribbling something in a small, battered sketchbook he'd pulled out of a pocket, so I assumed he was working out a new installation. I can't say any of it made sense, viewed upside down from the other side of the table.

Ned paused to say goodnight to me outside the café, while Jacob and Myfy wandered off, hand in hand, on their way up to the barn.

'Love's young dream,' Ned said with a smile, looking after them. 'Or undying dream: they were made for each other.'

The moon was silvering his mane of hair, ruffled as usual, but his eyes were dark shadowed pools.

'It's been a great day, Marnie, and having someone there with me who totally understands and shares how I feel about the Grace Garden made it even more special,' he said, looking down at me, and I heard the warmth in his voice and smiled up at him.

'It's wonderful to be part of it. I feel so lucky! The rose garden is going to be a little piece of Paradise, too, by the time we've finished with it. I want to stay here *for ever*!'

That last bit slipped out . . . leaving a space for my guilt at concealing I was a Vane to rush in and fill.

'I really hope you do, Marnie,' he said, his deep voice very serious. 'I've been surprised at how connected you feel to the village despite not having lived here for long. See you tomorrow.'

And he walked off before my sudden urge to Confess All and get it over with had quite formed into words.

I told Caspar instead, but he wasn't in the least impressed.

Lizzie

My sisters were already married, save one who was ill-natured and ill-favoured, though perhaps her nature had been soured by the lack of suitors and the realization that she was destined to be my mother's handmaid for ever. My brothers worked on the farm, or on other farms nearby, though one, Job, was gardener at the local big house, Risings, and lived in the lodge there. The age difference being such, they took little notice of me. My mother, harassed and worn down by constant work and childbearing, paid scant attention to me either, save to teach me my letters, so I could read the Bible, the only printed word in the house. She herself, being the daughter of a corn chandler in Thorstane, had been to Dame School, but there must have been precious little other call for her smattering of knowledge, once she married my father.

My experience of the world away from the farm was confined to Sundays, when the entire day was spent in Thorstane, at the meeting house of the Brethren, or the home of my mother's parents, who also belonged to this strict religious sect. This seemed quite normal to me at the time, of course.

There were many more Brethren then, and in bad weather my father would hold prayer meetings in the Red Barn on the farm, instead. It was even colder than the meeting house and no amount of threats that we would all burn in hell for our sins ever served to warm us.

26

Mr Mole

I woke early to what promised to be another warm, sunny spring day, but instead of heading up to the falls, or working in the lavender garden, I just pottered about the flat, playing with Caspar, until he vanished in search of his breakfast, and sat dreaming over mugs of coffee and a buttery croissant. They're not exactly the same as fresh French ones, when you microwave them straight from the freezer, but good enough.

The previous evening, Ned and I had grown even closer. We'd won through our initial misunderstandings to the friendship we'd once enjoyed and now were truly allied in a love of the garden and a desire not only to restore it, but to put our stamp on it.

He regarded me as both friend and ally . . . and yet, there was still this one secret I should have shared with him long before.

I finished my breakfast, put on my anorak and picked up my rucksack, ready to go – and with my mind made up. I'd *have* to tell Ned today, because the longer I left it, the worse it would be if he discovered it from someone else.

The koi were circling hungrily just under the water's surface when I passed the fish pond: Ned had usually fed them by now, but perhaps he'd been more tired than he admitted yesterday and was running late.

But no, when I turned into the courtyard there he was, waving his large fists about and turning the air blue, while the unfed peacocks skulked about his feet, unimpressed.

'What on earth's the matter, Ned?'

'*That!*' he said, dramatically pointing through the open gates to Old Grace Hall behind him and I saw at once that the usually immaculate small rectangle of lawn in front of the house was now pocked with large hillocks of dark earth.

'Moles?' I deduced automatically. 'They *have* been busy!'

'Not moles, unless they're giant ones who've learned to use spades,' he snapped. 'You can see the straight marks at the edge of the holes. This was *Mr* Mole – and I think we can both guess his real name – Wayne.'

I stared at him, cogs whirring and then, with a sinking feeling in my stomach, said, 'You think this was *Wayne*? But why – and when?'

'Must have been last night, while we were at the pub. He came in very late, if you remember. And as to why, I should imagine he was treasure hunting with that metal detector of his.'

'He looked muddy when he came into the pub, I noticed that,' I said slowly. 'And he *was* very interested in Nathaniel Grace's treasure . . . But I told him it wouldn't have been buried in the apothecary or rose gardens, because they were created after his time. So I suppose he thought this was the only place left to look where Nathaniel might have buried something.'

'He's mad – but I can't see who else it would be and I'm going to have it out with him, even if I haven't got any proof.

If I had, I'd call the police,' he added, still looking furious. 'No Vane is ever putting a foot on any of my property again!'

My earlier impulse to unburden my bosom on the subject of being closely related to Wayne and his family withered and died on the spot . . .

'How did he get in?' I asked.

'Must have been over the wall. He'd have ladders in his van anyway. He took a chance, though I suppose he knows I hardly ever miss a quiz night at the pub. Still, he won't be doing it again, because I'm going to fit security lights and a camera at the back of the house.'

'That's a good idea,' I agreed. 'Perhaps extend them to the office and courtyard area, too? It might even bring your insurance premiums down a bit.'

'That's a thought,' he agreed, starting to calm down a bit. 'It's a pity there's nothing I can do to bring the public liability insurance down as well. It's expensive, but I need it in case any of the visitors are daft enough to let their little darlings chew on the plants.'

He ran a hand through his hair, which already looked even more tousled than usual, and smiled ruefully at me. 'Sorry – what a greeting!'

'It's OK, I'm not surprised you're furious. Do you want me to feed the peacocks and fish, while you fill in the holes again, or the other way round?'

'I'll fill them in and try and smooth it over. Just as well the others are coming in later in the morning from today, or James would do his nut. Keeping that bit of lawn immaculate and planting out his borders are the only gardening tasks he's ever shown any true enthusiasm about, though he was always a hard worker until the rheumatism slowed him down.'

'I don't know why anyone fusses over lawns. It's like

outdoor housework, as far as I'm concerned,' I said. 'As much fun as vacuuming a carpet.'

'Yeah, me too,' Ned agreed. Then Lancelot gave a great, despairing wail. 'He's hungry, so if you could just feed everything – the scoops are in the food bins in the Potting Shed, two for the peacocks, one small one of fish food for the koi.'

Guinevere was so eager, she tried to come into the shed with me, but I shooed her out, distributed the food widely, so they both got a share and then spent a pleasant ten minutes by the pond, watching the huge silver, red and gold shapes of the koi circle, surface greedily and then sink back to the depths again.

Ned was still working on the lawn when I went back to ask him what he'd like me to do this morning, since I'd cleared the rose garden and it was ready for mulching.

'Could you start digging in the rest of the barberry bushes around the wetland area? I've put the pots where I want them to go.'

'OK,' I agreed, going to fetch my tools and looking forward to getting stuck in to the Grace Garden as a change from the roses.

Ned came to join me a little later, bringing two big enamel mugs of coffee. He told me the phone had been ringing off the hook again in the office, with people wanting to tell him they'd seen the piece about the restoration of the Grace Garden on *Look North* last night.

'Really? I didn't think they'd show it that quickly – or even at all, unless they wanted something upbeat to fill in,' I said, sitting down with my coffee on the steps that led to the Invisible Gazebo.

'No, me neither.' Ned lowered his large frame down beside me.

'Gert and James both say sitting on cold stone gives you piles,' I observed.

'Then they're taking their time arriving.'

'Was the TV coverage good?' I asked tentatively.

'Apparently. They used much more footage than I expected . . . But then, Clara, Jacob and Myfanwy are all celebrities in their own right, so newsworthy.'

'And so are you,' I pointed out, and he frowned.

'I was a *minor* one when I was presenting *This Small Plot*, but I hardly got mobbed in the streets – or not until I had that touch of notoriety to spice the interest up a bit.'

'You haven't been in the public eye since, though, so it's like I said: everyone will have moved on to something else long ago. I mean, the visitors yesterday were only interested in talking to you about gardening and how much they used to love your programmes, weren't they?'

'Yes, and they were all *really* nice. I think I must have got a bit paranoid.'

'That's what comes of thinking social media views represent those of all the ordinary people,' I told him. 'I felt better as soon as I'd stopped being on Facebook, though I'd hardly posted on there for ages before I left for France anyway, because I knew Mike read it.'

'I'm not on it any more, either. Lois used to check up on me that way, too, though she's long since moved on to another man now – and *your* ex has remarried.'

'Yes, and he didn't seem to be trying to find me after the first few months anyway, so I was being paranoid, too.'

'Well, there's no need for any paranoia now. We can just get on with our lives,' he said, getting up. 'Right – back to work, Ellwood.'

'Yes, Boss,' I said with mock meekness, following suit.

'Between us, we should have time to put the rest of these bushes in and plant the new quince in one of the tall beds, before the others turn up and we have to get ready to open.'

'James thinks we should spread the mulch on the roses early on a Tuesday, when there are no visitors, because of the ripe pong,' I told him, picking up my spade.

'Nonsense, it's a good country smell and the stuff has been rotting nicely for about five years now, so it's . . . delicious.'

'I know exactly what you mean, but only gardeners would appreciate it.'

We worked on, mostly in silence, but occasionally exchanging comments about which new types of lavender would do well in the garden and when we'd have a chance to try and source the roses that had died out . . . if we *could* match the old names with something recognizable, where they didn't presently exist.

The sun shone, fluffy white puffs of clouds chased each other across the baby-blue sky, the birds sang, and Caspar appeared and watched us, occasionally making a brief and indecipherable comment.

'There, that's everything in, until we get another consignment,' Ned said at last. 'I want more plants for round the pond and I seriously underestimated how many blue iris I'd need. I'll leave opening this area till the gazebo's up, anyway, and we won't open the paths in the rose garden until we've mulched it, either.'

'There are a couple of sections of the tile borders broken and in need of replacing, if you can get hold of any.'

'I think I've seen a few stacked in one of the outbuildings; I'll have a look.'

As we walked back, I said, 'The visitors are going to love the little temple in the rose garden, and enjoy spotting the names of the old roses.'

'You worked amazingly hard to get it to this stage in so short a time.'

'It was a labour of love. But now I'm going to have loads of fun throwing myself into helping you with the Grace Garden.'

'You might change your mind when we start marking out the long vegetable-style plots in the overgrown quarter of the mid-level garden,' he said. 'And Gertie's got loads more herbs in her greenhouse, ready for planting out.'

'A gardener's work is never done,' I said. 'Those big pots will want planting up too, when they arrive, won't they?'

'They might come on Thursday, but we'll just put them in position first: they're a statement on their own.'

We'd replaced the rope barriers across the entrances to the paths where we were working, so really, only the gravel needed freshly raking before the visitors came.

James and Gertie had arrived, though Steve would be in later. He'd come and go around his other part-time jobs, but it should all fit in quite well. I suspected that, like the rest of us, he'd end up spending a lot more time in the garden than he was paid for, simply because he enjoyed it.

When we opened up, although there wasn't the initial rush through the gates, like yesterday, it seemed just as busy whenever I looked up. Ned and I had started marking out those long narrow beds at the bottom of the garden.

Gertie, going past with pots of rosemary and tarragon, offered advice: mostly pointing out that nobody spray-painted grass in *her* day.

'I wonder where she's going with that tarragon?' Ned said.

'Where did you tell her to plant it?'

'I didn't,' he said with a grin. 'It's easier to just let her put it in where she wants to.'

'Coward,' I said, and he spray-painted a neat red line across the toes of my work boots, though at least it was biodegradable and would wash off under the tap.

At twelve and two, Ned reluctantly led a guided tour around the garden. So many people had asked if there was one that he'd bowed to the inevitable and a handwritten sign had been affixed to the side of the ticket window, giving the times.

'I sincerely hope Roddy Lightower will take over once he finds his way around the garden. He's very knowledgeable,' Ned said, returning from the second tour.

'They're not going to want his autograph, though.'

'No, well, I expect everyone can do without my name written on a bit of paper. I'm totally unexciting.'

That's not exactly how I'd describe him . . . especially when he'd ruffled his mane of hair and his amber eyes were glowing with enthusiasm . . .

We'd made a good start on digging out the first long bed when I left them closing up the garden later that afternoon and headed up the river, which, from a rubbish collection point of view, was much like the day before, though without the socks.

I'd noticed, though, that the force of the water cascading from the rock face at the top of the falls seemed less than before, exposing more of the fissure next to it – the cave of the treasure legend. But then, since the day I'd arrived, we hadn't had much in the way of rain, so I supposed that was why.

Elf called me in for coffee in the café kitchen when I got back. She'd just finished cleaning up with Daisy, who'd now left, but to my surprise, I found Ned in there, dipping a biscotti into a mug of coffee.

'We've put up the shutters and shut up the shop,' he said, looking up at me.

'That's an old tongue-twister,' Elf said. 'Though it's not as good as "I'm not a pheasant plucker, I'm the pheasant plucker's son, and I'm only plucking pheasants till the pheasant plucker comes." '

She managed that without a slip and we applauded.

One of the newer but still antique-looking ice-cream machines was chugging away to itself in the background and she said she had a box of strawberry ice-cream for me to take up with me.

'And I have some for you, too, Ned, which I was going to bring over, but now you can take it back with you. From frozen strawberries, of course, at this time of year, but very good, and I use some of my own bottled strawberry syrup in the recipe, too. You can almost taste the sunshine in that.'

It sounded delicious.

'I know it should be your day off tomorrow, dear,' she said to me, 'but you haven't forgotten that you volunteered to be the Easter Bunny in the morning?'

I put my mug down and gazed blankly at her: I had managed to forget it . . . and nor had I volunteered, it was more that I'd been press-ganged into it!

'Marnie's helping in the garden anyway tomorrow,' Ned said, then grinned wickedly. 'I'm really looking forward to seeing her in her floppy ears and bunny tail first, though.'

I gave him a cold look. 'Do I really have to put on an Easter Bunny costume? Won't we be hiding the eggs early, so there'll be no one about?'

'There may already be one or two random tourists, but we take photos of you hiding the eggs,' explained Ned, 'and I print a couple out and pin them to the fence by the entrance. The children love it. "The Easter Bunny, spotted this morning hiding chocolate eggs!" '

'Steve's got a big basket of eggs in the Village Hut and a load of little coloured paper flags to mark each clutch,' Elf said.

'Doesn't that make it too easy?'

'No, because the children will be all eight or under, and most of them tiny tots,' she explained. 'We want to make sure they all get some, though we have extras, so we can top up the cellophane bags they put their hoard in at the end.'

I sighed, resigned to my fate. 'OK, so I put on the bunny suit and hide the eggs all over the grounds, planting a little flag by each clutch.'

Elf nodded. 'Yes. Then the vicar comes over and opens the hunt at eleven.'

I hoped I'd be back in the apothecary garden, working away by then, my part in the proceedings completed.

Elf invited Ned to dinner and included me, but I said I felt like a quiet night in and she didn't press it.

Caspar was all for the idea and showed signs of interest in the strawberry ice-cream I sampled after dinner, though it seemed a very un-feline-like thing to want and I didn't give him any. I expect he'd stuffed himself full in Lavender Cottage and was just being both nosy and greedy.

He watched me from the sofa later, as I had a good rummage around in the decreasing pile of belongings in the corner. I'd soon discovered I no longer wanted a lot of my own things that I'd left stored with Treena, but I found another of the braided rag rugs of Mum's making, in soft shades of cream, pink and blue, which smelled of the lavender it had been packed with. I put that one down by the little armchair.

There was a box containing my school books, too, and every handmade card or little gift I'd given Mum as a child. I dithered a bit over those, then decided to keep them, putting them inside the small chest I was using as a coffee table.

Then I started on all the clothes I'd stored, though I couldn't now imagine why I thought I – or anyone else – would ever want to wear them again. But I repacked them for the charity shop in Great Mumming, where they would probably send most of them for recycling.

There were now only two small cardboard cartons I hadn't looked at, and I pulled them out before restacking the boxes of stuff to get rid of in their place.

They seemed to have been filled with Mum's old paperwork and odds and ends like that, so I thought I'd leave them for another day and pushed them under the big bookcase.

I don't know why Aunt Em had thought I'd want old utility bills and letters. Perhaps she'd meant to sort everything out a bit more later and never got round to it?

Over a cup of cocoa I had a riffle through the section of old photographs in Elf's book, lingering over the black-and-white ones of the Fairy Falls, then abandoned that in favour of curdling my blood a bit more with Clara Mayhem Doome's newest novel.

Lizzie

As soon as I could walk the distance, I went with my sister to sell our eggs around the village and since, once away from home, she liked gossip as much as anyone else, I was often left to my own devices outside in the street, to await her . . . in which way I sometimes came into contact with the village children.

I envied them their freedom to roam and to play . . . and they found in me a ready audience for tales of fairies and little folk, boggarts, goblins and even angels – for long ago, I learned, an angel had most miraculously appeared to a local child, when she was playing by the falls above the village.

This seemed to me a wonderful thing, and godly, so that I wondered my parents had not mentioned it, but when I said so to my sister Martha, and begged her to take me to this miraculous spot, she said it was but the Devil's work to put such ideas into idle children's heads and if I knew what was best for me, I would not mention the matter at home.

When I ventured to say that the children had told me there was a picture of the Angel Gabriel in the church window in Thorstane, she just snorted and I took the hint and said no more.

But I thought about it, as I trudged with her up the long, steep village street with our basket of eggs, and how I would like to go to the waterfall, and perhaps see a shining angel for myself.

I learned later that the three cottages along a rough track at the very top of the village were called Angel Row, since they were near the source of the waterfall.

Of course, I took every opportunity of asking the children for more details of the angels and fairies and learned that there was a rough path down to the falls, just beyond Angel Row, and if you continued on it, you came out by the old stone bridge that led to a row of cottages and the black and white house, where lived the Graces, distant relatives of the Lordly-Graces at the manor, Risings.

I was soon deemed strong enough to deliver the eggs alone, though my small legs and frame found carrying the full heavy basket hard work, so that my spirits lifted as the basket emptied on my ascent of the hill.

27

Rabbiting

I popped up to Toller's general store, which seemed never to close, even on Easter Day, for some supplies first thing in the morning (they have both *pain au chocolat* and croissants!), before Ned and I went over to the Village Hut.

Steve had already opened up and was pinning some of the bunting, which had been returned after the garden-opening ceremony, along the fence.

In one of the small back rooms, used as a dressing area when they were staging pantomimes, I donned the all-in-one bunny costume, and zipped it right up. It was quite a good fit, but in the mirror I could see my heart-shaped face surrounded by brown and white fake fur and topped with big, floppy ears, and I didn't think it was a good look.

Elf was waiting outside when I emerged and drew whiskers on my face with her eyeliner pencil, as the finishing touch. It certainly finished Ned off, because he couldn't keep his face straight.

I stomped out into the garden, observed only by a puzzled Japanese couple, who took a million long-distance snaps as I obeyed Elf's instruction to: 'Hop, dear, *hop*!'

Carrying the big basket of chocolate eggs, I half-heartedly

lolloped off, followed by Elf with the little paper flags, while Ned took a few photos before dashing off back to his office to print them out on A4.

The grounds of the Hut weren't extensive and just tussocky grass and small bushes, so the eggs were not really hidden, just laid down in clutches, or singly if large, marked by a flag.

It seemed to take ages, but finally the basket was empty, and by that time Ned had returned with the pictures of the Easter Bunny printed out in glorious colour. He and Steve fixed them to the fence by the gate, over which now rose a wire arch, covered in yellow tissue paper flowers. A sign had been put out, announcing that the annual Easter egg hunt would open at eleven, for children of eight and under, and a small table covered in a white cloth now stood just inside the garden.

On it was a stack of small plastic baskets, borrowed from the pub, a heap of triangular cellophane bags (completely biodegradable, according to Elf), and a collecting box for the fifty-pence admission charge. Under the table, hidden by the cloth, stood an open box of small chocolate eggs, ready for the less successful hunters.

With relief, I went back into the Hut to change and left the bunny costume draped over the back of a chair, like a very peculiar empty chrysalis. But when I attempted to remove the whiskers in the cloakroom, they proved surprisingly resistant. Elf must use waterproof eyeliner pencil. I managed to scrub them off eventually, though, leaving temporarily rosy cheeks.

Outside, there were now more people about and Elf went back to the café to open up, while Ned and I retired to the garden office for a well-deserved cup of coffee.

'There's plenty of time before we open. I expect James will be in soon, so you could pop over to the Hut just before eleven and watch the egg hunt start,' Ned suggested. 'I've seen it a million times so I'll stay here and give the gravel paths an extra rake, then we can carry on digging out the long beds when you get back.'

I was curious enough to agree and found Gertie there with Steve, and also the vicar.

The Reverend Jojo Micklejohn was a small, plump woman who might have been in her late sixties or early seventies, with short, silvery blond curls, bunchy pink cheeks and shrewd dark blue eyes.

On being introduced she said, rather alarmingly, that she'd heard a lot about me and that I would always be welcome at St Gabriel's, if Ned ever allowed me any time off.

'I've been told about your lovely angel window and I'm going to visit the church as soon as I get the chance, so I can see it,' I told her.

'It's a very old church, well worth seeing,' she assured me.

Apparently, she was semi-retired, and St Gabriel's, Jericho's End and a couple of remote moorland hamlets comprised her whole parish.

Elf, who'd reappeared, whispered in my ear, 'There's a big monster of a Victorian church in the middle of Thorstane. The vicar there has a much bigger parish to look after, but St Gabriel's has always been the Jericho's End church, even if it is only just outside the Thorstane boundary.'

She glanced back at the café, where I could see customers already sitting outside at the small tables and the stripy awning pulled out. It looked like another bumper day for ice-cream.

'I've left Charlie holding the fort, and Daisy's coming in shortly, but I must dash back after the hunt gets going.'

A queue of children and parents formed at the gate and the vicar stepped forward and gave a brief address, exhorting everyone not to forget the true meaning of Easter in a chocolate feeding frenzy.

'But Easter also heralds spring, time of rebirth and renewal, old traditions and new: and in that spirit, let us commence the Easter egg hunt!' she finished, to much applause.

Then the excited children rushed in through the gate, at which point I went back to the garden with Gertie, where James was already setting up the shop and ticket office.

After that, it was a day much like the two preceding ones, except that Ned and I were so engrossed in digging out our new long beds, which were laid out in a fan shape, that Steve had to come down and remind Ned to go and do his tours of the garden.

Paradise was proving popular.

That evening I ate my Sunday dinner in Lavender Cottage again, with Elf, Myfy, Jacob, Gerald and, of course, Ned. As before, the conversation was wide-ranging and entertaining. The only fly in the ointment was Ned's tendency to keep making bad rabbit jokes and puns. I suppose it was hard to resist, but eventually I rather snappily told him to stop rabbiting on and he took the hint.

Hare today, and gone tomorrow . . .

Replete and sleepy, I made my way back to the flat through the café, although Caspar had raced right through the cottage and beaten me to it.

I woke feeling an urge to walk up to the falls and see if anything there would like to communicate with me – perhaps even give me a small hint as to what Ned's reaction would be if I finally confessed to my Vane connection.

As I climbed up by the falls, however, I saw that Myfy and Jacob were already there, standing hand in hand on the railed flat rock next to the source.

They had the appearance of mythical beings, clothed in

magic: both tall, robed in black and with long silver hair lifting gently in the breeze.

I turned and crept quietly away.

The day grew cloudier, the sun intermittent, but it didn't seem to stop the visitors who, interested in gardens or not, appeared determined to drain every last drop of entertainment from Jericho's End that they could.

The garden had magic of its own and tended to draw people in, even when they'd only intended a saunter round the paths and a spending opportunity in the shop to prove they'd been there. Ned had already had to re-order postcards of the Poison Garden.

In fact, the Poison Garden had proved to be a major draw. People took it in turns to stand and read the information board about the deadly plants and their more grisly effects. Many of them wanted to go inside the enclosure, so Ned would have to organize his special Poison Garden tours soon. I didn't think he should fob that one off on poor Roddy.

The koi in the fish pond were popular, too, though we'd had to place signs around it, asking people not to feed them after we found whole sandwiches floating in the water, along with a Krispy Kreme doughnut with one bite out of it. We hoped that was a human bite, rather than fish, because it would probably be instant death to a koi.

Luckily, most visitors were sensible; it was just the odd one, or parents who thought it was fine to let their small children run about screaming at the tops of their voices, despite the signs warning them that they must be under parental control at all times.

Not all the plants with toxic effects were in the Poison Garden. It's surprising what some everyday garden plants can do to you, if brushed against, or ingested.

Some visitors, too, were frankly weird, trying to buttonhole Ned for long discussions on the history and uses of the mandrake, or taking an unhealthy interest in the effects of the rosary pea vine, but none was weird in the way *Saul* had been . . .

As the days had passed since he accosted me in the rose garden, I was feeling more relaxed about my encounter with him: nothing had come of it, after all, and there seemed no reason why our paths should ever cross again. And come to that, no reason, even if he *did* suspect who I was, why he should tell anyone else.

No, I thought it was safe enough . . . right up to the moment when, hooking the rope back across the path where we were working, on my way to lunch, I heard a faintly familiar woman's voice squeal: 'Marnie? Is that you? It *is*!'

And there was a small, raven-haired woman, looking at me over the top of her glossy garden guide with wide, startled hazel eyes.

It took me a moment to place her, but when I did, my heart sank: she was one of the veterinary nurses at Mike's practice.

'*Non* – you are mistaken. I am Genevieve, a student volunteer from France,' I said, hastily assuming a French accent, probably overlaid with a veneer of Lancashire.

She laughed and lowered the guidebook. 'Oh, you were always a joker! But I know it's you, it was just the short hair that made me look twice.'

I didn't think I'd ever been a joker, but I gave up on the French accent. 'Hi – Melanie, isn't it?'

'Melinda, Melinda Smith,' she said. 'And still working for Merchester Veterinary Centre, though I'm the senior veterinary nurse now.'

'Congratulations,' I said, without really being aware of what I was saying. 'I didn't know you were keen on gardens?'

'Well, I like them, but it's my mother-in-law who's really keen – she's trying to find Ned Mars, because she was a huge fan of his programmes.'

She was looking at me curiously now. 'You haven't been here all this time since you left Mike, have you? We all thought you'd gone to stay with that family of yours in France, but I heard Mike went over there to look for you and you weren't.'

'I've been travelling about,' I said vaguely. 'I've only just got this job and—'

'We didn't blame you for taking off like that; we all thought he was creepy,' she said. 'We still do. Was he violent?' she added eagerly.

'No, not physically violent,' I said, looking round to make sure no one else was within earshot, which luckily they weren't. 'I just . . . found it impossible to live with him any more and a clean break seemed the best thing.'

'He did tell us that . . . well, that you'd been ill and it had given you a sort of nervous breakdown, so you'd been sending out strange letters to people.'

'I bet he did,' I said bitterly. 'But I don't want to talk of the past, I've moved on – and so has he, hasn't he? What's his new wife like?'

Her hazel eyes went even wider. 'But Mike hasn't remarried. He was *engaged* at one time, but after she moved in with him, she changed her mind pretty quickly and broke it off.'

'Not . . . married?' I repeated numbly. 'But my sister, Treena, bumped into that receptionist, Sylvie, and she told her he *had* remarried!'

'Oh, that Sylvie! She only ever gets half of the story. She moved to a new job in Ormskirk soon after you went, but she's still friends with one of the other girls on reception and must have got hold of the wrong end of the stick.'

I expect I'd turned a whiter shade of pale, because she said, 'Are you all right?'

I summoned a smile. 'Fine – I just need my lunch. That's where I was off to when you spotted me.' I paused. 'Melinda, would you mind not mentioning to Mike that you've seen me? I mean, I don't suppose he'd be interested anyway, but I'd . . . well, much rather he didn't have any idea where I was.'

'Of course – you can trust me,' she breathed, and I could see she'd been unconvinced by what I'd said and still thought Mike was a wife beater. Which I suppose he had been, in a way, even if the scars were all on the inside.

I wasn't entirely convinced that Melinda would refrain from telling all her friends she'd seen me, but I hoped it wouldn't get back to Mike's ears. Perhaps it wouldn't. He'd never been one to socialize with his employees.

'Thank you – and it's been lovely bumping into you like this,' I lied, and then made my escape into the thankfully empty Potting Shed where I could try to get a grip on myself in privacy.

I thought I'd managed it, too, though it can't have been a total success because Ned asked me later if anything was wrong. I confessed to a headache, but nothing a quiet night in wouldn't cure.

'Good,' he said, 'because although it's your day off tomorrow, the builder I know is coming first thing in the morning to see how easy it would be to incorporate that outbuilding into the shop, and you're the one with all the bright ideas, so it would be good if you could be there.'

'OK,' I agreed, then escaped to check the River Walk, which was already devoid of any visitors. I suppose many of them had just come for the day, or for the weekend, and were now headed home. They had mostly been more thoughtful with their litter disposal, too, and I didn't linger over the walk, but dashed back to my flat as soon as I could.

There I checked the time, then managed to catch Treena on the phone before she went off to do the evening surgery. I hadn't yet told her about my meeting with Saul, but now that all came tumbling out, as well as today's unfortunate meeting with Melinda.

'Though perhaps she will keep quiet about seeing me,' I added.

'Perhaps,' she agreed, but she didn't sound convinced. 'Try not to worry, though, because he's got no hold over you any more, has he? And why should he care where you are now?'

'I don't know, but it would be like him to just suddenly turn up.'

'Don't worry, you can always hide behind this Ned of yours, if he does.'

'He's not mine,' I said quickly. 'Or not in that sense.'

'Just teasing,' she said. 'I think you can stop worrying about Mike suddenly appearing, so that just leaves the very odd conversation you had with this Saul Vane. But I think you're right and even if he's guessed who you are, he won't do anything about it now he's warned you off. Not that you wanted to acknowledge the relationship anyway.'

'Certainly not. I wish it didn't exist! You've no idea how horrible he and Wayne are!'

'So calm down and try not to worry. Luke starts his dig tomorrow, so I'm going to try to come over in the afternoon. Pop up if you get the chance – or maybe we can meet up in the pub later.'

'I think I'll have to go to the Friends of Jericho's End meeting first, so it'll probably be late, after eight,' I said.

'I suspect we'll still be there,' she said. 'See you tomorrow, one way or the other.'

I felt a whole lot better after unburdening myself. Tomorrow I thought I'd tell Ned about Mike's vet nurse spotting me . . . but my other worry would have to remain a secret.

'Oh, what a tangled web we weave, when first we practise to deceive,' I said to Caspar, as he slammed through the cat flap and appeared like an animated fur rug on the threshold.

'Pfht!' he agreed.

Lizzie

The cook at Risings was a kindly woman, who often gave me a cake to eat, or some other little titbit, and gossiped about the family – there was a little girl much my age and two older brothers – and many visitors, so that she was always baking and cooking and only had a respite when the family visited London.

I spent the day of my ninth birthday, like many years before, looking after the hens and then carrying the basket of eggs first to Risings, where I entered the kitchen to see a peevish, cross-looking little girl there, who I knew, from often seeing her go by in a carriage, to be Miss Susanna Lordly-Grace.

She was dressed in what I thought was a very pretty frock and pinafore and wore a pink ribbon in her hair. My own ill-fitting hand-me-down dress of rough black wool, with its high neck and long sleeves, and my close black bonnet, seemed even drabber than usual.

I curtsied and she looked me over and then demanded to know who I was and my age, and remarked how very ugly my clothes were.

'But I am bored, so you may stay and play with me,' she said imperiously.

'I am very sorry, miss, but I must deliver the rest of these eggs and then get home, or my father will be angry with me,' I told her timidly, which made her cross.

But I was adamant, being more afraid of my father than of disappointing her, and Cook came to my rescue.

'You must let her go, Miss Susanna, because her family are that strict you wouldn't believe, like all those Brethren, as they call themselves, and she has her work to do, same as I have.'

I left her and managed to empty my basket before I reached the top of the village street. I was about to turn dutifully for home when something took hold of me and, instead, I went on beyond Angel Row and through the wicket that I knew led to the path down the falls. My heart beat with terror, as if my father could see what I was doing, but the longing to see an angel, something free and beautiful and outside what I knew, drove my feet onwards.

And when I stood at the spot near the mouth of the river, which sprang from the rock face, I knew I had found what I sought and a great peace and happiness fell on me.

28

Angels and Demons

The builder had already arrived at the shop when I got there next morning and Ned had moved away a shelf unit that was hiding the blocked-up opening that had once led through to the lean-to building on the other side.

'Don, this is my new gardener, Marnie, who came up with all the bright ideas,' Ned introduced me. 'We just need you to tell us if they're practical or not.'

Don, who was a skinny, fair and freckled man, totally unlike my idea of a builder, gave an engagingly gap-toothed grin. 'We've looked at the outside lavs already and the plumbing part would be easy enough,' he said. 'And I've seen the blocked doorway, so let's go round and look what it's like from this outbuilding.'

We went out of the visitors' gate and Don cast a critical eye at the outside. 'Those stone roofing slabs tend to stay put, but the walls need pointing up and that door and the window frames replacing. That's a wide door frame, though,' he added. 'I reckon they must have kept animals in here, at one time.'

'A wide door is good from the point of view of getting wheelchairs through,' I said, and he agreed.

'Get one through there easy.'

He examined the interior carefully, especially the blocked doorway and the rafters, which, luckily, were dry and sound. Then he did some measuring, scribbling on a rough tablet of paper.

We watched him, then when he seemed to have finished and was contemplatively scratching his head with the end of his biro, Ned said, 'So, how easy *would* it be to make this part of the shop – *and* add a toilet at the back?'

'Oh, easy enough,' Don said breezily. 'Like when we did the shop, we'd take up the flags and damp-proof under them . . . replace the door and windows . . . electric update. I wouldn't even *try* turning on that single bulb – it's a deathtrap . . .'

He paused and scratched his head again.

'Knock through that old opening into the shop, but with some good supports and a proper lintel overhead, then make good all walls . . . install a ceiling . . .'

The list seemed endless *and* expensive, but he hadn't finished yet.

'Then there's the plumbing to the new big toilet compartment suitable for the disabled that you want and with a baby-changing area . . .'

'Is that all possible?' I asked.

'Yes, no problem. You need a good turning circle in the compartment for a wheelchair, so the partition wall would come to . . .' he pointed to a spot, 'about *there*. Maybe with an entrance through a partial stud wall in front of it, because you're going to have a display of garden stuff in the rest of this side, Ned says?'

'Yes, sort of a mini museum,' I agreed.

'Pictures of the garden through the ages and a few antique gardening tools in a glass case, maybe,' said Ned. 'The shop displays can extend into the other end, near the door.'

'The idea,' I explained, 'is that the visitors come into the garden through the gate past the ticket office, as now, but they'll have to exit by the new door on this side – meaning they have to pass through the shop to get to it, with all the tempting things on offer.'

'Smart idea!' Don gave me a look of approval and made a couple more notes. 'You'll need a small ramp outside both doors – the steps are low, anyway – and you'll have to leave a path clear that's wide enough for wheelchair access, right through the shop.'

He put the pen and pad back in his pocket. 'I'll put all that on the computer later, break it all down for you.'

'It sounds expensive – and it'll make a mess in the shop while you're doing it. We're closed only on Tuesdays.'

'Shouldn't cost too much. I'll give you a quote when I've worked it out. I'll have to send Larry and Jon over to look into the electrics and plumbing.'

'Don's got a trusty team of experts on tap,' Ned explained to me. 'He arranges everything.'

Don gave his attractive, gap-toothed smile. 'I wouldn't worry about the mess, either, because we can do a lot of the work on this side before we knock through, and then we'll seal off the opening with thick plastic sheet to stop any dust getting through while we open it up.'

Ned, initially reluctant to part with any more money on something that wasn't directly related to his beloved garden, now seemed to have moved beyond mere acceptance of the fact that he would need to install disabled facilities sooner rather than later and was warming to the idea.

'I'll wait for the estimate and, if that's OK, it'll just be a question of when you can start on it.'

'Fit you in fairly soon, I should think – and you know me, once I've started a job, I don't hang about.'

'Fair enough,' said Ned.

When he'd gone, Ned said to me, 'I'd better start looking out for some old photos and stuff for the museum! Once Don gets going, he's amazingly fast. He had the shop sorted in no time.'

'There's sure to be lots of interesting things in those boxes of papers you've got in your study – maybe even a plan of the rose garden!' I said.

'I know, but they'll take ages to go through. There's a big chest and then a box that's not much smaller – not to mention what's in that window seat – and Uncle Theo seems to have well and truly jumbled most of it up.'

'I could help you sort it out in the evenings, if you like?' I offered. 'I've almost finished going through my and Mum's things I brought to the flat, so I don't mind, and it won't take so long with two of us.'

Especially when at least one of us was longing to have a rummage through it all, in search of lost nuggets of garden history!

'OK, we could just rough-sort them first, looking for anything we can use – like your rose garden plan, though I doubt that exists.'

'Perhaps not, but there's bound to be *something* about the temple folly, if only in the accounts book for the materials and labour,' I pointed out.

'I suppose so, and maybe more planting lists, or plant orders, dating back to earlier times.'

The peacock must have said the wrong thing to his mate because she was chasing him around the courtyard, pecking viciously at him.

'On the wings of love,' I murmured, as Lancelot flapped in an ungainly way to the top of the wall to escape her, and Ned grinned.

'Where did you say you were going today?' he asked.

'I didn't, but I thought I'd have a look at St Gabriel's church and Thorstane, then perhaps see how they're getting on at the dig. Luke and his team start there today and Treena's got a day off, so she's going to come over at some point, too.'

To my surprise, Ned diffidently offered to drive me there. 'We've all worked so hard to get the garden open and it's been hectic all weekend, so I could do with a break.'

'OK, that would be nice,' I agreed, and he said he'd bring the car round to the front of the café in ten minutes.

I fetched my rucksack and applied a quick dab of lip gloss, then went down to find that the car was actually a big four-wheel-drive Jeep thing, which you probably needed in winter up there.

'I thought we'd go up the hard way, and down the easy, seeing as the weather's good,' Ned said, driving over the humpback bridge and turning right up the hill.

'But I thought the road from the top of the village to Thorstane was really steep and difficult,' I said, feeling slightly alarmed.

'It is, and there are some really hairy zigzags . . . but it all adds to the fun.'

He seemed to be looking forward to the challenge, which was more than I was, but I supposed it was better to be going up it, than hurtling down . . .

Mr Toller, standing outside his shop, waved at us as we passed. Unlike the day of my arrival, the pavements were filled with visitors, looking into the shop and gallery windows. The signs were swinging outside the guesthouses, advertising morning coffee, lunch and afternoon teas.

Beyond the last of the houses the road surface, as I had noticed on my walk, suddenly deteriorated, and as we headed steeply upwards towards the first bend Ned changed down a gear and grinned sideways at me.

'It's much more exciting coming down, but here we go!'

The road – which wasn't really worthy of the name – ascended in a series of sharp zigzags through thick woods. Where there were crash barriers, they showed ominous signs of vehicles having bashed into them, and a deep storm drain down one side of the road must have made things tricky if two vehicles met . . . assuming there was more than one mad driver living in the area.

Ned took a hand off the steering wheel to point out a half-ruined cottage, the Sixpenny Cottage of the treasure story.

'You'd have had to have been a keen treasure hunter to hike up here,' I said.

'Lots of people seem to find the lure of treasure irresistible, even when it's as unlikely to be as realistic as this one. I expect the cottage and garden were searched several times over before they finally found that box in the outbuildings, but I bet Wayne and his pals with their metal detectors turned it over later, just in case, too.'

'Do you think so?'

'I'm sure they have, though they'd have come up by Land Rover, not walked. His friends are like Wayne: after easy money with no effort. I'm off up to Risings in the morning to have a word with him about those holes in my lawn,' he added grimly. 'It's his regular day working there.'

'There's no proof it was him, though, Ned.'

'But I *know* he did it and I'm going to make it abundantly clear that if he ever sets foot on my property again, he'll be toast.'

For a moment, the usual easy-going, good-natured Ned Mars was overlaid with something older, grimmer and slightly intimidating. I thought Wayne would do well to keep his distance.

Eventually we emerged from the woodlands onto more level ground, on which stood a very small stone church with a square tower, surrounded by a walled graveyard. The surface of the road as we reached the gate suddenly returned to smooth tarmac and we stopped bouncing about, which was a relief.

'Here we are,' he said unnecessarily, pulling up at the side of the road. 'It's just outside the Thorstane parish boundary, one of those strange old quirks on the map, and it was always the Jericho's End church. I don't know why they built it up here, unless it was because there isn't much flat land down in the valley for a church and graveyard – or not land that doesn't flood, as those monks obviously found.'

We got out and walked through a wooden gate and up a gravel path.

'There's a Grace family tomb behind the church in the oldest part of the graveyard – two, in fact, because Nathaniel Grace built one there, too. The Lordly-Graces have a newer plot in the graveyard behind the Victorian Gothic church in Thorstane. It's a pretentious building with a door like something out of a Hammer horror film – we'll drive past it in a bit.'

The door to the church was open, as Ned said it usually was, only being locked at night.

'They don't have anything valuable, just a few pewter candlesticks and embroidered hassocks, and I don't think there's a huge market for those.'

Oddly, it seemed smaller inside than out. The walls had been painted white and the pews were plain, dark wooden ones, shiny with use and polish. One worn stone step led up to a simple altar.

It had the indefinable atmosphere of an ancient holy place, peaceful, serene and slightly scented with the lingering traces of flowers and Calor Gas heaters.

The Angel Gabriel window was small and narrow, with a pointed top. He stood in the centre of the large panel, his name on a banner near his feet, in case you'd missed the clue in the church's name or the large white lily he was brandishing. It was a very ancient window, the pieces of glass small and brightly coloured. The angel's somewhat androgynous face was calm but stern, and his wings were folded. Over his head, in the topmost section, a host of smaller angels in gaily coloured robes were swooping about, holding what looked like harps and trumpets.

'The Puritans never smashed this one: when the villagers of Jericho's End heard what was happening in other churches, they came up here and took it away and hid it.'

'Is that in Elf's book, too? I must have missed it.'

'I'm sure it's in there somewhere, but it's an old story and we all know it.'

'It must have been a lovely thing for the congregation to look at during services. I'm not surprised that that little girl imagined an angel at the falls rather than a fairy, if she'd grown up seeing this one.'

I looked up at the window again. 'The jolly little angels at the top look a lot more fun than Gabriel.'

'Oh, I don't know . . . The corners of his mouth look as if they're curving up and he's about to smile.'

We walked round the graveyard to look at Nathaniel's stone and I wasn't surprised to see a sailing ship carved on it. He lay under a lichened table tomb, surrounded by his descendants.

The older Grace tomb was half-hidden by grass and bushes near the back wall, evidently unused for a very long time and never visited.

Other than that, there seemed to be several local names represented, like Toller and Posset and even Vane – and a few Verdis, too.

'I think the original Verdis who founded the café were Roman Catholic, but the nearest church would have been Great Mumming, so they must have come over to the Church of England, instead,' Ned said.

We drove on into the very large village of Thorstane, which had shops, including a small supermarket, a Chinese takeaway and the horrible redbrick church Ned had described.

'It's the worst of Victorian Gothic, but over the moors there's a house in that style that's truly amazing, even if it is totally over the top: the Red House, where Clara Mayhem Doome and her family live.'

'I'd like to have a look at that.'

'It's in Starstone Edge, which is a nice place to visit in late spring, or summer. It's much higher than Thorstane and gets much more extreme weather in winter, though.'

He paused at the side of the road a bit further on and indicated a barn-like building opposite. 'That used to be where the Strange Brethren held their blood-and-thunder meetings.'

I couldn't imagine that the building ever looked church-like, but now there were cheery-looking posters on a board outside and the doors were painted bright red.

'It fell into disuse well before my time, when the last of the old Brethren died off and the new generation didn't take to the idea so much,' he said. 'But now, as the community centre, it's the heart of the village and all sort of things go on in there.'

Then he looked at his watch and said he was hungry and why didn't we go and have something to eat?

'There's a pub up on the edge of the moors, on the Starstone Edge road, where they do a good lunch, the Pike with Two Heads.'

'OK,' I agreed. 'But why on earth is it called the Pike with Two Heads? Is it some sort of heraldic thing?'

'You'll see,' he said mysteriously, and soon we'd left the last straggling cottages behind us and were driving up a single-track lane, to where a large, low old building stood alone, like an escapee from a Daphne du Maurier film, the sign painted with a two-headed fish flapping to and fro in the wind.

The pub took on a more modern and less creepy aspect as we approached, having added a new restaurant extension on one side of the old building, like that of the Devil's Cauldron.

A row of what were probably once stables had been turned into motel rooms.

The car park was surprisingly full and so was the pub, when we went inside. Ned insisted we detour en route to the restaurant, so he could show me the original of the pub sign: a huge and ancient-looking mutant fish in a glass case, which did indeed have two heads. It was not a thing of beauty.

'It looks fed up to the gills,' I observed.

'So would you if you'd been stuffed and varnished,' he said. 'Come on, let's see if we can get a table.'

A waitress found us a table for two by the window overlooking a stretch of gloomy moors under hurrying pewter clouds.

I'm sure when we got out of the car the temperature was several degrees lower than it had been even at St Gabriel's church.

We ordered food. I chose carrot and coriander soup with a tuna melt toastie, while Ned went the whole hog and had an enormous plateful of roast beef, Yorkshire pudding, roast potatoes, three kinds of vegetables and thick gravy.

'If I stoke up now, I'll only need something light tonight,' he explained, tucking in. 'I don't do much cooking, so if I get the opportunity of a decent meal and some fresh veg, I go for it.'

'Do you mean you *can't* cook?' I asked incredulously.

'Of course I can cook!' he said indignantly. 'I have an extensive repertoire of beans on toast, scrambled egg on toast, cheese on toast . . .'

'OK, just admit you can't cook. Those aren't meals, they're snacks.'

'I've never taken a lot of interest in cooking,' he admitted. 'There is always something more exciting to do and, anyway, it doesn't seem worth the effort for one, does it? Elf puts meals in my freezer sometimes, with cooking instructions.'

'I quite like simple cooking – casseroles and risottos and things like that, *and* soup. This one is really good – home-made is so much nicer than the stuff you get in tins.'

'That pasta you cooked the other night was really nice and it didn't seem to take you long to make.'

'It didn't, though I used bottled tomato sauce, which speeded things up.'

He evidently enjoyed his lunch now, anyway. I finished the soup and ate my tuna melt, then gazed absently out of the window at the moorland, feeling suddenly slightly disorientated as you do, sometimes, when you find yourself in a strange place, though at least I was not with a stranger.

Ned *had* seemed like one when we'd come face to face on

the day I'd arrived, but we were soon back on our old terms of friendship.

I turned my head and found that he'd finished eating and was regarding me with a faintly questioning look in his amber-brown eyes.

'Something's worrying you, isn't it? I thought so yesterday, even though you said you just had a headache.'

'You're right,' I admitted ruefully. 'And I was going to tell you today anyway, I just hadn't got round to it yet. It really isn't anything much.'

And I described how I'd been spotted yesterday by Mike's veterinary nurse, Melinda, and the shock of discovering Mike hadn't remarried, after all.

'Apparently his fiancée moved in with him before the wedding, which was bad for him, because she must have started to get some idea of what she was in for. But it was good for her, because she moved out again and called the wedding off.'

Ned was frowning. 'So . . . he's still single?'

'He doesn't seem to have found anyone else . . . and I admit I did somehow feel safer when I thought he was married,' I confessed. 'I'm not *afraid* of him any more, it's just that . . . if he found out where I was, he might turn up and try to make trouble.'

'I'll sort him out for you if he does,' Ned assured me. 'But you said this Melinda promised not to tell him she'd seen you?'

'Yes, and I don't think she will, because she doesn't seem to like him much, but she's bound to tell other people and then it might get back to him.'

'What does he look like, in case he turns up?' he asked.

'It's been a few years, so he might have changed, and he must be in his late forties now. He's medium height and has that deceptively slight, skinny build most runners have – that was his hobby. And short, spiky dark hair with some grey. He can be very charming and seems genuinely nice, so you'd probably like him.'

'He certainly doesn't sound very scary – but then, when Lois used to fly into a jealous rage she was pretty terrifying,' he admitted.

'It's hard to describe the effect he used to have on me once we'd been married a little while. Have you read the *Harry Potter* books, or seen the films?'

He nodded. 'Both.'

'Well, the effect Mike had on me was like a Dementor, sucking all the happiness and willpower out of me and leaving me feeling empty and helpless. But I think he found me a tougher nut to crack than he'd expected – unlike his first wife, who killed herself.'

'I'm glad you got away – and you needn't worry. If he tries to contact you, come straight to me.'

'I will,' I agreed gratefully. I thought Ned would be more than a match for Mike, however persuasive and convincing he might be. 'Treena knows about Melinda, of course. *She* said Mike couldn't do anything to harm me now, too.'

'It'll be fine,' he reassured me, smiling so that all the little sun wrinkles round his eyes spread out like rays, which I found rather endearing.

'Have a nice, comforting dessert: the chocolate fudge cake with whipped cream works especially well.'

It did, too, and his suggestion that we go back to the office and put in some orders for the old roses we'd been sourcing on the internet was a distractingly pleasant prospect: the icing on the cake.

Lizzie

A great change came upon my life only a few days later, for it seemed that my father had been summoned by Mr Lordly-Grace, whose tenant he was, and the upshot was that I was to go and live at Risings, there to be a maid and companion to Miss Susanna! On Sundays, though, I must return to the farm early in the morning, to spend the day at Thorstane with the Brethren.

I could see my father did not like the idea of my going, but he had had little choice but to accede, and soon I was installed at Risings in greater comfort than I had ever known. I had a small room off the nursery, where the nanny once slept, so that I could always be on call should my young mistress want me. She was inclined to be spoilt and pettish but, if sometimes thoughtless, not unkind to me. I think she liked having me at her beck and call, and I accompanied her to her lessons with her governess, which I found vastly more interesting than she did, and on walks, which usually tended to take us to Old Grace Hall across the bridge. There we might wander the paths of the walled garden, while the governess drank tea with the housekeeper.

Susanna had two much older brothers, George, who was already a young man-about-town and not seen much at Risings, and Neville, who was still at school and only came home in the holidays. He was a good-natured, merry young man and he won my childish heart immediately. He was destined for a career in the army.

29

Well Rotted

Thankfully, we drove back the long way, which might have been several miles longer than the back road, but infinitely safer.

Call me a coward, but unless I grew a pair of wings like Gabriel, I was never going to let myself be driven back to Jericho's End by *that* route.

We stopped off at the dig to see what was happening, if anything, and found the grass and soil had been neatly stripped back in several places, behind rope barriers held by metal stanchions.

The turf had been rolled and stacked nearby and now the volunteers were scraping soil away from the exposed areas with trowels. Charlie was among them and gave us a cheerful wave.

Luke and a thin young man with dark hair were standing in one of the shallow rectangles, laying down white measuring rods and taking pictures, while Treena, hands in coat pockets, looked a little bored. She must be a lot keener on Luke than she was letting on to spend her time off here, instead of walking the dogs or riding Zeph.

Ned, interested, went to see what they were doing but Treena came over to talk to me.

'So far, this is even more boring than gardening,' she said. 'It doesn't even sound as if there's going to be very much to show for it, either, as far as I can see.'

'I'm sure it'll all be infinitely exciting to Luke, though,' I said. 'By the way, I've just told Ned what Melinda said to me yesterday, about Mike not being married after all. He said much the same you did: that there was no reason to worry about Mike turning up and he'd see him off the premises if he did.'

'There you are, then – you've got your very own hero, though there's no reason to think Mike *would* turn up, is there? By the way, I hope you don't mind, but I've told Luke a little bit about you and Mike.'

'No, I don't mind,' I said. 'He seems a very nice . . . *friend*.'

She went slightly pink. 'Actually, we've sort of drifted into going out together. Or perhaps he steered me into it, because that vague manner hides a brilliant and devious mind.'

She raised her voice on the last part, so that Luke, walking back with the other two, could hear it.

Luke grinned at her and then introduced me to his assistant. 'This is Ken Lim – he was my postgrad student last year, so this is good experience for him. I can only afford to pay one extra person, so I wanted a good all-rounder.'

'You wanted someone who'd do the work of three people for a pittance,' said Ken.

'Ken's local,' Ned said. 'His family have the Lucky Dragon takeaway in Thorstane.'

'Yeah, Ned, and they think you've gone off their food, because you haven't ordered a take-out for ages,' Ken said.

'I think I'll be ordering one tomorrow night, though – Marnie's going to help me sort out a huge heap of old papers and photographs. Will you be on delivery duty?'

'Have to. I can't survive on what Luke's paying me,' he said cheerfully.

He went back to the hole and started taking more photographs and Luke said, hopefully, that if we were at a loose end, we could borrow trowels and help remove the surface layer in the hole of our choice.

Ned said, 'Since this is our only day off of the week, we'd like a break from digging things up.'

But Treena thought she might as well, so we left them to it, though we agreed we'd all see each other later in the pub after the Friends of Jericho's End meeting.

We found Caspar sitting on the steps of the office, as if he'd known we were coming and was waiting for us. He followed us in, settling on one arm of the angular sofa.

As he made coffee, Ned said that he'd spoken on the phone a couple of times to Cress's friend Roddy, and he was happy to come in in the afternoons and help with the garden tours and also in the office, or wherever he was needed.

'I'm going to move an old desktop and monitor down here, solely for the Grace Garden business,' he said. 'The landline phone number's just on the website; I've only ever used my mobile for Little Edens, so that's already separate.'

'Good thinking,' I said. 'You can leave any messages on the landline for Roddy to answer, as well as enquiries through the website.'

When we'd drunk our coffee, we had a fun session disagreeing over which roses were meant by the obscure Regency names on the metal tags. In earlier times, roses could be called by several different names and many of these changed during the Victorian era, so this was far from easy.

'But there must have been some kind of planting list

originally, because the metal tags are so much later than the Regency, yet have the old names on them,' I said.

'If there was, perhaps we'll find it among those papers when we sort them,' Ned suggested, and we continued pleasantly bickering about what should go into the empty spots where the original roses had died, but there had been no tag at all.

I returned to my flat feeling much more relaxed and certain there was nothing to worry about and everything would turn out fine.

By now, past experience should really have taught me to mistrust these moments of unfounded optimism . . .

The vicar was at the FOJE meeting that evening. She was a member, but hadn't been able to make it the previous week. And tonight's was short, because she had to dash back to Thorstane by eight to talk to a young couple about calling their marriage banns.

'Late, I know, but they both work in Liverpool and it's such a long commute,' she explained.

The business of the evening mostly consisted of reporting how well the Easter egg hunt had gone, and how much had been raised for the St Gabriel's church tower restoration fund, followed by the arrangements for the Great Mumming Morris Dancers to come and perform on the Green on Mayday.

'Though since Mayday is a Monday this year, we're having it on the Sunday before, instead,' said Myfy.

'Pagan, but fun,' agreed the Reverend Jojo. 'I can pop over after lunch and catch the second session. I doubt I'll make the earlier one.'

'They dance twice,' Elf explained to me. 'The Possets give them lunch at the pub in between. They're quite lively.'

'They're even more lively after they've been to the pub,' said Myfy.

'I often take my violin down and join in with their fiddle player,' Gerald put in.

'There's nothing much to arrange for that, except to make sure they have the right day and Steve opens the Village Hut for them to rest in, or put their bells on, or whatever,' said Gertie.

'And then there's only the jumble sale before the Annual Fête in July,' said the vicar, who hadn't taken her coat off so she could make a quick getaway. 'I do like that.'

'Yes, well, all these events are good for business, I suppose,' Myfy said, 'but when there are crowds about, I'd rather just go up to Jacob's place and hide out till it's all over.'

She and Jacob exchanged one of their intimate smiles, but I knew what she meant: I much preferred quiet and peace to crowds, too, but at least in the garden I was long acclimatized to letting the visitors pass me by, like a film whose sound had been turned down to a murmur.

In the pub we found Treena and Luke, who said some of the dig volunteers had only just left.

'Quite late, really, because most of them have quite a way to travel to get home and you can't drink if you have to drive,' he said. 'That's why I'm staying at Risings – to be on the spot – and I've let a friend have my flat while I'm here, so it's worked out well.'

Ned said he was going to order sausage and chips and I stared at him. 'You can't possibly want more food after all you ate at lunchtime!'

'But that was hours ago, and all I've had since is a sandwich!'

'It's just as well you work so hard in the garden,' I told him, 'or you'd be a tub of lard.'

'That's it, Marnie, don't pull your punches,' he said, grinning, and when his food had arrived and I tried to steal a couple of his chips, he wouldn't let me.

'Buy your own, Ellwood,' he said, covering his plastic basket protectively with both large hands.

Treena and Luke didn't stay long because although she had left the dogs at Happy Pets, where one of the staff would have walked and fed them, she wanted to pick them up and get home.

'The cats will give me hell,' she said gloomily. 'That new Siamese is ten times more trouble than any of the others, now he's settled in.'

'I know the feeling,' I sympathized. 'And Caspar has taken to coming to find me when I'm working.'

Once they'd gone, Ned and I reverted to our favourite topic – the garden – and there was no sign of Wayne that night to jolt my uneasy conscience . . . Not that it needed jolting, and when Ned suddenly asked me out of the blue if anything was still worrying me that I'd like to tell him about, it would have been the perfect opportunity to Confess All.

But call it cowardice, or simply a reluctance to spoil what had been a lovely day – maybe both – but I smiled at him and lied through my teeth.

'No, not a thing! I love living here and working in the gardens.'

At least that last bit was true.

I was early for work next day, but Ned had beaten me to it and had already tipped several barrow-loads of Gertie's best rotted compost on the rose beds, and there were three more full ones lined up.

We began spreading it out around the roots, but after an hour or so he left me to it, and went off to Risings to speak to Wayne about those holes in the lawn, and I carried on alone, feeling a bit uneasy. I hoped he wouldn't lose his temper.

Although he was very easy-going, he could be pushed too far . . .

I finished spreading the mulch and then awarded some to the Rambling Rector in the Lavender Cottage garden, though, goodness knew, it didn't really need encouraging. I spread the last bit on the Alchemist rose in the tall bed by the path leading to the arch, on my way to put the last of the barrows away. Then I replaced the ropes across the paths in the rose garden, ready for opening, though actually James was probably right about the pong and none of the visitors would want to venture down them.

There was still no sign of Ned, but when I found James in the Potting Shed with a cup of tea and a rock cake, he told me he was back and working down the other end of the garden.

'I suppose he thought I'd have finished spreading the manure on the roses on my own,' I said.

'Is that what you've been doing? It'll be ripe enough to floor a visitor at ten paces in there.'

'It is a bit niffy, but it's a good country smell and it'll clear their lungs a treat,' I said.

'It might clear the rose garden, till it wears off,' he said, then asked me what had been decided the day before about extending the shop. I explained what we planned and he said he hoped we'd be getting more stock in soon.

'People seem very keen to part with their brass before they go.'

'I know, there's something about looking round a stately home or garden that makes you want to try to take a piece home with you,' I said. 'A souvenir to remind you how lovely it was, I suppose. I do it myself.'

'Well, we need a bit more choice.'

'I know, I kept telling Ned, but he can see it himself now, so there's going to be a lot more stock soon – including some aimed at the children, with a galleon logo.'

Then I asked him if Ned had seemed OK, because he'd been to have it out with Wayne about those holes in the lawn.

'He didn't say anything but "thank you" when I took him a cup of tea down, but he'd been digging like fury and he's probably down to Australia by now.'

'Oh dear, that doesn't sound too good. Perhaps Wayne denied it all and they argued?' That certainly wouldn't make Ned warm to my loathsome relatives!

'Quite likely,' James said, a Job's comforter.

Ned didn't *look* angry when I saw him later, but his face darkened alarmingly when I asked him if he'd spoken to Wayne.

'Yes, he was up at Risings – and I'm certain the spade he was using was one that went missing when he was working for me. But I couldn't prove it, any more than that it was he who dug those holes all over my lawn, and he knew it.'

'So . . . he didn't admit he'd done it?'

'No, but I don't think he'll try anything like that again. I've warned him that if I ever find him on my property, he'll be sorry. I think I scared him, but he was still cocky, even when I'd finished tearing him off a strip.'

'I suppose he's just like that,' I suggested.

Ned frowned. 'There seemed to be a bit more to it than that, as if he knew something I didn't and then, when I was leaving, he asked me if I was happy with my new gardener and I said it was none of his business.'

'It isn't,' I said, feeling deeply uneasy. 'Did he say . . . anything else?'

'Yes, that perhaps I wouldn't be so happy with you, if *I* knew what *he* knew.'

I went hot and cold. 'What . . . did you think he meant by that?' I asked, trying to stop a slight quiver sneaking into my voice.

'I was about to ask him – or possibly shake it out of him – when we saw Audrey Lordly-Grace's car coming up the drive and he walked off and started digging again. So I thought I'd better leave before Audrey came nosing over to see why I was there.'

I must have looked odd, because he patted me as if I was a nervous dog and said, 'Don't look so worried, Marnie. Don't forget, Wayne does a lot of gardening jobs around the area, so he's probably picked up some version of the story about your resignation from the Heritage Homes Trust and thinks I took you on without knowing about it.'

That *was* a possibility, and I certainly preferred it to the alternative!

I smiled weakly. 'I suppose he must have, but I was hoping it wouldn't become common knowledge.'

'Local people will take you as they find you, and *we* all know the truth, so I wouldn't let it worry you,' he said reassuringly.

Little did he realize what I was *really* worried Wayne might know!

It was still the school holidays, so the village continued to be busy and, if we didn't get quite the hordes of visitors crowding in that we'd had over Easter weekend, it was still busier than we could have hoped for.

Roddy came in early in the afternoon and went round with the first of Ned's tours, to see how it was done. He'd already studied the plan, guidebook and information boards – in fact, he told me he'd taken pictures of the information boards so he could mug them up.

He and Ned seemed to be getting on very well and went off into the office to set up the old desktop for the business and induct Roddy into the ways of a PA. Roddy seemed a quiet, scholarly man, who said he'd be happy to work mostly in the office between taking guided tours around, but in any free time, he would work on his own laptop. He was writing a book about the legacy of Oliver Cromwell: the intermarriage of the Cromwell family into the nobility and their descendants. Or something like that.

Again, there wasn't so much carelessly discarded litter along the River Walk that day, now that the mad rush of Easter weekend was over. The last visitors making their way towards the turnstile seemed pleasant, too, wishing me good afternoon, which it might have been, if it hadn't been for what Wayne had been hinting to Ned . . .

A little magic was already creeping back in by the waterfall, where silence, except for a little sweet birdsong, reigned once more. I let the atmosphere wash like balm across my sore conscience and felt better for it.

Ned was expecting me at the Hall at seven, for our first session on the papers, which would be fun – and maybe even exciting, if we found anything relating to the garden.

When I'd showered and changed, Caspar appeared and I told him I was going out, then suggested he might like to go back and make up to Elf and Myfy for a change, since they were the ones feeding him expensive cat food and dealing with his litter tray.

This didn't go down well, especially my attempt to persuade him to return through the cat flap, and when I set off for the Hall, he insisted on accompanying me. In fact, he dogged my footsteps – you can't really say 'catted', can you?

So when Ned opened his front door, he found Caspar barging past him before he could say anything.

'Come in, why don't you?' he said, looking after the long bushy tail and marmalade rump as it made off down the passage.

Lizzie

I had no opportunity to visit the waterfall again, but treasured the memory of my experience there . . . But I did love the apothecary garden at Old Grace Hall, and Mr Richard Grace delighted in my interest and told me many wonderful things about the rare plants there, and how it had been set out so long ago as a physic garden.

Mr Grace's wife had died young in childbirth, so he was inclined to be melancholy, but I believe he found some solace in talking to me and telling me of the cuttings and seeds of interesting plants he hoped to obtain for the garden.

Susanna, bored, would trail behind us and was always pleased when her governess called to us to go home again.

These visits were some compensation for the long, dreary Sundays spent with my family and the other Brethren.

Other than Miss Susanna and Master Neville, the rest of the family at Risings seemed barely aware of my existence, though occasionally the master, a large, red-faced man with a loud, booming voice, would chuck me under the chin in passing, a familiarity he took with all the younger female servants.

30
Box of Delights

I'd only been in the Hall once before, with Treena and Luke, when Ned had showed us round. This time we went straight into the library, where the lights were on and the log-burner lit, making it look cosy.

An ancient, battered and metal-banded trunk and a plain deal box stood on the rug next to the coffee table, and neither was exactly small.

'I've dipped into the boxes a couple of times and found interesting things, but I'd say the heir to each generation has simply tipped his predecessor's papers into one of the boxes and started afresh . . . and then my great-uncle Theo came along and rummaged about in them, mixing the layers up. He did say that at one time he thought of writing a family history, but the way he was going on, it would have been a topsy-turvy one.'

'This could take a while,' I said, opening the lid on the trunk and finding it crammed right to the top.

'I know, and the other box is just as full,' Ned agreed.

Caspar poked his head into the trunk, then sneezed and backed off, looking affronted.

'Perhaps we ought to order some food before we start, from the Lucky Dragon?' Ned suggested.

'Mmrow,' approved Caspar from the armchair and listened intelligently as we discussed the rival merits of sweet and sour chicken, Singapore fried rice and prawn curry.

'Sesame toast and spring rolls,' Ned muttered, jotting things down before phoning the order in.

'That's enough for four people,' I pointed out.

'I *eat* enough for three,' he said simply, turning off his phone. 'There we are – we've got at least half an hour till it arrives, so we might as well begin.'

'We need a plan,' I said. 'Since everything's already mixed up, why don't we start by fishing out all the photographs and putting them on the table?'

'Good idea, and when we go through them later, there are a couple of photograph albums on one of the shelves, so we might be able to identify a few of the people in them.'

We worked away, one box each, *trying* not to let ourselves be distracted when we came across very ancient-looking documents written on parchment, and only stopped to devour our takeaway, duly delivered by Luke's assistant, Ken.

Ned suggested Ken stay and help us with the sorting, but he just laughed and said he had another delivery to make and then a hot date at nine.

Caspar accepted a couple of prawns from the fried rice, which I hoped wouldn't upset his delicate tummy, then Ned took the debris through to the kitchen and came back with a bottle of chilled pinot grigio and two glasses, which, if it didn't help speed up our search, at least cheered us along the way. Caspar, profoundly bored, went to sleep.

It was late before we were sure we'd found all the photographs, which ranged all the way from very early views of family groups, sometimes posed by the river or the waterfall, to hand-tinted portraits and Box Brownie snaps.

A few had names and dates on the back in pencil, but you could date some of them anyway by the clothes, or the vintage cars they were proudly grouped around. In the roaring twenties, there seemed to have been a vogue for people pointing at things in the garden, so the backgrounds of those were interesting – the sundial was in one.

The more recent photos were in the albums but I could already tell that Ned was a true Grace, tall and fair.

'There's a contemporary description of Nathaniel Grace as a fair giant,' Ned said, 'though in those times you didn't need to be very tall to be thought one.'

'You're pretty tall for *now*,' I pointed out, sifting through the heaps of photos on the table, looking for the more relevant ones.

There were some very atmospheric ones of the falls and I came across a whole packet just of the Grace Garden, taken before the lower part had been dug up to grow vegetables for the war effort.

'There's loads of material here for the museum display *and* the next edition of the guidebook,' I said.

'I think I'll have to update that annually anyway, as the restoration of the garden progresses,' he said. 'And we'll have photos of the rose garden in bloom to go in the next one, too.'

I stood up and stretched. 'I think we'd better call it a night, don't you? We can start rough-sorting the papers tomorrow.'

Caspar watched me put on my coat and then came to wind himself around my legs.

'I'd forgotten about Caspar – he probably needs to go out.'

'He followed me to the kitchen earlier and there's still a cat flap in the back door there, from my uncle's day . . . if he can squeeze through it,' Ned said. 'He didn't show any sign of wanting out then, anyway.'

He unhooked his own coat from the rack as we went out and said, 'I'll see you to your door.'

'There's no need – it's only a few yards away and it must be safe enough here!'

'I'd like to stretch my legs anyway,' he insisted, and we went back the way I'd come, by the road, which was a lot easier than unlocking every gate through from the back of the Hall to the Lavender Cottage garden.

As usual, a dim light burned at the back of the café and another came on near the side gate as we approached.

'Goodnight, then,' Ned said, opening the gate for me, as Caspar shoved through first in his usual mannerless way. 'It's been quite fun, hasn't it?' he added, as if in surprise and then walked off, whistling as sweetly as a blackbird.

And it had been fun, too. *Way* too much fun to risk spoiling it by telling Ned who I really was: first cousin to the vile Wayne.

The huge terracotta garden pots arrived early next morning, and Ned and Lex Mariner, who was almost as tall as he was, unloaded them and then moved them into position.

I watched them with Caspar and the peacocks, though Lancelot and Guinevere got quickly bored and wandered off.

The pots looked spectacular when four of them were placed at points around the wide circular gravel path, but they also somehow gave the impression of always having been there.

When the two men had finished, I had a closer look at the swirls of seaweed and barnacle-like applied decoration that Ned had mentioned, which was strangely beautiful . . .

'You'd fit easily inside one of those, Ellwood,' Ned

threatened me. 'Bear that in mind before you give me any more of your sarky comments.'

Then he introduced me to Lex, who was grinning. He was as dark as Ned was fair, with an aggressively Roman nose. In fact, he was very much like Clara Mayhem Doome; you could see the family resemblance.

Ned began telling him what we'd been working on recently in the garden and our future plans and something – possibly Ned's frequent repetition of the words 'we' and 'Marnie thinks' – seemed to have caused Lex to jump to the wrong conclusion about our relationship. He said he was glad Ned had found someone on his wavelength at last and we must all meet up at the Pike with Two Heads for dinner, when his wife got back from painting a portrait commission.

'Great,' said Ned, who didn't seem to have noticed Lex's mistake at all.

Roddy arrived early and Ned took him into the office, then later I saw him taking the second tour group round the garden, while Ned thankfully escaped to the half-dug long plots to join me.

'Roddy's amazing – he seemed to grasp what was needed almost straight away. He's going to have a chat later with James about what's selling best in the shop and what else we could stock.'

'Brilliant,' I said. 'I was just thinking I could do with some of the volunteers from the dig to start rolling all this rough turf back from round the beds, but you'll do instead.'

'You know,' he said, 'I seem to be under the deluded impression that *I'm* the boss round here.'

'Planks.'

'What?' he said.

'We need planks between the long beds, until we put down the new turf.'

'I know – I've got a stack of them in the stables. Two minds with but a single thought!'

And he picked up his spade and began to dig.

Caspar and I headed for the Hall again that evening. Ned had insisted he'd provide dinner – and this time actually cook something.

I hadn't got my hopes up too high, which was just as well, because he'd dashed up to Toller's and bought a huge pizza and a sherry trifle sealed in a plastic bowl.

Both were quite nice, though, even if the trifle was covered in slightly synthetic-tasting cream and the glacé cherries on top had never seen a stalk.

I ate too much pizza and was feeling distinct twinges of indigestion as we settled down in the library to sift the accumulated paper trail of centuries.

There were rolls of parchment and crackling sheets of thick, ancient yellowed paper, bundles of letters tied up with string or ribbon, miscellaneous official-looking deeds and documents, invoices and lists . . .

But we'd sworn not to start reading anything tonight, just rough-sort it all onto the floor and table, and we mostly managed to stick to that.

When we finally stopped, dusty, grubby and tired, Ned reminded me that it was the quiz the next night.

'It'll probably do us good to have a break from all this dust, and we can have another go on Saturday night if you haven't had enough of it?'

'Of course I haven't. I can hardly wait,' I said truthfully. 'It's been very tantalizing not reading what we're finding – when there's bound to be loads of stuff about the garden.' Then I added, more firmly, 'But next time, *I'll* bring dinner with me!'

On Friday I discovered that Ned had had the bright idea of carrying a box of the photographs we'd found and the family albums down to the office, so that if Roddy had any time to spare in the afternoon he could attempt to identify the subjects of some of them and pencil the information on the back.

I thought he'd probably prefer to get on with the book he was writing, if he had some spare time, but when I asked him later, when he'd finished taking the visitors round for the second tour, he said he was finding it very enjoyable.

'I like a challenge,' he said, and then, as if this had reminded him, remarked that Cress's mother had invited him to tea after the garden closed, or maybe he *was* tea, because now I came to think about Audrey Lordly-Grace, with her plump body and spindly arms and legs, she was a bit spidery and possibly might eat him alive.

But no, he escaped unscathed, because I saw him again that evening in the pub with Cress, sitting at the end of the next table, ready for the quiz.

Luke wasn't there, but that wasn't a surprise because Treena had told me he was going over to her cottage this evening for dinner. She'd be on emergency call tonight, so it made more sense that way.

We'd eaten our dinner and Ned was just telling the others about our delvings into the family archives, when I caught sight of Wayne coming in, followed by his father.

Elf spotted them too, and exclaimed in surprise, 'Oh, we don't often see Saul Vane in here!'

'The lure of mammon does seem to be too much for him to

resist sometimes,' Myfy said. 'Or maybe it's just curiosity to see what fun looks like.'

Wayne took his beer straight into the darts room as usual, but Saul stayed by the bar, sipping his pint and glowering at anyone who came near him, as if they might be thinking of stealing it.

Ned reclaimed my attention by teasing me about something, but when I looked up again, I found Saul's cold eyes fixed on me, under lowering brows.

Myfy noticed it to. 'Old Saul seems to be giving you the old "you'll burn in hell" look tonight, Marnie – what have you done to deserve that?'

'Nothing that I know of,' I said hastily. 'He's only seen me once before, on the day the garden opened, when he said some odd things . . . but Gertie told me he *is* a bit odd.'

'Daisy told me Wayne came into the café the other day, asking all kinds of questions about you, Marnie,' said Elf. 'But of course, Daisy doesn't know much about you and she wouldn't tell him if she did.'

'I warned Wayne on Wednesday morning not to come on my property any more,' Ned said angrily.

'Well, dear, although we're family, the café *isn't* your property, so I expect he thought it didn't count,' Elf pointed out. 'And he bought an ice-cream, so he was a paying customer.'

'What did he want to know?' demanded Ned.

'Oh, where Marnie came from and how old she was . . . if she was seeing anyone,' said Elf. 'Daisy thought he might fancy you, Marnie – and maybe he does and Saul's come to have another look at his prospective daughter-in-law.'

'I suspect Marnie could do a little better than Wayne Vane!' said Myfy.

'Yes, but it would account for Saul being weird to you in the rose garden,' Ned said, grinning. 'But if so, I don't think he's about to give you his blessing.'

'He can keep it,' I said and then, to my relief, Saul finished his pint, wiped his mouth on the back of his hand, and walked out.

But his sudden appearance and the way he'd looked at me had shattered my enjoyment of the evening. I wished I could believe that he merely was interested in me because Wayne had taken a fancy to me, but I couldn't.

But if he had guessed who I was and already thought he'd warned me off, why had he come tonight for what seemed to be the sole purpose of glaring at me? Was it just to reinforce the warning?

As if I needed it.

A bad conscience is a poor bedfellow, but luckily, a warm cat is a comforting one.

I didn't sleep very well, due to feeling that the Sword of Damocles was suspended above my head by a hair – and, deep down, I knew the only way I'd ever be free from it would be to tell Ned the truth about my Vane connections.

The trouble was, the longer I left it, the harder it became. We'd become so close now that I was afraid of seeing the change in his face when he knew, the sudden retreat behind that shutter, barring me from his friendship and confidence . . . and I didn't think I could bear it.

31

The Handmaid's Tale

Despite the lack of sleep, I'd still woken up just as early as usual, draped in a dead-to-the-world cat. My usually healthy appetite seemed to have vanished, but I drank two mugs of coffee before heading down to the bottom of the cottage garden, where I had a good weed under the bushes that edged the paving where the beehives stood in a row.

The shrubs there were all insect-friendly – winter-flowering mahonia, butterfly-attracting buddleia and a ceanothus – so it must be lovely on a warm summer's day when the bees were more active and humming happily round the flowers. I expect they'd be buzzing off next door to the roses, too, when their usual lavender-rich diet palled.

I went back up to the flat to fetch my rucksack and flask, just in time to see Caspar's furry rump vanish through the cat flap, on his way to breakfast. Then off I went to the Grace Garden, squashing down the feeling of impending doom. If it was going to happen, I'd dance like a butterfly right up to the brink.

Ned was in the Poison Garden, well covered up and weeding the beds around the angel's trumpet and the Irish yew. I hadn't actually been inside the claw-like enclosure yet – the thought of the rosary pea vine, just one berry of which was fatal, had slightly put me off. I had a mental image of it suddenly jumping out of its wrought-iron cage and grabbing me.

Ned said I was mad and there was nothing to fear, as long as you wore the right protective gear for the job and disposed of any harmful material on the bonfire.

'Come on in and have a look – just don't touch anything,' he invited me. 'It's not at its best at this time of year, but wait until the angel's trumpet's in flower, and the aconite and the foxgloves – I've got more of those coming, in pink, red and purple.'

'I'm sure it will be lovely,' I agreed, cautiously peering at the quite pretty ferny leaves of the rosary pea, which had red berries . . . all the better to kill you with.

It was enclosed in the Victorian ironwork aviary, and the mandrake was in a smaller one, though I couldn't imagine *that* escaping and wreaking havoc.

When he'd finished, he locked the gate carefully behind us. 'I'll start giving tours of the Poison Garden in summer, just to small groups of adults and maybe only at weekends,' he said. 'I can't really ask Roddy to do them, but if it's just one group a day, it won't take too much time up.'

'They'll be really popular,' I said. 'You might have to have a pre-booking form on the website. You should add a sign-up page for the Friends of the Grace Garden now, anyway, and perhaps another for volunteers.'

'You talk to Roddy about it,' he suggested. 'You're the one with all the ideas!'

'OK,' I agreed. 'When are the rest of the wetland plants you ordered arriving?'

'Early next week, I think,' he said, pushing the hair back

from his face. 'You might ask him to chase that up too, while you're at it.'

'Your hair wants pruning,' I told him.

'Stick to the gardening, Ellwood, you're not coming near me with the secateurs,' he said and, picking up the barrow handles, he headed for the gate to the vegetable garden where the bonfire patch lay.

Perhaps it was because it was the last weekend of the Easter holiday that the garden was almost as busy as the last one, but I was conscious of the ebb and flow of the visitors as I dug my way down a long narrow plot with Ned working from the other side, to meet, as we so often did with garden tasks, in the middle.

I didn't return after checking the River Walk, but instead went back to the flat to wash and change, ready to go over to Ned's later and get stuck into actually *reading* some of the papers we'd rough-sorted.

First, though, I whipped up a big risotto, which I ladled into a lidded container, wrapped in newspaper and put inside a freezer carry bag before setting off.

It had worried me that Caspar hadn't yet put in an appearance at the flat, but I found him sitting waiting on Ned's doorstep, like some misshapen heraldic beast.

'What kept you?' he said – or I *assume* that's what he said.

We ate first, while the risotto was hot, finishing off with some of Elf's ice-cream from Ned's freezer and coffee, before going through to the library and setting to work.

First, we put all the bundles of letters to one side, for later examination, except for one that had been labelled 'Tradescant', presumably by Ned's uncle Theo, and which we thought might contain some interesting insights into the early days of the garden. Of course, there'd probably be loads of interesting things in the other letters too, but it would take ages to read them.

That still left several other heaps on the table. Ned suggested we divide them between us, then put anything irrelevant to the garden back in the boxes as we went.

'I'll start with the oldest-looking pile and put my rejects in the trunk, and you put yours in the box. How about that?'

'Sounds reasonable to me,' I agreed, and we settled down to it, finding a few gems of information, but occasionally sidetracked by something irrelevant but interesting, like the contents of an ancient will.

Wills, marriage lines, inventories, lists, stray letters – the task seemed endless . . . as did Caspar's bubbling snores from his favourite armchair.

Ned had just come back with mugs of coffee to keep us awake, when I discovered a long brown envelope that looked quite new and had somehow found itself sandwiched between a bill for the refitting of a merchant ship and 'A Sovereign remedy for girth galls and Spavins', which didn't sound like a lot of fun.

'Listen to this, Ned,' I said as he put the coffee cups down. 'It looks like your uncle Theo's writing again and it says, "An account written by Elizabeth Grace, née Vane, to be given to her son, Thomas Grace, explaining the circumstances surrounding his birth." '

I passed it across. 'That's definitely Theo's writing,' he said, opening the end of the envelope to reveal another, older one, inside. 'I hope this isn't going to be like pass-the-parcel, with ever-smaller and older envelopes.'

'Don't be daft,' I said. 'And that must be the Elizabeth Vane in Elf's book, who ran off with a Lordly-Grace and then ended up married to your ancestor, mustn't it?'

The dreaded Vane connection had reared its ugly head again.

'I expect so. I can only think she must have had a charm about her that all the Vanes *I've* ever met have entirely lacked.'

I said nothing and he began to read what it said on the inner envelope.

I found this letter among the papers in my mother's desk after her death. I saw fit to keep it for posterity, who I hope will not judge her conduct harshly. My mother was the sweetest and kindest of women and her sins were only those of youth and folly.

Thomas Grace

'It's dated 1849,' he added, then gave me a quizzical look. 'I don't think I can resist reading this now, even if it's not relevant to the garden, can you? Elf will be cross that we found it after she'd finished writing her book!'

'It's irresistible,' I agreed, though little did he know I had a personal interest in it . . .

There were several stiff, crackling yellowed pages inside the inner envelope, closely written on both sides and not very easy to make out, especially when I was leaning over Ned's shoulder.

'Why did she use such tiny writing?' he complained, spreading them out on the table under the lamp.

'Have you seen the little books the Brontës wrote when they were children?' I asked. 'The writing is minute!'

He pulled out a pair of narrow, gold-rimmed glasses from his pocket and put them on: he looked a very learned lion now.

'I didn't know you wore specs?'

'Only for reading fine print, but I forget them half the time.'

'You should wear them more often; they make you look almost intelligent.'

'Gee, thanks! Now, perhaps you'd like to get out of my light and sit down, and I'll read it out aloud?'

He pushed the glasses up his broad nose, cleared his throat slightly self-consciously, and began:

I, Elizabeth Grace, once Lizzie Vane, have decided to set out this account of my life, which I will leave for my beloved son, Thomas, to read when I am gone.

I have survived my dear, kind husband by many years and only now, when I feel myself fading like the last rose of summer in the garden he created for me, do I feel this need to speak the truth.

My son is aware of my past misfortunes, but has never questioned me on the subject of this and the rift it led to with the rest of the family, the Lordly-Graces – and, indeed, the lasting estrangement from my own family at Cross Ways Farm. I have been as one dead to them since my elopement so many years ago.

I would like to tell the whole tale now, painful as it is, for I have known both the worst and the best of men, and would set the record straight. My husband, Richard Grace, knew the whole story and yet bestowed a lasting love upon me that I felt unworthy of.

Ned looked up. 'The plot thickens,' he said. 'But it confirms when the rose garden was created. Shall I read the rest of it?'

'Go on,' I urged, fascinated, and he set off again, forefinger moving along under the closely written words.

After a while, Ned looked up. 'This all sounds like a Victorian melodrama, doesn't it? The jolly squire, the younger son . . . But is she ever going to get to the point where she elopes, before my throat silts up with paper dust?'

'I'll make some more coffee, shall I?' I suggested. 'Then you can finish reading it. There can't be much more.'

'OK,' he agreed. 'And you're right, there's only a couple more pages to go . . .'

Lizzie

This fairly happy existence continued until the year I was to turn sixteen. Susanna was a year older and I began to dream of accompanying her to London as her lady's maid when she had her Season. While I secretly cherished romantic thoughts of her brother Neville, I knew very well that nothing would come of them, but hoped that perhaps one day, I might meet and marry a man of my own station in life, while in the service of my mistress . . .

But these modest hopes were to be shattered, for one Sunday my father informed me that as soon as I had turned sixteen, I was to be married to Mr Hodgekins, Minister of the Thorstane meeting house! He was not only older than Father and ill-favoured, but a harsh, disagreeable man of whom I went in fear, like all the women in his congregation. He had recently buried his second wife and I had secretly thought she must have been pleased to escape him, even by death.

Nothing I could say would sway his decision and his anger was terrible when, in my distress, I let slip some hint of my hope to accompany Susanna to London. He said the marriage would take place immediately upon my attaining my sixteenth year and, once the deed was done, Mr Lordly-Grace could have no say in my future.

I was thrown into great despair by this and did not know which way to turn, until it occurred to me that if Mr

Lordly-Grace were to learn of my father's plans for my disposal before the marriage could take place, he might very well intervene – for after all, I had been trained up as a maid in his house and Miss Susanna would be extremely upset should she have to do without me.

Next morning Master Neville, who was now an officer in the army and had been home on leave, was to return to his regiment, garrisoned near York. This would normally have caused me to weep into my pillow, but my present predicament was all I could think of, and I resolved to appeal to Mr Lordly-Grace to intervene with my father, as soon as he left the breakfast table for his study next morning, as was his habit.

But I was to discover that I was most grievously mistaken in my hope that he would have any desire to help me.

32

Flight

Ned laid down the sheet of paper and picked up the next. 'I think we can work out *why* Lizzie ran off with one of the sons, if it was her only hope of escaping marriage to a man she loathed,' he said.

'It certainly doesn't sound as if this Mr Lordly-Grace was prepared to help her, so I don't suppose she had any other option,' I agreed. 'I'm dying to know the rest now, and how she ended up married to your ancestor, instead of Neville – and whether the true story is the same as the version in Elf's book!'

'She's going to be really miffed if it isn't.' He pushed the glasses back up his nose again. 'Last lap: here goes.'

In my distress and agony of spirit, I ran straight out of the front door of the house, which stood open and must have passed the chaise that was to take Neville on the first part of his journey to rejoin his regiment, for as if in a dream – or a nightmare – I heard him call my name in a surprised voice.

But I did not – could not – stop. Without conscious thought, my feet took me down to the bridge over the river, and I only stopped when I had reached the highest point and was looking down over the low stone parapet into the cold, churning depths of the Devil's Cauldron so far below.

There was a pounding in my head and the rushing sound of the water reminded me of angel wings, though I was sure no angel would await me after I had committed the sin of taking my own life.

The chill striking into my bones through my thin stuff house dress woke me, shivering, to my purpose and I began to climb onto the broad wall.

I did not see or hear Neville's chaise turn away from the main road and stop nearby, or his running feet as he reached me just in time to snatch me back from the brink.

I struggled and begged him to let me go and when he would not, told him the reason I could not bear to live and that this was the only course open to me.

His face changed and darkened in a way I had never seen it before and he seemed for a moment unsure what to do, his hands still gripping me tightly, while I pleaded with him to let me go.

Then, perhaps seeing that I was beside myself and determined in my purpose, he declared he would take me with him and carried me off to his chaise.

It was a moment of impulse born from his kind nature, for his action was bound to get back to his father's ears. But during that journey I remained in such a state of shock and deepest despair that I barely took in his promise to look after me.

But this promise he carried out, as best he could, though his father immediately cut off his allowance. He established me in lodgings near the garrison, where he could visit as often as his duties allowed . . .

And later, when his regiment was sent to Portugal, he left me such money as he could and swore he would send more to support me – and the child that was to come.

After his departure I felt very alone and all too soon his letters ceased to arrive, so that I knew not what had happened, but feared the worst. Finally, a brother officer, who knew my situation, came to inform me that Neville had been killed in a great battle.

All too soon, my means were exhausted and, great with child, penniless and desperate, I felt my only course was to return to Jericho's End, for I could not take my own life when that would mean ending that of my innocent babe, before it had even begun.

I will spare you the difficulties of my journey there, in the dead of winter, but suffice it to say that my father refused me admittance to the house and threatened to set the dogs on me should I not depart forthwith, despite its being by then dark and the snow starting to settle.

I trudged on to Risings, for surely the master would take pity on my plight?

The butler denied me entry and told me to be gone, but beyond him I caught sight of the family leaving the dining room and, with one last desperate surge of energy, managed to slip past the butler and make my plea for help to Mr Lordly-Grace.

On my knees, I begged him to assist me, for the sake of the child, but he sneered and said there was no place for bold-faced strumpets in his house and told the servants to throw me out.

Half-fainting, I heard Susanna's horrified voice speak my name falteringly . . . and then the deeper, once-familiar voice of Richard Grace, saying, 'Why, it is little Lizzie – and come to this pass, poor child! Cousin, you cannot mean to throw her out in this weather. After all, the child—'

'May or may not be my son's by-blow,' said the master harshly. 'But it is nothing to me – the wench has made her own bed and must lie on it. Remove her at once,' he ordered.

'I wouldn't turn a dog out in this,' said Richard Grace, and I felt strong arms catch me as I fell into a deep faint and knew no more, until I regained my senses, to find myself lying in a warm bedchamber at Old Grace Hall, being tended by the familiar, kindly old housekeeper.

She said her master had told her that although I had behaved foolishly, I should be given all care until the child had arrived – and perhaps brought on by my travails, I gave birth to a fine boy only a few days later.

When I had recovered, Mr Grace came to talk with me and proposed that I remain at Old Grace Hall and help Mrs Higgins and Cook – and also, if I still had a love of plants, assist him in the garden, too.

This was kindness beyond any imagining and I was deeply grateful, especially when I discovered that his actions had led to a total breach between the families at Old Grace Hall and Risings and, I learned, was blamed for the apoplexy brought on by anger that confined Mr Horace Lordly-Grace to his bed henceforth.

I did all I could to repay Mr Grace's generosity to me and the child became a great favourite with all the household.

But I was sorry Mr Grace should think so ill of Neville, so finally resolved to tell him the whole truth of the matter and that Neville had acted only out of kindness, however misguided. It was difficult to reveal all to him and I could see it had made him very angry, though not with me . . . And only a short time later, to the astonishment and disapproval of the entire neighbourhood, he married me and adopted my boy, Thomas, as his heir.

Despite the hardships and rigours of my early childhood and the effect upon my constitution of what was to follow, I have survived my dear, kind husband by some fifteen years.

I often feel his presence when I walk in the rose garden, or sit in the marble folly there – and I long to join him.

It has been painful revisiting my past and I hope my son will not think too ill of me, for I was little more than a child when my misfortunes took place.

Neville's elder brother, George, proved to be a gambler and reduced the family fortunes to the point where they sold off their land in the valley and the London house, and settled at Risings in genteel poverty on the proceeds. Susanna married a poor clergyman and went to live in the North, and I heard no more of her.

I have no friends outside the household, but my son and his sweet wife and the little grandchildren bring me great joy.

I put my trust in a more benign God than the one the Brethren worship and for the intercession of angels.

Elizabeth Grace

Ned's deep voice stopped and he quietly laid the last sheet of paper on top of the others.

'Well!' I said, gazing at him and still taking it all in. 'This puts a slightly different spin on the old tale of elopement, doesn't it?'

'The version in Elf's book is right in all the main details, she just didn't know what had caused Lizzie to run off with Neville in the first place. I hadn't realized how young she was, either.'

'No, little more than a child – and she sounds rather nice, doesn't she? *And* keen on gardening,' I added thoughtfully.

'Nice for a *Vane*,' he grimaced. 'I'd still rather not be related to that family, however distantly, although there have to be some good ones from time to time . . . She obviously loved the garden and if it wasn't for her, the roses wouldn't be there, or the folly.'

'Yes, we know now when that was built, roughly. Richard sounds so sweet, rescuing her and then marrying her and adopting the boy. And actually, since Neville Lordly-Grace was the child's father, he was also related to Richard, wasn't he?'

'Nathaniel Grace was a cousin of the Lordly-Grace who sold him the Hall, even if they looked down on him for his buccaneering days and shipping interests – trade, but also lots of lovely money,' Ned said.

'It's odd to think that Lizzie's son, Thomas, was a Victorian, which wasn't really that many generations ago, was it?' I said.

It brought it all so much closer.

'We'll tell Elf and the others about the letter at dinner tomorrow evening, shall we?' he suggested. 'I'll print off a copy of the letter for Elf.'

'Could I have one, too?' I asked. 'I'd like to read it again. It's very interesting . . . and rather touching.'

'Of course.' He got up and stretched, then reached a hand down and pulled me up, too. 'It's getting late – I'll see you home.'

I didn't protest, even though it was definitely not needed in this quiet backwater, where the only thing to break the silence of the night once the pub had shut was the hooting of a hunting owl.

But this time I was wrong, for just as we reached the front of the café and Caspar was barging past me to the gate, in his usual gracious fashion, all hell seemed to break loose up at the monastic site: loud barking, shouting, car doors slamming and the revving of engines.

'Come on!' said Ned, taking my hand, and we ran over the bridge and up the hill.

But by the time we reached the car park, the excitement was over and there was just Steve, directing a powerful torch about, and his sheepdog, Bob, leaping excitedly round him. Gertie was peering out from the lighted door of the lodge opposite.

Steve turned at the sound of our footsteps and said, 'You were right to warn me that Wayne and those friends of his with the metal detectors might try and have a go at the site. There were two vans and they had sacking over the registration numbers, but I'm sure that's who it was.'

He shone the torch on the open gate, with the padlocks hanging loose. 'Bolt cutters, I expect,' he said. 'But they didn't know Bob was sleeping in there at night.'

'Bob was in the enclosure?' I said. 'Wasn't he cold?'

'Not him. He sleeps in his kennel in the garden all year round; asks to go out last thing at night, he does. I brought it over and put it in a nice cosy spot out of the wind, between the hut and the wall and he had the run of the site.'

'I don't suppose there's anything we can do?' Ned asked. 'I doubt that even Wayne and his cronies are stupid enough to leave fingerprints on the padlocks and chains.'

'No, there's no point calling the police, but I don't think they'll try it again,' Steve said. 'I've another chain that'll hold the gate tonight and I'll see about something a bit more heavy duty tomorrow.'

Ned helped him fix it while Bob was awarded a large rawhide bone by Gertie, who came across in her dressing gown and slippers. Then Bob retired back to his kennel, where we could hear loud gnawing noises.

When all was secured, we walked slowly back down the hill home.

'What are you doing tomorrow?' Ned asked.

'If you don't really need me in the garden first thing, I'll go to the supermarket in Great Mumming and then pop in to see Treena.'

I really, really, *needed* to talk everything through with her!

'But then I'll come and help in the garden,' I promised.

'You don't have to.'

'Try and keep me away!' I said, and he laughed.

The sky looked like darkest indigo velvet, speckled with silver sequins, quite beautiful. And my *life* would be quite beautiful, too, if only I didn't have a big, fat, horrible secret squatting like a spider in the middle of it.

33

Unforgotten

I got to the supermarket in Great Mumming just as it opened and filled my trolley up with staples. Toller's were good for extras, treats and things I'd run out of, but their prices meant I couldn't afford to do all my shopping there – or not unless Ned suddenly doubled my wages, which was highly unlikely.

I bought sushi and fresh cream doughnuts for lunch, though if Treena didn't fancy hers I'd probably manage both . . . Overnight, I appeared to have switched from no appetite, to comfort eating.

Treena had only just got back to the cottage when I arrived, after a night on duty at Happy Pets. There'd been an emergency admission late in the evening and a couple of pets recovering from operations. She was exhausted, but still feeling wired and not at all sleepy.

An early lunch of sushi and doughnuts, washed down with coffee, seemed to be exactly what she needed and, over it, I told her how Ned and I had found Elizabeth Grace's letter last night and about the later alarms and excursions up at the dig.

'It was very late by then, so Luke must have been fast asleep, because there was no sign of him,' I said. 'But I expect Steve's told him all about it by now and I shouldn't think Wayne and his friends will try that one again.'

'Are you positive it was Wayne?'

'I don't think there's much doubt,' I said, with a sigh. 'I keep *meaning* to tell Ned I'm related to the Vanes, but the moment never seems right – and every time I do screw my courage up, Wayne does something else dreadful. *And* he was hinting to Ned on Wednesday that he knew something about me that Ned didn't. Only Ned thinks he must have found out about that loopy resignation letter.'

'But he *could* be right about that and the Vanes haven't guessed who you are,' she said hopefully. 'And Saul only talked to you in the garden that time because Wayne had shown interest in you and he wanted to suss you out.'

'And pigs might fly,' I said. 'No, I keep trying to stick my head in the sand, but it's not really working.'

Then I looked up and said, despair suddenly welling up, 'Oh, Treena, Ned and I've been getting on so well together and having such fun working in the garden! It's just like old times, when we were at college.'

'What, when you were just good friends?' she said disbelievingly.

'Well . . . no, perhaps we've grown a bit closer than that,' I admitted. 'But once he knows who I really am, that's all bound to go totally pear-shaped.'

'Maybe not. I mean, you can't exactly *help* being related to the Vanes, can you?'

'No, but if he dislikes the idea of having a *distant* Vane ancestor so much, then he's hardly going to . . .'

'Welcome you into the family with open arms?' she suggested with a grin.

'What on earth do you mean?' I demanded. 'As far as the

Grace family tree is concerned, I'm barely a bud on the smallest twig.'

'Oh, come on! Even Luke could see that you and Ned have fallen for each other and he's usually totally unaware of that kind of thing.'

'I'm sure you're wrong and Ned only thinks of me as a good friend, and now a close ally in the restoration of the garden . . . and that's fine by me. I don't *want* anything else,' I said firmly.

'Yeah, right!' she said.

'And you've some need to talk, Treena, because you and Luke—'

'Are in a relationship,' she said calmly. 'I did say we were going out together and now . . . well, we've just sort of slid into something that might turn out to be more. But it's early days yet and I don't want to rush into anything. He's coming over Monday night to stay,' she added, slightly ruining the effect of this declaration. 'He's decided to close the dig on Tuesdays, now he knows everything else in Jericho's End is shut then.'

'Good idea,' I said, leaving it vague about which I meant – the sleepover or the closing day.

'Some of the volunteers can only come at weekends, so it wouldn't have been logical to have their one day off then.'

'The full-time ones seem to work even longer hours than I do,' I said. 'In theory, I get Sundays off as well as Tuesdays, though I told Ned I'd give him a hand this afternoon.'

At the thought of him, all my worries came crashing down on me again. 'Treena, what on earth am I going to do about Ned?'

'Well, you could wait and see if the Vanes really do know who you are and threaten to tell Ned, out of spite . . .'

I shook my head. 'I don't think they would tell him because, after all, they disowned Mum when she was pregnant, so they wouldn't want to acknowledge me, would they?'

'So, if Saul did guess who you were, he was just warning you not to try to claim any relationship with him.'

'Possibly – not that I ever wanted to!'

'And if that's so, then he's not going to do anything else about it and you can stop worrying, can't you?'

'Not if Wayne knows too, and keeps dropping hints to Ned, because he's bound to realize it's something more than the resignation letter. It would be like carrying an unexploded bomb around with me all the time. It feels a bit like that now,' I added. 'Only, when I'm really happy I manage to forget it, or convince myself everything is going to be all right.'

'There you are, then, you've answered your own question: you need to have it out with Ned, or it'll always be hanging over you,' she said firmly.

In my heart, I'd always known that would be the inescapable conclusion.

'Yes . . . but things will never be the same between Ned and me again.'

'Don't be daft – you've blown it up out of all proportion. Though it might be a shock to Ned, once he's got over that, I'm sure it won't change how he feels about you.'

I wished I could feel as sure about that as she did. She must have seen the doubt on my face, because she added cheeringly, 'On the bright side, it doesn't seem like Melinda's told Mike where you're living now, does it? I mean, there's been no sign of him, has there?'

'Mike . . .' I echoed vaguely. The question of whether he knew where I was or not seemed to have faded into insignificance next to my preoccupation with how Ned would react to my revelation . . . if I ever actually managed to pluck up the courage and tell him.

'Mike, your controlling ex-husband, remember?' prompted Treena.

'He doesn't matter any more, because Ned knows all about him,' I said simply. 'Perhaps he did find out from Melinda, but isn't interested?'

'Perhaps, but if he knows, then I wouldn't put it past him to try to jerk your strings a bit, just for the fun of it.'

I hoped she was wrong: he'd be one more blast from the past I could do without right then.

When I'd got home and put my shopping away, I changed and went to join Ned at the bottom of the garden, where our veg-plot-style beds were coming along nicely, even if the surrounding ground did look a bit of a muddy mess at the moment. Once we'd finished digging out, enriching and planting up the long beds and replaced the walkways and borders with new turf, it would all look entirely different.

The garden had opened by then, but was not yet very busy, so we spent a peaceful hour with just the two of us, working together . . . and it would have been the perfect moment for my confession, except that every time I looked up, the words forming on my lips, he'd catch my eye and smile at me, amber eyes warm and happy, and I simply couldn't bring myself to do it.

To add to the problem, after my talk with Treena I was seeing him with new eyes – and she'd been quite right, because my feelings *had* been changing towards him and unacknowledged hopes were now struggling to the surface. Perhaps how *he* felt about *me* was starting to change, too?

How could I speak the words that might put an end to all that?

He looked up at me again and grinned. 'Stop daydreaming and put your back into it, Ellwood,' he said.

*

That evening, over a Sunday dinner of roast chicken with all the trimmings, Ned told the family about the Lizzie letter and gave Elf her copy.

'I've sent one over for Cress, too, since it's about her branch of the family as much as mine,' he told them.

Elf pored over it, exclaiming and wishing it had come to light before she'd written the book. 'Though the bare outline is correct, of course. But it would have been nice to have the human element, to have fleshed out the character's motivation.'

'The poor girl sounded very nice, for a Vane,' said Myfy, who'd been taking the pages from Elf as she'd read them. 'Witty and clever, too.'

'Yes, but they can't all have been horrible. There are always some nice people, even in the most disagreeable families,' Elf said. 'Only think of that lovely Martha Vane, who was our Saturday girl in the café years ago, just as Daisy is now. Such a clever, sweet-natured girl – everyone liked her.'

I inadvertently swallowed my last bite of treacle pudding the wrong way and Ned patted me on the back rather too heavily with one large hand, then poured me some water.

'You know, I'd forgotten about her,' Myfy was saying, when I resurfaced. 'But she was a little younger than me, so I'd have been off to art college by then, I expect.'

'Before *your* time, Ned,' Elf told him. 'She was a beautiful girl too – tall and Titian-haired.'

That was Mum – and she'd worked in the café! Not only that, but she, a Vane, had been universally liked.

'What happened to her?' asked Myfy, ladling custard onto Jacob's second helping of treacle tart.

'She went off to train as a nurse, against her father's wishes, but her teachers encouraged her. Then I think there was some family breach later, because she stopped coming back to visit after a while. And I think . . .' she furrowed her brow in concentration, '. . . someone told me she died quite young. Tragic, if so.'

I couldn't have spoken if I'd wanted to, but my mind was working furiously. No wonder Mum's last words had been 'ice-cream and angels', because they'd probably been her two most favourite things about the valley.

There were two more plant deliveries next morning and, since Ned had gone over to Formby to see the site for a garden design commission, Gertie, James and I had moved all the pots to the bottom of the garden. Or rather, since his rheumatism was playing up, Gertie and I had moved them and James had directed proceedings, before going to get the shop ready to open with Steve. The school Easter holidays were over now and I couldn't guess how many visitors we'd have in the lull before the bank holiday weekend.

Gertie left me to arrange the new batch of wetland plants where I thought they would look best, while she went to fetch more of the small pots of herbs from the greenhouse, to put outside the shop.

I was finally heading for the Potting Shed and lunch when Ned, who must have returned at some point, called me over to the office.

Roddy was in there, too, sitting at the other desk with a stack of opened mail in a wire basket.

'Hi, Roddy,' I said, thinking this must be something to do with one of the orders – the roses, or perhaps the new lines for the shop, but although he returned my greeting he looked rather grave and . . . sort of embarrassed.

Ned closed the door. 'Marnie, when Roddy was opening the mail, he found something disturbing. I suppose you'd call it a poison-pen letter and it's certainly anonymous.'

'After all this time?' I said, surprised. 'I expect you had a few last year, when all the scandal blew up, but by now—'

'It's not about me,' he broke in. 'Or in a way, I suppose it is . . .' He ran his hands through his hair in that familiar gesture and then picked up a sheet of paper and passed it to me. 'You'd better read it.'

It wasn't handwritten, just a printout, and warned Ned that I'd gained employment with him under false pretences because the writer was sure I would have concealed my previous resignation from the Heritage Homes Trust, after making a series of unfounded allegations of misconduct against my employers and work colleagues. The writer then added that in light of Ned's own difficulties last year, if I made false accusations against *him*, too, it could cause him a lot of embarrassment he'd probably rather avoid.

It was signed, 'A Wellwisher'.

'Mike!' I said wearily. 'So Melinda *did* tell him she'd seen me here, after all.'

'I thought it must have been sent by him,' agreed Ned. 'I hope you don't mind, but I've told Roddy about you escaping from a controlling ex and him sending that resignation.'

'No, if Mike's going to do this sort of thing, it'll all come out anyway, won't it?'

'I don't see why it should,' said Ned. 'I *do* know the truth about it all, and the stories about me were disproved last year, so as you keep telling me, no one is going to be interested in that old news!'

'I'm sure Ned's right, now that he's given me the whole picture,' Roddy said. 'The writer doesn't know you've already told Ned, so he's expecting it to be a bombshell.'

'It was just an attempt to make trouble for you – he's a nasty, vindictive sod, isn't he?' said Ned. 'We'll simply ignore it, though I'll keep the letter just in case any more come and we want to involve the police.'

'I sincerely hope it won't come to that!'

Roddy, who had seemed lost in thought, suddenly said, 'You know, I've just remembered something disquieting that Cress told me the other day. A man rang up making enquiries about room availability, because he was keen to visit the Grace Garden. He said he'd heard that an old friend, Marnie Ellwood, was working there. So Cress, in all innocence, probably told him all kinds of things you'd rather she hadn't, if it was this Mike.'

I could imagine. Mike could be very charming and persuasive, so by now I was sure he'd know I was living over the café and working in the garden there, as well as at Old Grace Hall. I hoped Elf and Myfy hadn't had a letter, too!

When I said so, Ned said he thought they couldn't have, or they would have told him already, but in any case since they already knew all about my coercive former partner, it wouldn't make any difference to them.

'I think we'll warn Gertie, Steve and James, just in case he turns up,' Ned said. 'And I'll give Elf a ring, so she can beware if anyone appears asking about you.'

We left it at that, though when I checked my mail later, on the way back to the flat, I wasn't altogether surprised to find a short note from Mike awaiting me, saying how hurt he was I hadn't got in touch when I was living so near and that we should meet up for old times' sake.

Yeah, right – he must be entirely mad. And deluded, if he thought he had any power over me now.

Besides, I had Ned's support and strength behind me. When I went round to the Hall that evening and showed him the letter, he gave me a warm, reassuring hug and told me not to worry.

Which I wasn't – or not about Mike, anyway. And our dinner was again from the Lucky Dragon, with encouraging messages in the fortune cookies, so perhaps that was a good omen?

34

Folly

On Tuesday, my nominal day off, there was no time to sit worrying about anything, because it was a case of 'all hands on deck' at the Grace Garden. Not only had Don the builder and his team arrived to make a start on the shop extension, but Ned had roped in everyone he could think of to help put together the gazebo.

He assembled his troops – me, Jacob, Charlie and Steve – in the stableyard, where the door to the barn was thrown open, revealing the various pre-cut and formed pieces, which were already painted the same pleasing pale greeny-blue as the bridge.

Charlie had unpacked it a few days ago and now he took the huge instruction manual from Ned, who was looking at it rather blankly, and told him, 'You can ignore the first five pages of this. It's just about unpacking everything. The pieces are all numbered, so we just need to carry it all down to the water garden and lay it out in the right order.'

'It'll be a doddle,' agreed Jacob. 'Who needs instructions anyway?' And he seized a curved piece of the roof and bore it away towards the visitors' gate. We all followed suit, though we left the six heavy columns that would support the roof for Ned.

It did all go together smoothly and easily too . . . unlike flat-pack furniture. But then, as Ned said, it was stately-home quality from a special firm, so you got what you paid for.

Myfy drifted in and out occasionally, and Gert came to bring us all sandwiches at lunchtime and see how we were getting on.

And by mid-afternoon, the gazebo had risen like a pale mirage above the pool, an airy dome on six round pillars. There was a curved seat inside and low lattice walls between the pillars. All it needed, in my opinion, was one of the more delicate climbing roses growing up it.

Once we'd all admired our handiwork everyone began to drift off, until only Ned and I remained . . . and the builders, who sounded as if they might be mixing cement.

'I call that a good day's work,' Ned said, leaning on the column next to me as I sat on the seat looking out over the garden.

'You were right, this is the only point where you can see the whole of the Grace Garden,' I said. 'Or all of it that isn't hidden behind trees and bushes. You can even see down into the sunken herb bed.'

'That was the plan,' he agreed.

'You could let the public into this part tomorrow,' I suggested.

'I'd rather get the last of the planting done down at the pool end and around the waterfall, first.' He checked his watch. 'Though, actually, we could finish that today – unless you're doing something else?'

'I wasn't planning on it,' I said, and I wouldn't have been able to resist his eager expression even if I had. 'OK, let's do it. But we'll have a cup of coffee in the office first and you can go and check on how the builders are doing while I make it.'

*

We only remembered it was the Friends of Jericho's End meeting that evening when the light had begun to go and there was no time to shower and change out of our working clothes. We had scrambled eggs in Ned's kitchen, then just made it as the others arrived. I don't think I was the only one sitting in a semi-doze as the arrangements for the May revels next Sunday were finalized, an estimate to replace a cracked washbasin approved and a date pencilled in for June for a talk Clara Mayhem Doome had kindly agreed to give, on epigraphy in ancient Britain. The subject was her idea and no one had had the nerve to suggest anything racier.

But then, I thought, in Clara's hands any subject was likely to be much more entertaining than it sounded.

When the meeting broke up, Ned and I decided we'd like to see the effect of the new gazebo in the twilight, which was rather beautiful, with a little silvery sliver of moon appearing above it. Then we walked through the rose garden, silent except for a slight popping noise, as one of the koi broke the surface of the water.

'I feel weary and grubby, but it's been a really fun day,' I told him as he let me through the Lavender Cottage gate.

'I couldn't have finished everything today without you, Marnie,' he said, giving me a brief and unexpected hug, before heading back the way we'd come.

The night was so still that as I unlocked the back door, I could hear the rattle of the Grace Garden gate and the distant wail of a peacock.

Over the next three days, Ned and I threw ourselves into finishing the great fan of long narrow beds at the bottom of the Grace Garden, preparing the ground round them for returfing.

The visitors seemed to love the new wetland area and the gazebo, and all in the Garden of Eden appeared perfect – no serpents of any kind rearing their ugly heads. And perhaps, now, I told myself, they never would?

Paradise regained.

By now, Caspar was quite resigned to my evening visits to Old Grace Hall, where we had managed to sort most of the papers from the boxes and had quite a collection of interesting and relevant material to add to both the future museum display and the next edition of the glossy guidebook.

The only thing that I was disappointed about was that no planting list for the rose garden had turned up.

At quiz night on Friday evening, Cress thanked Ned for sending the copy of Lizzie's letter and said she'd found it very touching.

'She was little more than a child, and both her own family and mine treated her very harshly when she came back, poor thing. Thank goodness this Richard Grace took pity on her and it all had a happy ending.'

'You're a romantic,' Roddy said to her affectionately, and she went slightly pink. She'd abandoned her usual attire of polo-neck sweater, gilet and breeches in favour of jeans and a Liberty cotton shirt in soft shades of blue and green and was looking not only younger and prettier, but much less harassed.

Roddy would appear to be a good thing – *and* he'd clearly survived tea with Audrey Lordly-Grace, so he must be tougher and more resilient than he looked.

Treena, who had come to the quiz night with Luke, also looked glowing, so perhaps love was in the air? They sat with Cress and Roddy at the next table to ours and didn't seem to get many quiz questions right, so if there *was* love in the air, it didn't sharpen the intellect.

I sat back, looking around at the now-familiar faces and

feeling relaxed and happy – especially when Ned caught my eye and gave me his slow, deep smile, the one that seemed to warm me right through and do strange things to my heart rhythm . . .

I found myself smiling back – and then, beyond him, caught sight of Wayne, standing at the bar watching us. He made an indefinable little leering grimace and I felt as if I'd been drenched in icy water.

'What's the matter?' asked Ned.

'Nothing, I'm just a bit tired,' I said quickly as Wayne vanished towards the darts room.

Elf, Myfy, Gerald and Jacob had left together as soon as the quiz finished and Treena and Luke then took their place at our table.

When Luke went to order more drinks, I decided to pop to the ladies, then wished I hadn't when Wayne sidled up to me and shoved a piece of paper into my hand.

'From our dad,' he muttered, then slunk off again.

I looked back furtively, but I didn't think anyone had noticed and I bolted into the loo, where I unfolded the note, which said, without any preamble:

> Come to the farm tomorrow night at eight – I know who you are and we got things to discuss. Come on your own – you won't want Ned Mars to hear what we got to say.

It was signed just with his initials, S.V.

I read it twice, my mind in a whirl and my stomach churning, then pushed it into my pocket and went out of the cubicle, where I found Treena leaning against the wall with her arms folded, waiting for me.

'I saw Wayne pass you something as you came in,' she explained. 'It looked like a piece of paper.'

'Did anyone else see?' I asked quickly.

'No, I'm sure they didn't. What is it? You look a bit weird.'

I fished out the note and handed it to her and she stared down at it, puzzled.

'This seems to be a bill for something called pig nuts . . .'

'Other side,' I said, but she'd already flipped it over.

'It's from Saul – he must have told Wayne to give it to me,' I said. 'They know who I am – or at least, Saul does, but I expect Wayne does now, too.'

She gave it back and I tucked it into my rucksack.

'What are you going to do? You're surely not going to go there on your own tomorrow night?'

'Well, it would be a chance to have it all out, wouldn't it? I can make it clear that I don't want anything from them, not even to tell anyone I'm related to them, so there's no need to threaten me with telling Ned.'

'Maybe, but you'd be much better off telling him the truth yourself, and then ignoring them.'

'But if I can make them see reason tomorrow night, I might never *need* to tell him,' I said obstinately. 'That would be an end of it.'

'Your mum was too terrified of her family to ever return here and warned you not to, either,' she pointed out. 'They must have threatened her with something bad, to make her so afraid.'

'Her parents might have done, but they're dead now. Besides, it's the twenty-first century, not the Dark Ages, so what can they possibly do to me, except rant a bit, before I can explain?'

'I don't think you should go on your own,' Treena said stubbornly. 'I'll come with you. I'm not on duty tomorrow evening.'

'If you're with me, Saul probably won't talk to me at all!'

'Then I'll drive you there and wait in that layby near the farm gate with the bus stop,' she said. 'You'll have your phone and if you haven't come back or rung me in half an hour, I'll call Luke and then come and get you.'

I have to say, this suggestion came as a relief, because the whole scenario was starting to feel just a bit too much like a horror movie. You know, the 'please don't go down in the basement on your own' moment.

'I'm sure you've got other things you'd rather do tomorrow evening, Treena.'

'I expect Luke will still be in the pub waiting for me afterwards, and we could probably both do with a stiff drink by then.' She looked at me. 'I really do think the best thing you could do is tell Ned right now. You're making too much of it and I don't think it's going to be the horrible shock to him that you imagine.'

'Yes, but he loathes Wayne and doesn't much like the rest of them,' I said. 'And having kept it from him so long, I think he's going to be angry about that, too . . . and just when we're getting along so well. No, I'll give tomorrow a shot, first.'

'I know that stubborn expression,' she said, with a sigh. 'OK, I'll pick you up at the bridge tomorrow about ten to eight.'

We went back to our table together. There was no sign of Wayne, and Ned and Luke didn't seem to suspect anything was amiss, even if I wasn't very chatty for the rest of the evening. Eventually I pleaded a headache, which by then was the truth, and went back to the flat, telling Ned not to bother when he would have come with me.

He gave me such a puzzled look and I think would have come with me anyway, except that Treena said something to him just as I was getting up and I made a fast getaway.

When I got back to the flat I asked Caspar (once he'd finished telling me off for being out) if he thought I was doing the right thing.

If only I spoke Russian Cat, I might have had the definitive answer.

I had dark circles round my eyes next day and Ned commented that, apart from the fact that I hadn't got a tail, I looked like a lemur.

This made me laugh, but though I *tried* to behave normally, my mind kept going back to where I was going that evening and wondering if I was doing the right thing . . . But it couldn't do any harm to have things out with Saul, could it? And it might just resolve the matter once and for all.

Ned asked me later if I'd heard anything more from Mike. 'Only if you have, or you're worried about anything at all, you know you can count on me, don't you?'

'Yes,' I said. 'But there's really nothing the matter at all – just the headache and then a bad night. But I think perhaps I won't come over to the Hall this evening.'

I summoned a smile. 'If I don't lavish a bit more attention on Caspar, he won't be speaking to me any more!'

'You probably do just need an early night,' he said, then added guiltily, 'Perhaps I've been working you too hard!'

'Oh, nonsense, I'm having the time of my life,' I told him, and his expression cleared.

'Well, I'm glad to hear it, because I hoped that's how *you* felt, too,' he said and gave me his warm, all-enveloping smile.

35

Misery

'Are you absolutely sure about this?' asked Treena that night, when I got into her car.

'Yes,' I said, even though I wasn't any more and telling Ned suddenly seemed a much better option than a night-time rendezvous at the pig farm with my obnoxious relatives. There was a cold, shivery feeling in my stomach about it, but I am nothing if not stubborn.

'OK,' she said, driving off, but when she parked in the layby opposite the rutted, dark track to the farm, which showed only a glimmer of light from a downstairs window, she turned to me and said, 'You've got exactly one half-hour. Then if I don't see or hear from you, I'm leaving Luke a message and coming to find you.'

'Agreed,' I said, glad she'd insisted on coming with me, then resolutely set off up the track, the torch I'd brought sending a warm yellow circle of light in front of me.

I'd been able to both smell and hear the pigs as soon as I got out of the car and I could see the large, low buildings on either side of the track that must house them, as I made my way up it and across a paved farmyard. Dogs began to bark from a nearby outbuilding when I knocked on the door next to the lighted window and it was opened at once by Wayne, who grinned unpleasantly at me and moved aside just enough to let me through.

I was in a big, untidy kitchen, where someone had made a brave attempt to introduce a feminine touch, with flowery curtains and matching cushions in the wheel-back chairs and a rack of brightly painted decorative plates.

'You've come, then,' said Saul, stating the obvious. He was sitting in an upright wing chair by the fire and, with his large head and torso, looked more impressive sitting down than he had standing up.

'Yes, though I don't know why it had to be at night, in the dark, like this,' I said.

'We don't want people seeing you come here – and it had to be tonight, when my eldest, Sam, and his wife have gone off to her brother's wedding down south. He don't know nothing and she's a blabbermouth.'

'Right,' I said, not moving any closer. He didn't suggest I sit down, or have a cup of tea – or hemlock. Wayne had closed the door and I was conscious of him standing just behind me.

'But *I* know, don't I, Dad?' Wayne said eagerly. 'I'm not a blabbermouth and—'

'You shut up, our Wayne,' Saul snapped. 'You'll be sorry if I ever find out you spoke a word of it outside this house.'

'Look, can we keep this short and civilized?' I said brusquely. 'I assume you've realized I'm your sister Martha's daughter?'

'Her bastard,' Saul nodded. 'Knew it was by an Eyetie, too.'

'He means an Italian,' Wayne translated, in case I hadn't got it.

'So, how did you recognize me?'

'Our Wayne said you looked foreign, but sort of familiar and that set me wondering, even though your name was different. And then, when I saw you, I knew. Our mam kept a school photo of Martha hidden away – I found it after she died – and you look just like her. Same eyes, too.'

My likeness to her didn't seem to be a recommendation, since he practically spat the words out.

'That explains it, then. I wasn't sure at the time that you'd realized who I was, but I hoped not,' I said frankly.

'I told Dad you and Ned were sweet on each other, but he wouldn't have been so keen to take you on, even as gardener, if he'd known who you were,' Wayne said unpleasantly. 'He might fancy you now, but things'd change if he knew what we know.'

'But what's it to you?' I said, turning to Saul. 'I know the Vanes disowned my mother when she was pregnant, so presumably you want as little to do with me as I do with you?'

Saul continued to glower silently at me from under his bushy eyebrows, so I added: 'I'm not interested in you, or your family, so let's just forget the relationship, right?'

'It's not that easy, now you're here – and I thought your mam would have warned you off ever coming back.'

'She did, but I didn't come back to the *farm*, I came to the valley because I was offered a job here.'

'You came sneaking in under another name, to see what pickings were in it for you,' he said harshly. 'You heard the pig farm was prospering and thought you might get a share of it.'

I stared at him in astonishment. 'Of course I didn't! I didn't even know it was a pig farm till I got here, and I'd no intention of telling you who I was, let alone coming to the farm.'

'So you say.' His jaw was working and a fat vein throbbed in his forehead like a mad worm. 'And maybe you'll put your money where your mouth is and sign that paper on the table, saying you give over any property rights in Cross Ways Farm to me.'

I felt a wave of relief. 'Of course I'll sign it, if you want me to, but I'm sure I don't *have* any rights anyway – and I don't *want* them. Or better still, let's get a solicitor to draw up a more official document and I'll sign that, too, if you're really worried about it!'

'Ah, but then you'd have time to think things over and change your mind.'

'OK, then I'll sign this one, now,' I said, picking up the sheet of handwritten paper and glancing over it, before signing it with a biro that lay near. I was unsure how legally binding an unwitnessed document like that would be, but if it made him happy . . .

He watched me sign, then said, 'Good. The lawyers didn't know Martha had a child and I didn't think you'd any rights in the farm, but I found out later you had. Got someone to ask for me.'

He got up, glaring fiercely at me and I took a step back.

'You, by-blow of my sister, to take what I worked all my life to build up? That's to pass on to our Sam, when I'm gone?'

His eyes burned with hate in his mad prophet face and he took a step towards me, pointing, as if he expected a thunderbolt to shoot out from his fingertip and annihilate me.

'Now, Dad,' said Wayne, sounding nervous. 'She's signed the bit of paper, hasn't she? And she's got bigger fish to fry now. She won't want us to tell Ned who she is and spoil her chances.'

'Maybe . . . maybe not. But it might be best to make sure,' Saul said in a low voice that made my blood run cold. 'I told Martha if she or her bastard ever turned up on the farm again, I'd feed her to the pigs. There'd be nothing to show you'd ever been here, by morning.'

'Now, our dad!' exclaimed Wayne, horrified. 'You shouldn't say stuff like that!'

'I'll say what I like – and I'll do what I like. This might be the best way . . .'

He took another step towards me and I backed off, though Wayne still blocked the door.

'Don't be silly,' I said, with a shaky laugh. 'We're not living in a Stephen King novel. I've signed your paper and that's an end of it. I never want to see any of you again, or set foot on your farm, either.'

'So you say now, but it might be a different story if I let you get away,' Saul said, and I was just about to tell him that his threats were empty, because Treena was waiting for me in the layby, when it suddenly occurred to me that then he might send Wayne to fetch her on some pretext, which would put *her* in danger too!

Or was I just being over-credulous in taking his threats seriously?

Saul seemed to have made his mind up. 'Right then, Wayne, give me a hand,' he said, reaching out to grab me, but even as I dodged behind the table, the door suddenly burst open, sending Wayne flying past me and Ned's deep voice demanded, 'What on earth are you doing here, Marnie? And why does Treena think you need urgently rescuing?'

'Oh, *Ned*!' I exclaimed thankfully, casting myself into his arms and clinging to him. 'Don't let Saul feed me to the pigs!'

'Feed you to the pigs?' he repeated incredulously.

'It's to stop me claiming any rights to the farm,' I babbled. 'I don't want them, but he didn't believe me.'

'It was only a joke,' Wayne said quickly. 'And our Marnie was just visiting.'

'*Your* Marnie?' Ned said slowly.

'She's my late sister's daughter, out of wedlock,' Saul said, as if the words scalded his mouth. 'I knew as soon as I saw her, even if she was sneaking around under another name, seeing what the pickings were.'

'Ellwood is the name of the family who adopted me and I wasn't sneaking round, I came here to work. Mum told me never to come anywhere near you and I didn't intend to.'

I was still shaking, but though Ned kept an arm around me, he held me away slightly so he could see my face.

'You're a *Vane*?'

'My mother was – Martha Vane, the girl that Elf told you about. But I don't want anything to do with them or their precious pig farm.' I shuddered.

'Looks like you got rid of one Vane and hired another,' said Wayne, grinning. 'Only she didn't tell you that, did she?'

Ned looked down at me again, an unusually bleak expression on his face. 'No, she didn't.'

Then he seemed to come back from whichever bit of inner Antarctica he'd been visiting and snapped, 'Come on, Marnie, we're leaving.'

He swept me off into the darkness, one arm clamped almost painfully around me, half-supporting me as I stumbled over the uneven flags of the yard and back down the rutted track.

Treena's car had vanished and there was only Ned's Jeep in the layby.

'Where's Treena?' I asked. I couldn't seem to stop shaking, and my voice wobbled. 'What were you doing here?'

'Luckily, I spotted her in the layby and stopped to see if she'd broken down. She said you'd gone to visit the farm but it was dangerous and since she seemed to be panicking because you hadn't come back, I said I'd fetch you. She's gone to the pub to find Luke. You'd better tell her you're OK.'

'I . . . I'm not sure I *am* OK,' I said, 'just very glad you came when you did.'

'Your *relatives* didn't look exactly friendly, but you didn't *really* believe Saul was going to feed you to the pigs, did you?'

'Not at first,' I agreed. 'But then Saul suddenly seemed to make his mind up to do it, and he was just trying to grab me, when you got there!'

'But probably not to feed you to the pigs,' he said, opening the door for me to get in.

'*Wayne* thought he was serious, too,' I said, fumbling my seatbelt so badly he had to lean across and fasten it for me. 'He was trying to stop him.'

'Saul's a forceful personality; you both let him scare you,' he said, turning the car expertly in the narrow lane and heading back to the village.

We were silent for a minute, except for the faint sound of my teeth chattering. Something skittered off into the hedge – possibly the remains of my courage.

'So you're the daughter of Saul's sister, Martha?' he said evenly.

'Yes. She died when I was twelve and the Ellwoods adopted me – you know that.'

'True, though you somehow forgot to mention who your mother was, or that you had any connection with Jericho's End.'

'I did *mean* to tell you, only at first we got off on the wrong foot because of that resignation letter. And then,' I swallowed hard, 'I wanted to tell you, but the longer I left it, the harder it became, especially once I'd realized how much you disliked the Vanes.'

'I thought we trusted each other,' he said, staring straight ahead over the steering wheel. 'Yet all the time, you were keeping this secret from me. I suppose it was what Wayne was hinting about the other day . . . gloating over.'

'I think so,' I agreed miserably.

'So no, you couldn't expect me to be pleased to find you and Wayne were first cousins.'

He slammed the gears and shot over the bridge, then halted so suddenly outside the café that I jerked forward like a rag doll. He leaned over to open my door, obviously expecting me to get out.

'But, Ned,' I began, pleadingly, 'I'm so sorry. I really wanted to tell you but—'

'You didn't trust me enough – I get it.'

'It wasn't that—' I began, but he interrupted me.

'Look, this has been a bit of a shock and I don't want to talk about it any more tonight. We'll discuss things in the morning, at work.'

I got out, my knees like jelly and my hopes shrivelling to ashes. Perhaps he'd also fire me in the morning . . . and then maybe Elf and Myfy would feel differently about me when *they* knew, too?

I closed the door and he shot away. I watched the car turn into the stableyard beyond the Hall and then trudged round the back of the café and up to the flat.

I was still cold and shaking, and now in such despair that I cried into Caspar's fur for a whole ten minutes, before I gathered myself together enough to text Treena, before she came looking for me.

Back in flat, talk to you tomorrow. Xx

Then I turned off my phone before she could suggest she came straight over now.

Caspar dried himself off on the sofa cover, with a few unfeline-like remarks, but when I'd made a mug of cocoa and sat down again, he came and draped himself on my lap and headbumped my chin, which seems to be a slightly painful gesture of affection.

'I've blown it with Ned,' I told him. 'If I'd been completely open with him from the start, or at least as soon as we became friends again, then it would never have come to this.'

'Pfzzk,' agreed Caspar.

I doubted our relationship would have developed any further than friendship, if he'd realized who I was, but he'd probably have kept me on as gardener.

And that would have been fine . . . But now, I'd grown to want so much more.

The cocoa dispelled a little of the remaining cold shivery feeling. Ned might have dismissed what Saul had said as mere ludicrous threats, but he hadn't seen his expression, and I wasn't so sure.

I rinsed my puffy red eyes in cold water and wondered what to do with myself. It was getting late and tomorrow I was sure Ned would tell me he didn't want me to work for him any more, that he couldn't trust me.

But meanwhile, there were several hours to fill and I certainly wasn't likely to sleep tonight.

What do you do when your world has come crashing down around you like a house of cards?

I could start to pack – and I'd have a lot less to take away with me, now I'd sorted out the stuff I'd had stored at Treena's, except for the two small boxes of old papers under the bookcase.

I drew them out and put them on the coffee table, then made another mug of cocoa, before opening the flaps on the first box, to reveal a stack of old, yellowing bills. There couldn't be anything more likely to numb my mind than sorting these.

Caspar, very bored, settled down on the sofa next to me, with a long sigh.

36

Hidden Messages

Most of the contents of the first box were old utility bills and the like, which went straight into a bin bag for recycling, and when I started on the next, it looked like more of the same.

I was just beginning to think that Aunt Em had mixed up two boxes intended for the bin with the ones to save (and perhaps consigned two that *weren't* rubbish there, instead?), when I came on a big, sparkly, hardback Paperchase notebook.

It was more Aunt Em's style than Mum's, so I wasn't surprised to see from the inscription inside that she'd given it to Mum one Christmas.

I leafed through it and found a random selection of jottings in Mum's familiar hand – she seemed to have used it as a kind of journal. She'd dated the entries, and I saw with a pang that they'd all been made during the last few months of her life, to write down whatever thoughts and memories came to her – and her hopes for my future and how proud she was of me . . .

I didn't think she'd have been so proud of how I'd behaved recently – but I *did* think she would have understood. The diary was part of her legacy and I felt such love for her as I read her words from so long ago.

Time ticked on as I turned the pages, reading about her childhood memories, many of which she'd already shared with me, her happy days as a student nurse – and how guilty she'd felt that she hadn't known my father was married until too late . . . He'd been an Italian doctor over on a six-month exchange and he'd gone back home, never knowing about me.

The entries were not set out like a journal, but jumped to and fro in time, making me smile, cry, or laugh by turns, but I really sat up and took notice when I came to a page where she'd described her last visit to Jericho's End when, pregnant with me, she'd gone to tell her parents.

> Em insisted on driving me to the farm when I finally summoned up the courage to break the news of my pregnancy to my family. She waited for me in her car in the farmyard and I was glad she was there, because the interview with my parents was more awful than I could describe. They still held to the old, strict religious tenets they were brought up to obey, and disowned me, saying I was no longer any daughter of theirs. I was never to return to the farm or contact them again. But worse was to come, for when my older brother, Saul, saw me out, he made such horrific threats about what he'd do to me if I ever set foot on the farm again that my blood ran cold – especially when he added that the same went for my child! I was sick with horror, because I was sure he meant it and I hope Marianne never goes back to Jericho's End, even though I haven't been able to resist telling her stories of my happier times there as a child, especially playing up by the Fairy Falls.

'But you might have been a bit more *specific* about the danger, Mum!' I said aloud, and Caspar opened one eye, looked at me and then shut it again. The bubbling snores resumed.

From that point, her writing was shakier and most of the entries shorter, until I came to a description of how, in her last year of school, she'd had a Saturday job helping in what was then called Verdi's Ice-cream Parlour, though the last of the Verdis had married the artist living next door and was by then Gina Price-Jones. They had three daughters and the middle one, Elf, also worked in the café.

So far, this was very much what Elf had told me of the family history and I knew that the eldest of these daughters, Morwenna, had married Ned's great-uncle Theo and gone to live at Old Grace Hall. It was the next part that really caught my attention.

> One Saturday I was sent to the Hall with a message for Morwenna and found the housekeeper turning out a big glazed kitchen cupboard. The top shelf was full of musty old household account books dating back years, which were to be moved to one of the window seats in the library, which already held other family documents.
>
> I wasn't very interested in them, until one of the books, leather bound and thicker than the rest, slipped from the pile and fell open at my feet. Picking it up, I saw the name of Elizabeth Grace written on the flyleaf.
>
> Well, though never mentioned in my family, I had heard of this disgraced ancestor of mine, who'd eventually married into the Grace family, so seeing the book was full of handwritten recipes, I asked if I might borrow it.
>
> I had to keep it hidden from my family, of course, but I pored over it whenever I could. There were cookery recipes, but also remedies of all kinds. She'd seemed interested in the medicinal uses of herbs. There was, too, a list of the

roses that had been planted in the small garden that separated the cottages and café from the grounds of the Hall, though it was now so overgrown on either side of the path through it that you could see nothing other than a thick tangle of briars. I was a romantic, imaginative girl then, though, and loved the old names of the roses.

I turned the page over eagerly, hoping she'd written the list down, but saw with a pang of disappointment that she hadn't – though, of course, if she'd returned the book to the Hall, then maybe it was still there to be found.

That was the last thing Elizabeth Grace had written there and I was about to close the book, when I saw that a corner of the endpaper had come unstuck and there was the edge of a piece of paper covered in writing underneath it. I managed to ease it out without damaging the book further. The writing was faded and small, but it seemed to be part of a letter – and when I'd read it, I wished I'd left it there, because what it described was so horrible!

My eyes widened as I read on and I nearly dropped Mum's journal. I wasn't surprised when she finished by saying that she'd almost burned the page, but in the end replaced it in the book and stuck the endpaper down more securely, before returning it to the Hall.

Where, presumably, it still was . . .

I sat back, thinking that it had been a night of revelations, none of them good.

If *only* I'd opened this box first and read Mum's journal, it would have saved me the scene at the pig farm tonight and probably I'd have told Ned my secret ages ago.

And the journal also revealed something that, however awful, Ned ought to know. That he *must* know.

Suddenly it seemed urgent that I tell him right now: I couldn't keep *this* from him, too.

Without even stopping to put on a coat, I abandoned Caspar to his slumbers, rushed out of the flat and ran straight down the dark road, to hammer on Ned's door.

It must have been after midnight by then, but the lights behind their heavy curtains still glowed and when he opened the door, Ned was still dressed in the clothes he'd worn earlier. His face took on a wary, shuttered and angry look when he saw it was me.

'I wasn't expecting *visitors*,' he said coolly and it was only then did I realize that Caspar must have hurtled like a comet through Lavender Cottage and out through the cat flap in the back door, to have arrived before me.

Ned's face changed as he looked down at me and he said, in a gentler, concerned voice that brought tears to my eyes, 'What is it, Marnie? What's happened?'

'I've found something you need to see,' I said, thrusting the sparkly notebook at him and he stared down at it, and then at me, as if I'd run mad. Then he hesitated, before drawing me in and closing the door behind us. Caspar had already sneaked past and was making for the open library door.

'I shouldn't have left you like that, earlier,' Ned muttered. 'You're still in a state of shock.'

I shivered and he drew me into the library, where he made me drink a glass of brandy, which I loathe, and when I'd insisted he read that last entry I'd found in Mum's journal, he poured one for himself, too.

'It looks from this like Lizzie had second thoughts about revealing the whole truth, after all, and hid a page away,' he said.

'I did think, when I read through that copy you made for me, that the account jumped a bit abruptly from the end of one page to the top of the next,' I said. 'Do you think this book

Mum found would have been put in the window seat in here with the others that were moved?'

'I don't know, but we'll soon find out!' Ned was already across the room and lifting the lid from one of the large window seats. He removed a bundle of old newspapers and then the first of a mouldering stack of old books.

'She said it was leather bound and quite thick,' I reminded him, looking on. 'Unless your uncle Theo had been rummaging in here, it should be fairly near the top.'

Apart from the addition of the newspapers, it didn't appear that the earlier layers of documents had been disturbed and we found Lizzie Grace's recipe book very easily.

I put it on the table and opened it at the back, while Ned fetched a saucer of water and a kitchen sponge, with which he began carefully moistening the edges of the marbled endpaper.

Finally, it began to lift away from the back board of the book – and there lay the paper, just as Mum had said.

We knew it was part of Lizzie's account, even before we compared it with the original – and now we could also see how the new page followed on from the bottom of the one describing her decision to appeal to Horace Lordly-Grace to intercede with her father – and what a terrible and catastrophic decision this had been! For, instead of helping her, he had instead, in her own words, 'most grievously assaulted me – then laughed at my distress, saying it did not matter, since I was to be married almost immediately . . .'

It was all too easy now to understand why, when she'd finally escaped the room, she'd been in such a state of distress that killing herself seemed the only option open to her.

'Poor girl,' I said, with feeling. I remembered that Horace Lordly-Grace had had a stroke later, after Lizzie had returned, pregnant, to beg his help, and I felt he deserved it.

'She was still a child of fifteen when this happened, too,' Ned said sombrely. 'It's not surprising if she got cold feet at the last minute and decided she couldn't bear to reveal the *whole* truth to her son, after all. But at least she didn't destroy this page, just hid it away where she probably thought no one would find it.'

'It makes everything fall into place, though. She obviously told Neville the truth of what had happened, when he caught her on the bridge, and that's why he took her away with him. And really, he behaved very kindly to her, but you can see he couldn't very well offer to marry her when she was having his own father's child.'

'No, he did what he could and I expect would have continued to support her, if he hadn't been killed in action in Portugal,' Ned agreed.

'She must have told Richard Grace the whole thing, too, when he asked her to marry him. She said she didn't want him to think too badly of Neville, didn't she?'

I'd long since stopped shivering – the warm room and the brandy had seen to that – but I still felt the shock of this discovery on top of my earlier one.

But I had escaped from my danger, and poor Lizzie hadn't. My heart ached for what she'd been through.

'Neville must have been the best of the bunch, because his father was obviously a complete monster,' Ned said. 'First rape, then refusing to give her any help when she was pregnant and desperate – and then, when you think that he was the father of the Thomas Grace I'm descended from, it feels pretty vile.'

'Well, *you* can't help that,' I said.

He gave a short, bitter laugh. 'Maybe not, but being the direct descendant of a rapist does put the fact that you're related to the Vanes into a different perspective.'

Not if Saul had managed to dispose of me to the pigs . . . I thought, but I kept that to myself.

'But, Ned, you're related to the Vanes too, don't forget, through Lizzie – and that means you and I are also distantly connected.'

He pushed back his hair and stood up, wearily. 'So we are – and your mother and Lizzie seem to have been the best of them, don't they?'

He bent and pulled me to my feet, then took me in his arms and said, into my hair, 'I'm sorry about what I said earlier when I was angry. I'm an idiot. What does it matter who we're related to?'

'I suppose it doesn't, really, but I should have told you myself, much earlier. Only I was so happy and we were growing to be such good friends . . .'

'And more than friends?' he questioned tentatively, holding me away a little so he could see me. 'Marnie?'

I looked up and smiled into his dear face and he kissed me . . . or I kissed him, I'm not entirely sure on that point. But I definitely heard Caspar make a disapproving noise, so it was no surprise that when we surfaced some time later, he'd vanished from the room.

'Caspar's gone – shouldn't we look for him?' I asked worriedly.

'No, he knows where he is,' Ned said vaguely. 'Now, where were we?'

I suddenly sat bolt upright in bed – a large and unfamiliar one – and Ned, drowsily trying to pull me back down again, said: 'What's up?'

'I've just remembered the most wonderful thing!'

'Thank you,' he said modestly.

'Not *that*,' I told him. 'It was Mum saying in her journal that

Lizzie had written down a list of the roses she'd planted somewhere in her recipe book! Shall we go to the library and—'

'No,' he said firmly, pulling me down again. 'There's a time and a season for everything.'

It was Ned who woke up next, exclaiming, 'Mayday!' which seemed rather rude, until he reminded me that the Morris Dancers were going to come and perform on the Green this morning.

'I said I'd go over early to help Steve rope it off, ready – and look at the time!'

'Sorry if I've distracted you . . .' I said, admiring his broad and well-muscled back and then running a finger down it, which might have caused us to be even later, had not Caspar nudged the door open and jumped onto the end of the bed, where he stared accusingly at us.

'Have you been here all night, Caspar?' I asked.

'He probably squeezed through the cat flap and has only come back to make you feel guilty,' said Ned heartlessly.

Whichever it was, having a cat stare fixedly at you in this sort of situation is very off-putting, so we got up. I declined Ned's offer of breakfast (I'd probably have been the one cooking it) and left for a shower and a change of clothes in the flat.

Caspar came with me, but then vanished into Lavender Cottage in search of his own breakfast, with a few parting remarks that it was probably just as well I couldn't understand.

I didn't rush over breakfast or my shower – I no longer thought my boss was going to fire me for being late . . . or any other reason. My head was filled with a rosy vision of the future: the two of us, rooted here in the garden, for ever . . .

I felt full of boneless wellbeing, and also, light-headed from lack of sleep . . . or something.

Humming ('An English Country Garden'), I got Treena on

the phone and said, 'Have you got half an hour to spare?' and when she said she had, told her all that had happened the previous night – or *almost* all. There are some things you don't tell even your best friend.

When I finally went to look for Ned, he was alone in the garden lining up pots of dwarf lavender to put in the low bed near the wetland area, his back turned to me. And a very broad, familiar back it was, too . . .

For a moment I felt suddenly shy, but then he turned and saw me and a happy smile lit his face.

'Marnie!' He loped over and hugged me, so that my feet left the ground and the breath was squished out of my lungs, before kissing me. 'Did I tell you I loved you?'

'You might have done,' I admitted. 'I don't know why you should, though, because I've behaved like an idiot!'

'Never mind – you're *my* idiot,' he said fondly, which was strangely comforting, now I could see how I'd turned a Wayne-sized molehill into the most enormous mountain.

I helped him put in the lavender and then, just before ten, he insisted we go and watch the Morris Men.

'This first session is really just for us, the villagers and locals. You'll see – everyone will be there.'

They were, too: Elf, Myfy, Jacob, Gerald . . . loads of faces I recognized from the village. Even Cress and Roddy, though not Audrey Lordly-Grace, who I expect only turned out if there was a celebrity in the offing.

The middle of the Green had been roped off for the dancing and the bunting brought out again to decorate it. We all gathered round to watch, Ned and I next to Gert and James, and then a man playing a lively tune on a fiddle led the stamping, jingling troop of dancers out of the Village Hut.

They were all big men and their strange garb of beribboned straw hats, brightly patched waistcoats and white trousers tied in at the knee with more ribbon and bunches of small bells should have made them look silly . . . and yet, they looked oddly impressive, instead.

They took up their places in the centre of the Green and began an intricate dance that involved much waving of red handkerchiefs.

Gerald appeared and started to play his violin along with the fiddler and the tempo picked up for the next dance, in which the Morris Men hit each other with wooden sticks – or at least, crashed them together with a lot of loud noise.

I found it all quite riveting and then, when they'd finally finished, the fiddlers struck up a different tune, one that set my feet tapping.

'Circle dance time,' said Elf, whose turquoise head had bobbed up next to me. 'We all join hands – this is Sellinger's Round.'

Ned took my other hand and everyone began to circle, though I'd have had no idea what I was doing if one of the Morris Men hadn't been shouting instructions. Ned was surprisingly light on his feet and had evidently done this before.

'That was fun,' I said as we headed back to the garden, where James was already getting the shop ready to open. I'd seen him earlier, watching the Morris Men, but I don't suppose dancing is his thing any more and he must have slipped away.

'The Morris Men will go over to the pub for an early lunch and a lot of beer,' Ned said. 'Then they'll come back and do it all again – but that one will be more for the tourists.'

I'd agreed with Ned that I should break the news about my being a Vane to the others here, while he would go over to Lavender Cottage later and do the same for the family – plus take a copy of the page of the letter we'd found and share that unsavoury revelation, too. No more secrets to fester in the dark . . .

So when Gert went into the Potting Shed to make the first brew of the day, I followed her and revealed that I'd been born a Vane and ghastly Wayne and his father were my closest relatives.

'My mother was Martha Vane, Saul's youngest sister. I kept it quiet till recently, because they threw her out when she got pregnant with me, and I didn't want anything to do with them. Once I'd met Wayne, I felt even more that I didn't want anyone to know!'

She stared at me for a moment, kettle in hand, then said, 'Not surprised. Who would want to admit they were related to that shower?'

But then she added that she remembered Martha as a sweet girl, and she wouldn't hold my bad blood against me.

Then she said that it was a good day when I arrived in the valley, because I'd certainly cheered Ned up no end, and I could feel myself blushing so made my escape.

I'd left her to pass the news on to the others – and anyone else she liked. Saul might never mention it again, but I'd be surprised if Wayne could keep anything secret for more than five minutes.

When Ned returned from his mission to Lavender Cottage, he said Myfy had been there with Elf, so he'd told both of them and, although shocked about what happened to poor Lizzie, they'd taken the news of my identity in their stride.

And later, after another wonderful Sunday dinner, Elf said she'd had a slight suspicion about me at the back of her mind, ever since she'd told us about Martha Vane the other day. She'd realized I had the same unusual shade of light blue-grey eyes, the irises ringed with black, that Martha had had.

'And your face is heart-shaped just like hers was,' she finished.

I confessed the lengths I'd gone to, to conceal it from everyone, which now seemed slightly ludicrous . . . except my trip to Cross Ways Farm.

'Saul thought Marnie had realized she was entitled to some of his parents' estate and had come here under another name to check out what there was,' said Ned. 'But Marnie doesn't want anything to do with them, or their farm. I'll have to go and have a talk with the old fool.'

No one seemed to find Ned taking on this task for me at all surprising, even when he said, 'I'll get a solicitor to draw up some kind of legal document for Marnie to sign, giving up her rights to any inheritance.'

'I wish I could get rid of my relationship to them as easily,' I said ruefully. 'It came as a bit of a shock to Ned.'

'But finding that missing page of the letter and realizing I was descended from someone a whole lot worse than any of the Vanes put things in perspective,' Ned said wryly.

'Yes, and you and Marnie must be distantly related through Lizzie,' Gerald said thoughtfully.

'We know – it's weird, but it is very distant,' agreed Ned, and smiled at me, making me feel warm all the way through to my toes.

When finally I tore my eyes away from his, I found all the others looking at us with interest.

'We don't care whether you're a Vane or not, dear,' said Elf. 'We're just pleased that Ned is so much happier since you arrived.'

I blushed and Ned said cheerfully, 'Who wouldn't be happy, with a professional gardener working for them for a pittance?'

'*And* perks,' I said, before I could stop myself.

37

Blast from the Past

For some reason, Elf broke out two bottles of elderflower champagne after dinner, though none of the revelations seemed the kind of thing to celebrate.

But it was lovely, even if the alcohol did finish me off – too little sleep, too much excitement and quite a bit of digging in the garden.

Though Ned came up to my flat for coffee . . . and a snuggle on the sofa – or maybe that should be a *struggle* on the sofa, since a large, hairy and disgruntled cat kept trying to insert itself between us – he could see I was practically asleep on my feet and didn't stay late.

'Tomorrow, we'll get the ground round the long beds ready for the new turf,' he promised, as if offering me a treat.

'I can hardly wait,' I said. 'But if any of those old roses turn up, you've had it till I've put them in.'

'It's a deal,' he said, and, kissing me again, went off home.

Caspar seemed delighted to have me all to himself once more, but he was going to have to learn to share.

*

A good night's sleep worked wonders and the next day I was so full of euphoria born of relief and happiness that after a morning's digging and raking, I practically floated across the courtyard towards the Potting Shed in search of lunch, wondering what Gertie would have put in the sandwiches.

The inner woman was unromantically ravenous: preparing the ground around the new long plots had been hard work, especially since Ned had had to go back to the office an hour or so earlier.

I'd sort of half noticed a knot of people at the ticket office window, but it was only when a hand grabbed my arm and swung me round that I realized I knew one of them. Enclosed in my bubble of joy, it took me a moment to register who it was.

'Oh, it's you, Mike,' I said disinterestedly, because he'd receded into the past like a bad dream and now not only did he seem a total and unwelcome irrelevance, but I found I felt no trace of the fear he'd once held for me. This didn't stop me wishing I had those butter paddles handy, though . . . He'd changed, too – his once-skinny frame now looked stringy, his spiky hair more grey than black and the skin of his face as sharply folded as origami.

'Well, Marnie, long time no see,' he said tritely, and gave me the smile that had once seemed so charming . . . I couldn't imagine why. And his dark, bright eyes looked as cold as a hunting stoat's.

I shook off his detaining hand. 'What are you doing here? Decided to deliver your letters personally, this time?'

My attack seemed to take him by surprise. 'I just wanted to see you. When I knew you were so near, I thought it would be good to . . . catch up. Somewhere more private, perhaps – maybe in that shed you were making for?'

His smile this time was chilling, but no longer had any power over me.

'No, thanks, we've nothing to talk about.'

'Oh, I don't know, there might be a few things you don't want your boss to overhear . . . though since you're still here, he mustn't have taken any notice of the letter I sent him. Did you spin him some story?'

'*You're* the spinner of stories,' I said coldly.

'So I am – and a better one than you. So perhaps you ought to have that little talk with me – here, or maybe later, wherever it is you're living now?'

'Oh, for goodness' sake, Mike!' I snapped as he reached out to grab my arm again. 'Haven't you got the message yet that your threats don't work any more? Just go away and leave me alone!'

'Having trouble?' asked a deep voice as Ned emerged from the office in time to hear this. He came and put an arm around me and it was only then that I saw we had an audience: the visitors might have moved on into the garden, but Steve had come out of the shop and James was leaning over the ticket counter, to watch. Roddy hovered uncertainly in the open office doorway.

'It's Mike,' I explained succinctly.

'I thought it might be,' Ned said, looking him over with disfavour, and I was pleased to see Mike back off a bit.

'You write a nice line in slimy anonymous letters,' Ned told him.

Mike seemed to rally and pulled the remnants of his old, practised charm around him. 'I can't imagine what stories Marnie's been telling you, but she was always a convincing liar. I could tell you a few—'

That was as far as he got before Ned, without any warning at all, punched him straight on the nose.

Mike didn't so much fall as folded up onto the cobbles and lay there, making gibbering noises, so I knew he wasn't dead.

It must have relieved Ned, too, because he said ruefully, 'Whoops! I don't often lose my temper like that.'

Lancelot and Guinevere walked slowly through the arch and approached Mike, looking down at him in a puzzled way. Guinevere pecked experimentally at his jacket, as if she hoped he was concealing something edible in the pockets, and he pushed her aside and staggered to his feet, his nose bleeding copiously.

'I'll sue you for assault! You'll be sorry for this,' he threatened Ned, thickly.

'What, because you weren't looking where you were going and walked into that notice board by the arch?' said Steve. 'We all saw you.'

'Yes, *what* an unfortunate accident,' agreed Roddy in his frightfully posh voice and Mike swung round to look at him.

'It's a conspiracy!' he yelled.

'I do think, you know, that you might find a charge of assault difficult to prove,' Ned said. 'However . . .' he looked at the results of his handiwork, and said reluctantly, 'you need a bit of first aid before you leave. You'd better come into the office so we can stop that nosebleed. You can't walk about like a bloody Niagara.'

'Nicely phrased,' I said as he put a hand under Mike's arm and propelled him, willing or not, up the office steps.

I followed and Roddy suggested Mike sit down and put his head back, then pinch the bridge of his nose.

'That usually works.'

I passed Mike a wad of tissues and he leaned back with a theatrical groan, though the flow of blood had already begun to cease.

'Sorry about your *accident*,' said Ned. 'But you shouldn't have said that about Marnie.'

'He got off a lot lighter than he'd have done if I'd had my butter paddles handy,' I said, and he grinned at me.

'Did you say "butter paddles"?' Mike said. 'What on earth are you talking about?'

'I've got a pair of giant wooden butter paddles and I've had this fantasy that if you turned up, I'd clap your head between them as hard as I could,' I explained.

'You're mad!' he said, but cringed back slightly as if he thought I might whip them out from somewhere and actually do it.

I wish.

'Have you really got giant wooden butter paddles?' asked Roddy with interest.

'Oh, yes, I brought them back from France and they're unusually big. I thought they might look nice in the garden museum.'

Mike was now edging away along the sofa as if he was thinking of making a run for the door. I dampened a bit of kitchen towel and handed it to him.

'I'd clean your face a bit, if you're thinking of leaving, but otherwise, *hasta la vista*, baby.'

'Yeah, stay not upon the order of your going, or whatever it was Shakespeare said,' agreed Ned. 'And if I were you, I wouldn't come back, or make any more attempts to communicate with my fiancée, because I wouldn't take it very well.'

'Fiancée?' Mike looked as surprised as I felt – until I realized Ned had just said it to protect me.

He put his arm around me and said, 'Yes, but don't bother congratulating us – just go.'

'You were the one who insisted I come in here!' Mike got

up, throwing the smeared damp wad of kitchen paper on the floor. 'You totally misjudged my intentions. I only wanted to make sure that my wife – ex-wife – was all right and to give you a friendly warning—'

'I really wouldn't say anything else, if I was you,' Ned advised him, dangerously, and Mike backed towards the door – which suddenly burst open, sending him flying back into the room again.

I expected to find a tornado had struck but no, it was just a skinny teenage boy.

He was pursued by Steve, who was shouting, 'Come back, you!'

The boy ignored him and, fixing a pair of glowering blue eyes on Ned, flung out a dramatically pointing hand and demanded: 'Are you my father?'

'Oh God, that's all we need, the Bloody Child,' said Ned wearily, 'though it's clearly Melodrama Week, not Shakespeare. Who are you and why on earth should you think I'm your father?'

'Because that's what Mum told that journalist last year – I overheard them. But she said she could only reveal it now because my dad – the man I *thought* was my dad – was dead. He'd been paying maintenance, you see.'

'Well . . . not really,' said Ned, still frowning.

'Then the story came out and some of my friends said stuff – but Mum wouldn't discuss it with me and I didn't know where you were until I saw you on the telly the other week,' the boy finished in a rush.

'Right . . . so you're Sammie Nelson's son?' he ventured.

'Yeah, the one she was pregnant with when you threw her over and she had to leave college,' the youth said accusingly.

Now I came to really look at him, he did remind me of

Sammie, though fairer. But he didn't look a bit like Ned, which was hardly surprising.

Out of the corner of my eye, I saw Mike sit back down again, with an expression of enjoyment on his face.

'Look—' I began, then broke off. 'What's your name?'

'Jonas,' the boy said sulkily.

'Right, Jonas, I'm Marnie Ellwood and I was in the same year as your mum at Honeywood Horticultural College. Ned was in the year up and, though they did briefly go out together, *she* threw *him* over, because she'd got off with the presenter of a documentary that was being filmed there. Is that the man you thought was your father?'

The boy, who looked very young and very angry, nodded. 'He thought I was his, too, and he lived with Mum for a bit, but then he went back to his wife after I was born and I hardly saw him. He had a heart attack.'

'I'm very sorry,' said Ned gently, 'but . . . I'm afraid he *was* your real father. How old are you?'

'What?' Jonas looked taken aback, then said, 'Fourteen,' then added his birthday and Ned and I both did some rapid arithmetic.

'She met your dad in late April the year before you were born and dumped me within the week – so there's no way I could be your father,' Ned said.

Jonas took some convincing, but when Ned said in exasperation that he'd even take a DNA test, if that made him feel better, he finally gave in. 'But why would Mum sell lies to the newspaper?'

'I think "sell" is a bit of a clue,' I suggested.

'Yes, she must have needed the money badly,' agreed Ned. 'And she didn't actually come out and say I did all those things to the journalist, just suggested them. But none of them was true and I can prove it.'

The boy slumped and Steve, presumably deducing that the drama was over, slipped back out.

'I hitchhiked here and it's taken me all day,' Jonas said accusingly, as if it was our fault. 'No one seemed to be heading in this direction. It's the back of nowhere.'

'That's why we like it,' said Ned. 'But hadn't you better let your mum know where you are? She must be worried sick.'

'I left a note, but I turned my phone off so she couldn't call me,' Jonas said. 'Not that I expect she's even noticed I'm not there yet.'

But there he did her an injustice, for the door burst open for the second time and a woman threw herself at him, shrieking, 'Jonas!' and tried to shake him.

I'd have known her anywhere, even if she was about twice the size she'd been at college. The excess weight was all well distributed, though, and she probably still looked pretty when she wasn't snarling.

Jonas fended her off. 'Leave me alone! I know the truth now.'

'What do you mean?' she demanded. 'I've never told you anything but the truth!'

She whirled round on Ned. 'What have you been telling him?'

She hadn't noticed me, and started when I said, 'Hello, Sammie – fancy meeting you here.'

'*You!*' she exclaimed, eyes widening. 'I've heard all about you and the Heritage Homes Trust! What—'

'You really shouldn't believe all you hear,' Ned interrupted. '*Or* read.'

She looked at him in a baffled way and then turned back to Jonas. 'What were you *thinking* of? Didn't I tell you—'

'He says he's not my dad and I believe him.'

'All right – I never said he was, did I?' she snapped.

'You let that journalist think he was.'

'Well, I needed some money, once the maintenance from your dad stopped,' she said, as if that excused it. 'And now I've had to fork out a fortune for a taxi from the station to get here.'

'No car?' asked Ned.

'Lost my licence,' she snapped. 'Just what I need when I'm trying to run a business.'

'Oh, yes, it said in one of those articles you had a garden design business,' I said. 'Willow Wand Garden Transformations.'

'You were speeding again, Mum,' Jonas said, but she ignored him and turned to Ned.

'The least you can do is drive us back to the station,' she told him, as if it was all his fault.

But before he could reply, Jonas said wistfully, 'Seeing I'm here, couldn't I at least see the garden first, before we go?'

Ned looked at him with interest. 'You like gardens?'

'Yeah, and you've got one full of poison plants – cool!'

'OK then,' Ned said. 'Come on – we'll sort out that lift when we get back.'

He went out, followed eagerly by Jonas, and Roddy, who had been effacing himself in the background, murmured an excuse and followed suit.

I didn't blame him – I wished I could, too.

Sammie seemed to catch sight of Mike for the first time and they eyed each other curiously. Since there seemed nothing else to do, I said, 'Sammie, this is my ex-husband, Mike Draycot.' Then I added brightly, 'Anyone for coffee?'

'I've had a bit of an accident,' Mike told her and she sank down next to him.

'You poor thing, you're covered in blood!' she said, sympathetically.

'I'm all right,' he said bravely. 'But . . . if I've grasped things right, hasn't something you said to the newspapers about Ned Mars been twisted out of context, so it's led to today's unfortunate contretemps?'

'Yes, you're quite right. I sold a little human-interest story about Ned last year, when I was very hard up, and it wasn't my fault they twisted it to suggest something else, was it?'

'Not at all. Funnily enough, *I* was just explaining to Ned that all the stories Marnie's been telling him about me were just made up to get his sympathy . . .'

I tuned the rest of the conversation out, but when I'd drunk my coffee I broke in and said, 'I can hear them coming back, so if I were you I'd pipe down before Ned hears you, Mike.'

When Jonas came in with Ned, he looked about five years younger and pink with excitement.

'Mum, the Poison Garden's got a deadly plant in a cage in the middle – a rosary pea – and in the other corner, there's a waterfall with some steampunk metal flowers that open and close and—'

'He's a real gardener,' said Ned, smiling.

'Ned says when I'm sixteen I can come and do work experience in the garden for the summer, if I want to,' Jonas said.

'Well, that's very nice,' said Sammie weakly. 'Now, about that lift . . .'

'I have a car parked just over the bridge and I'd be happy to drive you anywhere you like?' suggested Mike, as smoothly as a man can who is covered in crusted gore.

'Would you really? That's very kind of you,' said Sammie, fluttering her false eyelashes at him.

For a minute, I wondered if I should warn her not to accept anything *other* than a lift from him, but then gave a mental shrug. She was more than a match for Mike, I reckoned.

When they'd gone, Ned and I looked at each other and said, simultaneously, 'Phew!'

'I wonder what's next, Plague of Frogs?' he said.

'I'm sincerely hoping Plague of Exes was the last one,' I said. 'And by the way, thank you for pretending we were engaged when Mike was being obnoxious. That was kind of you.'

'Yes, wasn't it just?' he agreed blandly. 'Do you fancy coming round later for another session of *paper sorting*?'

'Only if you promise me it's going to be a Lucky Dragon evening,' I said firmly.

38

Something in the Air

Our usual work ethic seemed to have unravelled next morning, so it was just as well it was a Tuesday.

We spent a couple of hours sorting out the final selection of photographs, plans, lists and other interesting material for the museum display, had a rummage round the old stables where Ned was sure he'd seen several Victorian hand-blown glass bells for forcing vegetables and rhubarb (not that *ours* needed any forcing), and then went to see how the builders were getting along.

The new interior was already taking shape and Don said a few more days and he'd seal off the shop side of the blocked doorway with plastic sheeting and open it up.

'Put a bit of support in and a new, wider lintel,' he said. 'We'll knock through into the old outside visitor toilet at the same time. You'll have to manage with the staff one, till it's done.'

'At least it's a fairly quietish time to do it,' agreed Ned, and we left them to get on with it.

'There's nothing quite as romantic as a nice chat about sanitation, is there?' I said brightly as we walked towards the bridge – we were having lunch in the Devil's Cauldron restaurant.

'You're the one who was so keen on discussing the loo situation in the first place,' he pointed out. 'Look at it this way – I'm giving you everything you ever asked me for.'

We decided to walk off our very good lunch and Ned suggested we go up the track by the Village Hut and along the top of the hill above the woods, to the path back down to the falls.

'We can take in Jacob's barn on the way. You haven't seen it yet and, even if he's out, there's lots to look at outside.'

This proved to be an understatement, for strange kinetic sculptures were everywhere: driven by the breeze, or the power of a nearby stream. Some of them made faint, melodic noises, or whirred, chimed and fluttered.

'Jacob's a magician,' I said. 'I suspected as much.'

There was no sign of him, so we decided not to knock on the door in case we disturbed his work, and carried on up the steep, rough path till we came out above the woods.

It was fairly level going after that and eventually we reached the road that led to Angel Row, then turned off and made our way down the side of the falls.

'It's good to have the place to ourselves – no tourists today,' Ned said, as we stopped on the flat viewing area by the source of the river. 'Marnie, I—'

But I'd caught sight of something over his shoulder and alerted by my fixed, astonished stare, he turned suddenly and exclaimed, '*Wayne!*'

It was that familiar carroty head I'd caught sight of, emerging from the cave by the waterfall, which was more exposed than usual, because the weather had been so dry for ages. Only now did I notice a brown rope hanging down from the top.

Wayne had grabbed it and was using it to help pull himself out onto what was left of the ledge underneath.

This was a mistake: it unravelled in an instant and I had one brief impression of Wayne, poised with a ragged stump of rope in one hand, before he plummeted backwards towards the pool way below.

'Oh God,' said Ned, leaning over the rail to try to catch sight of him. 'If he's hit the rocks on the way down . . . No, he's just bobbed up again, but the current's got him! Come on.'

He grabbed my hand and we scrambled down as quickly as we could, then ran along the riverbank, trying to spot him.

We'd gone quite a way before we found him, washed by an eddy into a backwater half-enclosed by rocks, floating face down.

Ned pulled him out and turned him over. 'You see if you can get hold of Elf while I try a bit of artificial respiration,' he said, and began working on the unconscious Wayne.

I managed to get a signal on my phone by running a few yards downstream. Elf answered straight away.

'Wayne's had an accident. He was climbing out of that cave at the top of the waterfall and he fell in and was swept down-stream,' I told her. 'We've got him out and . . .'

I paused and looked over my shoulder as various uncouth noises told me Ned had managed to get most of the water out of Wayne. 'He's not drowned – he's just brought most of the water up.'

'I'll be right up to have a look at him. See you shortly.'

I waited where I was, till Wayne had finished retching and was sitting up against a rock, before I went back. Elf arrived only a few minutes later and she had James with her.

'What *have* you been doing?' asked Elf, looking down at Wayne like a bright-eyed sparrow eyeing a not very savoury worm.

'He'd tied a rotten piece of rope to a rock up at the top of the falls and managed to get across that bit of ledge to the cave,' explained Ned. 'Then he put his weight on the rope when he was getting out and it gave way – and down he went.'

'That bloody book going on about treasure!' Wayne spat, looking accusingly at Elf. 'There was nothing in that cave!'

'*I* could have told you that, lad,' said James, surprisingly, and we all turned to look at him.

'What do you mean – have you been in it?' demanded Wayne. 'Did you grab the treasure?'

'No, you daft ha'porth, there wasn't ever any treasure in it.'

'I think you'd better tell us how you know, James, before we all die of curiosity,' Ned said.

James scratched his head. 'All right, but it was something and nothing. It was this way . . . There was a drought one summer when I was a lad and the waterfall was about half what it usually is, so your uncle Theo and me decided to have a look in the cave. But we weren't daft,' he added, giving Wayne a scathing look, 'we used proper ropes and tied them round a tree up at the top. There was a bit more of the ledge back then anyway, so it wasn't that difficult to get along to the entrance.'

He paused to make sure he had our full attention. 'It's narrow to get into, but then opens up a bit, and we could see straight away that there wasn't any treasure there. But there *had* been something – or someone – there in the past because we saw there were a few bits of mouldering bones and the rusty imprint of a sword and helmet. Looked like someone managed to crawl in there to hide and never left.'

I shivered. 'How horrible!'

'I dunno, he was probably wounded and the effort of getting there finished him off,' said James. 'And he lay there peaceful enough for maybe hundreds of years. We didn't disturb anything, just got ourselves out again. We decided to keep it quiet, so no one else would go poking around.'

'Till Wayne,' Ned said.

'And I did say plainly in the book it was just another legend,' Elf said defensively.

'Like the other one about Nathaniel's treasure being hidden at Old Grace Hall, that inspired you to dig up my lawn,' Ned said grimly.

'You can't prove that was me!' said Wayne quickly. 'Nobody saw me.'

'You're a complete fool, Wayne,' I told him.

'You said it,' agreed Ned.

Wayne hauled himself up, dripping and dishevelled. 'I'm off home before I catch my death,' he said belligerently, as if we were about to do a citizen's arrest for illegal stupidity, then squelched off towards the turnstile.

'Wet in more ways than one, poor boy,' said Elf. 'Well, James, I suppose I'd better get back to my ice-cream making and you to planting up the bicycle carrier.'

'We'll go back up to the top of the falls and remove what's left of that rope, so no one sees it and gets any silly ideas,' Ned said. 'Come on, Ellwood!'

He sounded cheerful and, really, there was no reason why the incident should dampen *our* day.

'We were wrong about the end of the plagues,' I said, following him up the steep path past the source of the falls. 'We forgot Plague of Idiots.'

Ned unknotted what was left of the rope, already half-frayed by the rocks, and coiled it over one shoulder like a mountaineer before we started back down again.

'I'll burn this on Gertie's bonfire when I get back.'

'Well, don't let her see you, or she'll say you're a spendthrift for not using it to insulate a pot, or something. You know what she's like on the subject of waste.'

'I did hear her telling you the other day that if you left your crusts you'd never have curly hair,' he said, halting on the flat rock by the river's source to ruffle my hair with one big hand. 'Bit late, though.'

'I'd only saved a bit for Guinevere – she's a peahen of character,' I said. I looked across at the gushing water and the dark, jagged slit of the cave entrance and sighed. 'Do you think whoever died in there felt comforted by the magic of this place?'

'I expect so. I think he must have been local to know about it.'

We watched the spray flung into the air to catch the last of the sun's rays, before it dipped behind the high hills and the atmosphere around us seemed to change and shimmer, too . . .

I had that feeling again that something winged fluttered just out of sight – and was that a faint, tinkling laugh, or just the sound of the water?

I turned to ask Ned if he'd heard it too – and found him looking down at me with such an expression of love that my heart seemed to stop and then start again, much faster.

'I thought Wayne had ruined the moment I'd planned, but it seems he'd only delayed it for the right one,' he said. 'Marnie, will you marry me?'

There was a rushing noise that might have been the water, or wings, or even birds taking flight towards their evening roost – or just the blood pounding in my ears.

I looked up at him uncertainly. 'Are you quite *sure* you want to marry a Vane?'

'I'm quite sure I want to marry this one,' he said, then pulled me into his arms and kissed me.

*

As we slowly walked back along the river, arms entwined, he said, 'Elf guessed – she gave me a ring that's been in the Verdi family for generations. It's a big flat ruby and looks a bit Borgia, so it might not be your cup of tea, but I'll show it to you when we get back.'

'I'd love a Verdi Borgia ring,' I assured him. 'I'd only wear it on special occasions, though, or I'd lose it in the garden, or in the pond, or somewhere.'

'We'll both have plain wedding rings we can work in and I'll make sure yours is tight enough not to fall off,' he said with a grin. 'We'll get married in St Gabriel's – we could go up in a bit to ask the Reverend Jojo about putting up the banns.'

'Just a little wedding, though – close friends and family,' I said, then caught myself up. 'Not *Vane* family. The Ellwoods, though – as many of them as can leave the château.'

'It should be soon – early June, perhaps?' he suggested. 'Better weather, but before the main tourist season and the school holidays.'

'All right,' I agreed happily. 'And let's make it a Tuesday and instead of a reception, have a Grace Garden party, instead!'

'Brilliant!' he said, and squeezed my waist. 'I'm looking forward to telling everyone – though I suspect most people have already guessed. There's just one thing worrying me . . .'

I looked up anxiously into his serious face and asked, 'What's that?'

'Who's going to break the news to Caspar?'

Epilogue

Flaming June

It had been a perfect little wedding and the Angel Gabriel had looked down on us from his jewelled window, austere but, I felt, approving.

Uncle Richard had given me away and Lex Mariner had been Ned's best man . . . and I hadn't worn white, but ruby-red silk, to go with my Borgia ring.

One of the smaller angels in the window was wearing robes the same colour, which I thought was a good omen.

Now the sun shone warmly on the Grace Garden, the throng of guests, the food laid out on trestle tables and the remains of a tall white cake decorated with real roses.

The Coronation bunting fluttered bravely in the warm breeze and there were pots of scented geraniums up the sides of the steps that led to the gazebo. Inside was a knot of people and I caught a glimpse of Aunt Em's bright turquoise linen dress. How lovely it had been to see her and Uncle Richard again and introduce them to Ned – and they'd got on so well. I suppose that wasn't really surprising, since we all shared a passion for gardening!

Caspar sat under a lavender bush dismembering a smoked

salmon sandwich and Lancelot and Guinevere hoovered up any crumbs.

'You know, this is the perfect place for a reception,' Cress said, towing Roddy towards us. 'You could hold them here as a side-line. We could have *ours* here, couldn't we, Roddy?'

'Yes, but only on a Tuesday, when the garden is shut,' he agreed, smiling at her.

'You can have yours here if you'd like to, but I wouldn't charge you,' Ned said. 'It's an idea, though – it would be pretty lucrative, I should think.'

'I expect so, but we might just want the occasional Tuesday off,' I pointed out before he got carried away.

'Marnie!' Treena said, appearing suddenly from the sunken garden, flushed with either the sun or champagne – or possibly both. 'Did Luke tell you he's found evidence that the monastic site was a really, really early one and abandoned ages before the Vikings? So apparently it doesn't matter if they haven't found much there – Luke's *delirious*.'

And when he joined us and slipped his arm around Treena's waist, he beamed and said, 'Just had an expert opinion on those bits of pottery back – I think this is the happiest day of my life!'

'I thought that was my line?' Ned said, grinning. 'Come on, Marnie, let's go and thank Jojo – I'm not sure I've ever heard the vicar give a speech at a wedding reception before, but it's going to be imprinted on my memory for ever.'

'And mine,' I agreed. 'Especially that joke about how we'd always stay true to one another, so neither of us would be tempted by the Poison Garden.'

'That was a joke?'

'I think so. Maybe it was inspired by the Borgia ring; she did admire it.'

The vicar had a smoked salmon sandwich in one hand and a glass of champagne in the other. She beamed at us.

'Everything has turned out beautifully, hasn't it? No more mysteries, alarms or excursions, just a peaceful life in our little Paradise on earth.'

'Actually, I suppose there is one mystery unresolved,' I said. 'Nathaniel's treasure!'

'Oh, I know all about that,' she said, and we gazed at her in astonishment.

'You *do*?' said Ned, doubtfully.

'Yes! It was one of those grisly and entirely spurious holy relics – St Peter's finger, along with a fragment of the True Cross – kept in a crystal box.'

'Yuck!' I said at the thought of the shrivelled finger.

'How do you know about it?' asked Ned.

'Because I found an account of it in one of my predecessor's notes. He thought it ought to be recorded. Your uncle Theo's father discovered it in a false drawer in a chest that must have been Nathaniel's. They decided together that the finger should be decently interred in the family tomb and a few words said over it. The box, with the bit of wood in it, is still in one of the vestry cupboards, the locked one with some very old pewter candlesticks.'

'So *that* was Nathaniel's greatest treasure?' I asked.

'Spiritual things so often are,' she assured me, and exchanged her empty glass for a full one offered to her by Charlie.

We moved away towards the sunken garden, to read the words on the sundial once more.

'*The sun is my treasure, it measures the hours in bars of gold.*'

'You're *my* greatest treasure,' Ned said, and then, as Caspar emerged from behind the sundial, expressing himself in a forceful manner and fixing us both with huge green eyes, added, 'I suppose *I* have to share the honours with that cat!'

'Got it in one,' I agreed.

Acknowledgements

I could not have written this book without the research carried out by my son, Robin Ashley. His wonderful plan and planting lists for the walled Apothecary Garden enabled me to walk around it in my head, step by step with my heroine, Marnie.

Recipes

Lavender Ice-Cream

300ml (10.5 fl. oz) double cream
200g (7 oz) light condensed milk
½ teaspoon fine ground dried lavender flowers
4 tablespoons lavender syrup
Splash of violet colouring

Whisk well
Put in ice-cream maker for 1 hour

(Sets very nicely. Very creamy. Strong taste, but nice. Quite a pale purple.)

Mincemeat Ice-Cream

300ml (10.5 fl. oz) double cream
200g (7 oz) light condensed milk
100g (3.5 oz) mincemeat (Robertson's Classic)

Whisk well
Put in ice-cream maker for 50 minutes
Sprinkle of sweet cinnamon on top when done

Ginger Ice-Cream

300ml (10.5 fl. oz) double cream
200g (7 oz) light condensed milk
225g (8 oz) dried stem ginger in sugar syrup (whole small jar)

Whisk well
Put in ice-cream maker for 1 hour
Layer of crystallized ginger on top when done

(Came out very thick and rich. Less ginger might be better, and adding it in stages through the chilling?)

Non-Dairy Coffee and Choc Chip Ice-Cream

250ml (8.5 fl. oz) single soya cream
300g (10.5 oz) sweetened condensed coconut milk
3 tablespoons coffee powder (strong)
Sprinkle of dairy-free choc chips (dark)

Whisk well
Put in ice-cream maker for 1 hour
Add more choc chips (and sugar snowflakes) half an hour in and on top when finished

Mulled Wine Ice-Cream

250ml (8.5 fl. oz) brandy cream, extra thick
200g (7 oz) light condensed milk
175ml (6 fl. oz) reduced mulled wine (from 1 full bottle)

Whisk well
Put in ice-cream maker for 1 hour

Loved escaping into Trisha's world?

Look out for the brand-new Christmas book from the heart-warming and uplifting *Sunday Times* bestselling author

ONE MORE CHRISTMAS AT THE CASTLE

Dido Jones' new job is to help elderly widow Sabine host her last Christmas in her beloved home, Mitras Castle. With housekeeping and catering to organise for the large gathering, Dido and her business partner Henry must stay at the castle for the whole of December.

But as Sabine's family arrive at the house – including Dido's old crush Xan – long-buried mysteries begin to unravel. And as Christmas day approaches, Dido's feeling of connection to the old house runs deeper than she first thought…

Available for pre-order now

Are you signed up to the

Trisha Ashley NEWSLETTER?

Trisha's newsletters are full of exclusive content and the first place to find out about book deals and competitions.

You will discover recipes and craft ideas inspired by your favourite characters and sneak-peeks into new books.

To sign up to the newsletter, search for Trisha Ashley on **penguin.co.uk**